Xen
Academy

Ste Newell

For Maria

ACKNOWLEDGMENTS

Thanks to Maria Newell, Keith Greenwood and all my friends and family for your continual support.

CHAPTER 1
The Rock

The craft trembled violently as the landing jets kicked into life, rattling the passengers around like rag dolls. The superstructure of the ship began to scream like a banshee as the pilot fought to keep the ship steady. The noise and turbulence only added to the emotional torment felt by the already tense group of students en route to the academy. One of the students, Daemon, looked nervously to his left and noticed that his burly friend Roz was gripping the armrests so tightly he was bleeding from his fingernails. He hoped that would be the only bodily fluid that would emerge from him as he had heard rumours of rookie passengers being involved in a chain reaction of vomiting during such violent descents.

"Is this normal?" he asked for no-one in particular as sweat cascaded down his broad forehead and he felt his jumpsuit starting to soak through and stick to the seat. Daemon felt as if he had already lost a kilogramme in weight through perspiring during the drop and Roz looked to be in an even worse condition than he was. He was about to remove his arm from the seat restraints and wipe his brow with the cuff of his sleeve when the ship suddenly banked sharply to one side making the majority of the passengers scream like startled children, himself included. The part of his mind that was, miraculously, not overcome with fear rationally told him that one of the four landing jets had failed and the pilot was probably attempting to compensate on the remaining three. Suddenly he wondered if this was an unannounced exercise to test the recruit's ability to withstand mental pressure but quickly reconsidered when he heard the unmistakable sound of metal being twisted up and felt the shudder of an explosion.

Red lights started to flash inside the passenger section sending each and every student into a fury of panic. The next few seconds were a blur of noise, movement and pain as the craft spiralled dizzyingly before impacting with the ground. Daemon was flung back and forth as the ship rolled a number of times before finally settling on its nose leaving all of the students hanging painfully in their restraint belts. Other than a sore neck Daemon didn't feel too badly hurt physically, emotionally he was shaken up but as his panic subsided and he peered around the strobing red room he realised that he had been lucky. The passenger who had been sat on his right-hand side was now hanging limply from her harness above him. He couldn't remember her name and it was too late to ask her now as he could see that she had taken a serious blow to the top of her head. Her skull had been flattened above her forehead and blood was streaming down her face. The strands of her long blond hair drooped down towards him and were quickly becoming crimson, rivulets of her lifeblood snaking their way down her locks before dropping off and splattering his face and jumpsuit. Her dead eyes glared at him as though he was somehow responsible for the crash and the steady drip, drip, drip was like a dreadful accusation that he had somehow ended her brief life. He closed his eyes and tried to ignore the awful sound of the rhythmic spattering. He thought, not for the first time, that maybe it had been a big mistake joining the Xen Corporation.

The ground crew from the Academy took three hours to rig up an umbilical from the ruined ship to the training facility. The crash had literally ripped the ship in half, tearing off the front section killing the pilots instantly. The emergency crash doors had sealed when the hull was compromised enclosing the passenger section and saving the students from an untimely death in the near vacuum. The precarious resting position of the ship had delayed the rescue process and for those students who were not dead, maimed or carried out screaming, morale was very low. They slowly made their way through the flexible tube into their new place of learning and were immediately granted twenty-four hours down time due to the traumatic event which had taken place.

In a rare show of compassion, they were spared having to endure the time-consuming screening process again. The students had already been screened for deadly pathogens at the Xen recruiting institution on Hanna Prime before leaving for the new academy and they had all been given clean bills of health.

This training centre was relatively new and had been constructed on a sterile moon which was commonly known as 'The Rock'. These moons had little corporate value and generally had weak nebulous atmospheres which provided the Xen Corporation with a dangerous and hostile environment to train new students. This Rock didn't even have a name as it was not visible from the planet it orbited; it merely had a signature of numbers that the majority of students had already forgotten by the time they had landed. The Academy itself had been fabricated from lightweight alloys and fortified glass which protected the students and staff from the hazardous environment on the Rock. It seemed to be a clumsy collection of drab grey buildings upon an otherwise featureless landscape of dust and stone.

The brief period of downtime passed quickly and before they knew it the thirty-nine remaining students were assembled in the briefing hall as two muscular females walked to a speaking podium. When the muttering and groans had fallen to a stark silence the smaller of the females began to speak.

"Welcome to the second part of your training. I am Mistress Suix and this is Mistress Jemm." She gestured towards her side kick who was as big as a bull and was only short of having a ring through her nose. Roz elbowed Daemon in his ribs and screwed up his face having witnessed such a brute of a woman.

"Look at that fucker. I tell you what Daemon, you can have her." He whispered as Daemon shot his friend a look of disgust while he rubbed his aching ribs.

"Today we will start with the basic fitting of your Environmental Combat Armour, otherwise known as an E.C.A. We will then move on to practical training using the armour correctly." The briefing droned on for over an hour before the students were even sent to the quartermaster to be issued with suits. Looking back Daemon remembered that day more than the rest of the students due him accidentally coupling his E.C.A. to the wrong gas tank and filled his air tanks with nitrogen instead of oxygen destroying the filtration units of his suit. He had spent the next two days in the infirmary having been subjected to a vicious beating by Mistress Jemm, a beating he would never forget. Even in the face of such abuse, he was deemed fortunate since he hadn't been given the more terminal punishment of being spaced.

A month went by as the students learnt the basics of repair, field maintenance and movement within the E.C.A. The suits themselves were standard issue training surplus, out of date hardware that had been superseded by the more advanced armours used by the Xen military CORE. They were matt black and made from numerous plates of lightweight alloys giving the wearer a bug-like appearance. When Daemon had first tried his training suit on after being released from the infirmary he had found it difficult to move in the bulky armour but after a week he could manage an awkward staggered trot. He was already well behind the majority of the other students who after a few more weeks practice could perform rudimentary operations. He found himself in the company of those who hadn't learned quickly and were punished until they did. Entombed in the bulky suit he soon found that he needed to relieve himself, his first piss in his E.C.A. was a sensation Daemon would never forget due to the powerful suction produced by the servo pumps. It was such an ordeal that he made a mental note that in future he would empty his bladder before climbing inside such an unforgiving piece of hardware.

At the start of the second month, the students were commanded to assemble in the briefing hall which had been lined with bare metal chairs. Each student was ordered to strip naked and sit and wait for Mistress Suix to arrive. Daemon noticed an air of silence within the hall and felt he could almost smell fear in the atmosphere. By the time Mistress Suix arrived cold sweat covered his body in a clammy sheen. She wore a simple blue gown covered by a medical apron and carried a serrated combat knife. The Mistress stood in silence while a large contingent of guards filed into the room; all of them armed with assault rifles.

"Today we will find out how much you have remembered from your lessons in the field of Pseudo-met," she stated in a passive tone. Daemon winced hearing the word Pseudo-met and remembered the intense teaching of this subject back at the Xen recruiting Institute on Hanna Prime. The course itself had lasted three months and was intensive even by the standards they had previously been subjected to. The reason for this was due to the nature of the subject which involved the practice of meditation to ignore pain. On the battlefield, wounded troopers who implemented their training quickly could markedly stem the amount of blood loss or even staunch it all together. But here, with his back against the cold metal of the seat, it seemed to Daemon that the stale stench of fear was quickly replaced with that of panic among the majority of the students within the hall. Daemon cursed silently to himself and wished he had sat at the back of the room with Roz and not right at the front facing Mistress Suix.

"I want you all to concentrate on Pseudo-met and begin your meditation. Clear your thoughts and focus upon the teachings you have received," she stated. Daemon thought she was enjoying this bleak moment as the students began to take control of their breathing. Distractingly he noticed Mistress Suix was a damn sight better looking than Mistress Jemm, in fact, he thought, she was really quite pretty apart from her shaved head

7

and flat chest. But this was no time for his mind to be wandering so he attempted to concentrate as Mistress Suix rushed to her first victim who was two seats away from where he was sat. Her blade sank deeply into the flesh of Frad, a female student he had met on Hanna Prime. Frad yelped in pain as Suix twisted the blade and removed it speedily from her flesh. The poor woman was shocked out of her state of meditation and tried to staunch the wound with her hand.

"No!" Suix barked, "You must concentrate. Focus on what you have been taught!" Daemon could see she hadn't stabbed Frad in any vital place but it clearly hurt a great deal and looked a total mess. Mistress Suix stabbed the next victim in the line and moved on towards Daemon, he cleared his thoughts and tried to relax as her hand thrust the blade into his stomach.

"Fuck me!" he cried in agony. It felt like a hot poker being rammed through him. Mistress Suix leant towards his ear while he continued to curse and attempted to recalibrate his thoughts.

"Maybe I will take you up on your offer, handsome," she whispered and then moved to her next target. The pain rushed through every nerve fibre in his body like acid burning through his veins. That hurt like a mother fucker! What a bitch.

For four hours the students had to endure the agony that had been bestowed upon them, praying for the torment to be over every single minute that passed. Daemon himself had initially been able to block out the pain and as his pulse had slowed the flow of blood noticeably staunched. Gradually though he found it difficult to maintain his trance as Frad took a turn for the worse and began moaning loudly at first then gradually quieter and quieter. Suddenly she went into a series of violent convulsions due to her inability to apply Pseudo-met and Daemon found it hard to find solace while Frad thrashed around on the floor nearby before finally dying. His lapse in concentration caused his wound to bleed freely again and blood pooled on the floor below him until he regained his composure. Finally, the allotted time passed and each student was taken to casualty and treated using advanced drugs and serums. Frad was taken to the morgue and was never seen again, there was no funeral for her and no mention of the fact that she had died during the test. Her life was of little consequence to the corporation, all that mattered to Xen was that they had proved that many of the students understood Pseudo-met and would remember the traumatic event from that day onwards. It was a literal case of what didn't kill them would make them stronger.

When the students came out of casualty they were granted a twenty-four hour period to reflect on what they had learnt. Daemon made his way to the shower room to wash the stink of medical detergents from his body. It was in the shower room where he overheard a couple of students speaking about Tomri. Apparently, he had taken his own life the previous night by injecting air into his veins, Daemon hadn't known Tomri very well but he had seemed to be a nice guy, maybe too nice for all this shit. He made a mental note that the initial head count of fifty was down to thirty- seven and shook his head in wonderment that they had lost so many already. After showering he made his way to the communication department and sent a long distance video message to his ex-girlfriend Florin on Jodie III. The communication was short and detailed his misery at making such a terrible mistake by joining the Xen Corporation. He could almost hear Florin's answer of "I told you so" but he gained no message in reply.

Over the next few months, the students learnt various methods of armed and unarmed combat and became so adept with the E.C.A.'s that they could get into them in a minute flat. All of them, that was, with the exception of Beck, a physically imposing but somewhat clumsy individual who despite numerous punishments still could not accomplish the one-minute E.C.A. operation. Eventually, the instructor's patience wore out and he was taken from the training room and spaced. Daemon couldn't even imagine the concept of being spaced, to be placed in an air lock and instantly decompressed. It sounded as horrific as it was barbaric.

During these months Daemon had befriended one of the female students called Cian, she was tall with an athletic build and had a seemingly insatiable appetite for sex. Many of his off-duty hours were spent in Cian's room where they fucked the stress of daily training out of each other's bodies. However, he couldn't help feeling a little guilty that using his time like this meant he neglected his friend Roz who had been struggling with some of the more intellectually challenging training sessions that had been spliced into the daily schedules. Although his guilt seemed to lift every time he climaxed inside Cian it soon fell back on his shoulders whenever he saw Roz being led away for punishment. In one of those moments of post-coital euphoria, Daemon decided he wanted to pursue a full officer career arguing with himself that it was the reason he had signed up for Xen training in the first place. He tried to convince himself that his decision had nothing to do with the fact he was making love to one of the most beautiful females in the academy and that it was more to do with finding himself a true calling. He believed he would make a fine officer and a great leader and told himself that it was his fate to be a Xen officer.

At the end of the initial six months of training, Daemon signed up for an extra curriculum program. The students that signed up were allowed to study another career, just in case, they failed the primary Xen program. Daemon did not think for one moment that he would fail the training but opting for the extra curriculum studies meant that he would be allowed one day off each week to learn something from the large list of subjects available. He chose engineering because he was interested in the subject and had already accumulated some technical knowledge from early school. Daemon found it fascinating to work in the maintenance department repairing broken machines, vehicles and equipment. It was an extra benefit that having time away from the regular Xen training meant

11

he did not feel as mentally and physically fatigued as before.

It was one of the strange festival periods on the Terran calendar, the reason for the celebrations had been lost throughout time but Mistress Suix granted a holiday as a reward for her hard working students. Daemon rushed straight to the academy bar, he knew he had forty-eight hours down time to get stupidly drunk and sleep off the inevitable hangover the next day. Under normal circumstance, he would have headed straight for Cian's room but the previous day she had been involved in an accident and was in casualty. Apparently, her E.C.A. had unexpectedly gone into RAGE mode and had proceeded to inject her blood stream with a hideous drug called Quat. Under its influence, she had attacked one of the members of the group she was assigned to and had actually managed to rip off the arm of Fali's E.C.A with his arm still in it. The exposure to the vacuum and freezing temperatures cauterised the wound almost instantly but Fali still died quickly. The drill instructor at the scene shot Cian five times before she was finally put down. Fortunately, her armoured suit had taken the brunt of the damage and it was patched up quickly by the other students saving her life for the meanwhile. She had been in danger of being executed for what had happened but it was quickly established that the suit was faulty and she had been cleared by the tribunal, much to Daemons relief.

The academy bar had been decorated with coloured balloons and large silver stars had been bolted to the ceiling. The bar itself was full of revellers celebrating the unknown festival and getting drunk in the process. Daemon spotted Roz at the bar and together they found a table in a quiet spot at the back of the room so they could talk without having to shout over the din of voices.

"Is Cian going to be ok? I heard the drill instructor didn't hold back with his pistol." Roz asked between mouthfuls of beer.

"I hope she is alright, they won't even allow me to visit her." Daemon replied morosely before being distracted by three students dancing on one of the nearby tables.

"Don't worry my friend they will have her patched up soon enough, but in the meantime let's make the most of this downtime; I haven't spoken to you for a while." As Roz finished his sentence an odd looking man sat down at their table. Compared to the physiques of most of the other recruits the man was slight and he sat in silence for a while as Roz eyed him suspiciously.

"I'm very sorry to intrude, but I wish to talk to you Daemon, I'm Miles." the man eventually said. Daemon noticed that Miles had eyes which were completely black, like the eyes of a predator fish which he found very unnerving. Miles offered his hand to be shaken but Daemon wasn't feeling courteous and simply ignored the gesture.

He was about to turn his back on him when he remembered overhearing a conversation between two students in one of his classes. "Wait a minute. Aren't

13

you a Doctor or something? I seem to remember overhearing your name being mentioned a few months back. Are you the Dr Miles they were talking about?"

"Yes, but we aren't supposed to use titles here, so please, just call me Miles." he nervously looked over his shoulder to see if anybody else had heard. "I have a doctorate of V-science but please keep that information quiet," Miles whispered across the table.

"V-science? That means you fuck around with viruses and contagious bacterium to make them even deadlier doesn't it?" Daemon asked while he screwed up his face in disgust.

"We also made cures!" Miles barked and then apologised for his raised tone. "Look Daemon, may I call you Daemon?" Daemon merely shrugged and drummed his fingers on the table. Miles realised he was pressed for time. "I can see you are busy but I have a proposition for you. I think me and you should partner up."

"I'm not that way inclined." Daemon stated, grinning and started to chuckle. Roz was a little slow on the uptake but he eventually understood the joke and laughed.

"I don't mean like that! I know a lot of that kind of thing goes on in the academy. What I meant to say is that we should team up." Miles said as his pale face flushed red.

Roz was still giggling and patted the odd man on his shoulder.   "Daemon is many things, but he is definitely not a shower room soap dropper."

Miles clearly didn't find the conversation funny in any way and his anger could be read on his face. "Your girlfriend nearly died today due to a faulty suit and I have a hunch that Xen has rigged each and every E.C.A. in this fucking Academy!" he spat.

The laughter dried upon Daemon and Roz's lips almost instantly at this statement and they considered him warily. Daemon leant across threateningly and whispered, "Wait a minute have you been spying on Cian and me?"

Miles shook his head from side to side, "Everybody knows you are sleeping with Cian." He paused and added, "Especially the occupants in the rooms nearby." The moment's pause brought a grin to Miles rodent-like face, before he continued, "You need help with your science studies. I hacked your file and you didn't score very well."

"You hacked my what?" Daemon said incredulously.

"You have access to equipment found in the maintenance department." Miles continued unabashed, "In return for certain items that I need I'm willing to help you pass your science papers."
Daemon knew he hadn't done very well in the science field of his studies but he resented the fact that Miles had gained access to his results. Roz looked at Daemons face, he had seen that terrible glare a number of times before and he knew Daemon was about to turn nasty.

Miles too noticed he was skating on thin ice and pushed a slip of paper towards Daemon before pleading, "Please at least think about it. The items I need will be easy to take and I need you because I don't have access to the maintenance department." He then looked entreatingly at the two men before him and scampered away. Daemon snatched the slip of paper from the table and placed it in his pocket.

"What a weirdo," Roz muttered, he had only ever seen Miles once before and he sincerely hoped he would never have to again.

"Yeah, he's strange alright. Did you see his eyes? Like a feral animal." asked Daemon, Roz nodded in response, "I've seen things like that before in the medical encyclopaedias. They are bio-eyes, manufactured by Xen unless I'm mistaken. They're state of the art kit, they cost a small fortune; I wonder what happened to his original eyes?"

As Daemon was speaking a pretty woman had approached their table and without asking sat with them. She was tall with dark red hair and had a beautifully structured face, although Daemon had seen her around in the academy he had never spoken to her before. Without introduction, she addressed the two men, "If I were you I'd stay well away from Miles. Apparently, he's been chipped and has already passed the great test. Nobody knows why he has been sent back to the training academy."

Roz was gawping at her beauty and sat in silence so it was left up to Daemon to talk to her. "You say he has been chipped?" he asked. The woman nodded. "Yeah, a standard Xen idea chip, so the rumours go." The blank expressions on the faces of both men indicated that they didn't understand. "In other words," she continued, "Whatever Miles designs or constructs, every goddamn idea can be claimed by the Xen Corporation as their intellectual property."

Daemon only half registered what she had said and was busy staring into her wondrous blue eyes. "Why would he let them do that?" he asked.

"How do you think he got those eyes?" she said as if speaking to a simpleton.

Daemon sat in silence thinking about it for a moment; it seemed that there was a lot to take in about the strange doctor. As he sat in contemplation the woman stood to leave them, he looked up at her and said eagerly, "Thanks for the heads up. By the way, I'm Daemon, who might you be?" He waited for a response.

"Hmmm, my name is Sherry." she said with a wink before she walked off into the throng of dancing students.

Roz was still in awe of her beauty and continued to watch her dancing erotically with one of the male students.

"Fucking hell she is stunning." Daemon finally blurted out but his words were wasted as his friend seemed to be more preoccupied with staring at her arse.

When Daemon awoke the next day he was still clothed in his black jumpsuit and had an acrid taste in his mouth. He tried to raise his head from the pillow but found every movement was like being kicked in the skull. He managed to elbow himself up on to his side and was greeted by the sight of a pool of vomit on his bed making his stomach roll upon itself. The liquid was hours old and congealed but he had no recollection of being sick during the night. He peered at his watch and realised he was late for breakfast, not that he really felt like it but it was best not to miss it. He grabbed some toiletries and a spare jumpsuit and made his way to the shower room. By the time he got there it was long abandoned so he showered by himself and hoped the canteen was still serving breakfast.

The canteen was only half full with many of the students looking sickly and trying to force down the breakfast of green coloured mush. Daemon realised it was Tuesday because Monday night dinner was always green in hue.

Leftovers what joy! He thought, feeling a little ill again. However, he managed to finish his breakfast without bringing it back up but his body had already moved to the second stage of a hangover. Every movement he took made his stomach heave and his brain feel like a merry-go-round. Daemon spent the majority of the day in his room sleeping off the pain which he had brought down upon himself. He was just grateful that he had the day to sleep the fucker off.

Morning call ripped Daemon from his slumber, his head still felt like he had been opening doors with it but his stomach growled with hunger which was a good sign. He decided to skip showering and head straight to the canteen instead, it had been nearly twenty-four hours since he had eaten he realised. When he entered the canteen he saw Cian sitting alone, he grabbed a bowl of orange gunk and sat himself down next to his lover. Cian smiled weakly and then winced in pain, it was clear that she was still suffering the after-effects of the Quat and the impact damage of being shot five times. Although he wished above all else to embrace her he refrained from touching her to spare her any further discomfort.

"I've missed you so much," he claimed as he pulled an overly sad face like the mask of a clown. Cian tried to giggle but the pain ate at every nerve fibre.

"Heaven only knows how I'm going to make it through today's exercise," she said and brushed her hand on his thigh. Her merest touch forged a fire in the pit of his stomach that he couldn't even describe. "I can't remember anything of that day," she said as her eyes glazed with tears.

"I have heard Quat can do that," Daemon said reaching down and placing his hand over hers. "In fact, it's not surprising you can't, remember it's a military drug manufactured to promote aggression. They won't want you remembering," he faltered for a second, "what the drug made you do." Daemon had read up about Quat after the incident and found its effects disturbing but he knew that sometimes it was necessary to go to extremes to properly serve the Xen Corporation.

As he had been trying to comfort her Daemon had not noticed Mistress Jemm stood behind him until she spoke. He had smelt a stench in the air but assumed it

19

was coming from himself as he hadn't had time to shower.

"These are for you Cian, they should help you through today's exertions, you know, make the day more bearable," Jemm stated holding out her hand which held multi-coloured pills.
Cian stared at the pills in her hand for a while. "What are they?" she asked with undertones of distrust.

"Well, what the fuck do they look like? Pills! They're a cocktail of painkillers, stimulants and antibiotics, all a growing girl needs to make it through a horrible fucking day of a drill!" she barked.

Cian physically jumped at the outburst and took the pills out the instructor's hand and swallowed them with the aid of water. Mistress Jemm sneered before marching off towards the canteen bar leaving a trail of body odour in her wake.

Dust rose up behind twelve students and a single drill instructor as they jogged on the surface of the Rock. Daemon had more or less ironed out the encumbering technical flaws of wearing the outdated E.C.A, which allowed him to keep up with the drill instructor. Cian ran at ease at his side seemingly fuelled by the cocktail of drugs she had taken. The drill instructor had cut all transmissions so Daemon was unable to talk to his lover and was, instead, forced to listen to his laboured breath and the beat of his heart. Now and then he reached out and held Cian's hand as they stumbled through the thicker layers of dust on the moon's surface but through the segmented gauntlet he could feel Cian's warmth. By the time they reached the outer marker it was late in the day if you could actually call it day on this dimly illuminated moon. The marker was the only landmark around other than a feature which had been nicknamed Sherry's Hole; a deep crater left from a fallen meteorite which had got its name because Sherry had a reputation for putting it around a bit in the academy. It was a running joke for the majority of the students with the noticeable exception of Sherry herself.

The outer marker was a slab of graphite that had been erected by one of the earlier groups as part of their heavy vehicle training. Daemon rested his back against the monolith and Cian rested the faceplate of her helmet against Daemons so they could talk in an oddly distorted, muffled conversation. Around them, the other members of the group stood or sat recovering their breath for the return back to base. The two of them chatted while their bodies recuperated after the physical exercise, after a few days apart it was mostly filthy bed talk they spoke to each other but they both found it comforting. The drugs had seemingly had the unexpected side effect of increasing Cian's libido and she was enjoying teasing him with what she would do to him once they got back to the academy. Daemon, in turn, was beginning to feel equally lustful and couldn't wait to vent his sexual frustration on her.

The brief rest period was ended when the drill instructor broke the communications silence to give the order to return to base. Cian picked herself up gingerly and could feel that the stimulants were wearing off.

Daemon noticed her struggling and wondered if she could make it back at all. He tapped his com-line and opened a private link to the instructor.

"Drill Master, I don't think Cian has the strength to run back, could we arrange for a four track to pick her up?" He asked through the interference from the moon's background radiation. The instructor called for an immediate halt.

"Arrange a what?" he addressed the entire group through the standard band, "If she falls down you carry her if she endangers the group's survival we leave her behind. Now is that clear enough Daemon or do you want me to call up your daddy so he can pick you and your girlfriend up from school?" Daemon set his teeth at the dress down and linked his arm with Cian's to comfort her, he looked into her faceplate and raised his eyebrows as if to say that he was sorry but had tried his best.

The Drill Master set a brisk pace and it was not long before the two of them started to lag behind. Daemon's breathing was becoming increasingly laboured as he expended more and more energy just keeping Cian on her feet. Just as he began wondering what he would do if she couldn't continue he noticed a figure was lumbering back towards them. As he got closer Daemon recognised that it was Bann, one of the guys from the dormitory next to his, a real high flyer in the academy. As he joined the two stragglers he grabbed hold of Cian and placed her arm over his shoulder gesturing for Daemon to do the same on the other side. He patted

Daemon on his upper arm plate to reassure him he was only here to help and not attempting to get in bed with his girlfriend. Even though Daemon had only spoken with Bann a few times in logistic class he had already come to the conclusion that he had a chip on his shoulder due to his small stature; he conceded that he may have judged him harshly.

Even with the two men bearing most of her weight the run back to the academy had taken its toll on Cian and she had all but passed out. As they approached the Academy, Daemon and Bann were joined by two other students who took her legs and helped them carry her the remaining distance. Through the com-line, the drill instructor mocked them for not leaving her behind. The outer parameter of the academy could just about be seen on the highest setting of the E.C.A's vision intensifiers and their struggles were nearly at and end.

As they got within five hundred meters of reaching the airlock Daemon noticed a problem with his suit. The ambient temperature inside his suit had risen to forty degrees Celsius and was climbing rapidly. At first, he thought his suit had been ruptured and his E.C.A. was attempting to compensate, either that or his temperature harmonics had overloaded. He let go of Cian and attempted to recalibrate his suit but the suit's controls were not responding and sweat pissed from his pores as he tried to initiate an emergency vent procedure. For some reason, the failsafe monitors on his suit failed to comprehend the need to perform such a manoeuvre and refused to respond. Daemon screamed as alarms flashed in his helm but he no longer understood any of the statistics and words that were being relayed on his helm plate. He stared uncomprehendingly at the information he should have understood and reacted to. His panic was short lived as his vision turned to darkness and he felt the comforting hands of unconsciousness embracing his thoughts.

CHAPTER 2
A friend in need

Daemon awoke. His vision was groggy, but he recognised Mistress Suix's face. She smiled as she dabbed a wet cloth on his brow. He looked down and saw an abundance of tubes penetrating his body through which all manner of multi-coloured liquids were feeding in to him.

"How long have I been out?" he managed to say even though it hurt his parched mouth to do so.

"About twenty hours, maybe more. You actually fell into a coma for a while; I thought I was going to lose you. But you're..." her eyes swept appreciatively down him, "muscular body fought its way out of that dark sleep." She brushed her hand up his arm in a very deliberate manner. Daemons reaction was to pull his arm away and her mood changes instantly.

"What was it? Was it a faulty suit? Daemon said…" He didn't manage to finish his sentence as Mistress Suix turned on him angrily.

"It was a field test Daemon!" she hissed "That is all! You were showing far too much compassion to that skinny girl so I decided to use you for a training exercise to see how the other students reacted to an emergency situation. By the way the students did well; in fact, you might want to thank Bann, he was the one who actually saved you while your pathetic girlfriend lay unconscious." She threw the wet cloth at his bare chest and Daemon yelped as the cold icy water splashed over him. His sudden movement ripped out an I-V tube and he yelled in pain as blood welled up from the hole in his arm and he had to bite back a flurry of curses.

Suix leant over him, her face inches from his and a fixed smile came over her face, "I suppose I better tell you," she said in a surprisingly seductive tone, "Cian is to be spaced at dawn, her body is weak and she compromised the other students in their training." Her bright grey eyes probed for any sign of weakness that he may have betrayed and her smile softened as she saw anger twisting his body and contorting his face into a picture of hate.

"You can't murder Cian just because she's ill! You know that it was a faulty suit that pumped her full of that shit. You know that was what made her kill Fali. And it was your drill instructor that shot her so many goddamned times that it made her sick!" His eyes began watering but he could see that his words hadn't penetrated Mistress Suix's cold heart.

Without answering him she stood up and made her way to the door of the medical wing. She stopped at the door and spoke without turning.

"If you wish to alter the sentence I have issued upon your girlfriend then you know what you must do. My room number is four. My personal guard will let you in." Without another word she left and closed the door behind her leaving Daemon to consider the predicament she had placed him in. He despised the fact that she was attempting to blackmail him but what choice did he have, he couldn't let Cian die. He steeled himself to what he must do and took comfort that it would only be the one night.

News travelled quickly around the academy regarding Daemon's deeds in Mistress Suix's private room. His acquiescence to her demands had prevented Cian receiving the death sentence but she was still sentenced to a public flogging in front of all the students. He had stood with them feeling every stroke of the lash to Cian's bloodied and torn back wishing he could have switched places with her so she wouldn't feel such pain. To his dismay he found that any hopes he had that all would be well between the two of them were shattered when Cian wouldn't even speak to him in the dinner queue at the canteen, probably hearing about his deeds with Suix. Daemon sat with Roz and

Bann while Cian sat with another group of students, mainly male in gender. Daemon glared at the vultures flocking around Cian, they were already homing in on his beautiful girlfriend, comforting and petting her after her ordeal with the whip.

"Leave it Daemon, from what I've heard you had no choice in the matter," Roz said as he stole a piece of somm-bread from his plate. Daemon ignored the petty theft and tried to avert his vision from Cian's table.

"So come on? You can't leave us in the dark. Is Mistress Suix good in bed?" Bann said, eagerly waiting for some sordid details.

"Mind your own fucking business!" Daemon growled but as his thoughts drifted to the night in question, which had involved the best sex he had ever had, his face gave him away. Mistress Suix was a very passionate lady and had kept him up through the majority of the night.

A howl of laughter from Bann and Roz made Daemon realise he was grinning like a child with a new toy. "Your face speaks volumes, my friend," he said before bursting into more laughter.

Daemon unsuccessfully tried to stifle his own laughter by drinking a tumbler of fruit juice but only succeeded in coughing out a stream of bluish liquid before joining in with the Bann's mirth.

Roz didn't quite understand the reason for their laughter and wished he had retired to bed earlier. He had never made love to a woman before and had no knowledge of such an event and felt embarrassed at the fact. "I will see you tomorrow, I'm off to bed," he said before leaving. When Roz had departed the canteen, Daemon and Bann headed off to the bar for a few beers before retiring for the day.

Daemon finally collapsed on his bed like a sack of lead ingots. One drink had led to another until both Bann and he had drunk themselves into a state of intoxication. His pillow felt like it was made out of wood so he punched it a few times trying to knock the lumps out of it and settled down to a drunken sleep. He was on the verge of passing out when someone rapped three times on the door to his room. In his drunken state Daemon thought it was some practical joker running the corridor so he ignored the noise but it persisted to the point he had no option but to find out what the commotion was. Groggily and with his mind warped with alcohol he entertained the thought that it might be Cian at the door ready to forgive him and wanting to climb into bed for some makeup sex. His disappointment was palpable when he opened the door and saw Miles standing in the corridor.

"Miles? What the fuck do you want? Do you know how late it is?" he mumbled. Miles didn't answer and just elbowed past him and sat down on the edge of his bed. Daemon looked up and down the corridor to check that no-one had seen Miles enter his quarters as the last thing he wanted was a rumour spreading of a man sneaking into his room in the dead of the night. After all, he reasoned, the rumours of him and Mistress Suix had already apparently destroyed his relationship with

29

Cian. What slim hopes he had of patching things up with Cian would surely lie in tatters if word of him taking a male lover got to her. Undoubtedly she would take it as a personal affront. He turned to tell Miles to leave but before he could speak a word the black eyed doctor began questioning him.

"Did you get the parts I asked for?" He asked abruptly, his eyes narrowed with suspicion. Daemon was taken aback by the question and he hadn't thought the small man would have the nerve to wake him up at this time of night and start demanding contraband. He felt he was being treated like a two-bit drug dealer.

"Yeah I got your parts, why are you in such a hurry?" Daemon replied his annoyance plainly showing in the tone of his voice.

"I think the administration is closing in on me. Look what happened to you, one minute you're happily wandering over the surface of the moon and the next Mistress Suix presses a series of buttons and your left helpless in your E.C.A. Well that isn't how I'm going to check out Daemon. No chance! I'm going to prevent anyone doing the same thing to me. Damn them!" Miles rant built him up into a violent fury and he punched his balled fist into his palm. Suddenly his tone changed and he looked slyly at Daemon, "Did you tell anyone about what I said about the E.C.A.'s?"

Daemon who had just wanted to get rid of Miles had wandered over to his locker, punched a serial code into the device and opened it. He was leaning into it to retrieve the parts he had stolen when Miles asked the question so his face was obscured as he realised that he may have mentioned something about it. He instantly used his Pseudo-Met training to remove the tension from his face and turned to face Miles.

"What?" he asked as innocently as he could manage. Miles was looking directly at him trying to gauge his reaction then opened his mouth as if to ask him again when suddenly he seemed to lose interest and burst into a broad smile as he looked at the contraband Daemon held.

"You got all of it?" Miles inquired.

"Yeah," laughed Daemon, "I can't say they were as easy to steal as you said but here they are. The full list of stuff of everything you gave me!" Daemon passed him the first items and started emptying various electronic components from the locker of onto his bed. Miles quickly filed through the components inspecting some of them carefully to see if they were damaged. His mood was now completely different to what it had been only moments before and his smile nearly enveloped his face.

"I can't even begin telling you how thankful I am. I owe you and I'll make good on our agreement, I'll help you through your science papers and before you know it you'll be on your way to becoming a full Xen officer." Miles gathered up the components and placed them in the pockets of his jump suit. He stood to leave but found that Daemon had moved to the door and had placed his heel against it to block his exit.

"Now that we are partners in crime," Daemon said, "I

think I should learn a little more about you."

Miles wriggled his head like a cornered rat which made him appear even more feral than he looked normally. "What do you mean?" he asked showing his disquiet, "This isn't the time for discussion, I've got to ready my E.C.A. with these parts. I have a lot of work to do, time is of the essence." Miles tried to worm his way past Daemon and open the door but Daemon easily pushed him away and gestured for him to sit down again. Miles looked at the larger man as if weighing up his options then reluctantly took a seat.

"This doctorate of V-Science you claim you have. You know that some people say that it's bullshit don't you?" lied Daemon.

"What?" blurted Miles obviously taken off guard.

"Oh? Didn't you know people were saying it? Well assuming you do have it, did you create any deadly viruses?"

Miles slapped his hands down onto the bed like a spoilt child. "Yes I did as it happens; the corporation even lets me name it after myself. Haven't you heard of the Miles Virus? Anyway, why do you want to know? Are you one of those who don't believe me?" Miles said scowling.

"You named a deadly pathogen after yourself? What kind of sick fuck does that make you?" Daemon said with disgust.

Miles shrugged and cocked his head to one side looking slightly confused. "I created it so why not name it after its creator?"

Daemon shook his head and finally understood

Sherry's warning to stay clear of Miles. "Did the company ever release the Virus?" Daemon prompted as he averted his eyes from the sinister man.

"Not as far as I know but I seriously doubt it. Xen certainly wouldn't have field tested it and I doubt they ever will. You see it wasn't really what the company was hoping for. It killed far too quickly and they wanted something they could use to make money from the cure." Miles seemed to be swelling with pride.

"Make money from the cure?" Daemon asked not comprehending.

"Yes, you know? They'd drop it on a planet then miraculously come up with a cure after a few million had died. Planet-wide vaccination at an astronomical cost, the profits would be incalculable."

"And you helped them with this?" Daemon could hardly believe what he was hearing.

"Well strictly speaking what I did didn't actually help them with it. Like I said it killed too quickly." Then Miles actually smirked, "That and the fact that they couldn't come up with a cure. I dare say they have kept it on ice to use as a death weapon."

Daemon was stunned that Miles was so blasé about what he was saying and although he claimed ignorance of the status of his beloved virus his tone suggested he knew otherwise. Suspicion crawled up Daemon's flesh leaving goose bumps in its wake and he realised that he was a good deal soberer than he had been when Miles had entered his room.

Exhausted and bemused by the turn of the conversation

Daemon slumped down on to the bed next to Miles. After a brief pause, he merely stated, "Fucking hell." The two of them sat in silence for a minute before Daemon continued. "That stuff I've stolen for you, you're going to rig your E.C.A. so that no-one else can control aren't you? Well, I want you to do the same to my suit. I'm not risking having someone put me into a coma again."

Miles smiled and light glinted off his dark orb-like eyes, "Certainly Daemon, get me those parts again and I will rig your suit. We shall also begin your tutoring of science tomorrow at seven sharp as we agreed." Daemon was about to object to the time but felt too tired to argue.

"Miles," he said, as the slight man opened the door, "don't get caught with that stuff. The last thing I want is a visit to the airlock to be spaced!" When Miles left and the door was closed once more, Daemon settled down on his bed and stared at the glaring overheads. Miles seems to be a useful friend to know in this dangerous academy but he was seriously deranged one.

"You stupid, ignorant, bastard!" Drill Instructor Gidd yelled and kicked Roz in his groin. Although his armoured suit stifled most of the damage it still hurt like hell, a kick to the balls was still a kick to the balls no matter how much protection you had. Roz fell to the floor and curled into a foetal position while his eyes filled with water. A horrible sickly sensation flared in his stomach and then crawled its way up his throat. The instructor continued to shout out insults but his words were blocked by the wall of terrible pain. Roz finally picked himself up from the dusty surface whilst the instructor tapped his foot impatiently. Despite the crippling pain Roz automatically responded to his training and searched his groin plate for any punctures in his E.C.A. The students had been planting simulated explosives in Sherry's Hole and Roz had accidentally wired up the wrong connector. If the explosives had been real it would have turned the students into a fragmented matter which would have been liberally scattered over the moon's surface.

Gidd hadn't finished with Roz yet, "The next time you fuck up like that initiate, I will personally flog you until I can no longer hold a whip." Gidd heard some of the students giggling through the comms but decided to let it ride. He was an ex-captain of the Xen CORE and was renowned for his physical endurance and capacity for brutality but he knew violence worked best in small unexpected bursts.

"Sorry Drill Master," Roz mumbled through his private comm-link, "I will study harder in the technical class."

"You're a sorry son-of-a-bitch, Roz. I do hope your momma is proud of you because I sure as shit am not!" Gidd growled and pondered how to dole out punishment for the laughter that had taken place.

"Right then ladies since you all have enough energy to laugh at Initiate Roz's incompetence it seems clear to

35

me I haven't worked you hard enough. Run to the outer marker and then back to the academy, if you set off now, you might get back to the base by midnight." Gidd turned to the students who had giggled and addressed them directly, "I expect you guys to keep up with the pace I set." This was met by a series of groans as they knew he would run them into the ground. He left the rest of them to move as fast as they liked, the longer they took the less rest they would get.

Roz didn't feel especially fortunate but unknown to him Gidd had gone easy on him because he had a good understanding of combat and weapons training and Gidd felt a kinship with him. Roz set off at a brisk run and looked at his clock calculating his personal best running time to the marker and back. It seemed it would be a close call for a midnight arrival at the academy.

As Roz ran his mind wandered away from the physical stresses his body were being subjected to and he began cursing to himself. He tried to suppress the anger that boiled inside, at making such a simple mistake. He knew he didn't really understand all of the technical side of Xen training but he had somehow struggled through the majority of the tech classes. Daemon had helped him along on a few pointers and showed him the basics of field stripping but absorbing the bombardment of information was far too much for him. Two hours into the run to the outer marker his desire to rip off Gidd's head had subsided, slightly. He hated to admit it but he knew who to blame for this punishment and it wasn't the Drill Master, it was his pig-shit brain.

"One of these days you are going to get us both killed. All you had to do was connect up a few wires? But no, that is far too difficult you, you dumb ass." he grumbled. As was standard for punishment runs the drill instructor had shut down the comm-links so each cadet only had their own thoughts for the company so all Roz heard was the echo of his own voice within his helmet.

He began castigating himself again as he found it helped to pass the time. "Here we go again using my body to save my skin yet again. Goddamn useless shit for brains. Always getting me into these situations may as well just scoop the useless thing out and leave the rest of me to muddle through." Through gasps of breath the abuse continued, he estimated he had another two hours of running before he would even see the outer marker.

In fact, it took him a little less than that to get there and as Roz rested against the outer marker he glanced at his suits internal clock and realised he had pushed him-self hard and beat his personal best time by one minute and thirty-three seconds. His E.C.A.'s internal ambient temperature was a little high so he flicked a switch on his arm brace which injected a nitrogen pellet into his suits harmonics. The wash of cool air on his skin quickly cooled down both the E.C.A. and himself. He watched his heart rate steadily drop and reflected upon why he had subjected himself to all this in the first place.

"This is shit." he thought, "why did I sign up for Xen training when I could have stayed at home and worked on the farm. Mind you, I would probably have become a drug addict like my father, smoking stimulants to counter the boredom when not working in the fields. There again I might have been married by now with a rake of kids." As usual, Roz tried to remember exactly which of the many reasons was mainly responsible for making him leave home. Was it the insults from his intoxicated father or was it down to the fact he had grown to hate the stench of animal shit? He had trodden this same line of reasoning so many times it was like walking through the fields on the farm in the pitch black, he might not be able to see where he was going but he always ended up in the same place.

"This is your entire fault, Daemon. I would have never of signed the dotted line if it wasn't for you." Roz remembered the exultation he had felt when he and Daemon had decided to join up with the Xen Corporation. It was all fun and games at first, standing in the Xen recruiting station having travelled from their home world to Hanna Prime. It had been a welcome change from the drudgery of their home planet. Roz remembered how they had both scraped together the funds to pay for the expensive space flight even though they would be refunded after joining up. He had sent his refund credits back home using his newly established Xen account. His father would have probably smoked the money away by now. He focused his attention on his clock and realised he had been sat for longer than he had planned and he wouldn't make it back to the academy by midnight.

As he checked his suit before beginning the trek back he noticed something unusual in the ink black sky. A fiery plasma trail had appeared over an outcrop of rocks near horizon and was arcing through the sky on a path that would take it close to where he was. Suddenly he realised that it was actually heading directly towards the monolith and he felt uneasy. He moved around the great stone not wanting to be seen and waited as a small craft came close and began descending to the moon's surface. Dust billowed around the craft as its thrusters slowed to a stop obscuring the markings on the tail that identified it. When the dust had settled Roz he could just about make out a corporate symbol on the side of the ship.

"Seinal Corporation?" he said aloud, "What the fuck are they doing on a Xen Rock?" Roz froze and switched off the comm-link transmitter on his suit even though he was pretty sure nobody else could hear his voice. The Seinal corporate signature had been burnt into his mind by the numerous film reels that Xen had force fed every student. The Seinal Corporation, they had been taught, were an evil and twisted group of villains, mercenaries and arms merchants. Roz tapped his communicator to see if he could establish a direct line to the Drill Master but all he heard was a hiss and the crackle of static.

"Nice one Gidd," he whispered sarcastically, "you've left one of your students unarmed in the middle of

nowhere, without even an emergency line of contact."
Roz hoped the Drill Master or one of the mistresses was
monitoring his transmission and would respond before
he shut down the line again. The gang plate on the
Seinal craft began to descend as Roz ducked back into
the cover of the monolith.

"Fuck, fuck, fuck." He repeated over and over like a
mantra wondering what to. He could make a run for it
and hope they didn't see his dust trail or wait to see if
they noticed his presence. He didn't feel he was in any
state to outrun them even assuming that they were
forced to follow on foot. That settled it, he only had one
option. The next thing to do was to establish if they had
life scanners. He forced himself to take another look
despite the risk of revealing himself and, to his horror,
witnessed three armoured soldiers making their way
towards the monolith. They didn't seem to be in any
hurry and seemed to be following a standard patrol
sweep pattern. That knowledge somehow calmed him
and he put his back to the monolith feeling the sense of
panic that had been building start to dissipate. If they
were following a standard pattern it could be predicted,
he estimated the time the Seinal troops would take to
zero in on his position and began to count the time
down on the internal clock. At no time did it occur to
him, that for once it was his much-maligned brain that
was saving his skin.

When the count reached zero he punched in a serial
code on the harmonic control pad attached to his arm
and activated RAGE mode. The display asked him to

input a number to represent the dosage he wanted to use. He wasn't sure what dosage was required as the students were not allowed to engage RAGE mode and had not received training on it. "Fuck it." He muttered as he told the suit to use three out of the four injectors.

He winced as the needles of the Quat injectors penetrated his lower back and then nearly vomited in his helm as the filthy drug raced through his veins. His teeth clamped down as if he had been given an electric shock and all of his muscles began to spasm as the drug took hold. He was aware of a strange roaring sound coming from somewhere but couldn't place where it came from. His head was pounding and felt hot as hell as if it was being scalded and crushed. His vision took on a vibrant blood red tinge and he could sense his mind entering some primal state. His rational thoughts were subsiding and were being replaced with the urge to tear and rend flesh; his anger increased exponentially.

He sprang from behind the monolith and ran towards the three men hoping, before the Quat took complete control of him, that he would never again feel so much anger and hatred towards another human being.

CHAPTER 3

What time is it? It's Quat time!

"Red leader six here, we are approaching the marker, yeah, this looks like it. It's non-indigenous. It must have been put here for training purposes. There is no Xen activity here at present, repeat, no activity. Awaiting orders commander, are we to proceed?" The corporal said into his communicator. The three Seinal troops moved towards the monolith as they waited for confirmation.

"Ok red six, proceed to the depot on foot. I'm going to take the ship back into orbit and collect supplies. I'll meet you back there." the Seinal commander replied as the ship quickly ascended on a plume of plasma fire.

"Shit! It looks like we are walking back to the depot boys." The corporal announced to the two soldiers as the ship disappeared skywards.

"Walking? That's eight kilometres, probably more." One of the soldiers complained.

"Yeah, well quit complaining and set a bearing for fuck's sakes, or we won't be eating tonight." the corporal growled. He was about to turn away from the monolith when a man rushed from behind it and leapt towards him. He tried to raise his assault rifle but it was violently kicked from his grip. Before he could react he saw the man raising a gauntleted fist towards him. The thought flashed through his mind that the guy was crazy, who in their right minds would try to punch an E.C.A. To his horror the first blow cracked the visor, his eyes widened with shock as he saw the second blow smash through the face plate exposing him to the almost complete vacuum. His breath was torn from his lungs and quickly turned to ice crystals as his head began decompressing. He dropped to his knees feeling himself freezing as his compromised suit left him at the mercy of the unforgiving absolute zero temperature.

Roz ducked down and grabbed the freezing corporal using his body as a shield against the other two Seinal soldiers who opened fire. Shots peppered the corporal's suit, some deflecting off the armour and some penetrating. Roz threw the man at the two troopers then rolled across the dusty ground and snatched up the corporal's firearm. He emptied the magazine into one of the soldiers from groin to head. The soldier dropped down in a pink mist of escaping gas and tissue from the ruptures in his E.C.A. The other soldier was reloading his exhausted weapon which allowed Roz to leave his makeshift cover and charge towards his foe. He kicked him squarely in the chest sending him flying backwards in a slow zero G tumble. Before he had even hit the ground Roz had thrown himself onto the panic-stricken soldier. Dust and sand bloomed up as the two combatants grappled in a violent melee. Roz managed to grab the soldiers air pipe and crushed it before ripping it from the helm manifold. The soldier thrashed around on the surface vainly reaching out to grab the tube which writhed around like a dancing snake as the air rushed out of it. Roz got to his feet and peered down at the doomed man for a few seconds before he lashed out with his boot buckling the neck ring around the soldier's throat. Blood spattered inside the soldier's face plate obscuring his agonised features.

Roz made his way over to the soldier he had shot and discovered he was dead also. Amazingly he had succeeded in applying several field patches that had staunched the escaping air but other ruptures in the E.C.A. armour had allowed the life supporting gases to seep away as his life had done. Roz felt an overwhelming disappointment because he hadn't had the opportunity to apply a coup de grace. He reached down and tore one of the Seinal insignia patches from the corpse and shoved it into one of the pouches in his E.C.A. At least he would have a trophy of what he had done.

Back at the Academy Drill Master Gidd stood cracking his knuckles as Mistress Jemm shook her head wondering if the Drill Master had calculated the timescale correctly. "Where is that numb nuts son-of-a-bitch? He should have been back by now." Gidd said exasperatedly.

"Stop worrying, Initiate Roz is probably caught up in a dust storm, they've been occurring all day. He'll be back soon enough, his suit contains enough O2 for three days." Jemm said trying to calm him down. Drill Master Gidd was worried which was unlike him and Mistress Jemm could see his torment. "Roz isn't the brightest of students after all; it wouldn't take much to disorientate him. I certainly won't be losing any sleep over his absence." She tapped her foot impatiently.

Gidd shot her a glare and shook his head, "He might not be the brightest star in the universe but Initiate Roz is a fine student. He has guts and he follows orders to the letter, he might not end up being an officer but you can't overlook his potential for the military core." Gidd barked then wished he hadn't raised his voice against Mistress Jemm.

"I haven't overlooked anything! You and your precious military core can wait. It's my job to make agents, officers and valuable personnel for the Xen Corporation, not two-bit soldiers." she ranted. Her eyes were bloodshot with anger and Gidd quickly found a reason to avoid them, he refocused his attention to the viewing screen that overlooked the docking bay in the academy. Mistress Jemm was about to retire to her quarters when her communicator buzzed.

"Mistress Jemm, we have initiated Roz in the rear airlock. He seems to have some bodies with him. Two bodies to be exact, both wearing E.C.A.'s with corporate signatures on their helms." The auxiliary stated.

Mistress Jemm clicked her communicator so Drill Master Gidd could also hear. "Repeat, did you say Corporate signatures?" she prompted. Gidd cocked his ear towards the speaker section on the communicator.

"Yes mistress. Seinal Corporation, I believe." The auxiliary replied.

Mistress Jemm scowled at the communicator as Gidd shook his head in disbelief.

"Are you sure it's a Seinal corporate symbol?" she asked.

"Yes I'm sure, why don't you come down and take a look." the auxiliary came back with a hint of annoyance in his tone.

"Well let the initiate in and we can find out how and why he has managed to find and drag a couple of bodies to the academy." Mistress Jemm commanded. Beside her Drill Master Gidd nodded in approval.

"Negative Mistress, the initiate is dusted to the eyeballs. His suit shows that three Quat doses have been administered." The auxiliary said as he double checked his reading.

Gidd leant over Mistress Jemm and spoke in to her comm, "Did you just say three?" he asked.

"Affirmative sir," came the reply.

Gidd looked at Jemm and cursed under his breath, "It's

a miracle he hasn't died from an overdose already." she said with a look of amazement on her face.
"Hold steady," Gidd said into the communicator, "I'm coming down." He looked at Jemm and spoke quietly, "They make them from stern stuff in the Core." Before she could reply he raced off towards the airlocks.

News about Roz travelled quickly in the academy, Daemon heard about what had happened in the shower room where most of the early morning gossip took place. The rumour going around was that Roz had killed six Seinal corporate troopers with his bare hands near the outer marker and dragged two of them back to the academy. Someone claimed that one of the auxiliaries has told him that Roz was in such a state a dozen instructors had been unable to restrain him and they had had to override his E.C.A. via remote and shut it down to immobilise him. After that, he had immediately been put into cryogenic still wearing his E.C.A. and medical experts had been summoned from Hanna Prime.
If it was true, Daemon realised, Roz would remain frozen for many months as it was a hell of a long journey by starcraft to get to the Rock. The more people he asked the more different versions he got about what had happened.

That morning the students were formally briefed about the incident by Mistress Suix and Mistress Jemm.
"First things first, it has been decided to remove all but one of the Quat injectors from all training E.C.A.'s,

this will be done by each student today instead of normally scheduled classes. It is clear now that students can no longer be trusted with military hardware, especially brainless students such as Initiate Roz. Quat is not some kind of recreational pharmaceutical to be used as and when you see fit, it is a very dangerous stimulant with hideous side effects if used inappropriately. The damage caused by an overdose of Quat, for those who survive one, is largely unknown. We don't even know if student Roz will ever fully recover from such an overdose. He will be removed from the academy as soon as he is stable enough to travel via starcraft." Mistress Suix paused for a breath and then continued.

"Secondly, E.C.A. and lunar surface training will be temporary put on hold until the Xen military declares this Rock safe and free from Seinal Corporation interference. Xen has a tyrant class starcraft close by and The Lazarus should arrive within the week. Temporary billets will be set up in all available spaces in the academy to house Xen troops, some students will be forced to share rooms to free up more space." A rumble of dissent greeted this as the students mumbled and groaned.

"Stop your banter at once!" Mistress Siux shouted, "You will all do as you are commanded." She took out her pain baton and began waving it around daring anyone to continue. Mistress Jemm started to circle the room watching out for trouble makers.

"Due to this temporary setback in outdoor activities,

you will all be signed up for another month to catch up on your training as soon as it's safe to do so. And before you begin asking dumb questions Xen Corporation will not be paying you for the extra month in question." A few of the braver students began to voice their opinions about the non-payable month of duty.

"You! You! And fucking you! Get your carcases up front!" Mistress Jemm shouted pointing at the rebellious students. The three students walked nervously to the head of the assembly where Mistress Jemm quickly subjected them to a beating. Daemon winced at every stroke of her pain baton and was sickened to see that Mistress Jemm was clearly enjoying each strike she delivered with her muscular man like arm. Several auxiliaries rushed into the briefing chamber and dragged the unconscious students away to the medical wing. Mistress Jemm calmly put her baton away and prompted her companion to continue speaking.

"I will take this opportunity to inform you about the great test. Now I know you were briefed on Hanna Prime of the great test but as you know the exact details were left out." Mistress Suix stated and cleared her throat before continuing.

"The great test will be performed by every student of the Xen Corporation at some point in their academic training. When this will be done is decided by high ranking Xen officials only. It could be next week or it could be a year from now. Some of you may already know that student Miles has already taken the great test and passed." Mistress Suix waited while the students who did not know this had finished gasping and pointing out Miles in the midst of the assembly. Miles blushed violently and nervously shied away from the whispers and pointing fingers.

"If student Miles wishes to share the details of his test with any of you then it is entirely his decision. However, the fact is, the great test will differ for each and every student in the academy. As you are all going to be confined indoors for at least the next week I can only advise you to take the opportunity to concentrate on your studies and be more vigilant with regards to your own safety." Mistress Suix paused and pointed to a nearby auxiliary.

"This auxiliary will provide you with the relevant forms to fill out if you wish to share rooms with another student. Remember we will shortly be housing a battalion of troops so volunteers are necessary. I don't wish to force people to do this but I will not hesitate to do so if need be!" With this Mistress Suix retired to her quarters.

Daemon spent most of the remaining day in the maintenance department aiding other students with the removal of the Quat injectors from their E.C.A. armour. At the end of his shift he wandered to his private quarters sleepily. He punched in his serial code and opened the door when he saw Miles inside his room he thought he had gone to the wrong room.

"Hello Daemon, or should I call you roommate?"

Miles said cheerily. Daemon couldn't even answer the question. He was busy wondering why Miles was in his room.

"Roommate, what are you talking about Miles?" He asked, and then he noticed his E.C.A. was on the floor next to his bed.

Miles followed his eyes and shrugged, "I've fixed your suit for you so it can't be activated by anyone but you." He grinned and sat on the extra bed that hadn't been in the room when Daemon had left that morning. Daemon glared at the pile of clothing and personal items stacked neatly by the side of Miles bunk.

"Forget it! You are not bunking in with me. Get your stuff together and get the fuck out of my room!" Daemon said as held the door open. Miles looked perplexed not understanding why Daemon was so angry.

"I'm sorry Daemon but all the forms have been filled out now, besides this makes perfect sense, I can teach you science a few hours every night before we sleep. And it's not as if you have a girlfriend at the moment. I've heard that Cian isn't even talking to you." Miles said with a frown.

"This has nothing to do with Cian, Miles! I just don't want to share a room with a man who develops hideous viruses in his spare time." He ranted.

"I only created the one deadly virus," Miles said meekly and cocked his head to one side studying his reaction. Daemon was seething but he knew once Miles had signed the relocation form there was no going back.

51

He stormed over to his bed and climbed in without taking off his clothes. Miles had fallen silent and Daemon tried to calm himself down, he enviously wondered if Cian had bunked up with another man and ground his teeth together. He hoped that she hadn't for the man's sake, in this mood he was likely to go all medieval on him.

Miles switched off the light and relaxed on his bed. "I bumped into Mistress Suix a few hours ago. She seemed delighted with me moving into your room. She said the move might prompt you to see her on a regular basis but I'm not sure what she meant by that?" Miles whispered in the darkness.

Daemon grabbed his sheets and rolled onto his side away from Miles. "For fuck's sake!" he called out. It seemed Mistress Suix was using any available advantage to get him between her thighs. He wondered if spending a few nights in Suix's quarters would make Cian jealous and drive her back into her arms, assuming that Cian wasn't already tumbling around in bed with somebody else.

"Shut the fuck up and go to sleep Miles!" Daemon hissed into the darkness as he imagined Cian in bed with another man.

The alarm call shook Daemon from his slumber. He yawned and stretched the sleep from his body before he crawled out of bed. He sat on its edge and sniffed the clothing he had slept in. The stench of stale sweat and machine lubricants filled his nostrils.

"Shit, I stink." He growled taking off his clothes. He

looked across and noted that Miles must be an early riser as his bed was fully made and his recreation clothing was neatly folded on the top of his foot locker. Daemon sneered at the neatness of his new bunk mate and gathered up the folded clothing and tossed them onto the floor before grabbing a towel and some soap from his locker. He was about to rush off to the shower room when he noticed Miles had left his foot locker unfastened. He knelt down and opened the box; it contained all the usual trinkets he had expected to find other than an old moth-eaten teddy bear. He picked up the tattered toy and examined it, an old faded tag protruded from the dusty seams. He had trouble reading the print at first until he brought it into the focus of the light.

"Dante?" he said puzzled. Daemon ran his finger down a freshly sewn seam on the back of the toy then shook it to see if it rattled. You are hiding something, Dr Miles, he thought. Curiosity was getting the better of him but he heard motion in the corridor outside and quickly returned the toy to the footlocker.

The spray of hot water soothed Daemon's flesh as he showered in the midst of numerous students who were also late up that morning. Bann was close by chatting to Sherry and another female student.

"Yeah, apparently the heads of Xen have passed Roz, they say his encounter with the Seinal Corporation was as good as any great test," Sherry said over the hiss of the showers. Bann seemed livid and kicked the nearby

53

wall.

"Well I hope my great test will be as easy as killing a couple of troops. Some people get all the luck," he claimed. Daemon shot him a glare and tried to refrain from striking out against him. Sherry giggled and started to pet around with Bann who clearly loved the attention.

"Not only that, but Roz is being shipped to a special academy when he is finally rehabilitated." she teased obviously attempting to get another reaction from Bann.

"So the dumb kids get all the preferential treatment?" Bann moaned.

"Nobody refers to my friend as a dumb kid, not even you!" Daemon roared before he rushed through the haze of shower steam towards Bann. Daemons footing was unsure on the wet tiles and Bann sidestepped the clumsy assault causing Daemon to slide uncontrollably into the wall. Bann quickly stepped over and lashed out.

A flash of white light bloomed in Daemon's vision as Bann's fist connected with his jaw. He tried to get back on his feet but his knees had turned to jelly and refused to follow the commands from his brain. He made it half way up before losing his balance and tumbled towards the wall. Bann tried to catch him as he fell but couldn't get a good enough grip to stop him. Daemon smacked his head against the wall, lost consciousness and cascaded down to a sitting position.

The lights had been dimmed as Daemon regained consciousness. He winced when he tried to move and realised his head had been bandaged.

"So the brawler awakes." He recognised Suix's voice in the shadows at the side of his bed. "Have you learnt nothing Daemon?" she whispered, "You attacked a fellow student and Bann has been let off with a verbal warning as he acted in self-defence. The next time you have a grudge against another student use your training and find a more suitable way to settle a petty argument." Daemon really didn't want to hear this and turned over so his back was to Suix.

"The problem is you started the fight so when you're done in here you will have to be publicly punished. I dare say Mistress Jemm will enjoy flogging you in front of your fellow students. There is a lesson to be learnt from this incident. I hope you learn never to attack someone while witnesses are present." He felt her fumbling around under his bed sheets, at first he tried to resist her warming touch but finally allowed her access to his cock. He suspected that this was going to be a long night

Mistress Suix had left the medical wing around midnight and sleep had been easy to find with the medication and his exertions taking its toll. He drifted into a dream where his father's house was a ruin as though it had been gutted by fire or subjected to some kind of explosion. He was unable to find his parents and wondered how the family home being ruined. Nothing seemed to make sense.

A voice called his name from where the kitchen was, it sounded sinister as though it was echoing from inside a cave. He walked towards the voice over a floor was strewn with rubble and broken glass. The next room was all wrong; he was somehow walking back into the room he had just left. Amongst the debris of smashed furniture, his eyes fell upon a burning creature that shouted his name over and over. The creature, although vaguely humanoid, appeared to be made of fire and was horned like some kind of mythical demon.

"Daemon," the demon cried, "you must wake up... NOW!" He felt his body surging with adrenaline and wanted to ask this thing what was happening but the ground rumbled beneath him.

CHAPTER 4

Forgetting all your troubles.

For the second time in as many days Daemon found himself in a hospital bed but this time he remained unmolested by Mistress Suix. His recollection of the events that had occurred was blurry, he could hardly remember leaving the medical wing as if his mind had somehow blocked out the entire incident. When he was given permission to leave the infirmary he was told to immediately get into his jumpsuit and report to the assembly hall.

He entered the room to find that it was as full as he had ever seen; it appeared that the full complement of the academy was present. As soon as he passed through the door everybody was called to attention and he was surprised to find that his name was being called out to present himself to the company. Mistress Jemm stood at the head of the throng and stared at him intently as he made his way towards her. For a second he wondered what was happening then felt a loosening of his bowels as he realised that it looked as if they were really going to make an example of him for his part in the fight in the showers. When he reached Mistress Jemm he saluted her and hoped she could not see that his hand was shaking. She looked him up and down slowly then spoke loudly, "Initiate Daemon, your actions can not be ignored," at those words Daemons shoulders drooped in resignation. Jemm paused apparently savouring his discomfort,   "You have shown outstanding bravery in the face of adversity. Your actions in rescuing your fellow students and securing the facility show the kind of fortitude that the Xen Corporation hopes each of its employees aspires to. I have great honour in presenting you with this medal in recognition of your bravery."

Daemon was stunned as a deafening round of applause rang out as the small black and red medal was pinned to his jumpsuit. He shook Mistress Jemm's hand after he had received it and grinned stupidly. Jemm motioned for him to remain where he was as she continued. "In light of events and the unfortunate loss of life we are also bestowing upon you the rank of acting sergeant of the Xen foundation, wear this pin with pride." As she attached the pin to him she whispered, "Your bravery and quick thinking saved many lives, well-done Sergeant." In the hail of cheers which echoed in the briefing chamber Mistress Jemm even surprised herself when she bear hugged him and shook his hand once more. Daemon returned to his place in the ranks dumbfounded shaking his head in disbelief. He listened carefully to the briefing as he wanted to know exactly what had happened the night before.

"Yesterday," Mistress Suix began, "the Lazarus arrived in orbit and performed a planetary scan that uncovered a secret Seinal base eight kilometres from the outer marker. Captain Lorex of the Lazarus immediately attacked the hidden base using space-to-ground bunker busting bombs. Although the Seinal base was wiped out a Seinal starcraft was in orbit and uncloaked launching a cowardly attack upon the Lazarus causing serious damage. During the ensuing battle, the Seinal craft sent a battle class cruiser to attack the academy. The Seinal battle cruiser caused minor damage to, the structure of the academy before it was brought down by our defence array. Unfortunately, when the battle cruiser crashed it landed in the living quarters of H block killing all five students and the three auxiliaries stationed there. In the hours that followed student Daemon and several of the trained Xen personnel were able to lock down most of the remaining living areas saving many lives, my own included. However, two more students and five auxiliaries perished during those hours of chaos." She paused and took several mouthfuls of water from a nearby tumbler. Daemon sat amazed, he really couldn't remember anything apart from having a terrible nightmare about his ruined parent's house. "You have all had a lucky escape thanks to the dedication and training of your supervisors, many of whom sacrificed their own lives to save yours." Mistress Suix left the podium and Mistress Jemm continued in her stead.

"In addition to the suspension of the activities already announced all studies will now be put on hold until we repair the academy. Captain Lorex is sending down any troops he can spare to aid in the repair work to the academy. Students who are fit for duty will be involved in the repairs. So the quicker we can get our beautiful academy back to an operational level the sooner we can all get back to training. The Lazarus will be sticking around for a few weeks while they investigate the Seinal Corporations presence on the Rock. That means you will still be forced to co-inhabit rooms." Mistress Jemm grimaced obviously anticipating somebody would complain but nobody did or dared to.

Miles patted Daemons shoulder and whispered to him, "That's good news isn't it roommate?" His glossy obsidian eyes probed for any reaction but Daemon merely shrugged. He was beyond caring as he would probably be spending long days outside the academy repairing the damage caused by the crash and the very few remaining hours in the company of Miles.

"One last thing people," Jemm was saying, "If you feel any loss for a friend that has been killed during this terrible assault please consult Mistress Suix who has kindly volunteered to council any traumatised students." Mistress Jemm could hardly disguise the distaste in her voice at this prospect.

It took six days to patch up the academy facility before it was fully inhabitable. Some of the amenities and the long range communicators were still offline but at least running water had been re-established. During the repair work, Daemon had witnessed Cian petting with Jaq and found out they were bunked in the same room together. He hated knowing that Cian had moved on but he grudgingly agreed on her choice of a male companion. Jaq was a very handsome man indeed, as Bann put it; he was like a gigantic chocolate cake that women couldn't help flocking to. The academy was bustling with heavily armed Xen troopers who took up more space than they strictly needed. The initial investigation into the Seinal base had confirmed that there was little left after the bombs had hit it so it appeared that the Xen troopers and the Lazarus would be leaving soon. From what Daemon had seen of the Xen troopers he couldn't believe how fanatical they were. They seemed totally unemotional, un-conversational and completely committed to the Xen cause. To his surprise, he found that because of his new rank he was often being saluted by them or finding that attention had been, called on deck even though he was still a student.

By the end of the week the investigation had been completed and the conclusion was that the Seinal base had been a way-depot for arms dealing in the localised zone of neutral space. He discovered that apparently it was not unusual for small scuffles to take place in neutral space between corporations but that it had never lead to an all-out corporate war. It was almost as if the major corporations had some kind of gentleman's agreement or unwritten rule that allowed them to take up arms against one another as long as they didn't openly invade corporate owned territories.

By the time The Lazarus finally left orbit the majority of the students in the academy had bonded with their roommates leaving a lot of rooms empty. Daemon had the option to move to one of them but declined, he had found that the late night science tutoring from Miles was working. He was starting to understand some of the more esoteric theories and even found he enjoyed wading through the mathematical formulae required to make sense of everything. He also found Miles to be quite a comical man underneath his reserved exterior and he often laughed at his open naivety to worldly experience. The guy had spent far too long cooped up in a laboratory.

"Never?" Daemon laughed half way through a conversation. Miles shook his head while he fumbled around with a clutter of glassware that he had assembled on a small table in their room.

"Well we will have to sort something out. I can't allow you to go through the entirety of Xen secondary training without ever experiencing the touch and caress of a woman." Daemon said while he drunkenly attempted to fill his glass from a flask of illegally distilled alcohol.

"No Daemon, I have never had the pleasure of a woman's touch but it's not surprising given my appearance. What female would be accommodating enough to bed me?" Miles stated matter-of-factly as he continued to fiddle around with a beaker half filled with coloured liquid. Daemon stifled a laugh and staggered over to Miles to sit with him.

"What about Crel? I've noticed she stares over at you in logistic class." Daemon slurred while the room span around him. The fatigue of the days work and the alcohol he had consumed was luring his tired body towards bed.

"Crel?" Miles exclaimed looking up, "She stares at me because she resents me being top of the class. It's more a glare of jealousy than a look of attraction I think." Miles screwed up his rodent like face in anger toward Daemon for even attempting to convince him with such falsehood.

"I'm sorry Miles, you're probably right. I think she does resent you but I will find someone to bed you if it's the..." Daemon didn't finish what he was saying because sleep had finally caught up with him. Miles sighed and manhandled Daemon to his bed. He covered him up and returned to his chemical apparatus with a feeling of utter despair.

Everything had fallen back into a steady routine of study, physical training and weapons programs. Months went by without any major incident happening in the academy, they were well enough drilled now for basic mistakes to stop happening. The only changes were in people's love lives. Daemon was now seeing Mistress Suix on a regular basis, he had also found out that Jaq had dumped Cian in exchange for a male student which she had taken very badly. He had been tempted to try and re-establish his relationship with Cian but decided to keep in with Mistress Suix. Dating the head woman of the academy came with its own perks. He couldn't remember the last time he had been subjected to toilet detail or any other demoralising duties. He had even scored eighty two percent on his latest science paper which he had thanked Miles greatly for his help in the late night studies. The chaos of the first six months seemed to have gone for good.

The Drill Master had planned a routine skimmer mission to the outer marker. Skimmers were fast transport crafts that hovered about a meter or so off the ground, they were very hard to pilot and very few students had any experience of mastering these wild cats, as they had been dubbed. Primarily they were used to transport special operatives to a target quickly as they were little use for direct assault missions due to their poor armour. Daemon understood the basics of piloting such a craft as he had sometimes had to move them when working in the maintenance department but he preferred not to pilot such a dangerous vehicle out in the open. The Drill Master had placed Daemon as sect leader for the day as he was the most senior ranked member of the team. Under normal circumstances, students would rotate as sect leader depending on the training missions, but this one was deemed important enough for his seniority to preside. The mission was simple, all they had to do was to skim out to the outer marker and plant a fake nuclear warhead then return to the academy. Luckily Bann had been placed in his sect that day and he was fully capable of piloting a wild cat so Daemon wasn't forced to pilot. Daemon and his sect of six students waited while the auxiliaries prepped the skimmer. It had been painted bright yellow to aid finding the bastard in the dark after they had finished planting the bomb. Daemon was doing a routine check on all his sect members to make sure their E.C.A.'s were functioning correctly when he noticed Bann was already trying to stir up trouble. Since the incident in the showers his relationship with Bann had soured, Bann particularly resented how Daemon had not been punished for his part in the fight and had instead been awarded his rank.

"Look I'm fully capable of checking my own suit!" Bann barked into the comms. Daemon clicked his communicator and initialised a direct and private line to Bann.

"Listen Bann, I'm in no mood for trouble today. Let's just get this mission over and done with and then we can go our separate ways." Bann just grunted and made a half-hearted salute before he attempted to annoy his sect leader.

"Hey! We can't all be fucking the mistress, apple

boy!" Bann whispered. Daemon nodded in his helmet and noticed the security com-eye on a nearby wall of the docking section. He decided not to rise to the bait with witnesses present.

"Sect. Load up!" Daemon commanded as he got the nod from the auxiliary that the skimmer was ready to take out. He decided to sit up front with Bann in the co-pilot seat to keep an eye on him.

The outer marker could be reached in a manner of minutes on an expertly piloted skimmer and Daemon sat quietly allowing Bann to concentrate on the controls of the deadly machine. When the outer marker appeared on the short range navi-com Bann started to drift the skimmer left and right dangerously.

"Cool it Bann. Just keep it steady and set her down south of the marker!" he said while his stomach began to swirl. It seemed that Bann had done his homework, word had got round that Daemon sometimes suffered from motion sickness and he was now playing on that knowledge.

"What's the matter Daemon?" Bann asked mockingly, "You're not going to throw up are you?" Pins and needles had already crawled up Daemons legs and the pit of his stomach bubbled as the G-forces that attacked him.

"Please Bann! Throttle down. Bring it to a stop. That's an order!" Daemon gasped and gurgled as his throat burned with bile.

"I haven't even started yet Daemon." Bann growled before he pulled hard to his flank on the control gear.

His judgement was impaired by his hatred and the edge of the responsive craft struck the ground violently. It bounced back upwards and now imbalanced began to bounce and jump around erratically. Bann tried to re-establish control but the craft was already tumbling across the surface of the moon and was on an inevitable collision course with the graphite monolith. The front of the skimmer collapsed as it struck it and as it was driven back into the hull it buckled and shattered against the solid lump of carbon. The sudden halt flung everyone out of the ship scattering them far and wide.

It may have been the adrenalin that had coursed through his body or the motion sickness that had kept Daemon conscious but he had not passed out as he struck the ground. He remained awake and steadfastly aware of the terrible situation they were in. He quickly assessed what was required and forced himself to his feet. Minutes passed as he pulled and dragged the students away from the wreckage as sparks flew from the damaged engine. As he was dragging the last man away the skimmer exploded in a mushroom cloud of ionic particles and debris gathered up from the moon's surface.

"You can't even comprehend how angry I truly am!" Mistress Jemm yelled to the assembled students. It was the morning after the skimmer crash and Bann had been issued the death penalty. Drill Master Gidd had monitored all communications of the mission in question as a standard operating procedure and found Bann was in gross negligence. Bann didn't even receive a trial as the evidence was so overwhelming; he was simply marched out naked in front of the gathered students in the briefing hall.

"This piece of shit will die this day and you will all witness and learn what Xen does with those who disobey orders and fuck with protocol." Mistress Jemm said with a bleak smile upon her masculine face. Daemon noticed Mistress Suix wasn't present, he assumed she had seen this spectacle many times before and didn't share the same sick affliction as Mistress Jemm.

"Initiate Bann will teach you never to place your team mates lives in danger. He will also teach you a fundamental tenet of Xen corporate law." Mistress Jemm said before two auxiliaries opened an air lock on the flank of the briefing chamber. The doors hissed open revealing a sizeable compartment beyond. Drill Master Gidd marched Bann into the chamber and nodded for an auxiliary to close it. The doors clamped shut but every student could see Bann stood defiantly though the plaz windows set in the doors.

"If I catch one of you little bastards not watching then you will join Initiate Bann after he has been spaced!" Mistress Jemm yelled to the gathered students. The two auxiliaries had probably seen this kind of event more times than they would care to mention. They swirled valves in their hands and put their backs to the wall to obscure the inevitable. Daemon wanted to look away but feared a reprisal if he didn't watch what was happening. Bann was already suffering, his veins stood out on the surface of his skin and his arms were already flailing around. His defiance was gone was and in its place came utter panic. Blood cascaded from burst capillaries as the pressure dropped in the chamber. Nobody could hear his screams as his blood showered the internal glass. Daemon couldn't help feeling sorrow at Banns death and thought that it was no way to end any human life.

It was drawing near the end of the students' term in the academy and everybody was excited about new prospects and further training on other worlds. The majority of them had passed the secondary training with high scores and only a few had opted for minor administrative or military jobs within the Xen Corporation. Daemon himself scored highly in weapons and combat, interrogation, engineering, tactics and espionage, he also hadn't done badly at science coming out with a class C pass. With his grades he could become a Xen intelligence agent but opted for a full military officer career. He had already sent the relevant forms to the academy on Vex II which was known as one of the top centres for training Xen military officers. Drill Master Gidd was pleased with his choice of career and had congratulated him commenting that he was following in his footsteps.

"You will make a fine warrior sergeant and a damned fine officer. Remember to take no shit from your squad members, be hard with them but fair. If you treat them firmly and with respect they will follow your orders like lap dogs." Gidd advised whilst he polished the sergeant's pin on Daemons tunic. The Drill Master had a look of reminiscence on his face and seemed more excited than Daemon was about his future prospects on Vex II.

"I will give it my best shot Drill Master." Daemon said as Gidd grabbed hold of his shoulders.

"Best won't cut it sergeant. You must rise above your best and excel. The last thing I want to hear is that your career is stalling. Remember I trained you and I have a reputation to maintain." Gidd patted Daemons shoulders and grinned, "Good luck Sergeant!" he smiled before saluting and walking away.

It seemed everybody had some advice for him and he soon tired of having the same conversations time after time. He was relieved when Suix contacted him and said that she had a surprise for him before his transport ship arrived in two days' time.

"Where are we going?" Daemon inquired, Suix smiled and made a gesture to hush. She had been quiet all morning while they prepped a ground crawler and suited themselves up in their E.C.A.'s. They had been playing around with one another to the point where they had been tempted to rip off each other's suits and make love on the floor of the airlock. Daemon found it uncomfortable being aroused inside his E.C.A., it just wasn't designed for it and wished he had taken a Dull-pill to calm his craving. Suix warmed up the engine of the open topped ground crawler and depressurised the airlock. Daemon checked the eight bulbous wheels on the crawler and then jumped into the passenger seat next to Suix.

She drove due north over the barren land while they made small talk. He asked many times about their destination but Suix remained secretive until after twenty minutes she brought the vehicle to a stop. He peered around but could not see anything but dust and small rocks. He wondered why she had brought him all the way out here.

"Come on," she said excitedly, "we walk from here." Grabbing hold of his hand she led him as they walked for a few minutes and then stopped again. Suix pulled a small device out from an armoured pocket on her battle suit, pressed a button and waited. The ground shook as a small piece of land opened up from which a shaft of light ascended from the stars.

"Quick. Inside now, before the light is spotted on the long range scanner!" she commanded. Daemon was dragged quickly towards the light and before he knew what was happening he was being rushed down a gang plate which descended into the moon itself. Suix quickly closed the door and then opened an inner air lock.

"You may never speak of what I'm about to show you!" she whispered into the comms before unclamping her E.C.A. She prompted for Daemon to follow suit and then opened an inner door. Daemon stood mouth agape as the door glided open.

"Well? What do you think?" she asked with a loving smile. He shook his head in awe as he looked upon a massive room filled with tall grasses, exotic plants and blossoms of all the colours of the rainbow. The scent of honey, jasmine and sweet blossoms intoxicated his senses with the remembrance of his home world bringing a tear to his eye.

"Words cannot describe such a place my Suix." He said with passion. Suix kissed his cheek and grabbed hold of his hand tightly before guiding him into what could only be described as a piece of paradise after the blandness of the last year in the habitat. He tried to pluck a large red fruit from a nearby tree but Suix pulled him into the long grasses and slipped off her underwear. The fruit in the tree no longer held his attention as his mouth gorged upon her femininity.

Sweat glistened upon the two lovers as they lay in the tall grasses shielding their eyes from the bright lights fixed on the ceiling. Fatigue burned in their lungs and bodies as they coiled themselves around one another feeding off their heat from the hours of physical love. "How did you find this place?" Daemon whispered into the nape of her neck.

"The last custodian of the academy was a passionate botanist and when he discovered this ancient crashed vessel he decided to use its cargo bay as a plot for his garden. When I arrived to take over from him six years ago he showed me this hidden paradise and made me swear it was for me and me only. He claimed the stress and pressure of running a Xen Academy could be subsided by regular visits to his secret garden."

She turned onto her stomach to face him, her face framed by the hair she had grown into a cheek length bob ever since she had been seeing Daemon on a regular basis. Her large hazel eyes were complemented by her dark hair which also feathered out her jaw line and enhanced her beautiful profile. "My heart is going to shatter as soon as your transport arrives." she said sadly, "You must forgive my absence on that day." Her voice trembled in pitch and Daemon embraced her wishing that time could stop so he could hold Suix forever.

CHAPTER 5

Goodbye shit hole

The transport ship was old and groaned audibly on take-off. Dust washed around its hull and obscured the viewing ports as Daemon tried to settle his nerves. The transports departure had coincided with the arrival of a passing comet that was liberally depositing its tail debris into the very thin atmosphere of the Rock, Daemon was hoping that he would get a good view of it. The viewing ports eventually cleared and he could see the streaks of fiery matter cascading to the surface and impacting with violent explosions of dust and shrapnel. He grinned at the thought of the repair works from the damage it would cause to the academy buildings. He knew the remaining students would have to spend the rest of the day patching up holes. However the rhythmic drumming sound of the hull being struck quickly removed his schadenfreude. He looked to the emergency bubble suit in front of his seat and noticed it had seen better days, even the hook that held it was rusty. He prayed that there would be no accidents today and looked towards Sherry and Miles who were sat close by. They too seemed absorbed by the terrible state of the emergency suits.

"We won't need them so calm yourselves down." He said hoping that he was not tempting fate. Sherry screwed up her pretty face making it clear that she resented Daemon outranking her. She had also opted for officer training on Vex II and Miles was heading there to further his studies in sciences that Daemon could hardly even pronounce. The transport ship finally cleared the trace atmosphere and started hurtling towards a tyrant class starship called the Caligula. Sherry unbuckled her safety harness and tried to get a better view of the vast starship through the viewing port next to Daemon. He gazed at her shapely behind and couldn't help revealing a filthy grin. Miles was also staring at her sexy curves but turned away flushing when Daemon smiled at him and raised an eyebrow.

"It's beautiful and so vast. I bet its engines are humongous," she said in wonder. Daemon sensed Miles was about to garble about astrophysics or something along the lines of zero-gravity drive engines, so he gestured him to silence which saved him and Sherry from an unnecessary lecture. Miles stayed quiet but looked like he was on the verge of sulking. Daemon ignored him and leant forward in his seat to peer through the viewing port towards the Caligula. It was a fine looking ship; the hull had been painted a dull black apart from its name which was written in gold paint that ran the side of its vast flank. People in the corporate universe spoke one standard language but this starship had its name written in an ancient language of some kind. He wouldn't have been able to identify its name if he hadn't already been told it. He noticed the ships array of weapons, it bristled with missile pods, plasma cannons and energy spurs. It was his first sight of a corporate warship.

"Something's wrong, we're coming in too fast. Why isn't the pilot slowing down?" Sherry cried with panic in her tone. Daemon had another look through the viewing port and gauged their velocity before he nodded in agreement.

"Sherry's right, get your bubble suits on now!" He barked as he grabbed his suit and rushed off towards the helm of the transport craft. He stopped at the crash door and punched the button to open it but the door struggled on its gears and only rose up a few feet. There would only just be enough space for him to squeeze under if he ditched the bubble suit. As he ducked under the door he spotted two troopers lying in their own blood, each with a gunshot wound to the back of their heads.

"What the fuck is going on?" he said, "Why didn't we

hear gunshots?" The only explanation seemed to be that the guards had been killed while the debris from the comet was hitting the hull of the ship. He slides under the door and plucked a sidearm from one of the dead guards checking to see if it had ammo. When he reached the helm door he found that it too had been locked so he ripped off the junction box housing and set to work to bypass the security lock. Sweat beaded his forehead as his fingers played swiftly across the circuit boards. He heard a mechanical click and began to manually crank open the heavy door. As soon as he had a large enough gap to squeeze through he rushed into the cockpit like a caged animal being freed after a lifetime of captivity.

The small cockpit was empty except for a single pilot who was still sat in his seat. "Engage autopilot now or I will spatter your brains all over the room," Daemon ordered with his pistol pointing at the back of the pilots head. The pilot did not respond and as Daemon took a step closer he noticed a silenced pistol lying on the floor in a pool of blood and brains next to his seat. Coming around the high-backed chair Daemon could clearly see the gaping hole in the top of the pilot's skull.

"Oh fuck." he moaned and tipped the corpse from the seat taking its place and scanning the complicated controls. The Caligula was looming larger by the second on the main viewer and the main nav-com was locked out with a security password and was unresponsive to anything he tried. He was running out of time.

Further back in the ship Miles and Sherry had

managed to grab hold of each other and secure themselves in a small space under the passenger seating. The transport craft barrel-rolled violently then began decelerating and pinwheeling out of control but they were prevented from being thrown against the walls due to the confined space. The aft jets continued firing and gradually brought the ship to a dead stop at which point the power shorted and darkness descended. Miles still clung to Sherry's hand while she powered up the headlamp in her bubble suit.

"Are you alright Sherry?" Miles inquired in a muffled but concerned tone due to his helmet. She patted down her rubbery suit and found it was still pressurised.

"I think so. Hang on a minute," she said as she clambered from beneath the seating. She helped Miles to his feet and brushed off some of the debris from his suit.

"Yeah, I'm fine just a little bruised. You?" she asked as Miles took off his helmet. His face was awash with sweat and the little hair he had was sleek against his pale scalp. He brushed his hand over the back of his head and then looked with horror as it came back covered with blood. Sherry took off her own helmet and took a look at Miles wound finding that he just had a small bump on his head which was bleeding lightly.

"You'll live." she laughed, "I've had bigger cuts on my clit. Now come on and let's find our glorious sect leader and see if he is still alive." Miles blushed as he still struggled with the idea of a beautiful woman using such language. They followed their torch lights into the corridor containing the dead troopers and Sherry stooped to pick up the remaining pistol and noticed another flashlight moving around in the helm section of the transport. She could also hear a familiar voice cursing and muttering. Smiling she stepped over the corpse of the pilot and scanned her torchlight under the main consoles. Daemon was covered with wires and had a screwdriver in his mouth as his hands fumbled around in the mess of wiring and circuit boards. The lights of the ship came back online but they were only dimly illuminated.

"I've had to dump the reactor core and we're running off the emergency battery. I don't know how long we have left on back-up but we're drifting." Daemon said before clambering from under the console. The main viewing screen had the tyrant class ship perfectly framed and its weapon arrays were pointed towards the transport. A clicking sound came from the console and then a hiss.

"Transport craft. This is Captain Hally of the Caligula. Would you mind telling me what has just happened and why we were nearly forced to atomise your craft?" Even through the communicator, her voice sounded on the verge of unleashing a volley of abuse. Daemon grabbed the main comms and flicked off the locking switch.

"This is Sect leader Daemon, sergeant of the Xen Corporation. The pilot of this transport murdered two guards, set up a collision course and then ate a bullet. I'm hoping you can tell me why he might have done this." He spoke through gritted teeth.

How many survivors do you have on-board sergeant?" Captain Hally asked with a curious tone. He looked at Sherry and Miles to reassure himself that they were still alive.

"Three in total but you will already know this from your ships scanners." he added with a little sarcasm.

"Watch your tone with me sergeant." came the abrupt reply, "I'm asking because our ship scanners are reading four life signs in total. Am I to assume that your group are upfront with you at the helm and the single life sign in the engineering deck isn't part of your party?"

"Sorry captain, and yes, none of my sect is in the engineering deck," Daemon said handing Miles the pilot's bloodied silenced pistol from the floor. Miles held the weapon between thumb and finger with distaste apparent on his feral features.

"I want you to remain at the helm of the ship sergeant and wait for the boarding party which is inbound now." Captain Hally said before the comms crackled back to static. Sherry pointed to the main viewer as a small limpet type vessel disengaged from the belly of the tyrant.

A loud metallic crunch echoed in the hull of the transport craft followed by the high-pitched howl of plasma cutters. Hot metal sparks showered inside the main corridor like a pyrotechnic display in the night sky of a festival period. A large oval of hull fell away crashing against the decking as a contingent of heavily armoured soldiers leapt through the glowing oval. Six of the squad immediately headed for the engineering deck while two remained to guard the corridor. Daemon approached the two troopers while they saluted.

"Please remain at the helm of the craft sergeant until we apprehend the target." One of the soldiers stated, the speaker on his helmet making him sound almost robotic. While Daemon backed off he noticed a woman climbing through the breach from the limpet craft. She had a captain's insignia on her tunic so he saluted quickly as she approached.

"You do speak the same language as I do don't you sergeant?" Captain Hally said with a peculiar smile. Daemon nodded, a little confused by the question.

"Then why the fuck aren't you in the helm section of this transport?" she raged. Now that she was in the light he could see the left half of her face was marred with burns and that she had bald patches in her long dark hair. Her left eye was dark and glittered like Miles's eyes which added to her disturbing appearance. "Are you in the habit of disobeying direct orders sergeant?" she said as she sucker-punched him in the gut.

Daemon's martial arts training had alerted him to the attack but he had thought it was best not to attempt to block or dodge. He hit the deck hard and gagged up a mouthful of bile. While he was prone he prepared himself for a kick to his ribs assuming she would lash out again but instead she stepped over him and entered the helm section. Miles and Sherry stood to attention while Captain Hally inspected the dead pilot.

"Last minute pilot changes," she said with disgust

toying with the hole in his head, "I knew it in my bones not to trust this fucker!" Captain Hally seemed to be speaking to herself rather than for the benefit of the room's other occupants. Daemon had managed to get to his feet and limp into the helm section.

"I take it this pilot isn't Xen trained after all?" he said through gasps of breath. Captain Hally shook her head and looked towards the mess of wires hanging from the main console. "I have to admit Sergeant, you and your sect were seconds away from an untimely death. Good work scuttling the transport by the way," she commented as she squatted down searching the corpse of the pilot.

"Yeah, I think this pilot is from the Seinal Corporation. We picked him up at Jurin's Gate along with an engineer. I should have gone with my gut instinct and never enlisted them. Then again they did have all the correct Xen credentials." She stood up off her haunches and placed her boot against the dead man's skull then crushed it under her boot. Grey matter and gore oozed from beneath her foot making an unnerving sound that echoed in the small room. Daemon turned away from the spectacle and wondered why she would do such a thing to a corpse.

"What we have here is a saboteur. Some low down Seinal agent on the same genetic level as a sewer rat." Captain Hally stated as she scraped her boots on the chest of the corpse. Daemon prayed for a distraction so that he wouldn't have to continue witnessing the gruesome scene before him. He thanked his lucky stars when a soldier entered the helm carrying an odd device.

"We found the engineer but he took a suicide pill before we could grab him. We also found this device attached to the main reactor core." The trooper reported and held out the device for his captain to inspect.

"Homemade, low-grade, trash. It's a good job you jettisoned the reactor core Daemon because this baby would have sparked the reactor core which would have blown us all to oblivion." The captain said with a smile while she patted his shoulder in an almost motherly fashion.

"Set charges corporal and then get your men into the limpet, I'm not going to waste my engineers' time trying to repair this transport craft." she ordered as the corporal scurried off to gather up the boarding party.

"That includes you and your sect Daemon!" she hissed as she made her way back to the limpet craft.

The interior of the limpet craft was cramped and had the stale aroma of sweat, engine grease and halitosis. As it was not fitted with gravity compensators the occupants had to strap themselves down securely before it unclamped from the transport ship. Daemon covered his mouth when one of the soldiers took off his helm and coughed violently. He could see the tiny globules of spittle floating around the enclosed space and hoped they wouldn't gather anywhere near him. Sherry was clearly excited by the close proximity of all the men and her smile was wide and beaming. Daemon assumed one of the reasons why she had ventured for officer training in the first place was that she loved being surrounded by so many men. He found it strange that she was attracted to them given that many Xen CORE troopers didn't have a sex drive due to the inhibitors placed inside them while they were grown in artificial wombs. Rumour had it that the female troopers also lacked a sex drive and that it was hard to tell them from their male counterparts unless you stripped a squad naked and realised some of the soldiers had tits.

It didn't take long for the limpet craft to dock inside the giant tyrant ship. The docking bay was full of drop pods, light attack interceptors and armoured ground crawlers. The auxiliaries and maintenance crews busied themselves in their duties as Daemon and his sect followed Captain Hally and the troopers through the hive of activity. He noticed the troopers and Captain Hally was speaking a strange guttural tongue which he had only heard once before at the Xen recruiting institution on Hanna Prime. Whatever language they spoke he didn't understand a single word. Sherry leant into him while they walked.

"They are speaking combat-cant, my father was a Colonel in the Terran CORE he taught me some of the basics," she told him as her ears twitched trying to pick out words she understood. "It sounds like Captain Hally is unhappy with the events that occurred on the transport craft. I think she doubts our story and intends to interrogate us." Sherry whispered.
Captain Hally stopped suddenly and rounded on Sherry

apparently having overheard her whispering.

"Button it little girl." the captain hissed vehemently as Sherry flinched in surprise, "Xen combat can't is a secret language exclusive to the warriors of the CORE. You have yet to earn the right to use such a language you little bitch." She walked up to Sherry and jabbed a finger at her in an accusatory manner.

I've read all your files and know who you are Sherry. I knew your father Colonel Sheridon from the battle of Norma'Imitula. I lost a lot of fine veterans in that battle due to your father's miscalculations and fuck ups. I'm hoping you have more of your mother's genetic information than his, the very last thing we need is another arse hole in this universe!" Captain Hally's face had turned purple with anger, Sherry's had also flushed but it was more out of embarrassment.

"I never said I was going to interrogate you," Captain Hally continued, "but I guess you don't know as much cant as you think you do. What I actually said was that it's a clear-cut scenario and there is no need to interrogate Daemons sect. It seems your daddy couldn't even teach you combat-cant correctly." She stormed off towards the bank of elevators leaving Sherry shell shocked. Daemon couldn't help laughing when Sherry turned to face him with flustered features.

"That wasn't funny Daemon. My father wasn't an arsehole. He had more combat medals than she has on her tunic." she complained.

"I'm sorry Sherry. It wasn't Captain Hally's words that amused me it's just the first time I have ever seen you speechless. You look quite cute when you're all embarrassed." he said teasing her. Sherry's face contorted with anger and he half expected her to lash out at him.

"If it wasn't for that nice shiny sergeant's pin on your tunic I'd drop you on the spot and dance all over your bones," she stated menacingly. She reached out and ruffled his dark hair

"And you can take cute and stick it where the stars don't shine!" Miles had remained silent during her outburst until he heard Sherry's threat against his commanding officer.

"Even a threat against a Xen officer is grounds for punishment Sherry!" Miles said with an aggressive tone.

"Shut up Miles!" Daemon and Sherry said in unison as they wandered off to find the on-board billets.

The filthy cramped room they were stationed in held twelve bunk beds and smelt like a factory animal pen. Condensation dripped from the metallic ceiling forming rusty coloured puddles on the floor. Daemon chose the bed nearest to the single wall fan which blew a slight musty smelling breeze into the warm and sickly chamber. Miles tested his damp bed finding that it rang with the sound of rusted spring coils.

"This room is a Petri-dish for germs!" He grumbled before climbing between the stale sheets. Daemon noticed him stripping under his blankets and then recalled he had never seen Miles change in front of him when they shared their room nor ever seen him in the shower room at the academy. He guessed that Miles was extremely shy and thought that it probably explained why he was always up so early everyday so he could shower alone. Daemon pulled off his clothes and threw them on top of his foot locker before getting into bed.

"These sheets are disgusting," Sherry said inspecting a mould ridden stain. She had kept her underwear and vest on as she wriggled into the bed sheets with a foul look on her face.

"At least we aren't billeted with the regular troops. Be glad that we have a room of our own." Daemon stated as he fluffed out his pillow.

"Lights!" he shouted at the room's voice recognition circuit making the overheads dim to darkness. He was trying to settle himself down to sleep when a pillow hit the back of his head.

"I can't believe I'm stuck in this room with you pair of wankers. To think I could be fucking Carl back in the academy. Instead, I'm stuck in this toilet with you two turds." Sherry said angrily in the blackness of the room. Daemon didn't rise to the taunt and instead commandeered the measly pillow stacking it on top of his own.

"Daemon." Sherry called in a girly tone after a few seconds of silence, "Could I have my pillow back?" Daemon grabbed the pillow and launched it randomly in a rage. He heard it hit the wall and mouthed a silent curse. "Should have been your face, bitch!"

"Why thank you very much Sect leader." she patronised him as he heard her padding across the room to retrieve it. He tried to envision her beautiful feminine curves in the dark and cursed the lights for being off. He had seen Sherry naked a few times in the communal showers in the academy and was always flabbergasted by her perfect body. He settled for the visualising her showering naked and grinned as he felt his cock harden against the mattress. Slowly he lapsed into sleep with erotic images running in his mind.

He was sixteen again wandering hand in hand with his first girlfriend Millie. She was wearing a stark white dress that stopped short of her knees and had thin straps over her shoulders revealing her tanned flesh. They had spent an hour or so walking out to the edge of her father's farmland where a glade of apple trees stood on the top of a low grassy hill. The summer's breeze brought a wondrous tonic of delicate flower blossoms and apple wood to their nostrils as their teenage hormones guided them to their favourite spot. The sun was high and filtered its warming rays through the canopy of leaves. Millie rested her back against the smooth bark on the trunk of the tree close to the heart and initials Daemon had carved into it months before. He cupped her freckled cheeks and gazed into her sparkling emerald eyes as the sun rays highlighted her strawberry blonde hair.

"We mustn't Daemon." she whispered as he brushed his hand up the inside of her thigh and touched daringly at her knickers. They kissed passionately her hands pulling him towards her, their tongues dancing like electric eels. Millie's scent masked the apple wood until all he could smell his beautiful Millie. He pulled at her knickers and felt her warm hands aiding their cascade down her legs. He ducked under her dress in a rush to taste his lover as her legs opened slightly to aid his progress. Millie's breath came in fluctuating bouts as his mouth and tongue washed against her bringing trembling jolts to her body. Millie's fingers brushed through his hair almost pushing him into her until she exploded with a cry that echoed around the glade and physically shook her legs. Daemon fell backwards into the grass and waited for Millie to catch her breath, her face illuminated with post orgasm.

She smiled and appeared to be a little embarrassed that she had cried out so loud. She looked around the tree line to make sure there were no witnesses before she crouched down and unbuckled his belt. He kicked off the rest of his garments and watched Millie slip off her dress. He felt abashed laid there with a slight breeze on his erection and was having second thoughts about the next move until Millie straddled over him and gently worked him inside her. Daemon felt the waves of heat washing up his body and he was already tingling while Millie settled into a rhythm. He could feel every inch of movement and it wasn't more than thirty seconds into the sexual event that the tingles came on in force.

"Millie I'm going to cum!" he cried as he rolled on top of her, withdrew and ejaculated onto the grass between her legs. She was shading her eyes from the sunlight and smiling lovingly at him.

Daemon was dragged roughly from his favourite dream

89

and it took him a few seconds to realise where he was until he smelt the sickly air in the billet cabin. Normally the dream carried on a while longer so he assumed a noise of some kind had rudely awoken him. He elbowed himself up and listened in the dark as the grogginess of sleep subsided. From somewhere in the darkness he could hear the rattle of rusty bed springs and heavy panting. The tempo of heavy breathing was rising with each passing second and a rhythmic sound of flesh slapping flesh echoed around the room. He wiped the sleep from his eyes and tried to connect the sounds until two shrieking orgasms reverberated off all the metallic walls.

No fucking way! I must be still dreaming. He quietly settled back into his pillow and heard the sound of bodies readjusting themselves followed shortly by heavy sighs.

"I take it that was your first time Miles?" Sherry whispered into the dark.

"Yes," Miles answered begrudgingly.

Daemon could hear the creaking of bed springs then the padding of Sherry's feet crossing the room to her own bed and the ruffling of sheets. It wasn't long before Daemon had to contend with the snores of post-coital sleep drifting to him across the darkness of the room.

CHAPTER 6

Tyrant class

The morning buzzer activated the overheads and half illuminated the billet chamber. Of the twelve lights only four came on fully, the rest buzzed and flickered creating a strobe effect that was painful to the eyes. Daemon feigned the actions and mood of someone who had enjoyed a sound night sleep even though the truth was otherwise. He had spent most of the night riddled with jealousy over Miles and Sherry pairing up with each other and wondered why she had favoured Miles over himself.

As he rubbed his eyes Sherry leapt out of her bed and stretched her limbs yawning widely. From behind his knuckles, he stole the occasional glance at her nakedness as she stood in the cold room. He could not believe what a lucky bastard Miles had been. Miles, for his part, remained in bed and was trying to find his underwear from the pile of clothing near his bed. Miles shot Daemon a guilty glance which was ignored.

"I hope we don't have to shower with the regular troops," Sherry announced with a wink and a smile that suggested she had hopes that they would have to.

"With any luck, we will, I dare say those female soldiers will be short of a good poke." Daemon replied with rancour. Sherry grinned at him and placed her hand on the top of her lovely hip line.

"You think so?" she asked, "I'd like to see you try it on with one of them. Even if they are medically suppressed and never feel the need for such activities you should feel free to apply your charms lover boy." She said before bursting into laughter.

Daemon pivoted himself out of bed grabbing his clothes and noticed Sherry wink again at his nakedness. He knew she was right about the female CORE troopers and realised that this space voyage would probably be a lonely affair on the sex front. Meanwhile, Miles had managed to find his clothing and was dressing under the sheets as Sherry paraded herself naked around the chamber looking for her underwear.

"I wonder if they serve the same food sludge as they did in the Academy," Daemon said while his stomach gurgled with travel sickness. He grabbed a box containing pills from his foot locker and swallowed three blue speckled pills to ease nausea from the drive engines on board the Caligula. Together they left the billet to find the canteen.

Breakfast turned out to be a bowl of grey mush and a hard lump of yellow soda bread. Sherry poked the sludge around her bowl with a spoon and her eyes rolled backwards as she covered her mouth.

"I can't eat this shit." she gurgled. Miles had sculptured the mush into a limp tower formation which made the food even more unappetising.

"It's probably the same crap we ate in the academy but the cook has run out of food colouring. Hey, you never know it might taste really nice." Daemon said trying to convince one of them to make the first move. Miles spooned up the top of his grey tower and shoved it in his mouth. He worked the food for a few seconds.

"It's not bad!" he exclaimed, his eyes widening, "In fact, it's better than the food we had at the academy." He smiled and took another heaped spoonful. Daemon and Sherry looked at each other, shrugged and begrudgingly filled their mouths with the grey stuff and instantly found their taste buds assaulted by the concoction. Miles spat his portion back into his bowl and laughed out loud.

"Sorry, but I couldn't help myself." He slapped the table with delight, "You should have seen your faces!" Tears started to form in his glassy black eyes. Sherry didn't look at all amused but she was too stubborn to spit it back out. Daemon, on the other hand, didn't like the stuff and spat it out and concentrated on eating the soda bread.

"I'm hoping I can get used to this stuff." Miles said, "It's like a cross between vinegar and eggs but the texture is all wrong."

The shipboard speakers pinged then announced "Sect leader Daemon, report immediately to training bay deck four. Bring your Sect." Captain Hally's voice was barely audible through the crackling old speakers.

"Deck Four?" Sherry asked shrugging while Daemon peered around the canteen for any signs indicating its direction. All he could see was some unusual scrawls on a board and he looked at them doubtfully. Miles followed Daemon's gaze and deciphered the ancient script. "It's Roman," he stated knowingly. Sherry screwed up her face in confusion.

"Roman? Is that a planet?" she asked looking from Miles to Daemon. Daemon smiled trying to look as if he knew the answer and waited for Miles to speak.

"No Sherry," Miles began using the intonation he reserved for lecturing people, "the Romans were an ancient tribe on Earth who conquered other nations then established their own technology on them. They were like an early corporation and it seems this ship and its crew have adopted the ancient language they used." As Miles spoke Daemon nodded his head as if in agreement then turned to face him. From the time Miles had spent tutoring Daemon the slight man instantly recognised that he did not have any foreknowledge of this and was attempting to show off in front of Sherry.

"I'd ask our exalted Sergeant to translate for us

Sherry but I'll save him the embarrassment of revealing his ignorance. You can stop pretending as if you know what I'm talking about now Daemon." Miles sneered. "Just be grateful that that I know how to read Roman."

"Thank fuck for that! Lead the way geek." Daemon countered while grabbing hold of Miles' tunic collar and thrusting him towards the signs.

Even though Miles had claimed to know how to read the strange written language they had still struggled to find their destination and resorted to asking numerous crew members for directions. The training bay was situated near the rear of the vast starship and it took them the best part of half an hour to find it via elevators and many identical looking corridors. The bay was grubby but spacious and smelt better than the rest of the ship they had navigated through. Two military Xen officers waited impatiently in the centre of the room against the walls of which were five freshly made beds. The rest of the room had been packed with numerous freighting crates and labelled storage containers. The two officers appeared to be veterans, both sporting facial scars and one of them had a mechanical leg. Daemon spotted their lieutenancy pins and called his sect to attention.

"Sect leader sergeant Daemon reporting for duty sir!" he saluted as both lieutenants grinned at each other.

"Well, it seems that Xen has been recruiting gutter trash again. Look at the state of this pathetic excuse for an officer!" Lieutenant Gracon barked.

"Yeah, he looks like he's fresh out of boot camp and still has the shit on his boots to prove it." Lieutenant Bryson said through deep laughter.

"Pleasantries aside sergeant, I wish to introduce you to two more shit-dicks who will be placed under your command." Lieutenant Gracon stated while snapping his fingers and readjusting his mechanical leg. A tall, heavily built man with blond hair wearing black fatigues wandered from behind a packing crate before standing to attention flanking the left side of the lieutenants. "This is former Corporal Hanz, who unfortunately for him was busted back down to initiate because he failed the great test. It would seem Initiate Hanz spent far too much time pumping weights in the gymnasium and popped a hernia but didn't bother to report his affliction until test day, did you, Hanz?" Lieutenant Gracon barked.

"No sir, I didn't and I was punished severely on grounds of incompetence!" Hanz shouted into the large metallic chamber, his strangely accented voice echoing round.

"However sir…" Hanz began to say as if to defend him but Lieutenant Gracon motioned for him to cease talking.

"And the next low life that will be under your command is this useless bitch!" Lieutenant Gracon snapped his fingers again as a petite dark haired woman with a round faced scurried from the shadows and joined the assembled group.

"Initiate Taku reporting for duty sir." she stated as

she tried to gain some height by standing on her tip toes.

"I would watch this one very closely if I was you, sergeant. She's a shining beacon of intelligence, a doctor of field surgery in fact." Lieutenant Gracon sneered as he shifted on his mechanical leg to face the tiny brunette. "However, it seems she couldn't even shoot a dog in its face with a carbine? A fucking hell hound, worth fuck all to the company and she refused to kill it. How smart is she if she failed the great test because of her compassion towards a canine?" Lieutenant Gracon shook his head in disbelief and continued.

"I've had unfortunate encounters with tree-huggers in the past but Taku here takes the goddamn biscuit. She seems to hold nothing but sheer contempt for Xen and all its fundamental beliefs!" He blasted each word into Taku's face and she held her breath against the onslaught of his dire halitosis. Lieutenant Gracon limped away and stared at a random packing crate before starting.

"Sergeant it's your job to aid these reprobates and prove worthy of your rank by pulling these people together as a team and as a fucking worthwhile sect of Xen. Normally you would all be heading for cryogenics right now for the journey to your next post of operations. But you lucky soldiers will bunk down in here, in this mighty fine cargo hold, and will get to experience all the thrills of un-frozen space travel." He laughed and grinned showing rotting teeth. Daemon balked at the prospect of full drive space travel without travel sickness pills and hoped that they would find a packing crate in the training bay filled with medical supplies he could rifle through. Why Xen was punishing them in this way was beyond him and sweat was already dripping from his hands as a cold unforgiving sensation crept up his spine.

"Hey sergeant, I hope these walls don't come crashing in on you when the Caligula goes into full star drive." Lieutenant Bryson stated through manic giggles as he elbow nudged Lieutenant Gracon. Daemon tried to control his breathing, it felt as if his body was no longer exhaling and his lungs were filled to capacity. His field of vision began to blur as a red mist slowly descended. He wondered what was happening to him and felt that as if his last meal had been spiked with Quat. Like a coiled spring being suddenly released he covered the distance to Lieutenant Bryson in a heartbeat and struck him in his throat with stiff fingers crushing his larynx. With his other hand, he then struck upwards connecting violently with the lieutenant's chin. The snapping of his spinal column was audible and Lieutenant Bryson's last view of the world was a two-second glimpse of the room behind him upside down before his knees buckled and he hit the floor. Daemon caught his breath and held his trembling hands in front of him as he tried to control the spasms and shock. Lieutenant Gracon looked down at his colleague who lay disturbingly contorted on the floor at his side.

"What the fuck have you done soldier?" he cried with

his mouth wide with panic. Miles rushed to check the floored man's pulse and shook his head before looking with horror at his friend "He's dead Daemon. You've just killed an officer." Daemon stared at his hands shaking his head from side to side. Lieutenant Gracon was shouting at him but he couldn't hear what he was saying.

"Has he listened to what I've just said?" Lieutenant Gracon asked the others around him. When they didn't answer his question he gripped hold of Daemons tunic and screamed into his face. "You will be court-martialled for this soldier, do you understand? Your trial will be swift and you will be spaced." Lieutenant Gracon was so caught up in his rage that he hadn't noticed a Xen agent had entered the training bay at some point. The tall agent had no need to flash any credentials even though he was dressed in a plain charcoal suit.

"Lieutenant Gracon, remove yourself from the training bay at once." The agent said sternly then pointed at the corpse. "Oh, and don't forget to take that lump of shit with you." The lieutenant paled as he spotted the agent and nodded before he began to drag out the body of his friend and colleague. Daemon froze as the man approached him and laid his hand on his shoulder before smiling thinly.

"You certainly did a number on that Lieutenant didn't you boy?" the man asked him quietly. His voice had a somehow disturbing quality which actually scared Daemon more than it would have done if he had shouted.

"Well calm yourself down Sergeant, because it's unlikely that he will be missed within the company. Besides, he was only a Lieutenant of the Military Core, even a sergeant of Xen out-ranks him... technically anyhow."

Daemon started to come around a little and he felt his heart rate returning to normal.

"Was I drugged?" he asked after a moment's silence. The agent shook his head with displeasure before he spoke.

"No, you weren't drugged. You were simply reacting to all the training you have received at the academy. You are all Xen special operatives and some of you will become agents. Others will become high ranking officers to keep the corporation in motion. Surely you know all this already?"

"Who are you?" Daemon asked him.

"I'm Agent Rowson, you'll find out that there are not many people around here who don't know who I am. Or what I can do."

"So are you going to court-martial me?" Daemon said, finally asking the one thing he wanted to know.

"Hell, you could have murdered both of those two-bit CORE lieutenants for all I care, just as long as you had a good reason. Did you have a good reason sergeant?" The agent stared blankly at him as Daemon shrugged not knowing how to answer the question.

"I don't think I had good reason to murder that man. I just." his words petered out. "Shit I don't know. The lieutenant was mocking us like students and I suddenly felt strange, and I - and I killed him." He drifted off into silence and only whispered the words "I killed him."

"I would have killed him too," Sherry said interrupting the silence.

Agent Rowson flashed a glare at her with his unforgiving eyes and studied her a while as she straightened her body.

"Yes, I believe you would have." The agent remarked before turning to face Daemon. "I like her. You should keep her close sergeant. Close enough to keep an eye on her because she is biding her time to watch you fail, so she can pick up the pieces." The agent said scanning his time piece and looking towards the exit.

"Well now, it seems your extracurricular activities are about to start. I'm heading for the luxury of cryogenics but you lot on the other hand, well, let's just say it will be a bonding experience for you all." The agent finished his words and headed off towards the pressure door closing it behind him.

Once Agent Rowson had left Daemon ordered the others to begin checking the inventory of the training bay before he sat down on one of the packing crates and tried to master himself. Slowly he started to feel more like a leader and began to think about what could be achieved before the star drives were engaged. He knew it would take at least a few hours to ready the regular crew into the cryo-tanks before the ship's nav-com kicked into drive. Meanwhile, precious time bled away as the sect performed the initial stocktaking of the supplies of water, food and sundries. Sherry had already returned from looking around and complained that there was only a single usable commode in the training bay. The others had ignored her and concentrated on things that mattered but she went straight to Daemon to continue her complaints. He had pacified her by saying that he would look in to what could be done then joined them to supervise the work. After a few hours of work, he felt the first tremor from the ships drive engines. So far he hadn't found any travel sickness pills in the bay and was cursing his luck. As he contemplated how sick he would be feeling soon Sherry walked over and linked her arm through his.

"How are you holding up murderer?" she asked with a girly giggle. He tried to wriggle out of her grasp but the strength of her arms lock had him pinned. He decided to change his tactics and focused on her large speckled blue eyes and smiled.

"Thank you for asking, but really I'm fine. By the way, I can smell Miles on you." Sherry's face contorted angrily as she ripped her arm from him, rubbing her wrist from the violent friction.

"So you heard? So what? We can't have a virgin in the sect." she growled and stormed off towards the water dispenser to cool her temper.

Daemon felt another tremor of motion as the Caligula warmed up its engines. His stomach rolled slightly and a bead of sweat trickled down his cheek. He noticed Taku and Hanz idly chatting and thought it might be best to bring them into line before the ship's motions made him too sick to effectively hold command. As he made his way over to Hanz he must have noticed his approach because Hanz wandered off towards a stack of crates to make it look like he was busy. Taku, however, remained defiantly stationary but stood to attention and saluted. He noticed her thin black suit was pulled taut over her petite but muscular body and her hair was cut in a straight line bob, framing her round face. Daemon noted that there was a bulge at her waist just under her tunic revealing that she was armed. Judging by its shape and size Daemon surmised that it was probably a knife but wondered why she chose to arm herself when no-one else had. He made a feint with his right hand and tried to grab the knife with his left but Taku countered quickly.

Much to his surprise, he found himself thrown to the floor by her and landing hard on his back slightly winded him. In the scuffle, the knife had been ripped from its sheath and had clattered across the floor. Daemon quickly crawled towards its resting place but Taku ran after him and aimed a kick at his kidneys. The first blow caught Daemon in his ribs and he quickly rolled over onto his chest and kicked her legs from under her. In the confined space Takus' leg got caught against the edge of one of the crates and having nowhere to go the momentum of the kick shattered her left ankle. She screamed and grabbed her wounded foot cursing several times as Daemon got to his feet. Hanz rushed into Daemon's flank but stopped short a few paces as he realised the attack would be futile now that Daemon was ready.

"Miles see what you can do with Taku's ankle." he said.

Sherry picked up the knife and circled around Hanz who was looking nervous at the prospect of facing two opponents.

"It seems we are already off to a bad start Hanz." Daemon said calmly trying to defuse the situation. "I think it might be best for all of us to back down and aid Taku before the Caligula goes into star-drive." Hanz nodded and saluted. "Agreed sect leader, maybe we could fight at a more suitable date?"

Daemon approached and shook his hand. "I will look forward to that time assuming we all don't die in this training bay."

Hanz laughed slapping him hard on his shoulders; he was tall and muscular standing twenty centimetres taller than Daemon. His blonde hair was spiked up slightly and his harsh angular face had the ice blue eyes of a killer. Daemon and Hanz lifted Taku onto a bed and Miles and Sherry strapped her down. Miles worked quickly splinting her wound and administered a high dosage of sedatives. It took only a moment before Taku passed out cold.

Daemon looked around at the drawn faces of his sect and realised he had made the worst possible start to his leadership of them. He had angered Sherry, incapacitated Taku and was due to have a fight with Hanz when the opportunity arose. Miles also looked disgusted as he tended to Taku. On top of all that they all seemed demoralised by the very idea of un-frozen space travel. He felt the need to address them so coughed and got their attention.

"I know I've fucked up today and made some bad decisions but I hope to make amends for them. But right now we need to think about what is going to happen once that star-drive is engaged. I suspect this flight is going to be very bad and we have no details of how long it is going to take. I want everybody to prepare for the worst and with any luck, we won't have any horrible surprises." Miles rummaged in his medi-kit bag and removed a pill tub. He shook it once and gave them all two pills.

"These will calm your nerves but they won't induce sleep. Daemon's right about un-frozen space travel. It's very bad. On the way to the Academy, the ship I was on developed a technical problem and we spent two weeks in star-drive with zero gravity. By the time the malfunction was repaired two of our number had died from brain haemorrhages." Miles said solemnly.

"For fuck's sake." Muttered Hanz.
Daemon looked away from everyone hoping to hide his face and mask his reaction to Miles' words. He was furious with him as he had hoped to bolster everybody's morale but the dickhead had just dissolved any strength they had left. The ship lurched sideways slightly and a strong humming sound vibrated through the deck.

"Well, here we go." he said, "At least we have gravity so there's hope yet." Privately he prayed that the gravity stabilisers would stay online which given the condition of the ship was by no means guaranteed. "I'm going to find something to hold onto, I suggest you all do the same." Daemon decided that lying in bed in full view of everybody was not a good idea so he wandered off towards the nearest corner of the bay hoping he could hide his travel sickness from the others.

The Caligula went into a series of violent motions as it moved into a clear path of space to engage its primary star-drives. Daemon's vision was blurred and his tunic was already soaked with sweat. He sat with his back against a cold freight box and held on for dear life as the ship banked, hurtled forwards, ceased accelerating then repeated the cycle. He tried to read his timepiece several times but his eyes couldn't keep up with his wrist trembling from the vibrations. They were only three or four minutes into the manoeuvre and already he felt like curling up and dying. He gurgled as bile crept up his throat and his knees felt like jelly. Miles had crawled over to where Daemon sat and dug in at the side of him.

"Once the ship goes into full drive the motion will subside a little," Miles said with a tiny amount of compassion in his voice. Miles didn't seem bothered by the motion apart from being unsteady on his feet. "Here drink as much of this as you can," Miles said as he pushed a plastic container of water into Daemons shaking hand. He gulped at the water and most of it spilt down his chin.

"Make it stop Miles! I can't take anymore. I want to die." Daemon sobbed as discoloured drool leaked from the corners of his mouth. Miles gripped Daemon's chin and narrowed his feral dark eyes.

"Pull yourself together sergeant. You have to be stronger than the rest. The pills I gave you should kick in a few minutes and you will feel calmer." After scolding him he stood quickly and nearly fell over, catching himself on the packing crate.

"Sherry is having a rough time as well. I will check back on you shortly." He walked off in the fashion of drunken man trying to maintain his equilibrium supporting himself on anything solid but as the ship banked steeply he had to resort to crawling. He could see Sherry throwing up at the side of Taku's bed while she held onto one of the fixed bed posts. He felt a strange sensation in his head, a dizzy feeling and his heart beat faster. He had an overwhelming urge to gather Sherry up in his arms and hold her close to him. He had never experienced a feeling like it before and could not comprehend how with Taku in obvious need of his care and attention he felt that looking after Sherry was the strongest of his priorities. It went against his logical manner and upbringing and he didn't understand or like it at all.

He managed to crawl to Sherry's side and hooked his leg around the bed post as a brace before embracing her. In return, Sherry vomited down his tunic and physically shook in his arms. He felt her warmth and pulled her even closer to his body even though he felt disgusted by what she had just jettisoned upon him.

"I've never felt this way before Miles," Sherry whispered into his ear. Miles braced himself as the ship banked again and he didn't know what to do so he simply patted the nape of her back.

"The ship is just setting up its galactic position. It will subside." He said cheerfully. Sherry pushed him away and crawled to the next bed post.

"You're an absolute arse-hole Miles. I was talking about something else." She turned to face the other way holding the bedpost. Miles was confused. She seemed upset even though he had tried to comfort her and he could not understand why. Shaking his head he grabbed another water cylinder and crawled back to where Daemon was hiding behind the crates. It took him a while to cover the distance due to the ship finalising its star-drive. He found Daemon cowered up in a foetal position using the freighting straps to brace his body against the packing crate. Miles sat down next to Daemon and rocked with the motion of the ship.

"I tried to help Sherry, but she got pissed off with what I said for some reason," he said but Daemon was too traumatised to listen. Miles resigned himself to not finding out what he had done wrong and instead prepared himself for the transition into star drive.

When the roar of the engines had subsided and the motion on the Caligula had died down, a whole new sensation afflicted the unfrozen crew members in the training bay. The violent actions of the acceleration had ceased only to be replaced by a continuous subsonic rumbling that seemed to resonate through the body. A full standard space day had passed slowly subjecting a new torment on Daemon and Sherry. Miles and Hanz had offered some food rations to them but they had refused to eat due to enduring nausea that crippled them. Taku was still unconscious and Miles had hooked up a drip to her bloodstream filled with a build-up formula and some sedatives.

"Is she going to pull through?" Hanz asked while he reapplied the dressing on her ankle. Miles shrugged and checked the dressings himself.

"Maybe, but it's not looking good due to the transit motion. I just can't get her leg still."

At some point, Daemon had managed to crawl over to Taku's bed to see how she was but he looked to have passed out leaning against Sherry's shoulder who was also unconscious.

"The sergeant will have a lot to answer for if she dies," Hanz grumbled as he moved over to Miles and leant his back against the smaller man. Miles didn't like the contact of another human being, especially a male but he found it comfortable for a while as it seemed to stop some of the vibrations.

"She's going to live!" Hanz hissed unexpectedly. Miles had his doubts that she would, the swelling on her ankle was the size of an apple and he worried that the broken bones had exposed the marrow infecting her bloodstream. He knew that he would find out soon enough.

"If she survives the next twenty-four hours we may be in luck," he said to Hanz, "I have found some meds in the supplies which will aid her recovery. However, we might have to prop her body up too aid circulation. Remember we are in full star-drive now and the ships gravity compensators aren't running like they should."

"I was born and raised on Xule." Hanz said with a smile on his face remembering his home world. "Our fleet didn't use gravity stabilisers until the Xen Corporation annexed Xule." Daemon opened one eye and was about to ask Hanz about Xule but Miles beat him to it.

"I figured out you were from Xule. I noticed your genetic code is almost identical to the standard clones produced for the Xen military core. I hope that doesn't offend you" Miles asked.

"No offence, taken my friend." Hanz laughed and shook his head. "I was a mere cadet when the Xen Corporation annexed my world. It wasn't long before Xen began to harvest our D.N.A to produce warriors for the Xen military core."

Daemon plucked up the courage to move closer to Hanz but only got about half way down Taku's bed before giving up. He wondered how it would have felt to be Xulen and to have Xen formally annex your world after using its propaganda machine to promise a new beginning for everyone only to find that they intended to use the people of Xule as cattle for their war machine.

"Don't you feel betrayed that Xen used your people? I'm surprised you joined up after what they did, making your planet and people weaker." Daemon said with undertones of pity while he held tight to his rolling stomach. Hanz frowned and gritted his teeth.

"You're wrong sergeant; the Xen Corporation has done nothing but makes our world stronger and our warrior creed and traditions have been embraced into the fold of Xen fundamentality. We are forever thankful. Xule has a high gravity due to its size and our resistance to the fairly high background radiation has made our race strong. We are used to evolving and this is just another step. Whatever you do, do not pity my race."

"I didn't mean to offend you, Hanz, I just thought you might have suppressed feelings about Xen annexing your world." Daemon blurted with embarrassment.

"Your ignorance betrays you, sergeant, as it did when you tried to take away Taku's knife. You should have known that she would try to stop you." Hanz looked over at the prostrate woman.

"What do you mean?" asked Daemon.

"Where she comes from at the coming of age you are given a ceremonial dagger. It is as much a part of her as her heart, as her lungs, as her soul and you tried to take it from her."

"But I didn't know." Daemon protested.

"No you didn't and your ignorance may have cost her life. As far as I am concerned your only redemption lies wounded in the bed to your side. If Taku lives then maybe you will take the opportunity to learn and I will see you in a different light." Hanz tapped Miles' shoulder to let him know he was going to stop leaning against his back and unsteadily wandering off to the other beds to salvage some blankets.

"What was all that about?" Daemon whispered.

"I think Hanz was referring to your lack of cultural education and to your pig-headedness. You didn't see the greater picture." Miles said and went to aid Hanz gathering blankets.

If Daemon hadn't felt so ill he might have understood what Miles had said but instead, he wallowed in his own misery hoping that Taku would make a full recovery.

"So I'm now the enemy?" he thought, "Well that's just fucking great. All I need now is Sherry to have a pop at me and that will be just about everybody wanting me to fail this fucked up assignment." He crawled over beside her and collapsed shivering in a state of exhaustion.

A few minutes later Hanz came to the pair of them and covered them with blankets until they could hardly be seen under the piles of furry fabric.

"Try and get some sleep." he muttered before he sauntered off towards the toilet. Daemon tried to thank him but the constant rumbling of the Caligula made him too ill to speak. Sherry awoke and started to weep, she held tight to his hand as her body trembled with shock and sickness.

CHAPTER 7

Choices, Choices

Daemon must have dozed off for a few hours. When he awoke Sherry and he were curled up in a ball on the cold deck of the training bay. The blankets Hanz had given them were wrapped and twisted around their bodies. He noticed Sherry must have cried herself to sleep as she had salty streaks down her pale, pasty cheeks. He was still clutching the water cylinder and made a move to take a drink from it. As the blankets fell away he noticed dampness on the trousers of her fatigues and thought the cylinder must have leaked. He checked it by sliding his fingers around the base and found no spillage indicating a leak. He suddenly felt a portent of trouble, he patted her clothing down near the crotch of her pants and his fingers came away sticky and red.

"Miles!" Daemon cried as he leapt out of the remaining blankets in panic. Miles kicked himself out of his bed, rubbed his eyes and rushed to his side.

"I think Sherry has haemorrhaged!" Daemon explained clearly upset. Miles exhaled a long sigh and in an unexpected show of strength gathered Sherry up in his arms and carried her to one of the vacant beds.

"Is she ill? Please, tell me she isn't going to die!" Daemon pleaded as he covered his face with his stained hands. Miles placed Sherry down onto a bed, covered her up and brushed the hair from her face. He quickly examined her and confirmed his suspicions.

"She will be fine." he told Daemon, "When a ship is in star-drive it can fuck around with the human body and it can also, well due to the polarity shifts it can mess around with a woman's menstrual cycle." Miles shrugged and he hoped Daemon understood without him having to go into further details. Daemon cursed silently to himself as the information landed home, he wiped down his fingers on his suit and hoped Miles had a short memory.

A week went by as Daemon's sect bolstered themselves against the motion of the star-drive. Taku still remained in bed as her infection had got worse and was starting to spread up her leg, this left Miles mystified as to why the medical supplies were failing to clear it. Sherry was eating well and claimed she didn't feel so nauseous anymore but Daemon was still throwing up the small amount of food he was consuming and Miles was keeping a check on his sergeant's health.

"You have lost a lot of weight Daemon, if you lose anymore then I will be forced to put you on a build-up drip."
Miles watched as Daemon disgorged his breakfast down the toilet. Daemon had hit rock bottom, he couldn't keep anything inside himself for more than an hour even though his body craved for food.

"I'm trying my friend," he said through gastric wind and gurgles of fluid, "I just can't keep anything down with the constant fucking motion of this ship." Miles had seen enough, Daemons health had deteriorated quickly and he didn't think he had any options left.

"I'll give you another twenty-four hours to show some improvement otherwise I will have to put you on a drip," Miles said as Daemon groaned in the toilet bowl.

"How is Taku getting along? Still no good news?" Daemon asked, his voice echoing in the bowl.

"Concentrate on your own health Daemon, worrying about Taku isn't going to help you. I am doing the best I can but she isn't responding to the treatment. If I didn't know better I would say some of the medical supplies are placebos, they just don't seem to have any effect." Miles shook his head slowly.

Daemon staggered out of the bathroom and leant

115

against a packing crate. "I looked at her ankle this morning. I'm no medical expert but I would say she might have to lose some of her leg." He said grimly. Miles nodded in agreement.

"If it comes to it I can do the surgery easily enough but I don't want to have to be the one who tells her." Miles took a long hard look at Daemon weighing his options. Daemon looked to be in no condition to argue with him so he risked adding, "I think you should tell her since you caused this mess in the first place and I don't see why I should be doing all your dirty work. It won't be the most pleasant of operations in these conditions." Sherry heard the last piece of the conversation and gasped as she appeared from behind a stack of crates.

"Operation? You intend to take off Taku's leg?" Sherry said angrily. "She's a fucking field medic. You know her career will be over without her mobility."

"We said that we might have to operate." Daemon countered. "We will look at all the options before we make a decision Sherry." He added in a low whisper, "But for fuck's sakes don't tell Hanz."

"What's this we business sergeant?" Miles scowled, "Unless I have absolutely no other option then I'd rather not operate. But if you think differently and want me to take action before the infection spreads further then it will be your call." Miles rounded on Sherry aggressively, "And Sherry, if she loses her leg the company will fix her up with a new one, which will probably operate better than her real one ever did." With that Miles turned his back on the both of them and went off towards the medical supplies to find the next batch of Biotics to try out on Taku.

"What's he all worked up about?" Sherry asked with her hands on her hips.

"Me I think. He says I've lost a bit of weight which knowing Miles is an under exaggeration. I think that coupled with the stress of Taku's infection has finally ground him down."

Sherry prodded his ribs and sighed. "You are looking a bit shitty Daemon. There's hardly anything left of you, you really need to eat some more."

"I'll try." He replied looking green at the prospect.

The next day had seen no improvement for either Daemon or Taku. Miles had put Daemon on a food drip and confined him to bed while Taku's infection had spread to just below her knee. Miles monitored them both and seemed pleased that Daemon was already showing some signs of improvement, his skin no longer looked so pallid. However, Taku had again lapsed into unconsciousness and Miles felt as if time was running out. He was sat with Daemon explaining the situation.

"She's running a high fever. If we have to do this, we need to do it now." Miles stated solemnly. The infection on her leg smelt very bad and the dressings had been changed twice that morning.

"Do it," Daemon said shaking his head.

Hanz smashed his fist into his other hand and growled like a dog when Miles came to attend to Taku. Hanz hadn't slept a wink that night holding her hand and

117

worrying about her health.

"So it's come down to this, has it? Oh, you're going to pay for this sergeant." He pointed a trembling finger at Daemon.

"She will die if we don't operate Hanz. What option do I have?" Daemon asked with an ashen face.

"And what option did she have other than to protect what was sacred to her? You had a choice but she didn't and now it's the same again." Hanz looked close to tears and when he saw Miles preparing the tools for surgery he walked away.

The operation took less than thirty minutes as Miles employed his skills. It was a messy affair without the support of trained nurses and Miles opted to work as fast as possible to limit the amount of blood loss she suffered. Even so with the lack of fresh blood Taku's chances of living was bleak. Sherry had offered to donate some of her blood but Miles explained that Taku had a rare blood type and that without access to a laboratory it wasn't possible to morph their blood to adapt to hers." Reluctantly, as Miles washed Taku's blood off his hands, he explained that to save time he had had to resort to cauterisation rather than suturing. Daemon squatted next to the sink with his hands covering his face

"Before you ask, I give her a twenty-five percent chance of making it through the next eight hours. And if she does then there could be some trouble giving her a new leg. What with the condition I was forced to leave it in." Miles said glumly looking disgusted with himself.

"You did the best you could do my friend and you have my thanks. There was nothing more you could do." Daemon said through the gaps in his fingers.

Over the course of the next four days Taku started to make a recovery and when she regained consciousness she thanked Miles for saving her life but refused to speak to Daemon or be in his company for very long. Hanz made her some makeshift crutches from metal rods which, when her strength allowed, gave her some mobility around the training bay. Daemon had already learnt to keep out of her way when she was hobbling around and had taken to keeping himself to himself in the corner of the great room.

During Miles' search for meds, he had stumbled upon numerous bottles of liquor hidden in a box. He had attempted to keep its discovery a secret but Sherry had witnessed him trying to hide some of the bottles in the medical supplies. She had soon liberated a few bottles and went off to find Daemon who was cooped up behind a large water tank, cursing and bending his drip-bag manifold so that he could sit down without it snagging his arm.

"Guess what Miles found today?" she said excitedly but Daemon didn't seem in the mood to play guessing games.

"Did he find a lifetime supply of travel sickness pills?" He said sullenly trying to adjust some of the tubes hooked up to his veins.

"Just close your eyes and hold out your hand," Sherry said and waited until he did as she asked. Daemon felt something heavy being placed in his hand, his eyes flashed open to see a large bottle of vintage Sigra III brandy.

"What? How?" He said with a beaming grin.

Sherry laughed and bent down to hug him. She smelled incredible, not perfumed but exuding a feminine musk he associated with Suix.

"I command you to get filthy drunk sergeant! Are you with me?" She said mimicking the tone of Drill Master Gidd. Daemon nodded and Sherry straddled him and pulled out the stopper from the brandy bottle before taking several deep gulps from the scented brandy.

"Sir, yes sir!" He responded in Gidd's voice. She kissed his lips and he could taste the vintage brandy on her lips. There was a moments silence as their eyes locked for several heartbeats. He guiltily wondered where this was going and where Miles was at this moment. Sherry seemed to be thinking along the same lines and took another swig from the bottle to break the moment.

"I hope there's enough to go around." He said and took a few gulps himself even though he knew his stomach wouldn't be up for this new challenge.

"There's plenty to go around." She said as she peered around to see if there were any witnesses present. He was about to take another hit from the bottle but she found his lips and kissed him. She finished her kiss and smiled before rushing off to find Hanz and Taku. He sat for a while listening to the cries of gratitude echoing around the training bay and tried to divert his lusty thoughts from the kiss they had shared.

Daemon groaned as he opened his eyes and quickly shaded them from the dimmed overheads. He tried raising his head but it was throbbing badly from the binge drinking of the night previous. His jaw hurt and he pawed his face for a while wondering why his lips were bruised. Sherry and Miles were curled up together naked near the beds, Sherry still clutching an empty brandy bottle. Miles' face looked heavily bruised and near them was a dubious pile of wet wipes.

"What the hell happened last night?" Daemon thought as he lifted himself to a sitting position and reached for a nearby wine bottle. The bottle was empty and he cursed silently to himself. Taku was sleeping soundly on one of the beds and he noticed the stump of her leg poking from under the blankets. He felt the motion of the ship but he was still drunk and numbed from all the alcohol that still coursed his veins. Hanz was lying face down in a pool of blood on the training bay floor and when Daemon nudged him with his foot he stirred slightly and groaned.

"Hanz? Are you alright? What happened to you?" Daemon said quietly holding his head. Hanz grumbled again and looked up towards Daemon. Looking down at the big man Daemon pursed his lips and sucked in air at the sight of Hanz's eyes being swollen shut and the bridge of his nose flat on his face. Blood had crusted around his mouth and a large bruise spanned the left side of his ribs as well as numerous other minor wounds.

"Did you do this?" Daemon scowled and pointed to

his bust lips. Hanz nodded and tried to smile but the expression was curtailed due to the pain it caused.

"Oh yeah, sorry about that. We had a little argument and I slugged you. But fear not Sergeant, you gave me a kicking in return then wandered off into a corner and fell asleep" He held out his hand and Daemon took it helping him to his feet.

"Don't apologise." laughed Daemon, "I can't remember anything about last night." He said shading his eyes from the lights. "So did I do that?" He asked and pointing to Hanz's smashed up face. Hanz chuckled for a while and shook his head.

"No, Miles did," Hanz said shrugging.

"Fuck off! Miles never picked a fight with you!" Daemon said between bouts of laughter.

"Yeah well, I kind of came on to Sherry and Miles went apeshit. I tell you what I don't remember anything after that last punch. I must have gone down like a sack of shit." Hanz said without any kind of embarrassment.

"So you picked a fight with me and then got into another fight with Miles? Didn't you learn from your first mistake?" Daemon said grinning.

"Yeah, but I kind of like a brawl after a good drinking session." he said rubbing the bruise on his ribs.

"Alright then tiger, let's get some food down you and sober you up before you kick-off again," Daemon said helping his wounded companion stagger towards the kitchen.

"Believe me, I won't be fighting with you lot again. Especially not with that psycho around," he said pointing a finger at Miles.

Breakfast was a sombre affair with everybody being hung-over and groaning with each bite of food. Hanz eventually broke the silence and apologised for being a drunken bastard, he even offered to stand still while everybody punched him. Luckily everybody declined his generous offer much to Daemon's relief.

"I don't think anybody has the strength to beat on you at the moment. Besides you look to have taken quite enough punishment of late." Daemon stated and hoped everybody else felt the same way. Miles looked up guiltily and avoided eye contact with Hanz,

"Sorry about your face Hanz, I really don't remember doing it but Sherry says I definitely did. I'll sort out your nose after breakfast."

Taku finished her breakfast and refilled her bowl.

"Damn Taku. You have an appetite this morning." Sherry said as she pushed her own half-eaten bowl away. Taku ignored her and began to eat her second helping of processed meat.

"Yeah but she's eating the wrong kind of meat." Hanz grinned grabbing his crutch and chuckling to himself.

"Quit it Hanz!" Daemon commanded but shouting forced him to hold his head as daggers of pain shot through his brain.

"Don't worry sergeant," Taku called out with a mouth full of food, "I served a tour on Mobraska with the CORE so I'm used to having arseholes working alongside me." She kicked Hanz in his shins under the table, he feigned shock and grinned.

"You served on Mobraska? When?" Sherry asked incredulously and tried to calculate how many years had passed since the Mobraska conflict.

"Six years ago, space standard. It was my first tour as a field medic before Xen pulled me out of the core and signed me up in the academy." Taku said.

"My father served at Mobraska." Sherry said with an amount of family pride. Taku stopped eating and looked towards the auburn-haired woman in a seemingly different light.

"Was your father a soldier in the Terran CORE?" she inquired.

"No. He was a Colonel." Sherry said with a beaming grin. Taku dropped her spoon which clattered onto the table top, her eyes filled with tears and her face contorted in rage.

"Colonel Sheridon?" Taku blasted across the table. She grabbed the spoon from the table and held it tightly in her shaking hands revealing an indescribable rage. Daemon's eyes went wide and he made his way around the table to try and restrain Taku just in case she attacked Sherry.

"Sherry I think you better check on the food supplies," he said as he hovered behind Taku. Sherry nodded and rushed off towards the food storage.

"Listen to me Taku. Sherry is not Colonel Sheridon. She may be his daughter but she had nothing to do with whatever happened at Mobraska." Daemon said in a soothing tone. Taku remained silent as she grabbed her crutches and hobbled off towards her bed.

"It would seem Sherry's father has made quite a lot of enemies over the course of his career. I hope I never meet up with him." Miles said before he left the table in search of Sherry.

Five uneventful days passed in the training bay during which Miles started to prepare everybody's meals using information gathered from an old data-spool he had found. The data-spool was probably over fifty years old and had been compiled by a frontline core-trooper called Private Lubeck. The writer had obviously only had access to rudimentary supplies of field rations and a few spices but had been able to create pleasant tasting food for the soldiers in service.

"Miles you have really outdone yourself preparing this meal," Daemon announced after he had chewed his first morsel. Miles had spent a number of hours moulding the protein rations into meaty shapes, including a delicate line of carbohydrate supplements which appeared to be fatty deposit around the meat. He had also made a spicy sauce and somehow produced several bulges that tasted like baked potatoes but didn't have the same texture. Sherry and Hanz agreed with Daemon and commented that now they even looked forward to meal times.

Taku finished her plate and moved on to a brandy sponge pudding, she was grinning because she hadn't waited for the rest to finish their main meal.

"Don't take this the wrong way, but on my home-world, we don't put much stock into the processed food industry. However, on the whole, I'm pretty impressed with what you have achieved Miles." Taku said and patted his hand. Miles blushed a little at the contact and Sherry watched him warily noting his reaction to Taku's gesture.

"Where did you say you come from?" Sherry asked in a neutral tone.

"I was born on the planet Dandibah. It's an agricultural giant on the edge of the Calos system. It's also a free-world. You wouldn't find any corporate meddling there and it's genuinely self-sufficient." she said proudly.

"There aren't many planets like Dandibah left in Corporate space," Daemon said as he poured himself a glass of synthetic fruit juice with a glazed expression of memory.

"I'm curious sergeant, have you visited Dandibah?" Taku said with a smile playing on her lips. He nodded and he noticed everyone was now staring at him.

"It was a long time ago. I was maybe eight years old when my father took me to Dandibah, back when the farm was actually making money. My father purchased eleven Doe deer and a mating stag. We didn't stop very long but I remember it was the most beautiful place I had ever seen." He smiled and pictured the rolling hills and forests in his mind.

Sherry shifted from side to side in her chair; she hated not being the centre of attention.

"It can't have been that beautiful or else Taku would have stayed on Dandibah." she claimed petulantly. Taku ignored her comment and asked Daemon if his father had purchased black or red Doe-deer.

"They were black, black as your hair," he whispered across the table. Taku ran her fingers through her shiny dark hair and laughed.

"Your father must have spent a lot of money on the herd because black Doe-deer is the finest breed. My parents kept obsidian deer and made a fortune exporting livestock to fine restaurants throughout the quadrant. Some were even transported to the greatest restaurants on Talon II." She grabbed her crutches to hobble around the table to sit closer to where he was sat. Daemon felt a twinge of guilt watching her struggle around the table but the feeling subsided as she touched his hand.

"You're the first person I've met in years that has seen the beauty of Dandibah. I know this will seem strange but it somehow makes me feel closer to home knowing you have seen it too." Taku looked at Daemon seeing that he had conflicting feelings about what was happening. She held his arm gently, squeezing it lightly. "I know you didn't mean to injure me in this way, it was unfortunate. Look, this is a troubling time for all of us and right now I need a friend to get me through this nightmare. I need something to hold on to." She leant her head on his arm.

Daemon wondered what to do. All his training had instilled the need to show as little compassion or humanity as possible yet he had an overwhelming urge to help Taku in this time of her need.   Something inside him gave way and Daemon suppressed all that he had been taught and finally hugged her. Sherry shook her head in disgust and grabbed hold of Miles,   "Come on Miles! Let's go and find a place to fuck and leave these lovebirds to their dreams." She dragged him off towards one of the beds roughly.

Hanz remained seated like a wooden manikin and watched the unfolding events between Sherry and Miles. He ignored the conversation at the table as Taku and Daemon reminisced and gathered all of the leftovers from the meal onto his plate.

CHAPTER 8

Gravity can be such a bitch.

That night as Daemon held Taku's sleeping form in his arms the motions of the star-drive seemed distant, almost far away and his nausea had subsided. Miles and Sherry snored loudly in a nearby bed and Hanz was exercising noisily somewhere past a stack of supply crates; Daemon wondered if Hanz ever slept. His thoughts drifted back to his duties and realised that he had let himself down as an officer. He had allowed the barriers that existed between himself and his sect to be broken down so he decided to re-establish authority over the sect the next morning. He would have to catch them off-guard and show them that he was still their sergeant. Xen expected this of him and he had let them down, there would have to be no more mister nice guy.

Taku moaned in her sleep and he felt obliged to cuddle around her to keep her warm. The feel of her body against him caused him to smile to himself and momentarily he doubted that he was up to the challenge of acting like a nasty bastard. Slowly he felt himself drifting off to sleep and he hoped that he would dream of Millie in the warm apple glade. He closed his eyes and listened to the soft purr of Taku's breath over the thrumming of the engines. As he began to drowse he was pulled back into wakefulness by a strong vibration through the floor. This was followed a fraction of a second later by the sound of a loud explosion. Daemon covered his ears as the main alarm screeched into the training bay and the lights dimmed turning a blood red.

Taku was ripped from her dreams and sat up in bed trying to find her crutches in the dim illumination.

"What the hell's happening?" she cried.

"Get yourself ready for combat, we may be under attack," Daemon ordered over the wail of the alarms as he rolled himself off the bed and grabbed his boots. Through a haze he spotted Miles and Sherry dressing quickly and realised that something was burning and he could smell an electrical fire in the air.

"Where's Hanz? And why can I smell smoke?" he shouted then noticed Hanz running out from behind a stack of crates with smoke billowing after him.

"The smoke is coming from the ventilation grilles," Hanz said pointing towards the east side of the bay.

"Well close the fucking vents, you idiot!" Daemon said dumbfounded by Hanz's stupidity.

Hanz covered his mouth with his tunic and rushed back into the smoke. The alarms subsided to a low bleeping sound and Miles headed across to Daemon to receive orders.

"What do you want me to do, sergeant?" Miles asked. But Daemon didn't answer; his brow was knitted with incomprehension. Miles followed his gaze and saw that Daemon was watching a cylindrical drinks holder slowly rolling across the floor. For a moment Miles didn't understand what was so fascinating about it until he realised that it seemed to be sliding up the gradient of the slightly tilted floor.

"Oh shit!" Miles exclaimed, "The gravity compensators aren't resetting, they must be stuck." he said.

"Stuck? Speak sense for..." Daemon didn't have a clue what Miles was talking about but didn't finish his sentence as the Caligula moved violently knocking them off balance.

This time some un-tethered crates defied physics and began sliding slowly across the floor. The pull of gravity on their bodies was undeniable.

"Grab something!" yelled Miles grabbing hold of one of the supporting struts. "Normally all of the gravity compensators align with the motions of the ship. In other words your feet will always be firmly on the ground, even if the ship is upside down compared to your starting position. But some of them must be damaged or malfunctioning or something they are holding the gravity in a fixed position. If more fail the pull with get stronger."

Daemon tried to understand what Miles was telling him but he couldn't quite piece it all together. He had copied the smaller man and grabbed the nearest sturdy object he could find which happened to be one of the beds.

"By the Gods Daemon, think about it!" Miles cried out, "Imagine if we were on a sea-faring craft on an open body of water and it capsized. The compensators are now acting like the gravity of the planet but the floor of the craft will now be at different angles and we'll be pulled towards the gravity." Miles said wondering how the hell Daemon had been put in charge of the sect.

"Alright, alright, I understand and the situation is bad. But what can we do?" Daemon said frantically as Miles shrugged in near despair.

"We have to hope the Caligula doesn't perform a lot of rolling manoeuvres and remains at this bearing. But lashing ourselves to something that is fixed to the superstructure will prevent us falling should the worst happen." It seemed like a plan of action so they began by tying Taku and Sherry down to a bed.

Hanz appeared dressed in smoke stained clothing and sporting a sooty face. He had to brace himself to stand up and from where the other four were it appeared that he was leaning at an unreal angle.

"All of the ventilation shafts are closed off sergeant but something weird is happening." he reported then stared at the two women in bondage on the beds, "What's going on here then?" He asked.

"No time to explain just tie yourself to something!" Daemon instructed.

Hanz rubbed the soot from his eyes and shook his head in confusion. Another explosion reverberated through the ship spinning the Caligula completely off its axis. Seemingly the explosion also caused more gravity compensators to malfunction failing to stabilise the correct centre of gravity. Daemon, Miles and Hanz were thrown off their feet and fell towards the new point of gravity, the ceiling of the training bay.

Hanz, totally unprepared for what was happening failed to react, he didn't even have time to cover his head with his arms. He impacted with the ceiling with full force, his skull shattered like an egg as the rest of his body crumpled upon the sunburst of blood.

Miles and Daemon had been luckier, they had managed to slow their fall upwards by grabbing the blankets on the bed Sherry and Taku shared. When their desperate grasp on the material failed their fall had been broken by other debris which had accumulated.

Daemon crashed on to the edge of a wooden crate and felt several bones shatter on impact before the crate settled back upon him taking the breath from his lungs. He gasped and tried to breath but the weight on his chest denied any conventional movement from his rib cage. His vision darkened and he could hear Miles talking to him, but his voice seemed distant.

"Is this it? Is this where I die?" he contemplated as he realised that he couldn't feel the pains in his body anymore. He felt thankful that at least his last seconds wouldn't be spent in agony and his mind had settled upon a peaceful death even though he had one last nagging thought. "Damn it! I would have liked to have fucked Sherry before I kicked off my boots."

"Forget it Daemon I'm not that kind of girl!" Millie cried shoving him away from her. Her beautiful face was contorted with hatred. He staggered backwards trying to keep his balance but his knees had turned to jelly and he fell into the grass. He tried standing but a searing pain in his chest jolted his body and sapped away all his strength. Millie was walking away peering over her shoulder with a look of disgust.

"Just wait until I tell my brothers and my father!" she said grinning evilly as she made her way down the small foot hill.

"Why Millie?" he cried but more pain crushed his chest forcing his legs to kick around spasmodically in the grass.

"You have brought this on yourself my boy!" Daemon looked up to see his father unbuckling his trouser belt and inhaling strongly upon a fat hand rolled Koll-weed cigar. Smoke billowed out of his father's ears as his mother stood silhouetted in the mid-day sun just behind him.

"You should have listened to your father son." she sobbed trying to cover a bruise on her eye with a fire charred hand.

"Mother?" he whispered with tears in his eyes. She shook her head and wandered away towards the tree line of the apple wood. He felt his father's vice like grip, the roughness of hard working farming hands around his neck, crushing the life from him.

"It's for your own good boy!" his father hissed as horns sprouted from his forehead and he brought up the belt strap high into the sun.

With each flailing of the belt strap came a terrible burning in his chest. Daemon quickly lost count of how many lashes his father brought down upon his flesh as he screamed for salvation. He looked to his mother begging her to stop the beating but saw that she no longer stood there; in her place was the demon with its skull aflame. The demon was laughing at him,

"Take your medicine boy!" it cackled, "It will make you stronger."

Screams of pain, panic and madness surrounded him. Daemon's eyes were being held open as someone shone a bright light in to them. He winced as stabbing pains penetrated his brain and struggled until he was released allowing him to close his eyes again.

A nearby voice issued, "This one's conscious doctor."

A strong smell of alcohol invaded the air and Daemon almost retched at it. He felt cold hands upon his chest and a dull pain as fingers probed his damaged rib cage.

"This one's pulse is strong. He will probably live, now get me some fresh gloves and some more adrenalin! I fear that one over there is going to crash any minute now."

The voice drifted away as bleeping alarms amalgamated with the screams of agony echoing from every corner of the chamber. He tried to escape the noise by sleeping but every time he drifted off a heart monitor machine flat-lined and brought him back into the living nightmare.

Daemon lost track of time and his mind waylaid him with confusing thoughts between bouts of sleep. He thought he had heard Miles talking to him a few hours before but it could have been a dream. It was quieter now; gone was the chaos and deathly rattles. Now all that could be heard was the humming and hissing of nearby medical machinery. He had lost count of the nightmares which visited him while he slept, strange recurring dreams of his childhood at his parent's farm with the dates and people muddled up. He knew that his father had never beaten him when he was a child. He hadn't started getting nasty on mother until he had got hooked on stimulants and by then Daemon was eighteen and leaving home anyway. A wispy voice to his left took away his thoughts.

"Hey buddy. Pssst." Daemon opened one eye and turned his head towards the voice. The man in the next bed was hairless and veins were prominent on his exposed body. Daemon assumed he had suffered decompression of some kind, probably from a hull breach.

"You're that student Xen sect leader aren't you?" The man didn't wait for an answer and continued. "Well take it from me buddy. You are one lucky son-of-a-bitch. The Caligula was sabotaged in full star-drive forcing it out of drive, right into an ambush. There's a big fucking hole where the Cryo-bank used to be. You and your sect would have died in your sleep. Instead you were doing some weird training in one of the cargo holds, you lucky bastards." The man stopped talking as though he was pondering over something else.

"Well you survived as well didn't you? So you can count yourself lucky too." Daemon said angrily. He didn't feel especially fortuitous stuck in a hospital bed with numerous broken bones and injuries.
The man levered himself up on the bed to face him.

"Look at me!" He cried thumbing to himself. "Do you think this is lucky? The doctors claim my hair will never grow back and my lifespan is going to be pretty fucking short!" The man ranted as the veins on his forehead bulged and pulsated with every word he said. Daemon tried to grab the alarm button to call for the nurse but his arms felt like dead weights.

"I was in maintenance when plasma fire ate through the hull. I ran for the pressure door." A vein popped on the man's head and sprayed a line of blood on to the bed sheets. The man didn't seem to notice the injury.

"My friends were in that room when I shut the pressure door!" the man said as tears of blood dribbled from his eyes.

Daemon summoned enough strength to grab the nurse alarm but his fingers couldn't depress the button.

"I could hear them screaming and banging on the door. But what could I do? I'd killed them as soon as I hit that button and they knew it. They told me they knew it too as they screamed their last!" The man kicked away his bed sheets and started to climb out of his bed.

"You had no choice!" Daemon shouted in a fit of panic. "Please, calm down. You're hurting yourself."

The man ignored him and stood up quickly. He appeared to be a human fountain as numerous veins ruptured over the surface of his body.

"You weren't there! You have no idea how it feels to survive when your friends didn't." His voice was becoming difficult to understand as he began choking on bodily fluids. The alarm buzzed in Daemon's hand and he prayed a nurse would come quickly as the man limped towards him.

"And you call me lucky? Look at you!" Spittle and blood flew from the crazed man's mouth. "You're practically unscathed. You goddamned academy scum. I will take you to hell with me!" The man sobbed as his fingers clasped around Daemon's throat. Daemon didn't have the strength to fight the man off and his ears were already humming with the pressure being exerted on his neck. His vision was failing as he saw an orderly running down the aisle of beds. The heavy set male nurse tackled Daemon's assailant to the floor and repeatedly punched him while the man screamed in agony. Daemon gasped for breath and tried to cover his face from the airborne blood sprays from each pounding fist the nurse dealt to the floored man. A sinister silence descended as the nurse stood up wiping his bloodied hands on his white tunic.

"Are you going to be alright Xen man? Do you need any medical assistance?" The nurse asked calmly as though he hadn't just beaten a man to death. Daemon shook his head and coughed.

"Well if you do need anything? Just press the buzzer and I will see to your needs." With no visible emotion he dragged the corpse away.

"Where am I? What kind of place is this?" Daemon shrieked with his last ounce of strength. The nurse ignored him and started to whistle a cheerful tune as he shouldered the door open and dragged the bloody corpse out

"Well you're a little malnourished but you appear to be on the road to recovery. In some ways you are in a better state than you were with your travel sickness. Apart from the odd broken bone, of course!" Miles stated as he browsed the medical display next to Daemon's bed.
Taku leant against Sherry's shoulder clutching her arm for stability.

"Xen fixed me up sergeant." Taku stated as she rolled her trouser leg up revealing a shiny metallic prosthetic limb. "But it hurts like hell."
Daemons face had obviously revealed his shock as

Sherry had fired him an unforgiving glare and gestured with her hand for him to offer some emotional support.

"It looks good." He offered, "They say that modern day prosthetic limbs are better than the organic limbs that you were born with. You'll be running circles around us all before you know it." Taku sighed and refused to believe such a bullshit claim.

"Not this one sergeant. This rudimentary model is the only type they have on board the Life-boat. I'd be lucky to run rings round you right now" she said grimly. Daemon scowled and looked at Miles who was busying himself with medical data.

"Lifeboat, what are you talking about?" He questioned.

"I take it nobody has told you we aren't on the Caligula anymore." Sherry said before laughing in disbelief.

"Nobody has told me fuck all." He confirmed.

"I suppose it's down to me to tell you what's been going on around here." Miles said as he sat down on a nearby chair and shrugged his shoulders. Daemon sat quietly as Miles described the events over the last week. His story started with the explosion in the engine room which had destroyed the star-drive engine and lead the Caligula into an ambush. The tyrant class star ship had been attacked by three Seinal battle-cruisers that had caused considerable damage to the Caligula including the heavy damage to the cryo-bank that he knew about. About ninety percent of the crew died in their frozen sleep during the first assault. Shortly after

Daemon had lost consciousness the gravity compensators failed completely and the entire ship had been thrown into zero gravity. Miles had managed to grab hold of Daemon and float his way to an empty bed. He had strapped him down and performed the first aid that had undoubtedly saved his life. By then the Caligula's auto-systems had come online and engaged the Seinal attack force destroying it after a brief battle. Even unmanned the tyrant craft was more than a match for the Seinal cruisers. It had taken six hours before the surviving personnel realised that a sect had been assigned to the cargo bay and a further four hours before they located them. Daemon and Taku had been taken straight to the huge life-boat in the belly of the Caligula. Surviving emergency medical staff had then been revived to deal with the mounting casualties. According to Miles the emergency staff on board the life-boat had probably been in cryogenic stasis for over six years. Apparently they were well paid by the Xen Corporation to endure such long periods on ice.

While Daemon had received medical attention, Sherry and Miles aided several groups locating survivors that were trapped in other damaged sections of the vast star ship.

Miles finally finished his account and sat in silence for a while with his head resting on his hand. Daemon noticed Taku was fast asleep on the bottom of his bed, she was snoring softly.

"So there was nothing you could do for Hanz?" Daemon asked again, he could barely recall what had happened in the last moments he had been conscious.

"Nothing," replied Miles shaking his head regretfully, "he was dead on impact. At least it was painless; many others suffered horribly before they went. It doesn't seem like much consolation though."

"Did Captain Hally survive?" Daemon said breaking the grim silence.

"She was in cryo. She died with the rest of the frozen crew in the forward cryo-banks." He mumbled as he readjusting his pose.

"That's a shame. I kind of liked her." Daemon said glumly. Sherry returned to the medical bay holding several bottles of ice cold beer.

"It's like a fucking funeral in here." She said as she distributed the bottles. "I've just been chatting to that Xen agent who closed the door on us in the training bay. By the sound of things he had a private room on board the Caligula with a private cryo-tank, he was one of the first ones out of cryo when the space-drive cut out." she said with a tinge of jealousy.
Miles frowned and appeared to be slightly unnerved.

"I've been trying to place him ever since we saw him. I think I've met that bastard before." He grumbled more words under his breath. Daemon prompted him for more information but Sherry was far too eager to tell her tale.

"As I said, I was chatting to Agent Rowson and he says we are being iced tomorrow for the final leg of the journey. But our destination isn't the academy on Vex II." She paused for effect as everyone looked at her.

"Instead we are heading for an assignment on another world but he refused to say which it was."

"Do you think Xen has chosen a great test for us?" Daemon pondered and hoped he was wrong. Sherry looked at her time piece and calculated how many hours the sect had until they were sent to cryo.

"I would say we have about ten hours before we are iced, why don't we finish these beers and get some more at the on-board bar." she said grinning.

"That sounds like a plan as long as you can carry me to the bar?" Daemon said as he kicked off the bed sheets grimacing with pain. The sect headed off to the bar to have a small wake for their dead colleague Hanz.

CHAPTER 9

Kommando

"I'll kill you all!" Roz cried as he punched the glass shielding with his bloodied, gnarled stumps. Blood was dripping down the interior of the holding cell as Roz marched up and down naked, smeared with gore. Drill-master Gidd flinched as Roz attacked the glass again with the fury of a wild animal.

"When is this shit going to wear off?" Gidd asked directing the question to Dr Kelum. The doctor readjusted his round spectacles and peered up from a handheld data-pad.

"Quat is a very dangerous drug and your patient has taken three times the standard dosage. I'm sorry but my field of expertise doesn't cover such an overdose."

Doctor Kelum started rubbing his sleep deprived eyes.

"Horseshit! Are you trying to tell me Xen hasn't experimented with Quat overdoses before?" Gidd hissed. He was clearly angered by the lack of progress and wanted results before he reported to Mistress Suix. He glanced at his timepiece and watched Roz flailing around on the floor of the cell like some kind of sub-human monster.

"It's very likely Xen experimented with greater doses of Quat upon laboratory guinea pigs in controlled environments but I have never seen any such reports." The doctor claimed scratching his balding head.

After a month in cryo Roz had been revived less than twenty four hours previously and it had been a long day watching him thrash around in the holding cell.

"I was escorted from my house in the middle of the night and invited to board a ship and come to this outer reach shithole." Doctor Kelum said in a fluster. "The Xen command didn't give any information apart from the fact they were experiencing problems with an individual at this academy involving Quat."
Drill-master Gidd curled up his lip and gritted his teeth as Roz began to howl like a dog.

"We need to sedate Initiate Roz before he causes any more damage to himself!" Gidd said as he tapped the glass wall to see if Roz recognised him.

"Well I'm certainly not going to risk any more of my staff! The patient murdered the last two auxiliaries who tried to sedate him. I suggest we either wait a while longer and see if the drug naturally wears off or refreeze him." Doctor Kelum said defiantly and glanced at the two pulverised auxiliaries lying dead in the holding cell. Gidd gripped the doctor in a painful arm lock and pressed his face against the glass wall.

"Time is running out Doctor. I have a meeting in less than three hours with Mistress Suix and I would like to attend it with good news about our patient." Gidd said as Doctor Kelum struggled in his vice like grip.

"You're hurting me!" The doctor wailed pitifully.

"And he is hurting himself. Unless you do something soon he might kill himself and that is not acceptable." Gidd increased the pressure on the doctor's arm, expertly judging the amount he could apply without breaking it.

"Honestly there is nothing I can do here." the doctor begged clearly panicked.

"You have two hours and if you haven't come up with something by then you'll leave me little choice but to put you in the cell with Roz to treat him personally; on a one to one basis." Gidd said with a menacing tone.

"No!" Doctor Kelum screamed then fainted with terror.

Gidd felt the dead weight in his arms and allowed the doctor to fall to the floor. He loomed over the unconscious doctor as Roz charged the fortified glass head first making Gidd involuntarily cover his face. The glass had bulged and was splattered with blood but it hadn't broken. Roz had bounced off before landing on the floor prostrate and it looked to Gidd that Roz had knocked himself out cold.

"Give me those sedating syringes." Gidd yelled to a nearby auxiliary who had cowered in to the corner of the room when Gidd had begun assaulting the doctor. Gidd snatched the syringes and popped the main hatch on the holding cell. Roz was laid prone on the floor but Gidd still approached him cautiously. He popped the protective lids off all of the syringes and jabbed them in to Roz's neck.

Roz's eyes flicked open as Gidd injected the sedatives and lashed out smashing the bridge of Gidd's nose before attempting to make an escape through the open hatch. Gidd held on to him and felt his struggles weaken as the drugs took effect. Roz finally collapsed half way to freedom several feet short of the door way.

Drill Master Gidd staggered out of the cell covering his bloody nose to find Mistress Suix had decided to make a surprise visit on the patient. She scowled as she noticed Roz slumped in the doorway of the cell and she elbowed past several auxiliaries and paced over to Doctor Kelum lying on the floor.

"What the fucking hell is going on in here? Is he dead?" She yelled pointing to the unconscious doctor.

"No Mistress," Gidd mumbled through his bloodied fingers, "he kind of fainted but Roz has finally been sedated. I suppose that's the good news." It was clear Mistress Suix didn't want an explanation judging by her angry face.

"Wake that idiot up and strap that patient down." She barked. The auxiliaries jumped at her command and followed her orders. Gidd tried to apologise for the mess but she gestured for silence.

"I have just received a transmission from the high command. A starship is arriving in thirteen hours' time to collect Initiate Roz. That time period is our window to make sure Roz is fit and calm enough to travel. Failure is not an option Gidd and I'm making you personally responsible for this task." She looked disapprovingly at the two dead auxiliaries in the holding cell.

Gidd squinted and wondered why she had suddenly made Initiate Roz his responsibility.

"You're asking for the impossible, look at him. Where the hell are they going to take him anyway?" He said negatively.

"They didn't say but I suspect someone in high command has been monitoring my personnel files ever since Initiate Roz brought back that Seinal corpse from the outer marker." Suix answered looked perturbed.

"Why put me in charge?" Gidd ventured. "I'm a drill master, not a doctor."

"Because I think that you have seen your son's qualities in Roz and I know you will do everything to succeed." She whispered. Gidd's eyes filled with tears.

"My son died in a terrible battle you bitch! You have no right to invoke the memory of my child, no right at all." He said through gritted teeth as a tear escaped his eye.

"We both mourned the passing of your son my friend but word gets around the academy. It's been made clear to me that you developed a bond with Roz." She reached out and held his arm. The rumours were true because Gidd had taken it upon himself to privately tutor Roz in a variety of subjects but had mainly concentrated on weapons and combat.

"This is your last chance to help him Gidd; I think you are the only one who can. The sands of time are drifting away my friend. I think it might be best if you organise what is left of the science team and get this patient back on his feet." She smiled at the Drill Master and squeezed his forearm. Gidd stood in silence until Mistress Suix left the room.

"Right then people, you heard the lady. We have thirteen hours!" He said clapping his hands to punctuate his authority.

The transport craft arrived at the academy on the Rock later than had been scheduled. Meanwhile Roz had been given a variety of sedatives and anti-toxins and had reached the point where he could recognise the drill master but was still prone to random acts of violence. Four armed attendants from the ship, dressed in full combat suits, came to escort the semi-lucid patient. Gidd accompanied them to the docking station to ensure Roz was not to be mistreated.

"Well this is it Roz my boy, they haven't told me where you are being taken but it might be for the best hey? After all, you weren't really cut out for the academy. You were never the studious type, you are more like me, a warrior!" Gidd said attempting to hide any emotion from his voice.

"Drill-master?" Roz mumbled though the haze of intoxication. Gidd made a quick check on the bandages covering what was left of Roz's hands and shook his head.

"You're a resilient little bastard and strong. I am going to miss our training sessions." He said but the escorts were already marching him up the gang plate to the waiting ship. The doors closed as Gidd walked slowly through the pressure door back to the academy. The guards on the door did him the courtesy of not noticing that he was weeping.

Later that day Gidd found Mistress Suix in the canteen eating a slice of lemon pie which she had procured from the supplies the transport craft had brought. Gidd sat in silence watching Suix savour the flavour of the pie with a heavenly smile on her face.

"Is it that good? I can't say I ever enjoyed the taste of lemons, especially in pies." Gidd said breaking the silence and screwing up his face as if he had just bitten in to a fresh lemon.

Suix laughed and pushed the last piece of pie across the table towards Gidd.

"This lemon pie is the chef's special, well it is when there are lemons in supply. Try it, you will like it."

"I'm not eating that shit!" Gidd growled.

"Listen to me very carefully, eat the fucking pie and that's an order! Besides which it won't change that sour look you already have smeared across your face." She said with a predatory tone.

"You can't order me to eat something I don't wish to eat." He laughed already picking up the fork and scooping up the last morsel.

"I can just about command you to do anything I desire." She smiled, "Now eat it soldier! Even if you don't like it, which you will, I have sacrificed my last piece and offered it to you, my friend."
Gidd peered at the yellow fondant leaking from the sandwich of limp pastry and sighed.

"I tell you what, we will do a small trade, you eat the pie and I will give you a fragment of information about Roz, how about that?" She stated.

"That sounds like a more than equitable arrangement." He said and then ate the lemon pie. At first he screwed up his face with disgust and then frowned as the flavours worked in harmony with his taste buds. "Okay you win, its nicer than the last time I ate anything with lemons in it."

Mistress Suix nodded smugly and sipped from a tumbler of yellowish dessert wine. "It works better with a delicate sweet wine but I see you are eager to trade. What I'm about to tell you remains between you and me!" She stated while she raised an eyebrow to emphasize her authority.
Gidd's face took on a serious expression.

"Of course, you have my word. Well I suppose I should come clean: I looked at the shipping data on the transport craft that Roz has just boarded. It's going to a planet called Talon II; that much I do know. I accessed the database and found out Talon II is a demilitarised free trade planet with a single Xen embassy. Somehow I don't think that Roz is a diplomatic resource so it begs the question as to what the fuck the corporation wants with an ex-farm boy on such a planet?"

"You appear to have done your homework," Suix conceded, "but with your security clearance there is no way you could know that there is a secret Kommando school on Talon II."

"Kommando!" Gidd blurted and shook his head. "I bumped into a few of them in a battle on Breaker. They were cold hearted killers! My battalion were ordered to dig in while three Kommando's entered the bunker head at nightfall. The bastards murdered everyone inside, women, children they didn't care. The rebels were desperate and we knew they would surrender in a couple of days but Xen wanted a quick victory and to send a message. We were part of the clear up crew the next morning." Gidd's eyes glazed over remembering the atrocities found inside the bunker. Mistress Suix leant across the table to hold Gidd's hand for comfort.

"I know. I was on Breaker too. Xen claimed its quick victory in hours instead of days. Back then I was only a first lieutenant leading a contingent of hired militia into the bunker to download information from the rebel data-base. It was pretty messy in there to say the least. I still wake up now and then with images of the inhumanity performed inside that lowly bunker." She whispered.
Gidd opened his eyes and trembled as he tried to forget the entire incident on Breaker.

"I can't believe the corporation wishes to transform Roz into one of them!" Gidd cried as he slapped the table with the sheer frustration of being unable to do anything to help his former student.

Some of the students in the canteen looked up at this outburst and stared at them.

"Well Gidd, I have a bottle of brandy back in my office. I think now is as good a time as any to go and drink it. Care to share it with me?" Gidd nodded but his face looked pale and drawn, for the first time she could remember he looked his age she knew him to be. Suix helped up the emotional Gidd and dragged him out of the canteen before the initiates saw him in such a state.

A young doctor checked Roz's vital statistics on a nearby data-stream. The doctor had just enough hair under his nose to be classified a moustache and his blonde hair was greased back into a small ponytail.

"It's time to make a move my man." The doctor said rocking his shoulder.

"What time is it?" Roz asked yawning. He felt a little groggy but was certainly in less pain than he had been previously. The injection he had been given an hour ago seemed to have numbed the pain in his hands.

"It's noon space time but your body clock will soon catch up. I see your hands have gone into the third stage of growth. You should have seen them last week. They looked like a pair of skinned cats." The doctor said chuckling.

"I don't remember what they looked like last week; in fact I'd forgotten I had new hands. Was I in some kind of accident?" Roz asked curiously.

The young man frowned and pulled out a syringe from

his chest pocket.

"You've asked that a number of times since you first came round. Don't you remember?" the doctor asked frowning. In response to the shake of Roz's head he continued, "To be honest with you I don't know myself. You may have been in an accident, we are hoping you will remember and be able to tell us exactly what happened. I was sent down here to perform a final diagnostic on you. Are you in any pain?"

"My hands feel a little raw but I suppose it's tolerable." Roz said looking down at them. They appeared skeletal with only a thin lair of tissue covering the bones. Purple veins pulsated beneath the thin lair of unblemished skin which was a bright pink colour like that of a new-born baby. The Doctor seemed satisfied with his answers and with the inspection of his hands and put the syringe back in his pocket.

"Well my friend, raw is good. It means your body has accepted the new growth. If you start feeling queasy or feel any pain what-so-ever press the big red button and I will come to aid you." The doctor said pointing to an emergency alarm button.

"So I'm free to roam around?" Roz asked. The young man nodded before wandering over to a patient in a nearby bed who had started to moan.
Roz pulled on a hospital gown and climbed out of bed. The floor was cold beneath his feet and he curled his toes up stretching them. He didn't know where he was or how he had got there and wondered where he should go. He thought about asking the young doctor

but he seemed busy with the other patient.

"Where am I?" He grumbled to himself as he made his way to the exit. His muscles ached as he walked as if they were unaccustomed to exercise so he assumed he had been bedridden for quite a while. He tried to remember what had happened to him but it was like trying to see over a large wall within his mind. His earlier memories seemed to be intact because the sensation of being on the verge of recalling something reminded him of a time when he was only eight years old. His father had built a wooden shed with a single window which was too high for him to peer through. He could hear strange noises coming from inside the shed and he tried desperately to shimmy up to the window to see what the noises were. But every time he got a good hand hold on the ledge he slipped and fell to the grass below.

"Wait until you are tall enough to see without trying." He whispered as he shouldered open the ward door into the bland metallic corridor beyond. The corridor went off to the left and right, he turned left following the luminous signs directing him to the canteen but soon found he didn't need to use them as he caught the drifting scent of cooking food.

To his surprise the canteen was busy with off-duty soldiers rather than patients. He made his way to a vacant table and realised that a number of soldiers were now staring at him.

"Are you lost?" a female voice asked to his flank. He turned to face a tall, heavy set, dark haired woman dressed in a green vest and army issue pants.

"I'm hungry." Roz said as he scanned the woman. She wasn't the prettiest woman he had seen but she seemed to have a way about her that he did find attractive.

"This canteen is for military personnel only. So I will ask you again whelp! Are you lost?" she asked through gritted white teeth.

"I am military personnel and in case you didn't hear me the first time, I said that I'm very hungry." Roz said masking the nerves he was feeling as he watched other heavy set military types stalking towards him.

The woman made a sudden movement and he was in no condition to defend against her attack. Something hit the bridge of his eye followed by a flash of white pain which temporarily blinded him.

His knees buckled and he fell to the floor where the assault continued. He tried to rise to his feet and defend himself but the attacks kept him grounded. He couldn't work out how many blows were making it through his defences due to the abundance of sedatives that circulated his blood stream and the fact that things were becoming fuzzy again.

The beating suddenly stopped and he heard gruff curses and laughter. He felt his weight shifting and then he was being lifted up onto a chair or table. Through swollen eyelids, he could see black clothing and a silvery symbol of a lightning bolt, set within a triangle. Roz finally looked up to the face of an aged man with wrinkled olive skin and piercing blue eyes.

"You took a bit of a beating there brother, are you functional?" The man said with little emotion in his voice. Roz thought the question to be odd and didn't really understand the use of the word functional.

"I think so." he mumbled with difficulty, "What the hell was all that about?" He spat out a bloodied tooth.

"It's some ridiculous CORE regulation, you don't go anywhere without your dog tags or you will become one of their prey." The man said prodding at Roz's swollen eye.

"Well I wasn't given any dog tags to wear." Roz said then noticed the man didn't even have a name tag on his fatigues.

"Come to mention it, you haven't any either. Why aren't they kicking the fuck out of you?"

"Because they know better than to mess with a Kommando, this symbol distinguishes us from the rest of the scum, brother." The man announced loudly pointing to the symbol on his left shoulder. "I heard you had been cleared from the medical bay and I was on my way down here to take you to cryo. Darn it, I wish I had got here sooner. We could have toasted those fuckers together."

"I wish you had been here too, it might have saved me a beating. Why are we heading to Cryo?" Roz wiped his mouth down on his gown.

"Too many questions my brother. All you need to know is that we are going to the cryo room to be iced. Your questions will be answered when we arrive." The aged man said as if he was speaking to a child.

"Arrive where? And why do you keep calling me that, I'm not your brother!" Roz said with rancour.

"You may not be my brother biologically but you will be in essence when you graduate. Names are unimportant in the clan of Kommando's, I must have had over a thousand names given to me by people I know or people that I have killed." The man said laughing. If Roz wasn't already confused he certainly felt it now.

"And what have I done to earn this honour? The last thing I remember is running to the outer marker at the academy. It's all a bit grey between then and now. I don't even know where this place is or how I got here." Roz said tapping the side of his head, as though the small impacts would jog his memory.

"You have shown promise and that is all you need to know. Someday, if all goes well you will understand and look upon me and your fellow Kommando's as brothers."

"Well until then what should I call you?" Roz said in annoyance.

"Call me whatever the fuck you like, you can call me Sue if you wish. Either way I wouldn't be a tiny bit bothered." The man said while winking. Roz thought for a few seconds and decided on a name.

"How about Brian? I had a friend called Brian who lived on the next farm down the road. He was a mad bastard too."

"Brian it is then." Laughed the man, "Now come on brother let's get you to cryo."

It took three months space time travelling to the planet of Talon II. Roz and Brian were kept in the cryogenic tanks and transported across the land until they reached the secret Xen facility known as the Kommando School. Brother Brian was thawed out some days before Roz as he was due to stand before a disciplinary committee to answer questions regarding the 'accidental' deaths of several military soldiers on the transport ship.

News had reached Talon II that each and every soldier who had attacked Roz in the canteen had died under mysterious circumstances shortly after. It was suggested that Brother Brian had sought out and killed them prior to being put in cryo himself. The disciplinary hearing was not concerned with the deaths of the Core troopers (including a sergeant) but Brother Brian's mistake of not hardlining his cryo tube. In other words Brother Brian had failed to cover his tracks when he went on his murderous spree. Hardlining would have provided him with an alibi as his cryo tube would have shown that, technically, he was sleeping soundly in his tube even though it was empty. It would then have been impossible to trace the murders back to him.

Roz was unaware of this as a week passed by quickly in the confines of the Kommando School. He received more medical attention for his new hands and by the end of the week they had fully grown and appeared normal to the naked eye. When he was not in the clinic he spent much of his time in the spacious gardens around the facility. The gardens themselves were a sight

159

to behold, delicate cherry blossom trees surrounded the lawns and water features. There was also a large root and herb garden where fresh vegetables and fragrant herbs were harvested for the Kommando School canteen. Roz had taken a liking to the food prepared in the canteen, spicy meals with rice side dishes and wild meats flown in by transport crafts on a daily basis. His particular favourite was roasted black doe-deer, which were transported live from some backwater planet called Dandibah and slaughtered onsite.

Roz had been told that his training would begin the following day and he was sat watching the setting sun in a small apple grove and meditating on the tranquillity of the sight.

"So my brother, you will begin training tomorrow, I was wondering; have you said your farewells to your former life?" Brother Brian had approached Roz silently while he sat watching the last crescent of the orange sun descending under the canopy of the forest.

"I think so. As a whole I am looking forward to forgetting my memories. They seem almost distant now anyway, as though my mind has already blocked them out. I think the only thing I will miss is my old friend Daemon." Rozs' voice sounded a little troubled.

Brother Brian sat down next to him and focused on the last straggling beams of the light.

"Think of it as a small trade Brother, you will lose a dear friend but will gain many kin: sisters and brothers that will give their lives for you. And you for them." Brother Brian's voice trailed off and they both watched the sky begin to bruise.

Somewhere in the trees a bird called out and Brian sighed, he leant a little forward scanning the tree line.

"I will leave you to your thoughts brother and the coming night. If you are silent you may hear the song of the night caller; it was she who called out then. She roosts somewhere at the edge of the forest but the predatory avian has eluded me for years. I have spent many nights trying to glimpse her splendour but she hides away. She is a solitary animal and though I have found the remains of many of her kills I have never seen the beast itself. She is a true Kommando of the animal kingdom." Brian left Roz alone in the brooding darkness.

CHAPTER 10

Rite of Passage

Roz had returned to his quarters in the dead of night and was woken early to be escorted to the Kommando School processing chamber. He was stripped naked and strapped to a cold metal table where medical attendants monitored him. Once they had satisfied themselves with their tests, powerful psychoactive drugs were administered to him and the conditioning began. For Roz time had no meaning at all during the process, and afterwards he didn't know if had been in that dreaded room for days, weeks or months.

During the mind changing conditioning, he was subjected to a myriad of images, odours and sensations. Tormenting pain and an assault of terrifying voices were his constant companions.

When, finally, he emerged from that terrible confining space he had lost almost twenty kilograms in body weight and was but an empty shell of a human being. Roz felt lost but cleansed.

"You have been processed Brother, you have no former life, you can never return to whatever existence you had. All you have now is the order and your fellow Kommando's." Brother Brian greeted him with these words as he exited the processing chamber. It was nice to see a friendly face at last.

"I remember now Brian. I remember the dirty Seinal troops I killed with my bare hands and I feel no remorse. I remember feeling the rage inside the cell and that I... I..." Roz cried, tears streaming his cheeks.

"Yes? You remember killing those medical auxiliaries while you were high on Quat? Remember Brother that they were trying to force drugs upon you and you fell to your basic instincts and killed them before they could cloud your thoughts. That is good my Brother. Why do you shed tears?" Brian asked fervently as though he was giving out a religious speech to fanatical followers.

"I do not shed tears for them Brother, for no more do I feel pain. No nightmare could rouse me from my waking sleep! My tears are of those of joy. My sight is crystal clear now." Roz wept and laughed in a rapture of hysteria.

"You are cleansed!" Brother Brian howled with elation shaking his fists. "Soon your mind will be filled with all that is good and righteous."

Roz accepted the nurture of Kommando training without thought like a blind newborn creature takes to the teat. Months flashed by as Brother Brian taught him things he had only read about in graphic spool-readers involving superheroes back when he was an adolescent. He would never have believed Kommando's could punch through the strongest armour with their bare hands and pluck out the beating heart of their victims. But his cleansed mind now absorbed information like a Cufa sponge. He learnt how to pilot space-faring craft, hardline cryo-tubes, how to convert an energy node into a weapon and what kind of basic components could be transformed into explosives. Everything fell into a calm routine, sleep, eat, learn, meditate and martial combat. In his spare time, he read poetry or travel journals and ended each day by watching the sun go down. Roz was at last happy, he was no longer confused or trying to find his feet in life but he still remained a quiet man around the opposite sex.

One day Roz had got up earlier than usual so that he could run to the edge of the forest and back before attending combat training. As he returned and passed through the gymnasium he saw that two of his fellow Sisters were sparing with wooden batons within the circular hall. He towelled himself down and sat on an empty bench watching the fighting styles they used which kept changing every few seconds. He was impressed how easily they were able to flow from one style to another without losing control or momentum of the batons.

Personally he preferred the simple efficiency of using his body over any mode of weaponry but was proficient at both methods of combat. It appeared that the two women were masters of weaponry and he found it hard to keep up with some of the different forms being used. In some instances when they used power attacks he had to cover his ears to muffle the din of the sticks hitting each other.

Before he had been cleansed he would have felt a competitive urge to prove himself against these women but now he chuckled to himself as he realised that he wouldn't stand a chance against either of them in melee armed combat. The door to the hall slammed shut and the sparring stopped instantly. Roz peered over his shoulder and smiled as Brother Brian approaching his bench. The two Sisters bowed and left the chamber drenched in sweat from their exertions.

Brian sat beside Roz with a strange expression on his face; he sighed and put his hand on his shoulder. "There will be no lessons for you today my Brother. I am no longer your tutor." Roz leapt up from the bench with a face of utter dismay.

"Why?" Roz said failing to hide the disappointment in his voice.

"You have learnt all that I can teach you. Today you will graduate. You have been a good pupil Brother. You have been conscientious and have learnt quickly. What has it been six, seven months?" Brian asked softly.

"Six months and nine days, but that doesn't make me a Kommando." Confusion had returned along with a feeling of betrayal.

"What can I say? Each of our kin, unique and is ready at different times, only the Masters can say when that time has come. You survived a terrible overdose of Quat and you survived the cleansing. Many do not. You have been diligent in your training and have proved yourself worthy of becoming a Kommando. What were you expecting Brother? A ceremony to commemorate your achievements. A show of appreciation? Do you not feel whole without them?" Brian chided. Roz thought for a second, "No, I do not feel whole."

"It is just as well!" Brian laughed for one of few times Roz could remember hearing. "The only thing preventing you feeling whole is your doubt. But come, our brothers and sisters are waiting to grant their blessings. Let us see if a ceremony changes your mind." Brian said gesturing with his hands for Roz to follow.

The ceremony lasted more than three hours and was followed by a small celebration of wine drinking. One of the rituals had involved all the Kommando's at the school drawing blood into a receptacle that Roz had to sip. It was passed to him by Master Vaul, one of the heads of the school and it was the first time that Roz had seen the tall man. As Roz had drunk from the chalice Vaul had congratulated him for joining the brotherhood and to Roz's surprise and pleasure told him that he had been keeping a close eye on him over the last few months. Roz had thanked him and listened as Vaul told him how the giving and accepting of blood symbolised the first rule of the clan: Kommando's would willingly give their lives for a fellow clan member. Roz was relieved that there was no similar ritual to represent the second rule: to kill a fellow clan member would be akin to taking your own life.

Later in the evening as Roz shared wine with a few of his new brothers he found that it was also customary to sleep with a fellow initiate clan member. However, on this occasion there were no female initiates present so Roz was allowed to forgo this privilege. Roz did not feel confident enough to ask where the two women he had seen earlier were. The party continued unabated in to the night but he decided that he would leave early as he always felt like an outsider at such gatherings. With the celebrations still in full swing he made his excuses and sought the tranquillity of his own room.

For some reason, he felt subdued about graduating rather than feeling the exultation he had expected. His idyllic routine had been interrupted and he felt regret that he would no longer be seeing Brother Brian on a daily basis. For the first time since he had been cleansed Roz found it difficult to get to sleep.

It was a summer's day and Roz was meditating in the chapel. The high noon sun shone through the stained glass windows bathing him in warm multi-coloured light as he centred on his breathing. It had been a week since his graduation and he was beginning to feel the first shoots of contentedness returning within him. As he turned his thoughts to attempting to divine the meaning behind a puzzling poem he had read that morning a member of the Brotherhood approached him. The woman gave him a brown paper box before bowing, departing and leaving Roz slowly opened the box and begin sifting through the papers inside. One of the papers simply gave a name and address, another was a cylinder train timetable and the last appeared to be star liner ticket destined for Krell. He had never heard of a planet called Krell, not even in all the travel pamphlets he had read but he was not surprised as they often only described the more exotic worlds. He realised that the information must relate to the first mission the Brotherhood wished him to carry out. Brother Brian had told him that the day would come when he would be asked to prove his devotion to the clan. Roz had asked if anyone had ever refused to carry out their first mission and Brian had smiled at him in an enigmatic way. He had explained that sometimes new initiates had doubts but they soon overcame them when given time to reflect on the situation. It was this confidence in the actions of the brethren that meant the brotherhood never imposed a time limit on the completion of the first contract. "Time grants Wisdom" was a motto of the Kommandos. Of all the first timers seventy five percent returned to the clan after their first assassination, one in four either died in the attempt, joined up with criminal elements or simply disappeared into society. On the receipt of his first mission Roz had no intention in joining that minority and hoped to make a favourable impression on those who would review his achievements. He decided that the best course of action was to prepare by committing himself to learning as much about Krell as possible so that he could blend in upon his arrival there.

For the remainder of the day he studied the notes and timetables that had been given to him in the pack until numbers, addresses and times floated before his eyes. That night he had trouble getting to sleep as he saw them running through his head. He started the next day with a long run and by practicing unarmed combat before heading to the Hall of Records to review literature regarding Krell.

There was little information for him to glean from these sources so he started to search through recent news articles for references to the planet. As evening approached he felt his head beginning to ache from the vast amount of information he was trying to saturate and returned to his room shortly after the evening meal. He popped a few pills to ease his throbbing head and got in to bed before drifting in to an uneasy sleep. His dreams that night were vivid, he revisited his encounter at the outer marker on the rock and the Quat induced bliss he had felt butchering the enemies of Xen. Each time he recounted their deaths his mind felt a little more at ease.

He found to his dismay that his head felt no better the following day, or the one after that. Medication seemed to have no effect and the only thing that seemed to ease the pain was physical activity so he pushed his body harder and harder until, exhausted, he would collapse in to bed. Each night his dreams became more disturbed and violent, he dreamed of carrying out his mission successfully and returning to Talon II with the blood of Xen's enemies dripping from his hands. On the third day, he felt he was in a waking dream and during combat practice, found his mind drifting and his body seemingly working autonomously from his brain. When he became aware of his surroundings again he was straddling a screaming Sister whose arm was contorted horribly. It appeared that he had broken it in several places and bone was jutting through the skin. Horrified he apologised and tried to comfort her as a medic was sent for but something inside him wanted to see what would happen if he pressed at the exposed bone. He knew something was terribly wrong and that he was a danger to his fellow Kommandos and he was frightened what would happen to him if the Brotherhood discovered that he was losing his grip on reality. He realised that the only option available to him was to leave the school before his erratic behaviour was noticed.

Roz packed light, emptying the contents of the mission box into a small rucksack along with some casual clothing, a knife, a small medical kit and some food. He ran through the paths in the forest heading towards a small paved road that led towards the nearest town twelve kilometres away. The afternoon sun was hot on his skin and soon a sheen of sweat stood upon his forehead as he briskly jogged down the rubble strewn road. He stopped once when he noticed a piece of carrion which could have been a kill from the Night Caller. It was a Brask rabbit that had probably strayed a little too far from the meadows and fields that flanked the left hand side of the road. The rabbit had been laid bare as if field stripped by a Kommando.

"Poor bastard." he whispered. But he couldn't help but salute the tree line hoping the Night Caller witnessed his hail. He looked at his time piece and increased his pace to make up the time lost he had spent peering at the dead rabbit.

He had never been to the town before and it seemed to be busy with merchants and farmers all trying to shove and push their wares to the waiting cylinder trains. The ambience was filled with the stench of animal shit and the banter of local voices. After the peace and solitude of the Kommando School the town seemed overbearing and full of unfriendly eyes. The overbearing heat and sensory overload of the town confused him making his head pound and spin. He felt the urge to run from the station and seek solitude where he could compose himself but something compelled him to head onwards.

He noticed an official in uniform winding his way through the bustling platform and Roz surmised that it was the train guard. He began shadowing him and watched as he jumped on to the section of the train that held parcels and letters. Roz popped his head through the open door and watched the guard enter a small cabin. He looked back down the platform to see if anyone was watching and jumped aboard silently sliding the door shut behind him and locking it. He walked down to the end of the carriage and checked that door was also unlocked then moved down toward the cabin.

The guard was pouring hot water in to a cup and looked up as Roz appeared at the entrance.

"Oh, I'm sorry sir this area is for staff only." the uniformed man explained. Roz feigned confusion.

"That's OK," said Roz, "I was just wondering if you could tell me where this seat is?" He pulled out a slip of paper which he obscured with his hand.

As the man leant forward to look at what he assumed was a ticket, Roz quickly wrapped his arm around the guards neck and with a thrust from his other hand, the guards neck snapped. He quickly placed the body upright in the seat it had happily been resting in moments before and then ran to the other end of the carriage to check that door was locked too. When he got back to the corpse the familiar smell of brewing tea was rising from the cup. Roz tasted it and smiled before sitting in the spare chair that faced the dead man. He felt the train starting to move and relaxed a little, he spent the next nine hours staring at the corpse occasionally wondering how the glazed eyed corpse talked to him now and then.

"It's all over for you my friend. You have been caught in a trap. It won't be long until the militia comes down on you. You MONSTER! People like you get it bad, you will be lucky if they don't just put your head under the wheels of the train and not bother with the red tape of a judge and jury!"

Roz ignored the words of the corpse to the best of his ability but he couldn't ignore the accent which sounded like Brother Brian.

"Shut up, you are dead!" Roz finally murmured and looked through the external window. Outside was the speeding darkness of the tunnel that led to the other side of the planet. For the first time in hours, the roar of the engine changed pitch and he felt the train beginning to slow down. Roz got to his feet and pulled open the manual override latch and tripped the security systems that overrode the safety functions on the external door. He pulled on the emergency door and it hissed open, the roar of the train became deafening. He waited a short while for the train to decrease speed further before he leapt out into the dark tunnel.

Roz ricocheted off the tunnel wall which bounced him back into the path of the rotating wheels of the train. He dug his fingers in to the ground to prevent himself getting sucked under the wheels of the train. He scrambled away on all fours, as he pushed with his legs, but something on the side of the train glanced against his shoulder and pain shot through his arm. He balled up into a foetal position in a subterranean pool of god only knew what as the train thundered past him. The scent of rat piss and mould surrounded him as a familiar voice shook his system and brought him to his feet.

"Darkness covers sight, patch the wound, gain new

clothing and relocate" Brother Brian's voice?

"Brian?" Roz whispered into the darkness, he readied his knife and searched the darkness cautiously. The only light source was retreating quickly down the tunnel from the rear lights of the slowing cylinder train. He felt sweat dribbling down his forehead as the whining of the lines faded.

"You arsehole, what would Brother Brian be doing down here!" he chastised himself as he put his knife away and set off down the tunnel feeling his way along using the slimy walls as a guide.

The station was quiet apart from two off-duty police officers dressed in casual clothing that had rented a pair of hookers and were getting their dues from them. Roz remained just out of sight in the doorway of the stations restroom watching. He could smell the cheap cologne in the air drifting from the two prostitutes and the heavy scent of alcohol on the officer's breaths. One of the girls was busy giving a blowjob while the other couple were pressed up against the wall fucking. Roz waited a while until the moans and groans were over and the girls had left the station platform.

"See I told you they would do it. They always do. Flash them the badge and give them the option of a night in the cells or a freebie and they always come to the same decision." The officer with the brightly patterned shirt laughed as he made his way to the rest room. The other officer agreed and nearly staggered off the platform on to the track below.

"Shit! Wooo that was close. Yeah we will come back

here definitely, that one could suck a bowling ball through a hose pipe!"

"And more besides too I bet. Right, I'm going for a piss." The officer shouted and laughed as he pushed open the door to the rest room.

"Well get a move on." His companion called back. "We've got to be back at the station in a few hours for the morning shift." Roz waited silently in a vacant stall and watched the officer relieving his bladder into a urinal.

"I never want to go back to work!" the officer said to himself in between a tuneful whistle. Obviously, shit faced from the night's debauchery.

"Your wish is granted." Roz whispered before grabbing the officer and thrusting his knife under the victim's rib cage. His brightly patterned shirt changed colour instantly as the officer slumped to the ceramic floor tiles with his legs kicking out. Roz held him as he bled out before he field stripped the man's belongings and found an ample amount of cash, a pistol and a much needed cylinder train ticket. He dragged the corpse into a nearby stall, bolted the door and climbed over into the next toilet cubical. Roz examined the pistol in the dim light and curled his lips with disgust. It was a low calibre weapon favoured for its compact size rather than its firepower and didn't incorporate any kind of silencing mechanism. He looked to the trash canister near the wash basins and began to rummage through its soiled contents. He soon found what he was looking for as he pulled out an empty mineral water bottle. He spent a few seconds forcing the nozzle of the pistol into the plastic bottle mouth, before leaving the restroom.

"I left my girly in Nasra, and sheeeee, sent me a spool! She left me no money, but I got her message! I would be damned if I'm being played for a fool!" The officer sang staggering around at the edge of the platform.

Roz approached him holding the empty mineral water bottle tight against the working end of his pistol.

"Falling for?" he paused mid-song with his face betraying his confusion, "Damn I've forgotten the lyrics already!" The drunken officer said before he stumbled and collapsed onto his arse.

"Son-of-a-bitch!" He muttered as he leant over to one side to rub his behind. Roz pushed the mineral water bottle against the base of the man's skull and pulled the trigger. A popping sound echoed around the station as the drunken man's head ruptured. The momentum of the impact forced the corpse forwards, tumbling onto the cylinder train track below. Roz collected the spent casing and discarded the smoke filled mineral water bottle before leaping on to the track and dragging the corpse into the darkness of the tunnel, where he stripped the man's clothes off. He then returned to the rest room to patch up his shoulder wound and change into his newly acquired clothing.

Roz used the stolen ticket and boarded the next express cylinder train to the starport. He found a seat, stashed his bag in the overhead compartment. It wasn't long before a waiter pushed a service trolley down the aisle. The waiter was dressed in a ridiculous pink all-in-one. The waiter smiled and showed a data pad of available services. Roz peered at the display of refreshments and quickly chose.

"I will have a tall, ground bean coffee and I think I will have the dressed foul salad." He said trying to avert his eyes from the gaudy outfit the waiter wore.

"Of course, would the handsome man want the optional red berry sorbet with that?" The waiter said with a sly wink.

Roz ignored the man and began to read the headlines on a nearby console. The waiter stood for a few seconds then wandered off down the aisle muttering under his breath "How rude!"

At the sound of the section train door sliding open, Roz looked up and saw a striking woman walk in. She was tall, slender and had long dark blue hair, her hips swayed like a hunting cat stalking pray. Roz couldn't see her eyes due to them being obscured by expensive looking sunglasses, but he got the impression that she was looking at him. She found a seat near to his seat and sat down crossing her tanned legs. She wore a black figure hugging blouse and a very short black skirt. He glanced once to her oval face with full red lips and noticed a slight nod before she booted up a small portable console. Roz returned to reading the headlines. He noted that the Seinal Corporation was presently in negotiations with the Xen Corporation trying to organise a peace treaty on several mining worlds. The console showed pictures of the two directors shaking hands making Roz laugh out loud. He knew damned well that the director of the Xen Corporation was nothing but a brain floating around in some kind of humongous machine which sustained her mind. The meal he ordered arrived or more accurately was dropped on to his table nearly spilling the coffee.

"I hope you choke on it!" The waiter squealed before parading away down the aisle. Roz couldn't help grinning as he tucked into the meal. The food was hot in places and lukewarm in others but he was hardly expecting the gorgeous food cooked at the Kommando School. After he had finished his meal and stacked the empty vessels in a neat pile, Roz looked up and noticed the stunning woman was staring at him. She uncrossed her legs and opened them slightly so that he could see a slither of her white knickers in the shadows of her dark skirt. She had finished working on the portable console which sat neatly shut on the seat table in front of her. Roz nodded to the rest room sign hanging next to the exit. The woman looked over her shoulder and he could see her beautiful profile beam with a smile. She picked up the handbag which lay at her feet before heading off to the rest room. She didn't bother to rearrange the short skirt she wore purposely so she could show just short of a centimetre of white laced knickers as she trotted seductively towards the exit. When she exited the train section he looked at his time piece, his hands were sweating and he felt trapped.

Maybe she is a high rolling executive and just wants

some fun? He thought but his instincts told him otherwise. He patted his pockets and performed a quick inventory check. The knife and pistol were well hidden on his person and he had kept his money and starline ticket in his boots.

He walked towards the exit she had taken and noted that the sign for the toilet had not changed to occupied. As he approached the toilet door the overhead light buzzed and flickered interfering with his eye's ability to adjust to the dimness. The door to the toilet was slightly open and inside it appeared dark and foreboding. As he passed he looked around into the shadows but couldn't see her and he wondered where she was. He knew something was wrong about the woman, his senses screamed out a warning to him. She was probably waiting in the shadows near the toilet with a fucking big knife to stick into his heart or worse. He decided to return to his seat and moved away from the rest room. He made his way back through the carriage and down the train to his seat. He sat staring at his time piece nervously.

"Not long to wait, just sixteen more heart pounding minutes until the next station!" he told himself. The passenger carriage had filled up with more businessmen since his meal in the café.

You can't wait can you Roz? Your already thinking about jumping out of the train back into the darkness aren't you boy! The voice sounded like Drill Master Gidd when he called him "boy" during the private training sessions back in the academy.

"Shut up!" Roz cried, ignoring the edgy looks he got from the other passengers. He was about to stand up and retrieve his bag from the overhead compartment when the train alarms suddenly wailed. He was up on his feet racing down the carriage fighting against the deceleration while the train wheels shrieked. Screams and angry shouts washed up around him like a high tide. He shouldered his way down the aisle through the throng of panic-stricken passengers knocking a few to the floor. The emergency doors cranked open and he leapt out once again into the darkness, this time he landed unscathed as the train had ground to a halt and he began running.

CHAPTER 11

The Solis Maria

The darkness welcomed Roz; its embrace was terrible and loving at the same time. He clambered around in its protective arms for hours using maintenance cul-de-sacs to evade passing high-speed cylinder trains and all the while his inner-voice guided him ever forward. Eventually, he found himself in a derelict station where, although the lights weren't working, the water lines were still connected in the restroom. He washed by torchlight and tended to his wounded shoulder trying to keep it as clean as possible.

Large rodents had made the abandoned station their home and Roz set about catching and killing a few. Eating their raw flesh was not pleasant but it placated his hunger. It was a strangely timeless place in the constant midnight of the tunnels. He took the time to gather his thoughts and gain some much needed rest.

"What am I doing in this festering place?" His voice echoed against the broken tiles. He felt cold and he could hear rodents pattering around outside the door on the station platform. They were probably wondering who he was and why he had chosen this place to co-inhabit.

"Nine more hours Roz, what are you doing wasting time eating rats and sleeping in this filthy place?" It was Brian's voice but it seemed distant as though he was standing at the other side of a plaster wall.

"My cover was blown! That bitch was going to kill me or report me to the authorities!" He answered unaware that he begun talking to himself. "I don't like this anymore! I don't want to be a Kommando. I want to go back home and be a farm boy again." Roz cried into the darkness with tears streaming down his face.

"You fucking pussy! I wasted my time on you boy! Your friend Daemon would be laughing at you right now. Now get on your feet wet nose!" The voice in his head was definitely that of Gidd, he had used the latter phrase a number of times before in the academy to get Roz moving when he felt that he was too exhausted to move. Roz felt angry and upset, his fist struck the floor tiles shattering pieces of ceramic across the washroom floor.

"Wait!" The voice hissed. Roz concentrated, his ears straining in the darkness; was that the whine of night-vision goggles warming up? He scampered silently to the platform door on all fours and pressed his ear to it. He thought he detected the soft stealthy footfalls of four or five people trying to move in silence. The muffled clinking of firearms being primed confirmed his fears. He span away and pressed up against the tiled wall just before the door was kicked open and something small rattled across the ceramic floor.

Roz covered his eyes with his arm but could still see a bright flash followed by a deafening sound like thunder making his ears ring. His actions had prevented him being blinded by the flash grenade and through the frame of the smashed door, he saw a glint of light shining off the muzzle of an assault rifle. Roz instantly snatched the weapon, pulling its bearer towards him, spinning him round as he grappled his assailant. He pulled the man tightly against him and moved his hand over that of his opponent. He squeezed the fingers of the man and four flashes from the gun illuminated his foes who were swinging their weapons towards the struggling pair. Roz instantly hooked his foot around the man's ankle and used his body weight to pull him to the floor using him as a human shield. He could feel the shudder of bullets impacting into the man's body armour but in such an intense volley of fire, it was unable to save the man's life.

Roz ripped the gun from the corpse's grip and fired

another quick burst into the darkness aimed just below the flashing muzzles of the automatic weapons. The recoil of the assault rifle fought against his single-handed grip with each squeeze of the trigger. Each time he saw a flash of gunfire Roz fired in that direction not knowing if his aim was true. The staccato bursts became more sporadic until it seemed only one gunman was still alive. A single flash from nearby caught Roz unawares and he felt the splatter of blood from the head of his human shield fly across his face. One more to kill, he thought, as he tumbled forward leaving the meagre protection behind and firing again in a scatter pattern. He lay on the cold floor wondering where to fire next. His ears were still ringing from the explosion and gunfire.

Silence descended and as the tinnitus in his ears subsided he thought he could hear a gurgling sound. He slid his hand to the still hot muzzle of the gun and found that the weapon had a small flashlight attached to it. Turning it on he stood up and followed the sound to a woman dressed in a local law enforcement uniform. She wasn't much older than Roz and she had three bullet wounds in her chest, the armoured vest she wore was obviously not made to withstand gunfire from weapons as powerful as that they used. Her hand trembled and reached out towards him. Roz shouldered the rifle and sat down next to her so he could hold her hand and cradle her head. Blood bubbled with each breath she took as she gripped tightly to his hand.

"I'm sorry." He mumbled.

"Don't be." Her words had to fight through the blood gathering in her throat. He understood what she meant; it could have easily been the reverse scenario. It seemed they were both out to kill each other and only one of them could be the victor.

"Am I hearing correctly? Is this guilt soldier? Have I taught you nothing?" The voice said angrily. Roz ignored Brother Brian's words as he felt the weight of her head increasing. She exhaled and her hand fell from his.

The tunnel was waterlogged in the final approach to the starport. The water pumps were old in this section and struggled to shift the sump water from the underground. In places it was stagnant and the disgusting water made progress increasingly hard as Roz made haste following the flash light on his rifle.

"Less than nine hours to catch the ship to Krell." he panted. The wound on his shoulder felt like fiery coals and it needed redressing yet again. He had changed into one of the law enforcement uniforms to save soiling the only civilian outfit he had left.

"This is so fucked up. The police must have been alerted when I jumped off the second train. And what the hell did that woman want with me? I bet it was her who set the alarms off on the train so she could kill me during the panic. I should have killed her while I had the chance." He went over and over with the same questions and assumptions but couldn't make any light of what was truly happening.

The starport train station was busy with people checking their baggage, relieving their bladders in the restrooms and staring numbly like zombies at the huge screens displaying the next arrivals for trains and starships. Roz had just enough time to change back into his civilian clothing and disassemble his Kommando blade. The blade could easily pass through security detectors because it was made of ceramic and not metal. The pistol he disposed of in a waste paper basket as there was no way he could possibly sneak it through. He made his way to the security check area and hoped he would get through without incident even though he was worried about the ill-fitting clothes he wore. His muscles bulged tightly under the fabric unlike the flabby flesh most of the other commuters had. The security arch way buzzed as he walked through but the bored security guard just pointed to his wrist watch. Roz had forgotten to take it off and he laughed with relief.

"Sorry." Roz shrugged and took off the timepiece and passed through the arch way again.

"Don't worry sir, it happens all the time." The guard said monotonously.

Inside of the starport was huge and filled with a throbbing crowd of people which made the town festival on his home world look like a small gathering. Whores of every description begged him for a service or spare money and claimed they needed to feed their children. Roz didn't see any children present but he did notice the signs of serious drug addiction the male and female prostitutes had on their withered arms. He finally arrived at the docking gate and took a seat amongst the hubbub of impatient travellers. A queue was starting to form at the boarding desk and Roz heard an educated female accent coming from the front of it. Amongst the rabble he had so far encountered this was unusual enough to pique his curiosity so he tried to isolate where the voice came from.

He felt a rising sense of dread, as he somehow expected to, he spotted the femme fatale from the train. She was wearing a brazen red dress and black leg tights which stopped inches from the fabric skirt line. There was no mistaking her beautiful profile and her long dark blue hair.

"What the fuck is she doing here?" he cursed silently as he joined the back of the queue. Although the docking gate had three ships and the gantries he knew that she would be on the same starliner he was getting. He kept his eyes on her as the queue started moving and watched which one of the three passageways she took once she had shown her ticket. As predicted she seemed to be heading to his ship, the Solis Maria, he fought back the urge to leave the starport and return to the Kommando School and gritted his teeth. It was better to tackle the problem head on he decided and started to mentally prepare himself for the troubles ahead.

Once Roz had passed through the boarding gate he headed up to the observation deck that stood above the great docking ring on which the three huge starliners were stationed. The ships drifted slightly on the electro-magnetic fields and were tethered to the port by massive metallic docking claws. He spotted the

Solis Maria, a luxury starliner for tourists for which he had a first class cabin. He looked down through the great plaz windows of the holding area in which people ate, shopped and drank before boarding the craft. He had hoped that he might be able to see the woman but realised it was a futile exercise when he saw the scale of the ship. Even by military standards it was huge, he guessed that it must be a kilometre long and at least a hundred metres high. On a ship that size he might stand a good chance of keeping out of her way but he doubted it somehow.

"Travelling first class are you? I suppose it's better than being a stowaway." The voice had a tone of jealousy and sounded like his father. He looked to the ticket again feeling a strange pang of guilt and then double checked the beautiful craft, silvery with its name printed in gold writing. His eyes were drawn inextricably to a flash of red at the entrance to the ship and he already knew what he was going to see. Among the throng of passengers boarding the vessel was the beautiful blue haired woman. She stopped at the head of the gang plate and unerringly peered over her shoulder directly up at him. There was a sense of inevitability about the course of events, he was certain that there could be no tracking device on him as he had changed clothes so often. What she was doing was physically impossible; it was as if she psychically knew where he was. He resigned himself to whatever fate awaited him and waved at her cursing under his breath. She smiled and blew him a kiss before disappearing inside the great hull of the Solis Maria. A host of laughter erupted in his mind; it was like a chorus of a thousand voices from his past all taking delight in his predicament.

"Fuck it." He sighed and shouldered his bag. With slumped shoulders, he made his way to the ship as his mind played over fanciful scenarios involving him becoming a stowaway on another ship. His curiosity was now too great and he wanted to know who this woman was and how she was able to find him so easily. Even more so he was intrigued to know why she was following him and what she wanted.

The luxury cabin was an insult to good taste. The room was flamingo pink with a red heart-shaped bed, laden with fluffy animal print cushions. It was garish and vulgar and the porter who had shown him the room couldn't keep the amusement from his face at Roz's discomfort. Roz had felt obliged to tip the orderly when in fact Brother Brian's voice was telling him that he should kill him and stuff his body in the overhead ventilation shaft. Once the man had left Roz quickly surveyed the room. The door was made from thick poly-alloy and was sound proofed, a small display screen booted up when the door was closed and displayed the outside corridor in full.

He was pleased that it had such a good security device and tapped the console to activate an alarm if the door was forced suddenly. The ambience of the room had been kept at a constant temperature chosen by the previous guest. He sniffed the air and then shut down the scent harmonics so the room wouldn't smell as flowery and lowered the temperature a few degrees. There was a walk in wardrobe with more than ample space for his few meagre belongings, he tapped the walls to check that they were solid then walked back in to the bedroom to get a chair. He returned to the wardrobe and stood on the chair looking at the highest shelves which were covered in spare blankets and sheets. Moving them to the side he worked loose a panel exposing the inner structure of the ship, he stored his knife in it and replaced the panel.

His exertions had made the pain in his shoulder flare up again so he went to the bathroom and took off his ill-fitting shirt to check the damage. The wound was showing signs of infection, no doubt caused by the filthy water he had waded through. The skin was an angry red colour and his shoulder was swollen.

"What a mess." He said as he patted down his trouser pockets as though they would somehow produce a treatment for his wound. He stripped naked and began to filter through the cabinets that contained various skin creams, hair products, complementary bottled scents and a basic first aid kit. The bathroom was furnished with wall to wall mirrors and a soundless reel-player depicting four humans copulating surrounded by computer generated fires. He grimaced at the reflection of his muscular body and searched through the kit and tapped out a few complementary pain killing tablets before running a tumbler of water to wash the pills into his system.

"You aren't giving up on me solider! Are you?" Gidd's reflection stood behind him, Gidd looked very angry.

"No sir! It's just a little infection. I will get it sorted!" Roz responded automatically saluting the fading image of Drill Master Gidd. It had been a long time since he had stared at his own reflection. He somehow looked different from the last time he had seen himself which was back in the training academy on the Rock. The Kommando School hadn't furnished any of its rooms with mirrors because it was said to be bad karma. He shuddered as he looked in to his own eyes because they looked unfamiliar, as if they were belonged to somebody else. They were a lighter shade of blue than he recalled and seemed to have a murderous intent like a feral wolf. As there was no electrolysis equipment like at the school he had to use one of the razors provided and began to shave off the stubble that had grown on his chin. Every so often he caught a glimpse of those terrible eyes.

"Who are you?" He asked the reflection remembering when Daemon had caught a hedge badger and thought it would be funny to put a mirror in the pen with it. The angry creature did not recognise itself in the reflection and attacked the mirror until it shattered while he and Daemon laughed at its stupidity.

"What kind of animal couldn't recognise itself?" he wondered as he looked at the stranger before him. The reflection shattered and pain shot though his fist. He stared at his trembling bloodied hand glistening with tiny silver fragments of glass embedded between his knuckles. Shards of the mirror had collected in the wash basin and drops of blood fell on them. He wrapped his hand in a clean towel and wandered into the bedroom to call for room service.

"Room service, how can we help?" A cheery voice stated on the other end of the internal network.

"I will have a bottle of Zhix!" Roz said knowing Zhix was a clear alcohol and high in proof.

"I will add it on to the rooms account. I'm sending it up now. Would sir like some company with the order?"

"No!" Roz said as he looked at the trail of blood dotted on the carpet from the bathroom. "But I could do with a cleaner. There's been a slight accident."

"Of course sir, glad to be of service." The voice answered. Roz sat on the edge of the bed and felt that the mattress gave too much under his weight for his liking. As much as he tried to relax on it, he could not get comfortable and thought that he may have to bunk down on the plush pink carpet tonight. It appeared that he wasn't used to the comforts of first class travelling

The door chimed tunefully as Roz quickly pulled on some trousers. "Come in." he said as the doors circuits opened revealing a petite dark haired maid holding a tray with a fluted glass and a bottle of Zhix. Her eyes widened as she looked at the half dressed wounded man. She was about to say something but Roz fanned his hand.

"Don't worry. I've had a bit of an accident. Nothing serious, it looks worse than it is." He said nervously due to the close proximity of the pretty maid. She paled as she looked from his infected shoulder along his muscular chest and down to the now bloodied towel wrapped around his hand. She also noticed the ceremonial tattoo on his chest and assumed he was military of some sorts.

"Are you ex-military?" She asked quietly as she placed the tray on the dressing table. He peered down to the Kommando tattoo on his chest, a lightning bolt set within a triangle.

"Err, yes," he lied, and then added, "I was a sergeant in the core but I was demobbed last year." He blushed because he was never any good at lies.
She nodded and peered at the small specks of blood trailing from the bathroom.

"Let me clean up those wounds of yours first then I'll clean up the room." She said pulling out some tissues from her pockets and grabbing the bottle of Zhix.

"No really I will be alright. I will nip down to the medical wing soon." He mumbled but he didn't stop her as she cautiously un-wrapped the towel from his hand. She smelt a little stale, masked only by a splash of cheap perfume, but her touch was delicate as though she had cleaned many wounds before. Her tiny digits plucked out slithers of glass from his hand while she wiped away the surface blood.

"You have such soft hands!" she exclaimed then blushed with embarrassment as she realised that it could be construed as an insult to someone from the military.

"They're new." He replied flustered.

"What?" she asked, her pretty eyes rising up in an arch.

"Nothing. Look, you don't have to do this." He whispered as he tried to remove his hand from hers.

"But I will. I've finished my shift and have nothing better to do." She shrugged and her cheeks flared again with red upon her olive tone.

Roz wasn't used to any female being in his personal space and felt torn between his attraction to her and his pathetic shyness.

"I served as a civilian auxiliary in the field hospital on Talon II during the brief Plutonium crisis, six years before Talon II became a free world." She said as she bathed the cuts with Zhix.

Roz shook his head as he hadn't been tutored on the past history of Talon II.

"My name is Karli by the way." she said as she looked into his eyes. Karli had light brown eyes flecked with tiny strips of crimson. He smiled dumbly for a second and was surprised she wasn't fearful of his ice blue murderer's eyes.

"I will return tomorrow with a medical kit and some anti-infection pads for that wound on your shoulder." She said.

He looked at his cleaned up hand and winced when he flexed it.

"Thank you Karli. Erm…" He was about to ask her if she would come to dinner with him but she somehow read his thoughts.

"I'm sorry but the lower staff cannot mingle with the

guests." She looked almost angry and then smiled before leaving the room. Roz stood staring at the closed door for a while before gulping down a few hits from the Zhix bottle.

Roz skipped breakfast the next morning and decided to finish off the bottle of Zhix instead. The lack of food and strong alcohol went straight to his head and he sat on the bottom of the heart-shaped bed giggling to himself at the ridiculousness of his surroundings. Here he was, a trained killer in a room made for newlyweds. The pain in his hand and shoulder were numbed from the influx of alcohol he had consumed and he ignored the stench of infected flesh emanating from his shoulder.

"What's troubling you soldier?" Drill Master Gidd sat in the corner next to the dresser holding a tumbler full of Zhix.

"Morning Drill Master." Roz said grinning in a stupor. Gidd saluted with his glass and smiled.

"It's these fucking voices in my head. At first I thought they were there to help me but now they are a bothersome background noise. They chatter all the time and I don't think they are helping me anymore." Roz said swaying back and forth on the edge of the heart shaped bed.

"They are nothing more than guides, they are there to keep you focused and to council you when you feel down or they can be just trying to warn you of present dangers." Gidd said before he finished his glass of spirit.

Roz hurled the empty bottle of Zhix at the wall, the bottle shattered into tiny pieces with a crash that echoed around the room.

"But it's all the fucking time! Why won't they shut up?" He stood shaking looking at the dent in the wall and the hundred pieces of glass scattered in a crescent on the carpet.

"Calm yourself soldier! If you wish for solace then cease invoking us to answer your questions." Gidd was stood in the doorway of the bathroom shaving with an evil looking combat knife.

Roz thought for a while, maybe he had been asking himself too many questions rather than putting trust in his training, he had never been one for self-confidence and belief. The room was silent now, Gidd had disappeared and all that was left was an empty tumbler on the floor near the dresser. He realised that he needed to pull himself together and place some trust in himself. He moved to the bathroom, forced himself to vomit up the contents of his stomach then took a long cold shower to try and sober up. What he needed, he decided, was to have a large meal and start acting like a Kommando not like a raw cadet.

The restaurant for first class passengers was found on one of the upper decks in a spacious ballroom on which professional dancers provided entertainment accompanied by a string quartet. Roz had found a table that was away from the ridiculously dressed travelling dignitaries and rich business types. The air had been saturated with expensive, overpowering perfumes and the acrid smell of bubbly grape wine. Waiters in white suits circulated among the tables all wearing the same false smiles and displaying a fatigued gait which suggested they had already pulled a shift in the kitchens.

Roz had already ordered a strong coffee and a starter of land crab salad. The news reels had a bold headline depicting a merger between the Xen and the Seinal corporations displayed on a large screen. The corporate wars on numerous neutral planets had finely come to an end and the side screens showed troops celebrating in various ruined townships and cities. One of the screens blinked on and showed a massive column of Seinal troops and armoured vehicles pulling out of a sprawling ruin which looked to have once been a mighty metropolis. He sneered at the green armoured troops and tried to suppress his anger at the mere idea of Xen joining up with the enemy.

The waiter wheeled a trolley to the side of his table and placed down his land crab starter, a large cafétiere of coffee and a bottle of chilled bubbling wine which had a blue triangle label with two golden cats leaping at one another. He frowned at the wine and was just about to ask why it had been brought over when the beautiful femme fatale sat down at his table. She smiled seductively at him before she ordered a starter of som-fruit. Roz immediately located the exits out of the restaurant should the need for a quick departure be required then took a long look at the woman. She wore a luscious figure hugging black dress with a deep neckline that met just above her stomach revealing the swell of her breasts with the material only just covered her nipples. She had also had her hair cut into a bob with a straight fringe but it was the same dark vibrant blue.

"Good afternoon Roz." She said in her educated accent.

He attempted to hide his anguish at her knowing his name by picking up his fork but his adrenalin was pumping so hard that his hand trembled as though two hundred volts had been channelled through it.

"It seems you have me at a disadvantage, you know my name but I do not know yours?" He said as he felt countless voices poised to speak inside his mind but he refused to let them comment on such a clichéd line.

She pouted a kiss with her rich red lips and winked. She was beautiful but this close he could see that she was a lot older than him. She smelled wonderful even though it was masked slightly with a delicate perfume, he suspected that she was wearing pheromones designed to entrap any red-blooded male. Roz was no exception, his body seemed to react in a primal manner and already he could feel his cock swelling. She lit up a Koll-weed cigarette, inhaled and blew the sweet scented blue smoke towards him. He coughed and wafted the smoke away like his mother used to do when his father smoked his pipe in the evening.

"My name isn't important." She said as she poured the strange nameless wine into two large crystal goblets.

"Poison?" A voice ventured in his mind but he relaxed when she sipped a little from her glass.

"Is this wine expensive?" He said sniffing the aroma above the glass as his nostrils filled with a wonderful scent of fruit and spices.

"It's not the best vintage; this is from a turbulent year to say the least. My family ceased production of this nameless wine a long time ago. Taste it. You are drinking history. Don't worry," she smiled, "I'm not in the habit of utilising poisons."

He was about to ask her a question when the som-fruit starter arrived. He watched her slice open the green pith to reveal the soft yellow flesh beneath as though it was his throat. He sipped the wine. It was like an explosion of berries against his pallet with the undertones of cinnamon which sweetened its progress over his taste buds.

"My goodness!" he exclaimed, it was all the words he could muster after taking a good deep breath as the wine massaged his tongue. He had almost forgotten where he was and whom he sat with for a few moments but reality soon crawled back.

"You left quite a trail for me Roz and made my job easy. I was hoping you would be a better adversary but I suppose you haven't been captured by the local authorities so there is hope for you yet." Her pupils dilated slightly as she leaned back appraising him. He felt her foot move up his leg then nestle against his balls as she took another long drag on her cigarette.

What's with this woman? Does she want to kill me or fuck me?

"Who do you work for? The Seinal Corporation?" He said aloud trying to take his mind off her foot rubbing against his groin.

She laughed out loud and waved her hair from side to side.

"No Roz, I'm just a contract killer like you but in my case I am better paid." she said between giggles watching his obvious discomfort. "I work for myself and my benefactor will remain secret until you are gasping for your last breath and then maybe I will tell you."

He nodded and felt a little ashamed that she had complete mastery of the situation. He decided that he needed to wrest her out of her comfort zone.

"Well I'm up for it right now, let's get this fucking thing over and done with!" He said leaning forwards and grinning.

"What and cause a scene? Have you not seen the six Sec-eyes in here? Let alone the abundance of trustworthy eyewitnesses." She hissed.

He noticed that an edge of fear had appeared in her voice and he took pleasure that she had been so easily rattled.

"I counted nine Sec-eyes. Seven in here and two in the corridor outside the main exit, the one you missed is behind that mirror over there." He said pointing to a glossy wall mirror near the drinks bar. She curled her lip but didn't bother to look at the mirror.

"It doesn't matter how many there are, they are still

there watching us!" She countered as a waiter placed down a salad and two small sugar brandies.

"Compliments of the house," The waiter said before wheeling away a trolley to the next table. She picked up one of the brandy glasses and raised it.

"Well we both know what is coming, shall we toast to mutual terms of engagement?" She said pondering over what terms Roz would decide upon for their combat. Roz picked up his glass and shook his head.

"No, let us toast to the uncertainty of life!"

"So be it." She smiled with a single nod of approval; she preferred it when her prey didn't meekly surrender to her.

"To the uncertainty of life," they said in unison as they clinked their glasses together. The two killers ate silently for the rest of their meal.

CHAPTER 12

Madeline

That night Karli called on to Roz's cabin and brought a medical kit and the anti-infection patches as promised. She was dressed in a grey woollen jumper and a floor length black velvet skirt. She wore her hair down around her shoulders as it was still damp from a recent shower. Roz could smell a rich perfume on her which he later found out she had borrowed from her roommate without her knowledge.

"You look troubled Roz?" She said as she patched up his wounds with her delicate hands. He had told her his name when she arrived but only after she had prompted for his name. The voices in his head were disturbed that he had given his real name but the alcohol that he had drank with Madeleine had subdued his instincts.

"I'm not troubled. I'm just not used to having such pretty company around me." He admitted.
She laughed and thumped him softly in his gut and then covered her blushing cheeks.

"You lie, I saw you having dinner with that beautiful blue haired woman. Who is she?" She said suddenly becoming serious. Roz closed his eyes and sighed.

"She, she is somebody from my past that I wish to remain in my past. To be honest with you I didn't even know she was on this ship until she came to my table." He lied and felt relief when Karli beamed with a smile.

"I brought some wine." She said rummaging through a cloth bag. "But it's not an expensive bottle like you are probably used to." She pulled out a cheap bottle of black grape wine called Khailoz. Roz recognised the label as it was his mother's favourite wine.

"It was all I could afford at such a short notice." She said with her hair covering her face.

"I can't honestly say that I know what expensive wines are like but you have just made me very happy. My mother loved Khailoz at festival time." He said nodding in approval.
Karli hugged him and kissed his cheek. He felt her

breath against his neck and was unsure what to do next. Luckily he didn't need to dwell on the matter as Karli started to open the wine. He felt uncomfortable that she mistakenly believed he was wealthy but with him staying in such opulent surroundings he was not surprised that she thought so.

"I have something to confess." He said to her taking her hand in his. She did not reply but stared unwaveringly into his killer's eyes. "I'm not a rich man. I won this ticket in a competition. I'm nothing more than a former farmhand and soldier. I don't want you to think that I'm something I'm not."

Karli smiled at him and returned to open the wine. "I knew you were an honest man when I first saw your eyes," she said. Roz did not reply.

Roz held Karli close to him as they chatted about their past quietly for what seemed like hours. Karli had admitted that her career tending to the wounded during the Plutonium crisis on Talon II was short-lived and jobs were hard to find after that due to the civil unrest. She had been forced to flee her hometown when rebels had stormed it. During the violence, she had found herself in the city along with many other refugees. After a few poorly paid jobs she applied for a post as a maid on board the Solis Maria Starliner and had been there for over seven years. The Starliner had travelled far and wide within corporate space and although the hours were long and hard she had been given the opportunity to see worlds she could only have dreamed about. Many of the planets she described Roz hadn't even heard about in the travel guides he had read. She described orange skies, mile high cliffs, alien animals and exotic people. Roz, in return, felt that stories of his farm boy days with his family and tales of the academy training betrayed his myopic view of the galaxy. He felt compelled to embellish the rest of his story by incorporating several military reel-films he had seen and graphic magazines that he had read as a boy.

"It must have been terrible for you at the academy." She whispered into the dim room and pulled his arm around her more for comfort.

"It was hard yes, but I had many friends that looked after me." He said basking in the warmth of Karli's body.

"Who is Daemon? You have mentioned him quite a lot. Did you grow up with him?"

"I went to the same village school with him and then when we were older we joined up together. I've only told you a fraction of the capers we did together." Roz chuckled drifting off and remembering the good times they had before they decided to join up with the Xen Corporation. He could feel the medications and the wine working in his blood stream. His wounds were a mere background irritation rather than a painful torment upon his flesh.

"He sounds like a good friend. Do you keep in touch?" She asked as a dull pain throbbed at the back of his neck.

"Why don't you just tell her everything you fool?" Roz bolted upright on the bed and swore he witnessed a shadow moving in the darkness. He shook his head and scanned the shadows of the room again.

"What's the matter? Was it something I said?" Karli said before she tweaked the light dial on the bedside cabinet. The light blinded him for a second and he noticed her face was clouded with worry.

"No, you didn't say anything wrong. " He stroked her cheek with his hand. "I think the meds are making me a little jumpy that's all." There was nobody else in the room apart from Karli so he tried to calm himself.

"Maybe I should go and let you sleep?" She said as she moved to the side of the bed looking for her shoes.

"Please stay!" He said quietly and touched the back of her neck with his fingers. "I don't want to be alone tonight."

She nodded without facing him and took off her jumper, tossing it to the floor. He wrapped his huge arms around her and kissed her neck. She breathed deeply, pushing her neck against his lips before she unfastened the clasp of her bra. His hands pushed under the fabric cups and gently caressed her breasts while he kissed her shoulder. The black laced bra fell away as she slid downwards off the side of the bed. Karli turned to face him, kissing his lips as she unbuckled his belt and tugged at his pants. He pivoted his body so she could pull the fabric free from him revealing what he had been hiding all of his life. Her mouth engulfed him and her tongue rolled against him. He had never witnessed such passion. She continued to work her mouth upon him, the lights of the room seemed brighter and his nerve endings played a sweet symphony to each tingle on his flesh. Her tongue picked up pace, her rhythm matched his increased pulse rate. He tried to push her away but she continued her regular motion and moved his hand from her cheek. He collapsed hard against the bed as he filled her mouth with a powerful ejaculation, the room span around him as Karli sat down on the floor. He panted for a while staring at the pink ceiling as his body relaxed into a calm that he had never felt before. Karli had settled onto the plush plink carpet she had a contented smile on her pretty face. He lifted himself from the bed and picked her up, cradling her onto the bed as she kicked off her skirt. She wore black knickers and thigh high leggings and her face was awash with anticipation as she opened her legs.

The following morning Roz was in the restaurant eating a breakfast of scrambled eggs and sipping a strong black coffee with a delicate pastry sat on a side plate. Karli had left early in the morning to prepare for her shift at work and Roz felt content but tired. A figure appeared in front of his table.

"You look like you have been up all night. Have you been worrying about how I'm going to kill you?" The blue haired woman teased.

Roz shrugged and hid a smile behind one hand. Little did she know what happened last night. He gestured to the spare chair and she sat down looking across at him. Roz ignored her and looked at the news reels that discussed the potential of a merger between the Xen and the Seinal Corporations. A number of minor corporations had consolidated to form a group called the Enclave which opposed the two major corporation's new agreement. Roz assumed the minors were fearful of losing sub-contracts from the major players.

"So are you ignoring me?" she said irritated that he seemed calm.

"Well I don't generally talk to people whose name I don't know." He replied looking at the vid-image of the Enclaves spokesman denouncing the chairmen of the two larger corporations, it was like a ridiculous faceoff between two heavy weight prize fighters.

"Very well," she answered, "You can call me Madeline."

"I can't honestly say that it's a pleasure to meet you, Madeline." Roz quipped. Madeline took a look at the article Roz was viewing and commented, "Look at how pathetic it is, Roz. You must feel like a pawn in some kind of intergalactic chess game."

"At least I know which side I'm playing for. That's more than I can say for you." He said before calling over a waiter. She glared at him for a moment.

"I told you, I don't work for anyone but myself. They can all piss in the same pot for all I care and often or not they do." A waiter drifted over to the table and waited patiently for an order.

"Could I have the smoked fish?" Roz said pointing to a menu card. The waiter bowed and glanced at the blue haired woman.

"I will have the fruit salad and some more coffee please." She smiled through clenched teeth and chimed her empty cup to emphasise her impatience. The waiter poured coffee.

"Why do you treat people so badly?" He asked as the waiter strolled away.

"Because they are scum and I'm rich. Besides he looks able bodied, he could easily get a better job than serving coffee." She said blowing on the steaming coffee.

"You have never done a days work in your life, how would you know what a shit job is like. You were born into a rich family owning vineyards and I would bet all the credits I have in my pocket that you were spoiled by your parents." He said and immediately noticed he had touched a nerve.

"I was an evil bitch when my mother spat me from her womb and very little has changed since. My family squandered their last credits trying to re-establish their precious winery while I sought my fortune. You can't even comprehend the wealth that I have earned and neither would my parents!" She was speaking passionately now with her voice raised.

Roz stifled a laugh and covered his mouth as he noticed other diners were now glaring at the blue haired woman with faces of disgust.

"Your face is flushed Madeline should I call the waiter for more water?" He said putting up a finger to call a waiter. She grabbed hold of his finger and squeezed.

"You fuck stain! I can't wait to crush your skull under my boots!" She raged and let go of his finger. He settled back into his chair grinning as she drank a glass of water dry.

"Where and when? Swords or pistols Madeline? Do we need someone there to make sure we obey the rules?" He joked.

She kicked the chair from under her and stormed off towards the exit. Roz turned and apologised to a nearby couple and waited for his fish dish. He knew she would come for him soon, probably this afternoon. He thought the sooner she did the better, if she came after him while she was angry she would be more likely to make a fatal mistake.

Roz spent the morning searching for a part of the Solis Maria where it was quiet and free from Sec-eyes. The last thing he could risk as a Kommando was being caught on surveillance equipment in a fight to the death. Most of the public areas of the ship were heavy on security, particularly those for the sole enjoyment of the 1st class guests. Outside of those, where the vast majority of passengers were present security was much lighter but it was not easy to find any place of solitude with twenty thousand people milling around. Eventually Roz tail-gated a member of staff through one of security doors which led to the otherworldly staff quarters. Although space was at a premium and the main corridors that ran the length of the ship were hectic. There were a huge number of storage bays and deserted rooms available most of which had little or no Sec-eyes watching over them. Roz found a series of rooms that suited his purpose and set about creating blind spots in them. He did not wish to risk directly interfering with the Sec-eyes and used one of the cargo loaders to rearrange packing crates and boxes to strategically block off their view. Before departing back to his cabin he stopped off in one of the communal showers and stole a pass from one of the crew members.

On route to his room Roz passed by one of the many reception desks. A sly smile came to his face and he approached the young lady stationed there. He explained that he had had a lover tiff with Madeline and wished to make amends. The receptionist who was petite like Karli but had blonde hair instead of the luscious dark cascades Karli sported, she suggested flowers and a message of forgiveness. Roz agreed and dictated the message he wished to be sent along with the gifts. The girl frowned as she finished writing it.

"It's a very odd message? Shouldn't you apologise in some kind of way and maybe tell her that you love her?" She asked helpfully. Roz shook his head and placed the message card on the flower bouquet.

"No, she will understand. It was a silly misunderstanding on my part; you know how these things are. Besides, that's where we met for the first time and it's kind of a joke between us."

"You met in a cargo bay?" She laughed and shook her head with a smile.

"Yes. It was a secret meeting spot for young lovers at the time. Her parents were rather strict and it was the only place we could meet in private." He lied. The receptionist shrugged and summoned a porter to

211

deliver the bouquet.

"You understand that for a man in my position it would be embarrassing if this became common knowledge." Roz said taking some credits from his wallet and placing it in the girls hand, "I'd rather that it remained a secret if that's okay?"
The receptionist slipped the money in her pocket and put her index finger to her pink painted lips nodding.

"Don't worry sir. We never record this kind of message. Our guest's privacy is our utmost concern. You have yourself a good night." She said winking.

The cargo hold was cold and only illuminated by a few yellowish lights, it smelled rusty like an old tin can and condensation had pooled in the shadows. Roz had been waiting there for about an hour dressed only in trousers and a loose fitting shirt with the Kommando knife hidden up the sleeve. The alloy floor cooled his bare feet and he felt the cold circulating around his body like a midnight tide. His timepiece displayed that is was five past midnight.

"Your late, bitch!" He whispered into the echoing chamber just as the door hatch hissed open and Madeline sauntered into the bay. She was dressed in an all in one gym suit, black as the night which revealed every curve of her feminine body. He stood motionless like a statue as she padded not ten feet from him and noticed her eyes. They were jet black, no iris was showing and they appeared bloodshot around the whites. He wondered if she was under the influence of Quat but thought her actions were a little too subdued for that.

"Do you need stims to fight me?" He asked as she bound up her blue hair into a top knot.

"They intensify the sensations I get when I kill!" She cackled like a villain from one of the old fashioned reel-films. Roz could see that she was living on the edge of her nerves, she seemed finely attuned to the muscles in her body.

Roz dropped into a combat stance to lower his centre of gravity and fanned his fingers wide to enhance circulation. "I wonder if they will intensify the agony of your death." He said baring his teeth.

"Thank you for the flowers by the way, not my favourite but very sweet of you." She said as she performed a couple of stretching exercises, which made her form appear to be a sleek muscular hunting cat.

"They were the best ones to hand. Shall we get this over with?" he said impatiently. Madeline levelled her eyes with his.

"Why do you need to be somewhere? Like, in the arms of a dark haired maid?" She said before grinning. Roz blinked and fear rose through his spine.

No! Please, not Karli! He thought.

"Yes, a strange kind of woman." Madeline continued, "I thought she was a little too old for a boy such as you and a little... lower cast!"

Roz's mind filled with tormenting images, he felt like something had been ripped out of him as he imagined a thousand different scenarios of Karli's demise.

"You killed her?" He choked, reeling in horror and

nausea.

"Every man has his weakness and I think I found yours!" She said before wheeling into combat.

Her attacks came like a shotgun blast, feet and fists exploded against him. He tried desperately to block every blow that she dealt but two landed hard throwing him off-balance and forcing him to retreat away from the bitch. He ran his hand down the side of his rib cage and felt a soft spot and a piercing pain.

"Not the best of starts Roz, she has cracked a rib already." Brother Brian issued deep from the corners of his mind.

"Shut up you fool, can't you see I'm busy!" Roz shouted.

Madeline was stood on the tips of her toes ready to attack again but looked momentarily confused at his outburst.

"Who are you talking to? Are you fucking wired?" She said angrily scanning the room to see if Roz had an associate hiding in the shadows.

"What?" asked Roz unaware that he had spoken aloud,   "Don't bother trying to use your mind games on me."

Madeline shrugged and leapt in clumsily, Roz thought it was a feint but he quickly decided that it could be the drugs that had made her attack sloppy. He ducked a powerful kick and kicked out sweeping her standing leg from under her. She crashed to the floor but rolled away from his next attack as he leapt at her trying to strike her with the point of his elbow. However, when she got to her feet Roz noticed that she wasn't putting her full weight on her left ankle.

Madeline grimaced as she wiggled her foot to see how badly damaged her ankle was then shifted her stance so that she would not have to bear too much weight on it. Roz crouched and struck out with a powerful fist attack but Madeline grabbed his wrist and wheeled around, grabbing his arm with her other hand and using his momentum to throw him.

Roz fell awkwardly landing hard on his face nearly knocked him out cold, he could feel that his front tooth was loose and he poked it with his tongue wincing in pain. He realised he had just fallen for the oldest trick in the book: Madeline wasn't as wounded as she had made out to be after all. As he picked himself up to his feet the room was spinning and he spat out globules of blood.

Madeline wasted no time in taking the advantage and tumbled into his flank slamming a fist into his kidney. If he hadn't had twisted away at the right moment he would have been dead but nevertheless intense pain shot through his body with every move he made, it felt like a knife blade twisting inside him. The damage had been done, Roz felt himself weakening and he knew he didn't have long to live and every second edged him closer to death. Blow after blow came in like a tornado but he managed to deflect, duck and dive out of the way of most of them, absorbing most of the damage on his arms and legs in an effort to protect his waning body.

Madeline's face was contorted with hate and she was obviously getting frustrated with his stonewall defensive tactics. She was tiring from throwing such a constant barrage of power attacks so she slowed down and pulled a slender blade from the sleeve of her gymslip hiding it under her forearm. She feigned another attack to his body and then the blade flashed in and out twice, nearly taking out one of his eyes. However, in doing so she overstepped slightly and Roz was able to sidestep her and stamped down hard using his full body weight to concentrate the attack on her ankle. After impact, his foot continued it's trajectory and connected with the floor as an audible snapping sound echoed around the cargo hold. Madeline shrieked and limped away from him dragging a contorted leg behind her.

"No! No! No! No!" She wailed as she slashed out wildly with the knife to stop him advancing on her.

Roz gasped for breath, the cracked rib had cut against his lung and his kidney felt like it was on fire. He wiped the side of his mouth and peered at the thick blood dribbling off his hand.

"I would cancel those dance classes if I was you." He said through coughs and splutters as he eyed the bone sticking out of her leg at an awkward angle.

"Look what you have done to my beautiful leg!" She sobbed pathetically as she dragged her foot out of the pool of welling blood. Her eyes looked deranged and her demeanour conveyed shock rather than agony.

Roz knew that if she had taken Quat she wouldn't be

feeling much pain at all and it was probably the sight of the damage that hurt her more. Madeline seemed to regain some clarity of thought and looked at the blade in her hand before stumbling forwards towards her target. She leapt off her good leg and Roz had to admire her effort and style but it was all too easy to counter her now. He ducked and moved across the plane of her jump grabbing her arm and unbalancing her, it was easy to snatch the blade from her hand. As she fell on all fours Roz completed his turn and cleanly slashed the knife across the back of her neckline, sweeping her beautiful head from her shoulders. The head thumped to the floor as her body remained braced in the position it had landed for a few seconds, spurting blood out of the severed arteries before it finally crumpled to the ground.

Roz crawled over to the medi-kit that Karli had given him and injected a cocktail of stimulants and painkillers before throwing the syringe into the shadowy corner of the cargo bay. The drugs worked fast inside him giving himself another surge of adrenaline but he knew that it would not last long. He needed to finish up here before heading to the medical quarters to fix the damage that she had done. He dragged her body to the trash compactor which made short work of Madeline's mortal remains and then jettisoned them out into space. He held up her head which stared wide eyed at him and spat in her face before disposing of it in the same way.

Walking over to where the pool of blood was starting to congeal, Roz set light to some cardboard and waved it under the smoke detectors. He had disabled the fire alarm before the fight to stop unwanted attention when the sprinkler system was activated and waited until they sprayed water to wash most of the blood away. Roz staggered through the rain of water cascading from the ceiling, his clothes clinging to him. He moved his hand up to his throbbing mouth and examined his tooth, it came loose as he probed it and walked off with the single tooth-clenched within his balled fist.

CHAPTER 13

To crush, a rebellion.

A menacing cloud of green smoke drifted over the sand dunes obscuring the rising sun. From the distant bunkers, shrieking alarms could be heard signalling another assault from the Free-Army of Kyson. Sergeant Morgan grunted and kicked himself out of a hammock rubbing the sleep from his eyes.

"What's going on? Are we finally attacking?" He bellowed reaching for a bottle of brandy. He was a beast of a man, well over six feet tall and almost as broad, he peered at the bottle and let it fall to the floor when he realised it was empty. It landed in one piece and seemed disgruntled with its stubborn refusal to break so he kicked it hard against the bunker wall until it did. Satisfied with the sound of shattering glass he staggered over to the corner of the room and began to urinate up the wall. Daemon eyed the huge sergeant and thought he wouldn't look out of place wielding an axe in a barbaric pit fight.

"Are you fuckers still here?" Morgan grumbled as he leant back seeing how high up the wall he could jet his piss.

"Yes, we are still here, and no, we aren't attacking yet." Daemon said through a long yawn. Daemon, Sherry, Taku and Miles had been dropped off in the Jiggeron desert on to a war-torn planet called Kyson. They had all expected to be put into the great test on arrival but nothing had happened for over a week. The Xen Corporation had been fighting against the F.A.K. for over a year. It was a war that Xen had confidently predicted they would win within a month of arrival but they hadn't foreseen the resistance that the people of Kyson had been willing to throw at such a large corporation.

As always this was a war over resources, Xen wanted to strip mine the uranium ore deep under the Jiggeron desert but the people of Kyson demanded a hefty percentage of the profit and an exemption from have to pay any operating costs. Xen had refused to pay the twenty five percent requested and when discussions ground to an halt the corporation was only too happy to use the crash landing of one of their freighters as a pretence for war. The war started with a massive air assault followed by ground troops being established within twelve hours of the outbreak of hostilities. It was usual procedure for Xen to destroy one of the major cities of its enemies to end any kind of resistance but Kyson had strong corporate allies and Xen couldn't risk going to war with other corporations. A protracted land battle over reparations was acceptable behaviour but the desolation of a valued spaceport impinging on the business of other corporations was another matter entirely.

"Nip over to the supply depot son and snatch a couple of bottles for me," Morgan said as he rubbed his bald scared head wincing from the pain of a terrible hangover.

"Get it yourself, we were told to observe the battle, not to run errands for a drunken sergeant." Daemon said cradling the assault rifle he had been issued. Morgan sneered and snatched some field scopes from Sherry's hand through which she had previously been watching the green smoke drift through the distant bunkers. Explosions and plasma emplacements bellowed in the distance, illuminating parts of the large mass of smoke.

"I can't see shit. The bastards have pumped the dunes with that irritant again. I'm glad I'm back here with you whelps. That stuff's itchy as fuck!" Morgan said trying to re-focus the field scopes. Sherry wandered over to sit with Taku and Miles who looked about as bored as she did. Miles held his assault rifle gingerly as though it was a newborn baby which Daemon found amusing.

"I'm so bored. I'm so bored. I'm so fucking bored!" Sherry sang intermittently irritating everybody in the dingy concrete room. She was about to start the song again when Taku elbowed her in the ribs.

"Will you knock it off! We are all fed up with waiting around. Why don't you do something useful like clear a mine field using a jack-hammer!"

"Silence!" Daemon barked as the bunker door opened revealing Agent Rowson. The man stood in the doorway shaking his head and dusting off sand that had collected all over his dark corporate suit.

"Well I've been to some shit holes in my time but nothing beats this cesspit." He said banging out sand from his shoes before he entered. Outside the bunker the howl of a lifter ascending was accompanied by an unwelcome sandy wind into the room. Sergeant Morgan spat on the floor and scowled at the agent.

"What's the matter with you? Isn't this bunker to the agents liking? I'm sure once the air conditioning and a nice desk full of pens arrives you will be comfortable enough." Morgan laughed.

"What a warm welcome from the common soldiery and to think an opening for a sergeant on the front line has just arisen. What do you think sergeant? Feel like you're up for a battlefront position?" Agent Rowson stated with relish as Sergeant Morgan suddenly felt the urge to leave the room.

"It's down to business then." Rowson said clapping his hands together as Morgan slammed the bunker door.   "Intelligence reports that the F.A.K. has just compromised their command post by sending out all their reserves in a futile attack against our frontline." Rowson peered at his timepiece and then continued.

"The F.A.K should be running into a carefully planned ambush and an air attack will be taking out four of their front line bunkers including a supply depot right about now," Rowson claimed as he pressed several buttons on his timepiece which made an audible chime.

"To cut to the chase this petty war is pretty much over and about goddamned time as well! This war has sliced into the corporate reserves more than we were willing to sacrifice."

"I take it the uranium yield that Xen planned to mine is no longer profitable?" Daemon said trying to look interested.

"You're joking aren't you sergeant? The current stock price for uranium is through the roof, especially due to the backward worlds rising to power. Selling expensive uranium to the backwards gives us profit margins only dreamt about a few years ago." Rowson said raising his fist as though he had personally won the war single-handedly.

"However, to get back to the point I want you to take your sect and lead an elite group of CORE troopers into the F.A.K. command post. Capture as many F.A.K. technical staff as you can. Kill the rest of the degenerates they won't be needed."

Daemon's team did not have much time to prepare for the assault based on the schedule that Agent Rowson had outlined. With the exception of Taku, who was left behind due to her mechanical limb slowing her down, they rushed across the dusty base camp and boarded an X.RAV armoured lifter. Ten CORE troopers all wearing similar light armour as the sect saluted as Daemon entered the vehicle. He knew they were mixed gender but he had trouble telling them apart due to the metallic visors they had drawn down over their faces and the fact they had numbers instead of names printed on their shoulder plates.

"We are going in quick and accessing the roof of the command centre." Daemon addressed them. "The X.RAV will provide air support if it's needed. Once we have infiltrated the bunker we need to take down the F.A.K. command network and capture a handful of administrators. Remember we need the technical staff not the commanders. If you see anybody with a chevron, gun them down."

"Yes sir," the trooper with the corporal badge stated robotically, "Got that troopers! Geeks only, waste the brass."

Daemon nodded and tapped a secure line into his communicator.   "Our assignation is Black Troop and we are on band 603 people, set your comms."

Sherry nudged him and grinned looking over at Miles before she threw down her visor. He saw that Miles was still holding his assault rifle as though it was an object completely alien to him.

"It's about time we saw some action hey sergeant? I can't wait to open up this baby and feel its vibrations in my hands!" Sherry said referring to her gun.

Daemon shook his head at her lust for battle.

The thrusters howled as the X.RAV took to the air creating a tornado of sand and dust around the aircraft.

As the X.RAV raced over the billowing clouds of smoke the carnage of the major ground battle escalating in the dunes below was obscured from view. Daemon tried to imagine what it would be like trying to fight through a thick fog and suspected friendly fire would claim many lives on both sides of the field. As the X.RAV banked sharply to avoid rocket fire his stomach churned and he wished he was down there with them.

"Stay behind the team sergeant and mop up anything we miss." The corporal said shouting over the din of the twenty-millimetre cannons firing off the nose of the X.RAV. As the ship took up position Roz hoped the firefight would be brief and that his Sect would come out unscathed. He attached himself to the drop ropes, lowered his visor and took the safety off his gun.

It had been a bloodbath. The elite CORE team had murdered just about every person in the complex. Corpses littered the corridors and rooms as they gunned their way to the central processing network. The bank of computers, communication terminals and display screens had been smashed, bombed and destroyed. Fragments of metal and glass mixed in with the blood that was awash on the floor of the command room.

Daemon leant his head against the cold alloy of his assault rifle as the troopers kicked the shit out of the four technical administrators they had captured.

"Enough! They have to go back for questioning." He commanded, the troopers backed away from the captives. The administrators were bound with hand-cuffs and lay bleeding on the floor, one of them had been so badly beaten that he appeared dead.

"And you!" he yelled at Sherry, "You sick bitch, what were you thinking back there?" he said gesturing with his thumb into a side room.

"I didn't know it was a family room." She shrugged as she reloaded her rifle. Daemon tried to understand her motives when she had shouldered her way to the front of the unit and joined in with the slaughter.

"Black Troop to base, Black Troop to base, we have smashed the network and gathered up four captives," Daemon said pressing a button attached to his ear. He took another look at bloodied face of the man who had taken the brunt of the beatings and tapped him with his boot. "Make that three captives."

Miles appeared at the doorway and looked at the scene of destruction his eyes only seeming to linger on the broken equipment.

"What the fuck? Why have they smashed up all the computer terminals? I thought we were supposed to cripple the command net, not destroy everything."

"It seems the good corporal was in a hurry so he just blew everything up," Daemon said knowing that there was something amiss.
Miles wandered over to where Daemon was sat.

"Do you think Agent Rowson wanted to hide something stored on these data-banks?" he whispered.

"Maybe," Daemon said gesturing to some of the old assault rifles scattered around the debris. "I wouldn't be surprised if Rowson had been selling arms or vehicles to the F.A.K. and lining his own pockets unknown to Xen."

"Sergeant," The corporal called, "Incoming news; the F.A.K. has just surrendered. The war is over!"

The Sect and the three captives ascended to the roof of the command centre and boarded a waiting starlifter. The starlifter quickly left the surface of the planet and docked inside the 'Hopes Lost' orbiting battle station. The Xen battle station had been in orbit around Kyson for over a year and now that the war was over it would probably stay for a while longer acting as a supply depot. The docking station was busy with transport ships being loaded with strip-mining equipment. It seemed the corporation had known the war would soon be over and was already prepared to reap the Uranium fields under the Jiggeron desert. Agent Rowson waited on the docking ring with a broad smile when Daemon's sect arrived.

"I hope you were taking notes down there kid." He said slapping Daemon on his shoulders.

"I certainly did sir; I've learnt not to trust any Xen agents in the future. Tell me Rowson, why did we capture the administration staff and not the officers? Did the officers know something that could compromise one of your dirty little secrets?" Daemon said glaring at the agent.

"Well now sergeant, it almost sounds as if you are

making dire accusations about an Agent of Xen. That kind of traitorous talk could quickly have you spaced or even sent to the plants." Rowson grinned evilly to hammer home his threat. "I'll pretend I didn't hear your little outburst just like I didn't see you murder the CORE sergeant on the Caligula."

Daemon bit his tongue and wondered what the plants were. He was lost in thought as Agent Rowson had the captives taken into custody.

"You are to accompany me to the prison sector. You will be happy to hear that a great test has been organised for your pathetic group." The agent said before following the guards and captives.

Taku was already waiting in the stale prison chamber wearing a short white smock which made her metallic leg look odd in comparison to her real one. At her side stood a tall, thin man wearing an all-in-one blue suit. He held a data-pad and his head had been recently shaved.

"Welcome to the great test. I will be your auditor." The man said bowing.

Like the rooms in most Xen craft this one looked like had seen better days, rust and stains coated the metallic walls and the floors were coated with grease and debris. In the centre of the room were three chairs, each holding a captive. Daemon noticed an air-lock in the corner and a long wooden table holding evil looking equipment.

Agent Rowson pulled out a hand held camera and walked over to a shadowed part of the room.

"Don't mind me, I will be recording this for training purposes and perhaps for personal viewings."   He chuckled.

The auditor bowed again and gestured to the three captives.

"You have learnt interrogation techniques in the academy and I wish for you to utilise the skills you have learnt upon these Kyson rebels!" He almost spat the last word with hatred.

Miles walked over to the table to scrutinise the equipment laid out on it.

"What do you need to know?" he said as though he was already eager to torture the captives. "Surely there is a line of enquiry you wish for us to pursue rather than asking random questions." The auditor scowled and banged the data-pad he held. "I was getting to that before you rudely interrupted me!" He sighed with disdain and continued. "The F.A.K. purchased some powerful nuclear weapons from the Seinal Corporation about six months ago. The Seinal Corporation have recently consolidated their company with Xen and have traded us this information. We need to find out where they have hidden the weapons before a splinter group uses them on our strip-mining equipment or upon our defence facilities." He paused.

"If the F.A.K. had nuclear weapons why didn't they use them during the war?" Daemon said wandering over to the auditor. He stood by his side and whispered, "If you wanted that kind of information surely we should have captured a couple of generals or other high ranking officers. These administrators are just computer geeks. They won't know where the weapons are hidden?"

"Sergeant, for the purposes of this exercise you are to assume that they do know. I would suggest that you get to work or I will report your weaknesses and you and your sect will automatically fail this test!" The auditor growled.

Daemon looked to Taku, Sherry and Miles and closed his eyes for a second or two.

"So we are to torture innocent victims to gain recognition within the Xen Corporation." He thought to himself.

He felt tempted to kill them quickly so that they didn't suffer but knew that doing so would mean that they would all fail the test and he couldn't let his sect down in that way. He stormed over to the captive on the far right and crouched in front of him.

"You heard what the auditor said, tell me where the weapons are hidden and I promise that I will use all my influence to make sure that you and your fellow personnel live."

The man looked into his eyes and shook his head. Daemon could see that he knew he was going to die.

"Really, we aren't soldiers and we don't have access to information like that. I didn't even know we had any kind of nuclear capability." The man finished his plea and began to cry, at first it was a small sobbing but it escalated into a tear streaming frenzy.

"Enough of this shit!" Miles yelled. He marched over

to the captive on the far left and dragged the seated man across the room towards the airlock. "One of you fuckers is going to talk or this man is going to be spaced!" He threw open the doors and dragged the captive in. The transparent doors to the airlock clamped shut as he operated the dials and controls.

"Just say the word sect leader and this man will be vomiting out his intestines." Daemon stood with his mouth open in shock. What was Miles doing? Had he gone mad? He wondered if he was playing the part of the aggressive interrogator or was genuinely going to go through with his threat. Again he was torn between pulling his side arm and blasting the captives knowing Xen couldn't torture the dead or putting Miles on report for failing to adhere to S.O.P.

Miles had his hand over the control panel and looked eager to begin spacing the man, Daemon had to make an instant decision.

Fuck my career! I can't do this! And fuck Xen and their test! He thought and reached for his sidearm to aim at the nearest captive. His heart was pounding furiously when the room suddenly dimmed. He looked round the darkened chamber and found it was absent of people and it was growing darker by the second. Daemon's eyes fell on the dark skull of the demon from his dreams skulking in the shadows.

"Help," Daemon croaked. The demon stepped forward and as it approached him its flesh pulsed with streams of lava that spouted small columns of fire over its frightening body. Daemon felt ill and wanted to flee

231

from its fiery glare.

"Should I take over now Daemon, after all you're not very good at hurting?" It asked cocking its great head to one side.

"Who are you? Where did you come from?" Daemon chattered with rising panic as he failed to see any exits from the chamber.

"I am you Daemon! Well at least I am a part of you." The demon roared. "Try to relax and rest a while." It said seductively.

Daemon felt a wave of exhaustion roll over him and the thought of sleeping seemed so tempting.

"I suppose a little sleep won't do me any harm?" He said to himself stifling a deep yawn.

The demon gathered him up gently and set him down onto a nice comfortable bed within the dark place.

"Wonderful! Sheer brilliance! I have never seen such carnage." Agent Rowson announced ecstatically while he checked his camera to see if it had recorded the whole event. The words echoed in Daemon's head but he was confused and felt dizzy. He was disorientated and felt like he was coming round after being unconscious. He staggered around for a while before he noticed he was covered in blood.

"Medic!" He cried as he patted his body down looking for injuries.

Sherry was throwing up near the auditor and he noticed Taku had turned to face a corner of the room.

"You're not injured sect leader. It's not your blood." Miles said grabbing hold of Daemon's trembling hands.

Daemon looked into Miles obsidian eyes and saw his own dark reflection within the lifeless orbs.

"Am I Me?" he asked the gaunt looking image looking back from the pool of black.

A scream of agony came from the corner of the room followed by a slushy popping sound.

"Oh!" Miles exclaimed, "I forgot about him with what was happening." He looked towards the air lock dribbling with gore.

Daemon looked around the rest of the room he wanted to cry. It looked like it had been decorated by some avant-garde artist obsessed with the colour red. When he was on the farm Daemon had seen inside an abattoir when his father had taken him to butcher the Doe-deer for what he had presumed was a life lesson at the time. His memory of that day bore some resemblance to the sickly room he looked upon but paled in comparison. Everywhere he looked a new monstrosity greeted his disbelieving eyes.

"That my man was torture on a whole new level." Agent Rowson proclaimed as he clapped his hands together in applause. "And to think, I doubted that you had it in you. This spool is going to make me a lot of money. People pay hard cash to watch shit like this."

"I need a drink!" Daemon said resting his head against Miles shoulder. The auditor finished his notes and cleared his throat to get everybody's attention.

"By the authority bestowed on me by the Xen Corporation, I'm very pleased to announce that this sect has passed the great test!" The auditor frowned as he looked at the state of the chamber and then continued.

"I must admit the methods were a little unconventional but I believe each member adhered to the rules and didn't compromise rank or step out of line while the Sect leader ruthlessly interrogated the prisoners." He bowed before leaving the chamber.

"Don't worry about the mess. The prison janitor will clear up all this blood and matter. Now go and enjoy some downtime you have clearly earned it." Rowson said before he disappeared through the exit.

"Did the captives know where the bombs were hidden?" Daemon asked quietly. Miles shook his head as he wiped sweat from his scalp.

"No Daemon. But I think we all knew that as soon as we entered this room."

The Hopes Lost battle station was currently being refurbished to support the abundance of radioactive material mined from Kyson. Starcrafts were arriving by the hour, unloading yellow cake processing equipment, prefabricated fortresses, mining operatives and additional troops to fortify the Jiggeron desert. The entire station was busy with people who had been called upon to carry out double shifts. This left the onboard bars almost deserted as the Sect discovered when they arrived there after the great test.

"You did what you needed to do to pass the test Daemon. I know Taku and Sherry don't understand at the moment but in time they will thank you." Miles said calmly.

Daemon glanced at Sherry and Taku propping up the empty bar, they were sombre and chatting quietly.

"I don't remember Miles. I don't remember what I did!" He ranted before he laid waste to the selection of shots on the table.

"I see." Miles said with an edge in his tone. "You're a hero Daemon. You got them all through the test. Damn I wish my test had been so easy." He trailed off as he watched his friend hitting another shot.

"Why was you," Daemon searched for the right word, "at the interrogation Miles? You had already passed the great test. And what did you have to do in your test if you thought that that was easy?" Daemon said narrowing his eyes, eager to listen.

"I chose to be there Daemon. If a sect is selected to attempt the great test collectively then a member of it who has already passed has the right to join them. I thought that you might need my help. After all you are my sergeant and my friend." Miles looked embarrassed admitting it.

"Is that why you spaced him?" Daemon asked.

"Well, it looked like you would not do what had been asked. I had a duty to protect the sect. I'm sorry I doubted you." Miles apologised. Daemon was not certain what to make of Miles words and as the effects of drinks set in he decided that it wasn't worth pursuing.

"So are you going to tell me what your test was? All the time I have known you, even when we shared the room at the academy you could have told me but never did. What did they make you do Miles?"

"I'd rather not say Daemon. The thing is I was never going to tell you because I feared that it might influence our friendship. After what you have just done I'm sure you appreciate that what is in the past is best remaining in the past. I'd be grateful if you didn't try bringing up the subject ever again." Miles said inspecting the drink he held.

"I can't work you out Miles, sometimes it sounds like you want to open up but then, just as quickly, you clamp up again. You are full of contradictions. You're generally the mild mannered shy type, sometimes you can be bad tempered of course but now and then you seem to be blatantly psychotic." Daemon said drunkenly and gulped another shot.

"It's called being human." Miles said shaking his head slowly, "And it's what Xen requires of us. On the subject of blatant psychotic behaviour, I would take a look at Agent Rowson's recording. You performed atrocities that I wouldn't be capable of." He said defensively. Daemon slumped in the chair and rubbed his eyes.

"Rowson can keep his spool. I don't want to see it and I'm glad I don't remember one second in that room. I'm having trouble coming to terms with all the Xen training, personally I think they manufacture monsters and I've been turned into one of them." He sighed and ordered another drink as Sherry wandered over to the table leaving Taku alone at the bar.

"They have offered me a corporal rank in the CORE. That agent claims he has received excellent reports about the assault on the command centre. He seems to think I would make a fine CORE soldier with the potential of becoming a front line officer." Sherry said with uncertainty.

"What? Are you just going to flush away your career because an agent thinks you could be a good field grunt? What about Vex II and your officer training. You are guaranteed the rank of lieutenant and a real military career!" Daemon said in genuine surprise.

"I've given it some thought but I haven't made my final decision. I enjoy the fighting and I think I'd like to gain my rank in the field, instead of studying at some academy where you're guaranteed a high ranking position upon graduation." Daemon thought he detected doubt in Sherry's voice suggesting that she hadn't finalised her plans.

"Has this anything to do with your father and his mistakes?" Miles asked worrying about the thought of losing his lover.

"It has everything to do with my father! I don't want to end up like him, being hated for the careless loss of lives because he never experienced what it's really like in battle." She said sitting down.

"But you are nothing like your father!" Miles argued.

"And I want to make sure that I never am." Sherry said. Miles knocked over his drink and stormed off towards the exit.

"I think I may have upset Miles." Sherry said stifling a laugh. "But he will get over me when I leave for the CORE."

"So you have made up your mind then? You're really leaving us for a life in the CORE? I don't want to piss on your parade but life expectancy in that outfit isn't good at all. Statistically speaking that is." Daemon said shaking his head and puffing out his bottom lip.

"I think that's what draws me towards a real front line career. The sensation you get in battle with bullets whizzing past your head, the soldiers around you working as one unit against the enemy. I would even go as far as to say it's better than sex!" She said excitably and banged the table with her fist shaking the clutter of empty glasses.

"How can you compare sex to situations involving death? I would rather be buckling the bed springs in the arms of a beautiful woman, than hammering it out in some fucked up battle. You must have had some shitty bed friends if you prefer war." He sneered and then wondered if he had insulted her.

"Well I have yet to find a man that could change my mind." she winked.

"I wish he was here because I think you are making a big mistake!" He shrugged and scanned the empty bar room as Sherry emptied a tumbler full of ale.

"We might as well get this out of the way, just in case we don't see each other again." She said grabbing his arm and lifting him up from his chair.

"Get what? Oh, I see." He said grinning drunkenly wondering if she was serious.
Sherry placed his arm over her shoulder and led him back to a small cabin she had rented as though she had

238

already planned what would happen that night.

Daemon didn't even feel guilty about betraying Miles as he rattled the bed frame with Sherry.

CHAPTER 14

The Neptus

Daemon yawned as he covered his eyes from the automated light fixtures that illuminated the small cabin space. He noticed Sherry had already gone as he patted down the mattress where she had slept. The mattress was damp from all the sweat and other fluids associated with a long night of fucking. His mouth was dry and his head ached from the alcohol and the dehydration from such a physical night. Sherry had been out early and left him a large bottle of water on the tiny bedside table.

"You are truly a gem Sherry!" He thought as he gulped down the water as though he had recently traversed a parched desert. When he got down to the last drop in the bottle he noticed a hand-written message stuck on the door.

It was nice, thanks for the fun but my mind hasn't changed. In other words, you aren't THAT man that could change my mind. (That's if you remember our conversation in the bar.) By the time you are reading this I will be on the next military transport destined for Xen Prime. I was never any good at goodbyes, so I'll leave it with you to tell Miles. I will try and keep in touch with you all and write as often the CORE allows. Keep well.
xxx S.

He recalled the conversation and grinned shaking his head. The sly little... He screwed the paper up into a tight ball and threw it into the waste bin as he headed off for a shower.

"Resigned? What the hell was she thinking?" Daemon said throwing his hands in the air with dismay.

"Yes Taku put her resignation form in this morning, it's been stamped and she is on her way home to Dandibah." Miles explained as he tested the weight of the bulging carry case that he clutched.

"Why would she do that after all the training and finally passing the dumb test? I thought she wanted to further her medical career?" He wanted to scream out in anger but the docking ring was far too busy and he didn't want to cause alarm.

"She didn't say why but I suspect it might have something to do with her new leg, she has been struggling with it ever since it was fitted. I also think the test may have also unnerved her." Miles suggested looking at his timepiece again wondering where Sherry was. "Where is she? The transport ship isn't going to wait for her if she doesn't hurry up."

Daemon winced and tried to think up a nice way to tell

him that Sherry wasn't going to Vex II.

"Sherry left this morning, she joined up with the CORE. I'm sorry Miles I hate to be the one to tell you." Miles dropped his bag to the floor and looked as though he was going to piss his pants.

"She didn't even say goodbye. Did she say she would write?" He asked fiddling with a button on his tunic.

"She will write as often as she can but I would try and forget about her, well at least for a while. Let her settle into the CORE. It's the life she has chosen." Daemon tried to comfort Miles but felt his words were ineffectual; they seemed to bounce off an invisible field around his friend.

"Rats and sinking ships hey Daemon?" Miles finally said with a wry smile and in an unexpectedly cheerful tone. It was almost as if he hadn't just lost the love of his life and had already forgotten her entire existence. "Well, I suppose I may as well get on board then." A Trident class transport craft was docked in the ring and was unloading a battalion of armoured soldiers, who all appeared to be very young. They looked like they were fresh out of boot camp and had not yet developed the intimidating presence of a group of highly trained CORE troopers. Daemon spotted the red circular insignia's they wore on their arms and chuckled to himself.

"Xen army regulars. Poorly trained colonial trash". He finished the thought and felt glad he had performed as well as he did in his training because if he hadn't he would have probably ended up as an officer in charge of the regulars.

"That's me then my friend. It's a shame we couldn't travel to Vex II together." Miles said offering his hand to shake.

"Yeah, I know. I have to stay back here a few days to

attend some debriefing meetings. But after that shit, I will be on my way to Vex II too. Try and get us a half decent room hey?" He laughed.

Miles was still holding out his hand but Daemon chose to ignore it and bear-hugged his friend instead. Miles squirmed around for a few seconds trying to get out of his friends embrace before relaxing and patting his back.

"I'll see you at the Vex academy, take care and travel well," Daemon said as Miles picked up his bag and then blended into the crowd of people waiting or arriving on the docking ring.

The next two days Daemon attended a string of mind-numbing meetings, none of which directly involved the actions of him or his sect during their short stay on Kyson. Attending meetings like these was a necessary evil of attaining the rank he had and it appeared that from now on he would have to attend more. On the night before he was due to leave for Vex II he was promoted to the rank of lieutenant class C. His new rank as a graduate of the Xen Academy gave him enough leverage that he could actually question an order given by a Captain of the CORE. He still didn't understand the labyrinthine ranking system within the Xen Corporation and laughed at the ridiculousness of the entire bureaucracy of it all. If he had become an Agent of Xen he would have had the authority to override any order given by a Xen Colonel or a General of the CORE. As it was he was allowed to question Captains of the CORE but had to obey orders from his superiors and any agents. He kicked himself at the thought because he had achieved the grades to become an agent but had chosen a military career instead. For him, the immediate future held endless meetings and following the orders of men he believed he was better than.

A huge star cruiser craft drifted through the air shields upon the magnetic fields of two tug-class vessels which struggled to keep the behemoth ship on course. Daemon waited patiently on the side of the docking ring carrying a small hold-all carry case. He had dressed in a tight fitting black shirt and trousers which clung to his muscular body like a second skin. The travel pills popped in his stomach and he could feel the calmness of the drugs smoothing out the turbulence in his gut. The Neptus would be dropping him off at Vex II and he now understood some of the perks of being an officer of Xen. First class travel on board a star cruiser rather than having to slum it in a military craft was the kind of preferential treatment he could get used to. He thought of Miles travelling in the shitty transport craft and laughed. The gang plate descended and he heard the engines warming up for an immediate take off. He looked around and noticed he was the only pick up for The Neptus so he rushed on board. A young woman waited for him and took his bag before bowing. She wore a simple green gown that hid her figure within the many folds of the garment and her dark hair was bound on the top of her head with numerous needles poking out.

"I am Yula your aid during transit." She bowed again before leading him off through the polished corridors toward his cabin.

"I hope I will not offend you but are you from Dandibah?" He asked noticing the woman had a similar appearance to Taku.

"Yes I'm from the Alteu province of Dandibah." She

said smiling at the thought of somebody noticing her heritage.

"One of my friends came from Dandibah, I believe she shipped out a few days ago because she missed her home world." He said not going into any real details of why Taku left.

"The friend you speak of is very lucky. It will be unlikely that I will get to see my home world ever again." She said solemnly as though she was suddenly carrying a heavy, invisible weight.

"Oh." He said lost for words and wishing he had never brought the subject up. The clean interior of the craft was remarkable it even smelt fresh and didn't stink of recycled people like all the other spacecraft that he had travelled on. In a few of the corridors they had passed were various religious shrines set in small alcoves. His family had never been religious and the school he had attended had no religious affiliations so he was largely ignorant of what happened in the shrines. He could, however, imagine the calming sensation which these tiny places of worship would bring to passengers with faith. He had to admit that although they didn't bring any ease to his soul they looked pleasing to the eye and added to the overall decoration.

"This is your cabin master." Yula stated as the CORE trooper flanking the door saluted to him after noticing his rank pins. Daemon made a show of the situation and inspected the guard's rifle before giving it back.

"Thank you Lieutenant!" The female trooper stated through the speaker on her armoured suit. He saluted and wondered if she was pretty under all of the metal she wore.

"Fear not! While I'm guarding your room, any aggressive force will only pass me upon my death." The trooper said as Yula rolled her eyes at the military banter and then opened the door revealing the luxury cabin space.

"This is a class B cabin with an en-suite bathing chamber and king-sized bed space. The reel-player display unit has thirty entertainment channels and also has a built-in spool reader. Spool-films are available on request but The Neptus library isn't extensive." She stated monotonously as she closed the cabin door. Daemon saw the guard taking notice of the room's dimensions until the door slammed shut in her face.

"My room is next door, so, if you need me to attend to you I'm only a button press away." She said pointing to the internal communication system on the wall near the door. Daemon smiled broadly and was on the verge of asking a question when Yula scowled at him.

"I will attend to you as your aid but not like that!" she said shaking her head before exiting the room and slamming the door behind her. He blushed and felt confused as he had been going to ask when morning call was. Then it dawned on him what she must have thought he was going to ask.

"Oh dear, what must she think of me?" He thought slightly shocked. He was tempted to rush out and explain to her that he wasn't trying to take advantage but decided that as he had done nothing wrong there was no reason to. Instead, he walked over to the mini-bar.

"Hmm, mead, I haven't had that in a long time." He said as he searched through the multitude of wines, beers and spirits. He plucked out a small ice cold bottle from the refrigeration unit and decided to make himself comfortable for the night.

The scent of Suix surrounded him, amalgamating with the herbal aroma of the plants inside the secret botany garden. He was deep inside Suix, her breasts glistened with sweat as they swayed groin-to-groin caught in the clutches of the dance of ages. He pulled Suix on him with every motion of her hips as her ankles caressed his lower back. With each breath in their mouths, every moan of joy, it was like time had no meaning at all. No haste in the embrace of motion, just two entities entwined within the harmony of love. A final thrust against one another, warm and fluid, whispers of true bonding echoing in their ears.

"It's time to wake up master!" Daemon heard Yula's voice dissipating the dream. He tried to protest but Suix told him it was time to leave as the dream faded.

"But I like it here." He said elbowing himself up from the pillow sleepily. Yula set a breakfast tray down on the side of his bed and smiled.

"You were moaning and I thought you were having a bad dream. But it seems I was wrong." He frowned at the tray holding two boiled blue eggs set in small yellow ceramic cups and a jug of red fruit juice.

"Are those real eggs?" He asked as he began to tuck into his breakfast. "You should have seen the slush I've had to endure for longer than I care to remember." He mumbled while he ate.

"Most of the new officers say just that." Yula said as she tidied up around the cabin. Once she had finished she walked over to Daemon who was savouring the taste of fresh food.

"I've brought you an itinerary if you wish to read it?" Yula said handing him a small yellow card. He scanned it while he drank the red juice which tasted sour yet with a sweet aftertaste. The itinerary card had small screens in the corners displaying advertisements for sugar-free soft drinks and holiday destinations for the very rich. In the middle of the card, it said he had two more nights in the luxury cabin and then he would be placed in cryogenic for just over four months.

"I had no idea how Vex II was so far, or how long it would take to get there." He said worrying about the considerable length of time spent in cryogenic.

"This is a cruiser craft, not a warship." She laughed. "Technically it isn't very far to Vex II, it's the speed of the craft which is the factor."

"Well, I hope I'm still paid while I'm iced!" He grumbled getting out of bed naked and then realised he was in polite company. Yula turned to face the door and made a tutting sound.

"Oh shit, sorry about that, I had forgotten where I was." He blushed and quickly clothed himself. "It's not something we really think about in the military."

"Try to be more careful in future. We got off to a bad start yesterday please think before you pull another stunt like that." She said tapping her foot and holding her hips.

"You're right and I apologise. I'm finding it hard to adjust to civilian life." He said as he entered the bathroom to clean his teeth. He switched on the shower to let it run hot and as he rearranged his balls. He laughed to himself thinking how Yula tended to act just like his mother, chastising him at every opportunity.

"Mind you," he thought, "I don't recall ever catching my mother taking a sneaky look at my cock." He had raised his voice so Yula could hear in the main cabin. He heard another tutting sound.

"I don't think I've been in a cryogenic stasis for so long before, are there any side effects?"

"Not really. Well, I suppose it depends on the type of cryo-tubes used. But The Neptus has the type seven series which are probably the best. I once did nine months on ice and felt a little nausea coming round but nothing serious." She said closer to the bathroom door.

"All the times I have travelled long distances they brought us in and out of cryo on a kind of rota system." He said washing off his toothbrush and remembering feeling nasty each time he was un-frozen.

"Can you keep a secret?" She said as she opened the door slightly to hear over the hiss of the shower.

"I can keep a secret." He replied wondering where this was going.

"I heard a rumour about new officers doing subliminal training while they are in cryogenic. Apparently, it's some kind of foundation course to speed up training at the various academies when they arrive."

"I've never heard of that before." He said worried at the thought. It sounded plausible considering everything he had already gone through and could possibly explain why he had been seeing the fiery demon. It would not remotely surprise him if Xen had already been subjecting the students to conditioning while they were iced.

"Well, if anyone asks? You didn't hear the rumour from me if that is okay?" She said with an undertone of a threat in her voice and closed the bathroom door. Disappointed that events hadn't gone in the direction he had hoped Daemon turned the shower to cold and jumped in. Once he had finished his ablutions he padded into the main cabin where he found Yula was sat cross-legged on the bottom of the king size bed. She was singing a tuneful song in a language he didn't understand and stopped as he entered.

"Is there anything I could bring to your room? Or maybe you would like a tour of The Neptus? The day is yours master." She said rising up from the floor and brushing down the fabric of her gown. She was a few inches taller than Taku and her face was more angular but her figure was more voluptuous and her breasts appeared larger.

"Does this craft have a drinks bar?" He asked her wanting to see how she reacted.

"The Neptus has many bars, take your pick!" She said showing irritation as if all the new male officers she had dealt with had asked the same question.

"Excellent, I think I will let you choose the bar." He said grinning.

Yula had picked the most expensive bar which was set in the entertainment promenade down in the belly of The Neptus. It served exotic wines collected from all over the corporate universe and the prices reflected the fact. Daemon didn't really care which bar they went to as long as could relax and drink himself into a stupor but he preferred to do it with Yula as company. The entertainment promenade was a bizarre of stalls selling frivolous electronic gadgets, hand-crafted jewellery, and mass-produced mementoes, all of which were extortionately priced. Off-duty officers and executives from all backgrounds of Xen and the other corporations circulated the marketplaces, bars and restaurants, spending their hard earned credits. His eye roved over a few attractive female officers amongst the throng but they appeared to have male attendants hanging off their arms, some of them even had two.

"It looks like you have more than drinks in mind." Yula

intimated with a sneer as she drank a weak lemon tea eying him over the rim of the cup.

"Not really, I just want to relax for a while and soak up the atmosphere." He turned his attention to this strange woman who appeared eager to judge him but willing to serve him. He did not know how to behave before her, whether to admonish her or encourage her.

"Good choice with the bar by the way." He said testing the water, "I would usually stay clear of wine but it's rather nice after a few glasses."

"And to think I could be showing you around the engine room or the onboard art gallery!" She said with what Daemon took to be a hint of sarcasm before she turned to concentrate upon a newsreel being displayed on the table top.

Daemon hadn't realised the table was moving with pictures from one of the Enclave sponsored news channels and decided to click the audio button to see what was happening in the universe.

"It's war on a scale you wouldn't believe and a civil war to boot!" The excited news reader claimed standing on the corner of a busy cityscape. "The meddling Xen Corporation has just felt the backlash against its aggressive policies and Sigra III is now in a state of emergency! The corporation backed government is presently under attack by the very civilians it claims to represent. Only one month ago Sigra III was a free-trade planet but now under the shadow of the oppressive corporation it stands in chaos!" A car in the background exploded as the newsreader ducked into cover.

"The people of Sigra III have stated that they have had enough, people on the street are telling me that they hope Xen is seeing this because the people are taking to their guns to defend their rights." The news reader was unable to continue his story as a Sect of Xen troopers appeared in the background firing wildly. The camera shattered and whined with static and the table display reverted to a spiral pattern as Daemon clicked off the sound.

"Well, that was heartwarming! I suspect The Neptus will be cancelling the visit to Sigra III because it's on our final leg of the cruise." Yula sighed and slumped back into her seat.

"Maybe not," Daemon conjectured, "by the time this cruise liner reaches Sigra the crisis may well be over. Like you said, it isn't a very fast craft after all. Xen will have put the population down by then."

"Go and fuck yourself!" Yula said quietly but not quietly enough to prevent Daemon from hearing. He decided that he would let her petulance ride and drained his glass whilst summoning the waiter.

Sweat dribbled off his Daemon's nose as he finished vomiting into a plastic receptacle that Yula held at arm's length.

"I'm so sorry I got drunk last night." Daemon said as he held tightly to the bowl of foul smelling fluid. She gave him a tumbler of water and rushed off to the toilet to empty the bowl before he started again.

"There's a limit to what a human body can consume, I think you stepped over the line last night. The sickness you feel now might alter your drinking habits in the future." She prattled as she returned with the bowl. Her features were blank but he could tell she was laughing underneath.

"The only lesson I've learnt about drinking is to stay well away from wine. I will stick to beer in the future." Even in such a delicate state he still managed to piss her off.

Yula screamed and threw the rinsed out bowl at him, it bounced off his head and rolled along the floor.

"Ow!" He cried in surprise rubbing his head. She winced and put her hands to her mouth.

"Oh no, I'm sorry about that! I don't know what came over me. Please forgive me." She appeared to be in a fit of panic, undoubtedly caused by the realisation that she could lose her job for assaulting an officer.

He waved her away as she damped down a towel and pressed it against the slowly forming bump.

"Let me see." She said tugging at his hand which he was now using to cover the lump. Once she was able to inspect the severity of the damage she sighed and commented, "Well, I'm as good as demoted now. They will probably have me cleaning out cabins when you file a report. Does it hurt?"

"Of course it fucking does." He said petulantly although in truth he was more embarrassed at his exclamation of pain rather than the injury itself.

Yula burst out laughing and Daemon, wondering what she was laughing at, he tried unsuccessfully to prevent a grin forming on his own face before starting to laugh too.

"Sorry, I just can't help myself. What a pair we are?" She said trying to control herself. "But you do look funny when you're in pain, almost child-like."

"Thanks a lot, now could you bring me a report form to fill in?" He asked with mock seriousness on his face and saw her smile fade and her copper eyes widen with the thought of him reporting her.

"Only joking Yula but I had you going for a second or two." He chuckled. She grabbed the pillow from the bed and pretended to beat him.

"That wasn't funny! I had visions of me cleaning out bathrooms for the rest of my life." She stopped the mock beating and hugged the pillow as though it was a long lost teddy bear. He could tell something bothered her.

"Tell me Yula, why are you here? I mean why be an aid on The Neptus? You're intelligent, cultured and good looking; I would have thought being a diplomat would have suited you more." She clutched the pillow tighter and rested her head against it.

"Please don't do this." She pleaded.

"Do what?"

"Ask me what I cannot answer. I would like to tell you but I can't. Let's just pretend that I enjoy my role as an aid for the time being and nothing else matters." She turned away from him her face burrowed in the pillow and there was an unnerving silence for a while before she allowed it to fall from her grip.

"Hungry?" She asked with her head bowed. He noticed a small damp patch on the pillow and suspected it could have been formed by tears.

"A little, but I couldn't stomach anything rich. I didn't mean to upset you. I can be an inquisitive little bastard at times." He said apologetically.

"I will go and get you something with rice. My father ate a lot of rice when he had been drinking. He claimed it soaked up all the badness." With that said Yula left the cabin.

The next day Daemon made an effort to cheer up his aid by sightseeing the places she wanted to show him. It appeared that he had been wrong thinking she was being sarcastic when she had listed the places she thought he would like to see when they had first met as she did indeed start with the engine room. It was a pretty standard configuration and he had seen his fair share of reactors cores when he volunteered as a maintenance operative at the academy. He had to admit however that he had never seen a triple-core fusion reactor with a duel nuclear and Ionic fuel lining before. It was hardly a subject to write home about and he feigned a moderate amount of interest.

The art gallery was a highlight for him that day, not the actual artistic endeavours posted around the walls, it was more to do with the life model posing naked while a group of budding young artists sketched her feminine curves. Yula noticed him winking at the life-model and dragged him away to see the navigation room when she saw the beautiful lady return his wink.

"Must you do that? Do you think because you are an officer of Xen that any girl you lay eyes upon will succumb to your will?" Yula said in a huff as she guided him toward the navigation room.

"No!" He said defensively. "But I do appreciate beauty when I see it. Why does it bother you so much?" Yula stopped suddenly and clenched her fists.

"It bothers me when I see bastards like you thinking that every woman you see can be objectified!" She raged as she prodded his chest with a stabbing finger.

"Yula listen to me." But she didn't stay to listen. Instead, she ran away down the corridor and left him wondering how he had upset her this time. He tried to catch up but she was swift and he wasn't used to the labyrinthine corridors of the star craft. He gave up and wandered back to his cabin.

Daemon knocked on Yula's cabin door and waited nervously trying to think up a suitable apology although he wasn't really certain what he was apologising for. The guard trooper in the corridor snapped her fingers and pointed at his cabin door.

"She's in my room? Why did you let her in?" He asked.

"Yula is your aid and is on the trusted list." The guard stated through her chest speaker. He pretended to strangle the air and directed his gesture to the guard in a joking fashion. He then took a deep breath and entered and found that Yula was stood in the middle of the cabin with her arms crossed.

"Oh great." he thought. "Is this going to be another lecture on decorum? I wonder what it will be this time, have I left the toilet seat up or something?"

"You are a drunk, a chauvinist and above all a corporate puppet." She said softly and held up her hand to show she hadn't finished. "However, when you aren't acting like an idiot you actually seem to show some consideration and humanity. In those moments I can't help thinking that you are the best client I have had in years. Really, I've had to put up with some real scum in the time that I've served on The Neptus!" Daemon stood open mouthed at her outburst; Yula looked at his expression and continued.

"I can see you are already bored so I will get to the point. Under that pathetic wall, you have been taught to surround yourself with I believe there is a good man skulking in the shadows. I know the corporation tells you that you need to act like a machine but you have your own thoughts and emotions. You don't need to act like they want all of the time, you can be yourself. Perhaps then you might find some happiness in the world." Her words hit him like machinegun fire and he couldn't help agreeing to the hurtful truth. He walked over to the bed and sat himself down upon it.

"The man in the shadows you speak of is still there." He tried to focus his words to explain what he meant. "But like you said I have been trained to keep him in the shadows. The majority of the time I cannot invoke him even when I'd like to. I think that now I keep him hidden to evade feeling the torment of the path I have taken. But, maybe, if you have seen glimpses of him, perhaps there is hope." He said crossing the room and holding his hand out as a truce. Yula eyed his hand suspiciously before she reached out to hold it.

"If I can give you hope with but a few words then hope has been returned to me." She said shaking his hand and bowing.
Daemon and Yula spent the rest of the day into the night chatting about their failures and triumphs. He told her about Suix and how he missed her warmth and touch. Yula slowly relinquished her secrets of how she had become an aid. He was horrified to hear that she was sold at such a young age, to the captain of The Neptus because her father was a hopeless gambler and drunk.

"It's a terrible universe if a father could sell his own daughter to rid himself of debt!" He felt angry and sick to the stomach.

"It wasn't all terrible, the captain sent me to the Al'Guhn school for three years to train to be a hostess and aid on this fine craft. He has never raised his hand nor beat me, even when several of my guests have complained in the past." She whispered softly in his ear as she rested her chin on his shoulder.

"Is this why you can't return to Dandibah because you are owned by the captain?" He tried to be cautious with his wording but they came out all wrong.

"Yes and no. The captain released me from duties five years ago and I was free to take up another career. Instead, I stayed because I am a prize that he won and I wouldn't wish to disgrace him, even when he begged me to go to find a new life. The reason why I can't go back to Dandibah is simple. I'm a disgrace to my own people." There was no vehemence in her tone only sadness.

Daemon wondered what his own people would make of him now. He suspected that they would no longer recognise him as one of their own. The more he thought about it the more uneasy he became so he tried to dismiss the doubts he felt. He changed the subject until they both fell into reminiscing about happy times in their respective pasts until the morning arrived.

Yula guided him, hand in hand, to the cryogenic bank in the top level of The Neptus Daemon was already shaking at the prospect of being iced. He had taken a couple of travel pills to try and ease his nerves but most of the symptoms he exhibited were psychosomatic. A queue of people had formed inside the huge white room the walls of which were obscured by an uncountable number of coffin shaped cryogenic tubes. There was a funny smell in the air; a mixture of pre-travel sweat and an alcohol tinged scent which he associated with embalming fluids for some reason.

"Why are most of the people waiting to be iced in couples?" He asked.

"We will be sharing the same tank." She replied with a wry smile. "I thought you read the itinerary?" She laughed and assumed he was joking when he shook his head.

Daemon looked to the single man directly in front of

them and wondered why he hadn't been coupled up. He must have sensed Daemon's stare and turned around cradling a domestic cat, he had the rank-pins of a 1st lieutenant of Xen on his tunic. The cat had silvery grey fur and piercing green eyes which appeared to be fixed on Daemon.

"Look at the pretty cat," Yula said in a sing-song voice as she petted it bringing a noisy purr from it with each stroke of her hand.

"Good morning Lieutenant. I see you are travelling with an aid." The 1st lieutenant said curling his lip with dissatisfaction. "But where are my manners, let me introduce you to my wife." He said excitedly. Daemon looked about the queue of people but failed to see the 1st lieutenant's wife.

"Meet my wife Tanya." He said proudly holding out the cat for Daemon to appraise.

"You're fucking what?" Daemon blurted. The cat flashed a claw at him and nearly took out his eye before the man stepped away hugging the cat with a frown on his face.

"There, there my lovely Tanya, the nasty man obviously doesn't like your beautiful form." He said petting the cat with comforting strokes.

"Why are you being so rude Daemon? That's his wife!" Yula hissed and slapped his arm.

"The cat is his wife?" He exclaimed wide eyed rubbing the sting from his arm before Yula dragged him away so they could talk in private.

"When military officers are married they are away from their loved ones for years at a time and often the partners cannot cope with the solitude. So sometimes a small percentage of married couples agree to take a procedure known as the Chione-pact. Its where..."

Daemon put his finger over Yula's lips and nodded.

"I think I understand what they do but I would never understand the motives involved." He whispered.

"That's because you have never truly been in love. His wife suffered terrible pain during the transfer of memory and personality imprinting. It is a tremendous sacrifice to make for someone. Not only because of the physical pain but because during the transfer you can lose memories and traits. You can literally end up sacrificing your personality, and if it happens it is irreversible." Her eyes were wide.

"I feel sorry for the cat! I wouldn't want some soppy bitch imprinting on my brain." He said jokingly.
Yula's eyes went cold and she struck him hard across his face.

"Why are you so heartless?" She screamed. "They have shown their love for each other by making this pact. The lieutenant has suffered too you know, his part of the pact is to become a eunuch." She explained.

"That's just weird! Is it to stop him fucking the cat?" He was obviously disturbed by the idea and grabbed his crotch to reassure himself, while he pulled a sickly face. Yula turned her back on him indignant with rage and noticed the queue had vanished and an administrator was rapping on a data-pad impatiently.

"Come on, let's get iced. At the moment I don't want to share a tube with you but as I'm contractually obliged to do so. Let's get it out of the way so I don't have to listen to any more of your mindless shit." She grumbled and led him towards their designated cryo-tube.

CHAPTER 15

The Plants

The secret academy on Vex II was a great deal bigger than Daemon had expected, it was effectively a small city installed in the very bowels of the sterile planet. The installation was so deep under the extinct volcanic rock that a full planetary scan wouldn't pick anything up, apart from a weak trace of iron coming from the indigenous rock. Yula was to be stationed on Vex III and gave Daemon a cold goodbye as he boarded the small shuttle craft that left The Neptus and took him down to the planet's surface.

After negotiating a tight volcanic tunnel the shuttle eventually docked in a very small port about three miles under the surface. From there he was taken under heavy guard onto a pod-tram rail which descended deeper still. The pod-tram was a rickety old contraption, rusted and dilapidated with only five millimetres of transparent windows keeping it pressurised from the manmade vacuum of the tunnel. He found a seat nearest to the only bubble suit available on the tram which upon closer examination didn't look to be in very good condition either. All of the guards that accompanied him on the tram were hideous to behold, they had mechanical parts replacing missing limbs and were so heavily scarred Daemon could barely spot a patch of unsullied skin. As he watched one of the wretched men changing a full artificial bladder for an empty one he realised that they were probably veterans who were no longer battleworthy. Daemon tried to ignore the guards and the trams violent shaking as it rattled along on the lines. Luckily it didn't take very long to reach the terminus.

The platform was quiet and the air smelt stale and sulphurous as he left the tram. His nose wrinkled in disgust and he hoped the entire installation didn't smell as bad. He shouldered his belongings and set off toward the flickering illuminated signs. The signs were faded and he had trouble finding the main reception in the maze of tunnels and storage rooms. A grubby man in overalls on his way to the dock stopped to help and lit up a koll-weed cigarette.

"You lost sonny?" The filthy man said between inhaling the pungent smoke.

"Just a bit," Daemon said trying to waft away the drifting smoke. "I'm looking for the main reception to the academy."

The man started to laugh and nearly choked on the koll-weed.

"Then you are more than a bit lost my man! You need to double back through that corridor and take a left." The man said pointing to the corridor he had just come from.

"Thanks," Daemon said wondering briefly if the man was deliberately showing him the wrong way for his own amusement. However, he did as the man said and found a side corridor that went to an area in better condition. The floodlit cavern had a huge arched double door set into one of the rock faces. Two bored looking guards checked his credentials and opened the doors after tapping a complicated code into a terminal. The reception area was small and had better air-filtration units installed, so it smelt a bit fresher.

"Ah, Sergeant Daemon I presume?" a sinister voice stated. Daemons eyes fell on a disgusting sight that he suspected was the receptionist. A bulbous man was half submerged in a tank of green water, small jets of water pumped over the mass of the man and dribbled back into the reservoir he sat within.

"I'm sorry, but my rank has changed recently. I'm a Lieutenant now." Daemon replied automatically as he tried to avert his eyes from the vile looking man. The receptionist shook his flabby head as he accessed the computer databank.

"Oh yes, I see now, your rank was changed on Kyson. Yes, by Agent Rowson. I will update the system so this won't happen again." He said waving a cherub-like hand angrily towards Daemon.

Daemon remained silent as the fat man's dainty hands floated over the computer's keyboard. It was news to him that his promotion had been based on Rowson's recommendation; the knowledge caused him some discomfort.

"Before you go, you need one of these." The receptionist spluttered as he fumbled around on the desk looking for something. Daemon felt sick as he noticed the man had gills pulsating along the sides of his chest, slurping up the foul coloured water. Whatever the man was looking for he found it.

"Wear this at all times inside the facility, if you fail to wear a security transponder then the auto systems will go live and gun you down."

Daemon grabbed the silvery badge from the monstrosity and then wondered where he was actually going to.

"Your room space is in area J, take the third elevator and then follow the signs until you reach the officer's wing. The room is outfitted with a terminal which will brief you about the academy and a study rota. Goodbye Lieutenant Daemon!"

It felt to Daemon that the receptionist had read his mind and he hoped it wasn't the literal truth as he walked off thinking, Yeah see you fish boy!

Daemon found his room eventually and was surprised with the cleanliness of it. It had a large bed, generous locker space, its own separate shower and as promised on his desk was a computer terminal that could access internal data-banks. He logged on and saw that he had been granted class four security clearance which allowed him to send messages off-world. He glanced at the briefing and rotas he was expected to read and was daunted by the quantity of data. Rather than browsing the material, he took a shower to wash away the sweat from travelling. The water was discoloured by a red tint even though it had been filtered through various chemicals that made it smell like detergent. It wasn't very hot but it soothed him all the same. Before he left his room he sent an internal message to Dr Miles, stating that he had arrived at Vex II. An automated response arrived instantly saying that Dr Miles was currently busy and the original message had been received. He turned off his terminal and headed off to the mess hall to tend to his growling stomach.

The mess hall was busy with student officers, far too many for Daemon to count with an empty stomach, so he rushed for the queue at the food bar. The food on offer was a mixture of steamed vegetables and protein-based slush that came in three colours. He presumed the brown, gelatinous paste was beef flavoured so he heaped a good portion onto his plate. When his plate was nearly overflowing with food he found a vacant table and tucked in. The vegetables were nice but the brown stuff didn't taste of much, for all he knew it could have been reconstituted shit. It certainly looked like it and it was a far cry from tasting like beef. He listened to the banter of a few students nearby and a blonde haired girl in the group took his interest. Her name was Juni and she had apparently joined up for officer training because her father had left her a vast amount of money in a trust fund. Providing she followed in his footsteps and became an officer of Xen then she would be granted access to the trust fund. She had hoped to graduate as an officer and leave Xen for a life of luxury, however, because she hadn't read the small print she had accidentally signed up for a ten-year contract.

Daemon had to suppress his laughter at her situation and thought it served the rich girl right. Daemon himself had signed up for life and the only way out he had was either a bullet through the head or punishment, which would mean death whatever the case. He chuckled at the hopeless thought that he might have retirement to look forward to. Compared to his future ten years seemed like a walk in the park.

The weeks went by in a flurry and Daemon concentrated on his studies and continued to send messages to Miles but received only one human response, stating; they had him working around the clock on some kind of breakthrough. Daemon didn't have the security clearance to be told of the project

Miles was currently working on and he apologised to Daemon for not coming and seeing him.

Sherry was also being allusive, she had sent a few long distant messages describing the harsh training conditions in the CORE, other than that she bragged that she could get into an E.C.A. in a flat thirty seconds. Daemon thought it more likely that the lying slut could get out of one in that short amount of time if she had some CORE troopers cock available.

This attitude was half born out of jealousy and frustration as the new academy hadn't provided much opportunity to forge sexual relationships. The career-minded students were all competing to become the best and had little time to waste on distracting love affairs. He had made a lot of new friends though, including the blonde haired girl Juni but even she avoided the bedroom like it had been infected with the Miles-virus. Daemon thought his balls would eventually explode with the lack of fucking that went on at the Vex II Academy.

Daemon's crestfallen attitude at this realisation had not gone unnoticed and one night a group of drunken students had decided to take Daemon on a tour of the various laboratories at the academy to try and cheer him up. Some of them had better security clearances than the others so they could access the areas where experimental projects were being conducted. The laboratory spaces were quiet and dark because it was around midnight and together, armed with flashlights, they wandered from one lab to another showing him odd looking machinery and prototype weaponry. He feigned interest and made the right noises at the right times but he didn't really care for science, he had only come along on the tour because Juni was among them. By the time they had reached the higher security rooms most of the students had made their excuses and gone back to their rooms leaving him alone with Juni and a geeky young man called Todd.

Daemon's attention had been riveted to the curves of Juni's jumpsuit as he stood behind her and he tried to imagine how she would look stripped naked on all fours with her face turned back to him. His train of thought was interrupted as he realised that Todd and Juni appeared to be in the middle of a whispered argument.

"Not tonight Juni. I don't like purgatory it always gives me nightmares whenever I go there." Todd whined.

Daemon had heard the students talking about a place they had nicknamed purgatory and he still didn't know what it was.

"But we must show Daemon, he has to know what the plants are." Juni pleaded as she pulled on Todd's arm.

"Look, I'm a bit drunk and I'm not really bothered by seeing anymore," Daemon said shrugging. Juni ignored him and had a desperate glint in her eye.

"Swap security passes! Just for tonight, I promise." She said fluttering her eyelids. Yeah, swap passes Todd, and then fuck-off and leave me alone with Juni! Daemon thought.

"Fine, but we swap back tomorrow morning and you

owe me one." Todd said begrudgingly exchanging passes before wandering off grumbling to himself.

"Look, Lieutenant," she said to Daemon as she waved the security pass in his face with a beaming smile, "I'm Dr Todd." She grabbed his hand and pulled him along the corridors until they reached a plain looking opaque door.

"So what is this place?" he whispered leaning closer to Juni feeling the warmth of her body in the cold ambience.

"Ssshh!" she giggled and placed her finger on his lips, "Listen." Daemon strained his ears but was unable to hear anything. Just as he was about to comment on the silence he heard a muffled moan followed by a faint scream of agonised pain coming from behind the door. His eyebrows shot up in the air inquiringly.

"This is where they keep the plants." Whispered Juni and dug her trembling fingernails into his arm. "They say that it's a horrible fate, even worse than being spaced."

Daemon's mind went back to the spacings he had seen and doubted that there could be anything worse.

"Have you ever seen a spacing?" he asked - Juri shook her head. "Well I have and it's not the prettiest way to die. I don't see how this plant's business can be worse." As he spoke he realised he really didn't want to know what could be worse than it.

"You will see." she said pressing the security badge against the reader plate of the security panel.

"Welcome, Dr Todd." A synthetic feminine voice

issued as the door slid open.

A tsunami of smells and sounds washed into the corridor making both of them step back involuntary. A powerful stench greeted the uninvited guests and a cacophony of screams reverberated around the room. As the two intruders covered their noses from the worst of the onslaught and stood at the threshold of the room the groans and screams could be discerned as containing words.

"Please make it stop."

"It wasn't my fault. I didn't mean to kill them. It wasn't my fault."

"Please, just give me some drugs. It hurts so bad." Many other cries were incomprehensible through the din that assaulted them at the doorway. Down the length of the long chamber were a large number of low tanks filled with viscous fluids. In each tank lay half-submerged abominations baring numerous tumour-like growths upon their chests. They thrashed around in agony as they cried for help or a quick death. As soon as Daemon stepped into the room the auto-systems clicked and began to sedate the poor vat-people. The shouts died down to a low murmur within seconds but the people still jittered around in their sickly baths.

"What the fuck are they?" He asked nervously.

"These are the plants. They are punished officers, criminals and sometimes misinformed volunteers. It's a living hell for them all." She said leaning against his tense shoulder wiping a tear from her eye.

"No, I mean what are they doing here and why are

they so disfigured?"

"They are forced to grow organs for transplantations, real organs, not the artificial types that fail after a few years. Each plant can grow five, maybe seven organs per week. The facilitators of this organ bank can program each 'plant' to produce kidneys, hearts, livers, lungs; usually what is needed or most profitable at the time.

"The last time I was here they were growing a lot of lungs to sell to planets with extensive koll-weed use. If there is a profit to be made then Xen will be the first to take advantage, even if it comes from something as twisted as this." She explained as he noticed one of the plants trying to lift itself out of its tank. Its arms were atrophied and it could no longer bear the weight of its chest where numerous sacks of flesh pulsated and throbbed with each beat of its sickly heart.

"Kill me!" The plant gurgled as it tried in vain to escape the vat which contained it.

"That's no longer human, it isn't even an animal!" Daemon couldn't tell if it was the demon speaking within him or it was actually his own thoughts.

A loud snapping sound came from the arm of the plant and bones splintered through pulpy flesh as the creature collapsed under its own weight. Blood snaked across the surface of the water as it howled in pain. Juni grabbed tightly to Daemon and they both took steps backwards as alarms started flashing around the chamber. A door at the far end of the room opened and a number of laboratory auxiliaries came running in.

They seemed to ignore the trespassers and concentrated upon the damaged plant. The auxiliaries grumbled to one another until one of them pulled out a shock-stick, striking out at the creature which brought more shrieks of pain.

"Come on we have to go! I'm not ending up like one of those!" Juni cried. Together they ran for the exit and heard the terrible crackle of the shock-stick again and again. That night Daemon's dreams were haunted by visions of ghastly apparitions straining to escape from eternal entrapment.

"Has it been three months?" Daemon scratched his head and double checked the calendar on his terminal screen. The dates were correct, he had been training on Vex II for that long already and it only seemed like a few weeks had passed since he had arrived. He thought about the amount of knowledge he had learnt and it was only then that he agreed to the electronic calendar.

"Oh shit! I'm late for A.F.E." He said noticing the time and rushing off to class. When he arrived at the Advanced Field Engineering workshop he was already dripping with sweat.

"You are late again, Daemon! Your time keeping is appalling." The giant tutor growled.

"I'm sorry Master Kelob but I lost track of time." He mumbled as the huge man stomped towards him.

"Lost track of time? One day you may find yourself leading an elite unit into battle having previously organised an air attack. If due to your poor timekeeping they find themselves in the midst of that attack, you're comrades exploding under the force of the air strike, do you think they will sympathise with your pathetic excuse that you lost track of time? Well, do you boy?" He rasped gripping Daemons throat and squeezing. "I don't give a fuck about your excuses!" The giant of a man yelled as Daemon started to lose consciousness under the tutors iron like grip.

Finally, Master Kelob let him go and allowed Daemon to breathe. His vision had tunnelled and he struggled to inhale as the huge man stalked off to the large display at the front of the classroom.

"Right then we are going top-side today so get suited up. And this time in FULL battle-kit, if anybody forgets a spare ammo clip or even a pulse pump, I will overload their E.C.A.!" Kelob roared.

The students rushed to their lockers and began to bench test the E.C.A.'s before they put them on. The suits were probably over thirty years old and every one of them had a minor glitch. Daemon had named his suit Sherry because he wanted to get inside it as often as he could. He smiled as the last light on the battery unit didn't come on, that was normal for the suit, it never came on. He could have spent some time changing over the light fixing but he kind of liked the little glitch, as though it somehow gave the suit a personality.

"Danny! What have I told you about your fusion kit?" Kelob yelled at a nearby student and slapped him round the back of his head. Daemon chuckled and began to get into his suit; he liked Kelob and found his tutorials interesting even though he could be a little unhinged at times. The prospect of going up-top was always exciting as not only did it provide a much needed change of scenery it also had an element of danger about it.

Vex II had two tiny moons orbiting quickly around the planet and usually had high wind speeds on the surface. The atmosphere was thin and poisonous, thin enough so that the students were in little danger of being thrown off balance; there was enough of it for the wind to stir up dust and other debris. Ten students waited at the drop zone for a lifter to bring them the day's assignment. A recent storm had abated and visibility had improved for the time being. As the students assembled some flood-lamps to illuminate the drop zone Kelob stayed inside the ground-crawler which was parked to the rear of the area. He monitored the students from there as he could no longer wear an E.C.A., ostensibly due to a traumatic event he endured in the past. Some of the students assumed he had claustrophobia but none of them had the balls to ask him about it. The lifter arrived and hovered above the drop zone for a while before dropping off three large containers. The students had to work as a team, no leader had been appointed but they were expected to act as an organised unit with no bickering among the ranks. As soon as the first container was opened Daemon knew just at the sight of the components what the device would look like fully assembled.

"A fucking fyr-spur? Aren't those out of date?" He

complained and then realised Kelob would have heard him because his com-line was open.

"I heard that Daemon. Any more moaning out of you and I will cut your balls off. You shit-dicks better get assembling that fyr-spur, you have twenty minutes!" Kelob growled through the communications.

All the students rallied around Daemon because he seemed to know what they were assembling. They all dug in and started to piece together the huge field weapon. Daemon had read about fyr-spurs before he joined up with Xen. These weapons were technically banned from the battlefield as they were considered to contravene accepted standards of warfare. Firing a fyr-spur against a battalion of charging soldiers would quickly render them all into boiling pools of plasma. For Daemon's part, he didn't understand why you couldn't use these weapons on the battlefield but could nuke an entire city. He wondered who came up with these ridiculous rules of conflict and where the boundaries of "common decency" started and ended. Daemon had often opined on the subject when drunk and summarised his thoughts with the argument that if you asked the corpse of someone who had died on the battlefield through legal methods and one who had been killed illegally whether they felt their death was justified by law? Neither of the fuckers would answer.

They had almost assembled the weapon when one of the students pointed out they had several bits left over, the bits which Danny had been in charge of.

"You were supposed to couple those up to the rail-forks and that needed to be hooked into the main power conduit!" Daemon said as he pointed to the pieces of machinery scattered around Danny.

"Well, I didn't know where they were supposed to go. I'm an officer, not a sapper." Danny said cockily.

"Why didn't you say you still had them?" Daemon asked incredulously.

"The twenty minutes are up." Kelob interrupted laughing. "Strip it down to its bare bones and re-assemble it. If it takes all night you will do it within the allotted time!"

The students glared through their helmets and if they could have shot lasers from their eyes then Danny would have been blasted from the surface of the planet.

"What are we doing this for? We are officers; shouldn't we have technicians to assemble field artillery while we supervise?" Danny moaned as they began disassembling the weapon. Luckily Kelob was too busy laughing to hear his gripe.

Four hours later and after a number of failed attempts the students stood panting and dripping with sweat around the completed fyr-spur.

"Twenty-five minutes and thirty-two seconds," Kelob said laughing again. "I can't believe you can't assemble that old lump of shit in twenty minutes!" he added rubbing salt into a wound.

Daemon had felt the anger building up inside him after

each failed attempt. With a couple of trained personnel, he knew that the task could be achieved in less than fifteen minutes but each time this group attempted it something went wrong. As they were all tired their efforts got worse and already Daemon had admonished Danny for making the same mistake twice. He could feel the demon stirring and no matter how hard he tried to shake away the sensation it kept on coming.

"Start again." Kelob stated, "You're not going anywhere until you've completed this exercise. I don't care if I have to send down for fresh air tanks to make sure you don't all asphyxiate!" This was clearly a jibe in their direction as even suits as old as the ones they were wearing had enough air for several days use. Something cracked in Daemon.

"Fuck you Kelob. And your mother! This isn't training, it's humiliation!" he cursed.

The Comms fell silent and the anger he had felt was quickly replaced by dread. He wondered if Kelob would disregard whatever impediment ailed him, suit up and come and kill him.

The other students were also silenced by his remark and stood around staring at each other. Daemon bit his tongue and ignored them setting about dismantling the device. It was a while before the others began to help him.

The students finally finished assembling the fyr-spur in the allotted time after another two attempts. The first had been hampered by a brief dust storm that had reduced visibility to the point they had trouble identifying the pieces of kit. They had all stood around expectantly waiting for Master Kelob to comment but he had merely called out, "Too slow, try again."

This time everyone worked as a team and they were soon left standing next to the large gun emplacement in utter silence. According to Daemon's chronometer, it had taken just over seventeen minutes but confirmation had not been received. Just as he toyed with the idea that Kelob had fallen asleep a burst of static announced that the Master was about to speak.

"You have successfully completed the task. Lieutenant Daemon you are now the squad leader. It's time to see if you have done your job correctly. Fire the weapon!" Kelob said through the crackles of the comms.

A few of the students complained about Daemon being the new leader but the majority seemed relieved with the decision. Daemon ignored a few comments about him being the off-spring of a gutter whore and tutors cock-sucker as he readied the weapon.

"Everyone clear the field. Test one. Firing," He commanded as he activated the weapon via remote control. Nothing seemed to happen, in fact, the gun didn't even charge up.

"Stay your ground people. Test two. Firing." He said, silently begging the machine to fire so they could go back to the academy for something to eat. The gun charged up but didn't fire.

"It's the focus grid. It has probably got some dust in it

during the storm." Danny said as he ran towards the fry-spur.

"Danny, get back here now! Daemon cried. But Danny was already climbing up the side of the machine and reaching for the focus grid.

"Bring that soldier back in line squad leader!" Kelob barked into the comms.

"I'm going to shoot you if you don't get your ass back here!" Daemon shouted as he chambered a round in his side-arm. A number of the other students had also drawn their pistols.

Daemon took a step towards Danny and noticed that a display on the maintenance panel of the fyr-spur was starting to flash. It took a moment for Daemon to realise what it implied.

"Oh fuck, it's going to blow!" he cried running for cover, "Everyone get away from it. For fucks sake, Danny get off it!"

"I'm telling you, it can't fire because there's dust all over the..." Danny didn't finish his sentence as the fyr-spur exploded. Daemon dived behind a jut of rock and cowered up into a ball like some kind of armour-plated animal. He hoped his fellow students had done the same as the blast-wave ate at the rock he desperately sought sanctuary behind.

"Suit compromised, containment levels dropping. Ninety-two percent. Eighty-six percent." The feminine voice of his suit informed him as he sensed the demon stirring again.

"Do you want me to take over kid?" The demon asked

as though it was as nervous as him.

"Yes, please. It's just down here isn't it?" Daemon said as he stumbled dreamily down a row of darkened cells in his mind. The demon nodded and rushed off towards the light at the opposite end of the tunnel. The demon claimed Daemon's body again and patched up the compromised suit within a heartbeat. It then raced off to aid any survivors from the aftermath of the fyr-spur explosion.

The damp stone felt cold against Daemon's flesh and the darkness of a small room surrounded him. He tried to ball himself up, to regain some warmth but his body was shivering too much to stoke his internal fire. A flickering light illuminated the stony cell when he opened his eyes fully and he noticed there was a door set into one of the bricked walls.   How long have I been here? He felt it had been a long time and the only company he had had during the unknown time period was his own thoughts and the demon inside him.

"I can help Daemon, if you wish me to aid you?"

"I'm probably in here because of you!" He hissed as he tried to remember how he had got into this miserable place.

"You're burning up with a fever, please try to calm down."

"Fuck you!" He said as he turned over on the stone slab to face the wall.

"That door isn't locked you know. They are waiting for you outside that door."

"How do you know that? I'm not stupid. They have put me in here for a reason but I will be damned if I know why?"

"I disabled the lock three days ago when you were sleeping. I have told you this many times now and you have given me the same answer each time."

"Please get out of my brain. It hurts every time you say a word. Just go and I will pretend you never existed. Not that I ever believed you were ever there." He said shaking his head in confusion.

"Open the fucking door and get out!" The demon roared in his head.

Daemon leapt at the command, his legs felt like jelly as he eased himself up from the stone slab. He had to fight the demon inside him for the complete control over his body.

"You win, I can't fight you forever. But if you're lying about the door being unlocked, I'm going to..." His words faded because he couldn't think of any kind of threat which would deter the imaginary creature.

He edged himself to the door and held the cold handle. He pulled and the door opened bringing bright lights which washed over him making him squint. When he reopened his eyes he could see that the hall outside was filled with people that he didn't recognise for a few seconds before his mind began to piece together the faces. The people applauded, clapping hands and cheering. Kelob, stood at the front of the crowd greeted him first.

"Welcome back Lieutenant Daemon!" He said and

continued to clap.

Daemon had been in solitary confinement for one month as punishment for firing an unchecked or unready field gun. The accident had killed two of his squad and though he had been punished he was also congratulated for saving seven of the squad. The surviving seven had healed up by the time he had served his sentence, they had suffered serious burns, decompression and toxic shock from the thin but poisonous atmosphere. Each survivor personally thanked him and gave him a yellow flower of peace. Juni had organised a celebration that night dedicated to him and had invited a number of students to it but Miles wasn't among them.

The party was in full swing when he discovered he had missed the funerals for the victims of the fyr-spur explosion due to his confinement. He was glad because he hated funerals and didn't really know what to say during them.

"So hero, have you got a kiss in that bloated head of yours for a fellow peer?" Juni asked, swaying slightly due to the strong cocktails she was consuming. She was wearing a sleek blue dress that clung to her curves, leaving very little to the imagination. He put down his drink and stood up nodding drunkenly. Juni threw her arms around him and cocked her leg so that her knee nestled against his balls. What first started off as a rudimentary peck soon changed into a heavy passionate kiss. Some of the other students in the canteen began to cheer when they noticed the luckiest bastard on Vex kissing the stunning woman. There were also a few jealous jeers which came from a group of geeky technical students. Juni finished the kiss and smiled.

"Wow." She said as she wiped her hand across her full red lips, smearing lipstick across her cheek drunkenly.

"There's plenty more where that came from." He said cockily but she was already staggering away.
His knees gave way so he sat down again wondering if that was all he would get from Juni.

"You have a lot of catching up to do Lieutenant, not just in my classes but the other studies you missed during your confinement." Daemon hadn't noticed Kelob sitting down at his table until he recognised his grave voice. He felt nervousness creeping up his spine when he remembered what he had told Kelob to do with his mother.

"Listen Kelob, I was in a rage when I..." Kelob cut him off with a gesture.

"We all have to do what is necessary when we are officers; you insulted me with vicious words but in doing so gained dominion over the other students who rallied to your banner so to speak." He peered around the room and then narrowed his eyes upon Daemon.

"It was all a test. You assembled a time bomb nothing more! We knew there would be casualties and we had a med-vac team waiting just over the ridge. When the fyr-spur exploded, you had patched up most of your

283

teammates before the med-vac team arrived. You saved the majority of them which is acceptable within the standards of Xen. As for your uncouth words towards me, I've already taken revenge for them. By making you the squad leader I knew you would get solitary for firing the weapon. That makes adequate amends for your insubordination. One day you will make a fine officer and for what you did up there you have made us all proud kid!" Kelob said before standing up to salute him. Daemon, remaining seated, responded with his own salute and didn't even see the punch that exploded against his jaw tipping his chair over and sending him crashing to the floor.

"However, that pays for your words towards my deceased mother you disrespectful bastard!" Kelob laughed before wandering off to the bar leaving Daemon groaning in pain.

Four more months rushed by before Daemon graduated. He had learnt so much at the Vex academy, advanced interrogation, engineering, sabotage, counter-intelligence, espionage, piloting and all manner of new combat techniques. He had hoped to date Juni during this time but she had fallen in love with one of her tutors who had pulled some strings and put her on a communications and linguistics course. She was very happy because it meant she would be more of an administrative officer and would be kept away from the battlefield. After the rushed graduation ceremony he was promoted to the rank of first lieutenant of Xen by

Kelob himself. He had one week of downtime to enjoy before his ship arrived to take him to his first real assignment at Sigra III where small scale guerrilla warfare was taking place in some of the cities.

Daemon was sat in one of the café bars available to the students nursing a glass of iced water after a heavy night. As he waited for his breakfast order to arrive he noticed a young officious looking man scanning the tables. Almost inevitably he headed over towards Daemon.

"Communication for you, Lieutenant." The runner stated and handed Daemon a sealed com-tube before standing nearby to see if a response was required. Daemon opened the tube by placing his thumb on the security checker verifying his identity. Inside was a simple piece of writing paper which was covered with a script he recognised. He dismissed the runner and checked that no-one was nearby before starting to read it.

Hello Daemon, its Roz here. They have taken me to a secret academy on a planet called [CENSORED 1 word *dir001a] they are treating me well and I'm learning as quickly as I'm able. You know me D, I was never very good at learning so it's taking some time. The food is unbelievably good and the tutors are amazing, they need to be I suppose to put up with me. I hope they haven't censored this letter too much, but I suspect they will have taken chunks out. You see they don't

really tell you what you can write about or not.
[CENSORED 33 words *dir012b]
They won't tell me where you have gone but I know you have left the Rock academy that much I have been told and I also hear you were promoted to [CENSORED 1 word *dir002c] I miss you a lot and I hope they are treating you as well as they are keeping me and I hope you eventually shook off that weirdo Miles. I didn't like him, I thought he was a bit of a prick! Oh yeah, did you eventually manage to bang that auburn haired girl, I can't seem to recall her name because of all the stuff I'm learning, but I remember that you found her attractive (Who didn't?) It's hot here and it has an extensive [CENSORED 1 word *dir001a] surrounding the [CENSORED 2 words *dir013d] but it's better than wearing an E.C.A. on some kind of sterile planet. It's much better having the sun on your back. I'm not sure how you reply to this message but I'm sure you could send it via Xen Prime, they will happen forward a message for you.
 Until we meet again my friend...
 ROZ

   He stared at the communications for a while, reading it over and over, trying to fill in the gaps which Xen had removed through censorship. He wondered how old the message was, it could be months old due to the actual freighting of the message. One thing was certain; wherever Roz was posted they obviously were not allowed to use the general electronic communications systems.

"I miss you too big guy." He said misty-eyed into an empty glass.

CHAPTER 16

Krell

It was around 3:00 a.m. when Roz stirred in the medical deck after checking himself in. All was quiet apart from the purrs of deep sleep coming from the other beds in the ward and the humming of machinery. The blind around his bed had been pulled back by one of the nurses as he was sleeping which he took to be a good sign that his body was making a recovery. He had been stuck in casualty for over a week after the encounter with Madeline during which time they had patched up his lung and transplanted his damaged kidney.

The doctor had been keen to point out that the kidney was organic rather than artificial since nothing was too good for the elite passengers of the Solis Maria. Roz was both impressed and pleased at this news as he had heard horror stories involving artificial organs being rejected by the host, being prone to malfunctioning or even failing catastrophically leading to the patient's death.

Roz asked who the donor was he as he wished to thank them or, if the donor was dead, their nearest kin. He was told that the information could not be released due to privacy regulations which struck him as being odd. He couldn't understand why any donor would ask to keep his identity a secret, but nevertheless he counted his blessings. He realised that the Kommando School had deemed him valuable enough to have provided adequate insurance to afford such an operation. The cost must have been astronomical and he wouldn't have had enough money to pay for the operation if he had been saving for twenty years.

A dull throb began to pulse in his chest and waist as the painkillers that had taken earlier that night began to wear off. He closed his eyes and attempted to fall asleep again knowing it would be a race against time before the pain kept him awake.

Early the next morning a pretty nurse wearing a pale green uniform with dark blue stockings began her rounds. Roz, who had lost the race in the early hours and had suffered a restless night, was already awake and waiting for her. As she came to check his charts he could smell her perfume which made a welcome change to the medicinal odours of the sterile ward.

"Morning Corel," he smiled, "I thought you were going to leave me here alone all morning."

"And good morning to you too mister, up nice and early I see. Are you hungry?" She asked as she checked the read out from the computerised monitors.

"Starving," He answered.

"I'm not surprised, had a rough night have you?" she said as she noted he had been awake for some hours.

"Yeah, pretty awful night's sleep. Can't you increase my dose of painkillers again?" he asked.

"You know we are trying to wean you off them, we don't want to turn you into an addict do we?" As she answered she pressed a button on the bedside table and a breakfast tray slid out which she placed upon the bedside. It had a large yellow egg, some tiny cucumbers and a pitcher of bluish fluid upon the tray.

"Eat all this breakfast and drink the build-up and Sandi will bring you your meds later. Don't you dare leave it like you did yesterday or you will get me fired." She laughed and tapped the breakfast tray with her fingernail. Normally Roz would have been crippled by shyness in front of such a pretty woman but Corel had a pleasant manner which he found settling.

"Sandi?" he asked mischievously and grinned like a naughty child, "Isn't she that really sexy nurse?" Corel suddenly looked stern but a smile formed slowly as she realised he was deliberately trying to get a reaction from her up.

"Whatever floats your boat mister, but while you are here can I suggest you get your eyes fixed because Sandi isn't very sexy at all." She claimed and then looked a little nervous. "But don't tell her I said that!"

"Of course not," He laughed easily, "Do you know when I'll be allowed to leave? I really do feel much better now and I have a lot that I need to do." He said changing the subject.

"You can leave soon mister, but we have to keep you under observation for a while, just in case your body rejects the new kidney." She said as she ruffled his pillows.

He sighed and knew modern day transplants rarely failed but he supposed they had protocols to adhere to.

"However, you wouldn't want to leave before it is my turn to give you your bed bath would you? After all, it's best that you have something to look forward to before you leave this medical facility." She said jokingly, winking at the same time.

"I wish it had been your turn last night," Roz returned, "the nurse was so heavy handed that I thought I was being beaten to the inch of my life." He grumbled and started to eat his breakfast.

Corel started to laugh and patted his hand.

"Yes I know. That was Wendi, the nurse with the muscles. I'm sure she used to be in the army before she became an auxiliary nurse here." She said through fits of giggles.

"She reminds me of one of my former tutors, Mistress Jemm she was a heavy set woman who enjoyed inflicting pain on others, just like Wendi." He said and immediately regretted mentioning his past as the chastising voice of Brother Brian started up in his mind.

"If you must speak of the past then make it up, don't go around revealing secret information!"

Roz had almost forgotten about the strange voices he

heard or the odd visions he witnessed.

"Who is Mistress Jemm? She sounds like a prostitute of some kind?" Corel said in a high pitched voice before laughing out loud.

"She was just a teacher at the high school I went too." He lied and blushed. She gave him a wiry look and didn't press the question.

"Anyway I have to go now if you need anything just pull that cord." She said and started to wander away as he immediately pulled the cord.

"Cut it out mister and try to get some sleep." She said without turning.

A few days later, when Roz was released from the medical wing, he rushed to his cabin and immediately checked the cleaning rota-board attached to the door. He scanned the list and to his surprise saw that Karli's signature was against the previous day's cleaner registration. He looked at his time piece and double checked the date.

"She's alive?" he said out aloud in his excitement. Hoping against hope he began thinking through what may have happened.

"Madeline must have lied to gain an edge during combat." He finally concluded.
He felt happy and sick at the same time and felt the need to get reassurance that Karli was really still alive. He tapped the reception button and waited for the receptionist to answer.

"Room service, how can we be of service?" The

receptionist sang.

"Please can you send Karli the cleaner to my cabin?" He asked nervously.

"Certainly sir, if you wish to make a complaint then you may issue a statement now, to me sir?" The female said.

"No it isn't a complaint I just…"

"I see sir! I will send her to your room immediately." The woman interrupted him with a disgusted tone in her voice before she hung up.

Roz frowned at the silent wall speaker then sat down on the side of the bed and waited. A few minutes later the door knocked and he rushed to answer it. Karli was standing in the corridor panting trying to gather her breath. He embraced her as she kissed his lips.

"I was told you had some kind of accident but my security clearance doesn't include the medical wing so I couldn't visit you." She said as she tried to adjust her body from the painful embrace. "Let go and let me catch my breath!"

He relaxed his grip on her and escorted her in to his cabin.

"So what happened to you? Why have you lost so much weight?" She said ruffling his chest with worried features.

"I grappled the wrong guy in a game of Ringball." He lied, remembering the Solis Maria had a Ringball court on board.   "You never told me you played Ringball?" She shook her head in disbelief.

"I don't. That's why I had an accident. I thought I

would give it a go. I had no idea how rough the sport can get." He claimed and hoped she would believe the lies he was spinning. He so much wanted to tell her the truth but he noticed Brother Brian lurking in the dimness of the bathroom for a few seconds.

"You had me so worried, please don't do that again!" She sobbed as she smothered his face with kisses.

"Forgive me, it will never happen again. I've missed you Karli." He said as he brushed her hair with his fingers. She looked into his eyes and read his thoughts.

"I'm still on my shift Roz. Oh very well just a quickie, then I will see you tonight." She smiled as she pulled off her cleaning tabard.

Three weeks passed quickly as the two lovers comforted each other nearly every night. When the Solis Maria finally docked at the orbiter at Krell, a rich gateway planet which had yet to be annexed by any of the major corporations, Roz kissed Karli goodbye. They had both made promises they probably couldn't keep: to see one another again in the future. There was an empty hole in his heart as he walked down the gang plate into the docking station. He was tempted to run back on board to begin a new life with Karli much to the disgust of the voices muttering in his mind. Instead he caught the next shuttle ship down to the planet's surface.

The sprawling capital city shared its name with the planet itself and was surrounded by humid marsh lands which made the cities atmosphere unbearable during the summer months. He had a window seat on the transport and could see the vast evaporating mists drifting from the swamps into the city like the smoke from a huge forest fire. The starport was situated on the city outskirts of Krell to avoid debris hitting the city should any accidents occur from the abundance of shuttle crafts that frequented the port.

He didn't particularly enjoy the brief flight because the shuttle craft flew far too close to the sky-scrapers below. He almost convinced himself that the craft would hit one of the communications antennae that spiralled above some of the larger buildings seemingly missing them by a hairs length. Finally he arrived at the starport which he guessed was the only one on the continent judging by the vast number of people saturating the massive collection of buildings. He had never seen so many ships docked in one place before, the entire docking ring had been filled to the brink of chaos with ships and people.

The journey down coupled with the overcrowding caused him to be irritable and he sourly thought that the soldiers, merchants and travellers milled around the waiting rooms and kiosks like flies round shit. He pushed and shoved his way through the many customs and security booths until he arrived at the grand amenity sector which thankfully didn't have half as many security forces present as the main hub. By now he thought his face would never shed the false grin he had been wearing to avoid unwanted attention during the checks.

An automated vending machine caught his attention through smell alone, a cooked meat aroma drifted from the machine inciting a number of customers to queue up at it. When his turn came he fed a few coins into the machine and it deposited a bread roll containing a bright pink sausage. It tasted synthetic but pleasing as he watched a large screen advertising a miracle drug called Forever Young. He sneered at the Seinal corporate symbol on the side of the drug syringe as he finished his snack. The advert claimed that the drug could lengthen the average lifespan by fifty years and subdue the aging process by seventy percent. People taking this drug could live to be one hundred and eighty years old and still appear relatively young. As the advert ended it was followed by a quickly scrolling health warning and disclaimer which moved too fast to read fully. He chuckled and felt happy that he would probably live until he was one hundred and thirty years old like any other healthy human without taking shit like that and risking serious side effects. He deposited the paper wrapping into a litter bin and headed off to the main exit.

Outside rain hammered down from the dark clouds of the morning sky drenching the starport vehicle park and washing the road clean of litter. He covered his head from the downpour using a Krell-Chronicle magazine which he had taken from the pile near the exit. He peered round and spotted a taxi coming into the turning circle. The taxi stopped in front of him when he put up his thumb and the back door hissed open.

"Where can I take you?" A fat man driving the taxi said from the side of his mouth while he smoked a koll-weed cigar.

"Ever heard of Pablo Way?" Roz said remembering the address of his target.

"Sure I have, it's in the glow right?" The man's flabby neck bulged as he turned to see his passenger.

"I guess? I've just arrived so I'm not entirely sure. I'm meeting friends." He said knocking the rain off his clothing.

"The glow isn't the friendliest place mate and I generally avoid it." The man warned him. Roz understood where this conversation was going and pulled out a bunch of credits from his wallet which the man took grinning, his eyes bulging at the amount.

"This should be enough mister. Anywhere particular you are heading?"

"Yes. Take me to an eatery. I'll find my own way from there." The taxi moved off and followed a small ring road before it entered a busy highway.

"I grew up on the outskirts of the glow." The fat man said concentrating on the traffic in front of him, "I think Mama's Kitchen is still operating, it's a nice eatery where my father used to take me. Pablo Way is just a few blocks from there, you can't miss it."

"Yeah that will do, take me there." Roz said as he surreptitiously began assembling his Kommando knife in the shadows of the taxi.

The taxi crossed a suspension bridge and entered the city main, the buildings loomed on both sides of the traffic ridden road and they all appeared built in the same way. Roz was trying to establish landmarks to help him get a bearing but the architecture made it almost impossible to do so.

"Does it all look like this?" he asked after a while.

"Pretty much," The driver said as slowly made his way through a busy intersection. "Krell city was founded by a socialist movement over a hundred years ago, each citizen was granted new prefabricated room spaces as part of the revolution. That's why most of the city looks the same."

The journey continued for another thirty or so minutes while the driver rambled on about this and that as Roz remained silent. Finally the taxi pulled up at a gaudy looking diner with Mama's Kitchen displayed in neon and a cartoonish illustration of the eponymous lady tossing a pizza. Roz jumped out of the cab and ran through the pounding rain before taking a seat by the window and placing an order.

As the morning progressed Roz watched the sky growing darker and darker. The rain was not subsiding at all and before long lightning filled the skies. As Roz ate some pasta with synthetic meat he looked down the street towards the area of the city known as the Glow. It was a seedy neon lit part of town where a person had to be on their guard at all times. Its reputation as a den of iniquity was well earned and Roz perversely thought that he would feel at home there. He drank coffee until the worst of the storm was over then set off wandering around the dark streets trying to locate the address he had been given.

It turned out that behind the neon lit facade of the Glow was a warren of back alleys full of dingy bars, sex clubs, vendors and cheap hotels rentable by the hour. Making his way down the short cut of a filthy alleyway he noticed three degenerates smoking under a makeshift shelter. Roz sized them up as a group of pimps and drug pushers who would probably be flush with cash. He grabbed his sodden clothing pulling it tight around the stomach line, hunched over a little and began to drag his leg as though he had been wounded. The men spotted him and, as if they had caught the scent of blood, started to move down the alley towards him.

"Hey there, are you in trouble?" One of the men with a face like a weasel and a scrawny moustache asked stifling a laugh.

"Yeah, lost your way have you?" added a youth with a face scarred with pockmarks from acne.
As the three of them approached Roz they produced what appeared to be baton's from the folds of their capes.

"Help me!" rasped Roz twisting his face with feigned distress waiting until they were close enough for them to attack him.

As they raised their batons Roz struck out with his

knife with lightning speed severing windpipe and slashing upwards from groin to sternum of another. Within a heartbeat, both were down and dead and the last surviving one started to run, screaming down the alley crying for help. Roz raised his arm and threw his knife; the man tumbled to the floor, the handle sticking out of the back of his neck.

The entire encounter lasted less than five seconds. Roz quickly searched the bodies ransacking them for cash and anything of use he found. He stripped a long leather jacket from the running man before removing the knife from his neck. There was only a little blood on the jacket from the wound and he quickly washed it away in a nearby puddle. He lifted the lid of a nearby dumpster before stuffing the corpses into it. A few minutes later he exited the alley somewhat richer than he had entered it and set off down the Glow in search of alternative lodgings.

I will find the address tomorrow, he decided. It's probably best to have somewhere else to fall back on just in case.

From the outside the Sunset Hotel looked more like a derelict building than a place to rest your head. It suited his purposes ideally; a strictly cash and no questions kind of place. The lobby of the hotel had a pen written sign stating "Rooms for rent, clean sheets daily". The yellowed wallpaper hung limply to the damp walls in the reception area and he heard a snorting sound coming from a security cage. The proprietor looked up from a few lines of yellow powder on the table top in front of him. His eyes were bloodshot and he still held a tiny metal tube to one nostril.

"You want a room buddy? Or something else?" He sniffed.

"I'll take a room, probably for a week, maybe more." Roz pulled out a bankroll and watched the greasy proprietors eyes widen. He counted out what he thought would be enough and slid it across the counter. The man motioned for another bank note before accepting the wad of credits.

The man tried to focus on the key he held.

"Room Eleven, it's on the third floor. Hey if you need a bitch for the night or maybe a gram of zwoot, just give me a holler." He said scratching at his arm pit and pulling at the string vest he wore.

"I don't think I'll need either. However, you might be able to help me with something else?" Roz said.

The man gave him the key and leant a little closer to the bars that separated them.

"So what do you," Roz grabbed his throat cutting off his words and dragged him into the bars.

"I want you to understand that I am not here, I was never here and I hate drug dealing, pimping scum like you."

The man's terrified features were contorted against the security bars.

"Okay! Okay! You're not here and if anybody asks for you I've never seen anybody that fits your description." He gasped.

Roz nodded and let go of him, he counted out five more bills and threw them at the man.

"Well it looks like we have an understanding then." He set off up the stairs.

The room was as substandard as he expected it to be, a stale stench of sex pervaded the air. The reel player had been kicked in and glass from the shattered screen still lay on the floor next to the hollow box. The humidity in the hotel was stifling and to his annoyance, he found that he couldn't open the small window that overlooked the noisy streets below. He sat on the rickety bed and curled his lip when he noticed a dubious stain spattered over the pillow.

Fucking great! He thought as he turned the pillow over.

He felt a familiar pounding in his head and closed his eyes as he pinched the bridge of his nose. When he opened them again he was not surprised to see Gidd sat on a corner chair.

"Back so soon?" Roz said.

"Well I thought I would check up on you. See how you've been getting along in this shitty city." He said shrugging.

"I'm a bit busy as you can see," Roz said before realising he was just sat on the bed. He stood up and walked across to the sink turning on the tap and letting it run for a while before filling a cracked tumbler.

"Do you want a glass?" he asked interested in seeing what Gidd's response would be.

"No, don't need one." Gidd replied smiling wanly.

"You handled Madeline better than I thought you would. At one stage during the melee I thought she would gut you like a pig."

"Well she's dead! And to be honest with you, I'm glad." Roz said as he remembered her beautiful head rolling off her shoulders.

"Personally I think it was a shame you had to kill her. Xen could have used a dangerous little bitch like her." Gidd said sadly.

"Yep, we could have used her in the Kommando's as well. Who's this by the way?" a voice from the other side of the room said. Roz turned round to see Brother Brian sat crossed legged on the toilet. He was gesturing to Gidd who looked on the verge of asking the same question about Brian.

"Listen I have a lot of preparation to do, so please go, the pair of you!" Roz whispered, trying to keep the noise down.

"Well if you need me you only need to call." They said in unison before walking through the wall leaving Roz alone in the hot humid room.

Roz slept the rest of the afternoon and through most of the following day. He went down the hall to the shared shower room and washed both his clothes and himself before heading out to the pavements of The Glow. It was busy in the evening but as the sky darkened people vacated it quickly apart from the most naive of the tourists who would be soon be prey to the criminal element that frequented the night.

Litter kicked up with every step he took as the sun went down and the rain clouds formed from the humid heat of the day started to pour. As he walked down the Glow he was approached by pushers and pimps who offered strange sexual experiences and illegal pharmaceuticals he had never heard about before. One of the drugs he was offered went by the street name of Sanctuary, it supposedly sent the user into a waking dream where vivid erotic or egoistical fantasies played out. Pushers claimed the drug allowed the user to control the fantasy and the small blue and red pills could be purchased alongside several erotic pamphlets to get things started.

Roz felt disgusted by people's weaknesses and the people who preyed upon them. He was tempted to murder some of the dealers for the cash they carried and knew these vultures would only be missed by decrepit addicts that were nothing more than walking skeletons. He refrained from doing so knowing that he needed to stay out of trouble tonight unless he was forced to defend himself.

Eventually, he found the address he was looking for and waited, across the street in the entrance of one of the alleys facing the large apartment block. The building was in similar disrepair to the majority of buildings in the Glow but it had heavy-set guards on the main entrance. Fast food establishments had been built out of the ground floor of the building, hugging to the host like parasites. A skinny man dressed in an odd suit wandered out of the Shink Burger Bite carrying a small paper bag of fast food. He rooted around in the bag with greedy hands then noticed Roz stood watching him. He threw the bag on the floor and began running across the street towards him and Roz ducked back into the alley. As the man approached he was ranting something that Roz couldn't hear over the din of the heavy rain. He pulled a pistol from his pocket and waved it around manically screaming.

"You're on my patch bitch!" he yelled.
Roz put his hands up and backed off further into the alley.

"Give me your creds and then get the fuck off my patch!" The man barked as he waved the gun in his face.

Roz nodded and reached into his pockets as if searching for some cash before he lashed out with his fists. The pistol rattled across the floor as the man crumpled to his knees, his head loping to one side on a broken neck. This was something Roz could have done without but he looted the corpse then hid it under a pile of sodden trash and retrieved the pistol which was a customised military side-arm. He undid the clip and whistled when he saw it was full of Red Devil's, expensive armour piercing ammo. The dealer must have been wealthy to have owned such a piece of hardware. Roz decided to find a new vantage point to watch the building and he walked off to find one.

As he emerged back onto the main strip of the Glow, rain dripped off his dark blonde hair. His eyes fixed on the security guards patrolling the entrance. So close to my target, yet so far away. He thought pondering over how he could slip past them unnoticed.

A group of whores made their way up the street, laughing and jostling one another, kicking up rainwater further drenching their sodden clothing. The guards started to call out seedy comments to them as Roz made his way across the street. The prostitutes stopped at the entrance and attempted to ply their trade by dancing erotically to the guards. Roz sensed that the guards suddenly seemed nervous and started to wave the girls away, voicing threats.

He made it to the sheltered entrance of the Shink Burger Bite without being seen, as the prostitutes not taking lightly to the threats, started to return insults and took out hidden blades. The standoff was just the distraction Roz needed and he began sidling down the street towards them. One of the guards stepped forward and fired twice into the air with a shotgun scattering the unsavoury flock from the entrance. As the other guards moved out waving batons Roz slipped in to the building while they gave chase to the fleeing girls.

The interior of the building was even worse than its exterior, refuse lay rotting, piled up in the corners of the reception hall and the night porter had fallen asleep watching animal porn on a spool-reader. He was snoring loudly cradling a BORE repeater close to his chest. Roz snuck past the sleeping porter and tried to ignore the horrendous sounds of a pot-bellied pig being raped by a guy in a leather mask. A hand written sign on the elevators stated they were out of order, so he made his way to the stairwell and entered.

It was dimly illuminated by cheap flickering light bulbs which were coated in grime and the unmistakable stench of urine was cloying. As he climbed the steps he avoiding touching the handrail and crumbling plaster walls aware that he must not leave any physical evidence. The target's address was on the thirty third floor of the building so he slowed his pace to counter the fatigue burning in his calves. By the time he reached the twentieth floor he was breathing deeply and could smell two drunkards who had passed out in the doorway to the flats before he even saw them. They were still clutching empty spirit bottles as he silently walked by them and continued up the ill lit stairs. Sweat was dripping down his shirt by the time he had reached the thirty third floor.

To his surprise this level seemed to be the most poorly maintained in the entire dilapidated building. He had been expecting his target not to be living in such squalor and quickly decided that he needed to remove all preconceptions from his mind. He entered the corridor leading to the rooms and suppressed a slight smile when he observed that only one light in the corridor was working and even that seemed dim, casting deep shadows along the length of the moth eaten carpet.

With silent footsteps he made his way to the door of

room 33E. It was made of plastic and had an old fashioned tumbler lock under a fake brass handle. He reached into his pocket and found his Kommando knife. Removing two ceramic prongs from the grip his hands worked the lock using the needle like instruments until he heard a mechanical click. Satisfied he tried the door handle and opened it fractionally. Light trickled into the corridor and he silently cursed.

So you are awake... or you fear the dark when you're asleep?

He looked at his time piece seeing that it was 01:06am then edged his ear to the gap in the doorway. From inside he heard the muffled sounds of rampant intercourse, a bed frame was thumping against the wall and he now recognised the feminine sobs of pre-orgasm. The door creaked slightly as he entered the elaborately furnished room.

A long comfortable arrangement of seats faced a huge reel-player which displayed a live-feed of some kind of orgy but the sound had been muted. In front of the longest seat was a glass top coffee table with an array of coloured powders set in lines upon the glossy surface. Roz moved into the middle of the room, knife in hand, trying to pinpoint from which of the three doors that lined the far wall the sounds of congress were coming from.

To his horror a toilet flushed from one of them and he stood rigid as the toilet door opened revealing a huge man waving his hand in front of his face and holding his nose with the other. The man's eyes were watering and he was muttering curses seemingly pre-occupied by the stink that he had just created. By some miracle he had not yet noticed that an intruder stood like a statue in the middle of the room. Roz realised that he did not have time to charge the man as his movement would surely give him away. He hurled his knife towards the man as he turned round and looked into the feral eyes of his killer, it pinned him through the neck and sank deep into the door frame. The huge man gurgled and then went limp, hanging off the knife. Roz looked to the other door, the noises inside had suddenly ceased.

"Gary?" A muffled voice from behind the door issued. Roz stood frozen, caught between trying to answer the query himself and going to retrieve his knife. His heightened senses detected a mechanical clinking sound which he assumed was an automatic weapon being primed. Instinctively he rolled behind the seating and levelling his pistol at the door. Molten plastic showered from the door and plaster flew from the opposite wall as machine gun fire made a jagged line across the room. Roz felt a bullet whiz past his ear while he kept the pistol targeted on the damaged door. The wall exploded with more bullets before his target leaped through the thin plaster into the room continuingly firing the machine pistol randomly. Glass and chips from the furnishings danced around Roz as he kept low behind the seat.

"Call up security bitch!" The naked man yelled as he fumbled around with the machine pistol, it had jammed or it was out of ammo and he was too drugged up to notice the difference. Roz was up and running closing the distance in a fraction of a second then pushing the pistol nozzle against the side of the man's head.

"Tell her everything is alright and don't call security!" Roz whispered.

The man turned to face Roz dropping the machine pistol and grinned at him.

"Fuck you big guy!" he spat.

The pistol discharged and his head burst open like a ripe watermelon. Roz watched the man topple to the floor before clambering through the large hole into the bedroom. A young girl, barely into her teens stumbled around the bedroom gathering up her clothing. Roz felt disgust in the pit of his stomach as he saw she had clearly been drugged and probably didn't know what day it was, never mind where she was.

"Did you call security?" Roz asked and noticed the phone dangling off the hook near the bedside cabinet. The girl started to sob and hugged the clothing she had gathered to her bosom.

"I don't know? A man answered but I didn't say anything because I was scared. Is Ralphy going to be okay?" She slowly mumbled without facing him.

"Well, I don't think all the wonder-glue in the world will piece his skull back together. So no, he isn't going to be okay." He said.

"Please don't kill me." She said while covering herself with a bed sheet.

"I have no reason to kill you. Tell me, was Ralph a good guy to you?"

"Sometimes, he bought me things. He looks after me. Why?" She said cowering under the bed sheet.

Roz felt something going cold inside him.

"He looks after you?" he asked trying to keep the rage out of his voice.

"When my Mom is away he takes care of me." She answered with tears streaming down her face.

Roz stood for a second trembling. He felt on the verge of losing control of himself. A mixture of loathing at Ralph's depravity and disgust at the girl's acceptance gripped him as he held the pistol tighter.

Suddenly the apartment door banged open and he heard security guards entering, crunching the plastic underfoot. The spell was broken and he rushed to the bedroom window, kicked it through, jumped on to the rusted fire escape and disappeared into the rainy night.

CHAPTER 17
Darkness is my friend

Roz was two stories down the fire escape when he heard the footfalls of the pursuing guards above him. He instantly let loose a couple of shots upwards to give them something to worry about in order to buy him some precious seconds. A few shots were returned blindly as Roz continued running down the metal steps. At each level he glanced at the windows to see if the rooms were occupied but at this time of night, all he could see was drawn curtains. A few floors down he saw what he was looking for, a bare window. He stopped running and smashed it with the butt of his pistol, knocking away the shards of glass left in the frame. Rather than climbing through it Roz continued downwards grasping the handrails and sliding down them in order to try avoiding making any noise.

Seconds later he heard the guards reach the broken window and come to a halt. He heard one of them speaking into his radio stating that the target had gone back into the building. It would take them a while to realise that it was merely a decoy and Roz took advantage. As he worked his way down the side of the apartment building he was careful to dodge the beams of light thrown up from the security personnel gathering in the street below.

Whoever he had just assassinated clearly had connections judging by how quickly the place was swarming with security. He soon came to a place where the steps had corroded through and was forced to leap across the perilous drop. On landing his footing slipped and he landed heavily against the far railings sending a vibrating metallic sound reverberating. He couldn't afford to stay outside much longer so when he noticed a broken window that led in to an abandoned apartment he kicked through the rotting wooden panel covering it and crawled through in to a room that smelt mould ridden.

It was almost pitch black inside with only a sliver of light showing from beneath the exit to the corridor. Noiselessly he approached it and pressed his ear to the cold damp surface. It was eerily quiet so he opened the door and headed towards the main stairwell. As soon as he pushed open the heavy fire door he was greeted by the sound of boots thundering up the stairs. He risked a quick glimpse over the bannister and saw a dozen or so men in body armour bearing automatic weapons snaking their way upwards.

Unless he could find another way out it looked to Roz that he would have to shoot his way out but a pistol against machine guns stacked the odds heavily against him. He silently returned to the corridor and started searching down it. At the very end he located an old maintenance elevator which, unsurprisingly, was out of order. He forced open the doors and looked down; it appeared the shaft was not blocked by the lift so he would be able to get down to the basement. He climbed in then, with difficulty, pulled the lift doors back together as far as he could manage before lowering himself down on one of the cables. By the time he reached the basement his hands were coated in blood and grease.

He made his way through a disused maintenance area which looked as if it was being used to store junk from numerous apartment clearances. Beams from flash lights revealed the presence of guards already searching the basement, he had only one option left, he prised up the cover of the storm drain and he leapt into the darkness below.

The drain was swollen from the heavy rain and it soon became apparent that the fast food establishments above discharged their sewerage in to it. He waded waist deep through the rapidly flowing water as a gurgling sound from above preceded a disgusting fallout that rained upon him until he moved away from the main tunnel of the sewer. Here the flow was lighter but for over a mile he had to force his way through the gathering mass of stinking effluent gagging with each foot step. During the ordeal he could feel the spectre of Brother Brian encouraging and chastising him in equal measure as if he was actually behind him with the folds of his fighting robes floating sickly on the bed of shit.

"I've been in worse places Roz. It was a good idea to come down here; the security forces won't follow you down these filthy tunnels." Brian's voice boomed stifling a laugh.

Roz ignored him and tried to speed up his pace.

"Leave me alone!" he shouted into the tunnel, his voice echoed for a while and he felt alone again at last.

"They're nothing but sprites, meanderings of past memories!" he tried to convince himself and continued down the river of human waste.

Eventually he found a rung ladder which he climbed and found that it opened up into another storm drain. On the walls glow signs were mounted which he followed until he recognised a street name. Dripping and stinking he climbed another ladder but found that the man-hole cover at the top of it was stuck. He had to use all his weight and strength until it popped open and he clambered, exhausted, into a deserted alley. The rain was heavy enough to wash away the worst of the filth from his clothing but he would need to change into fresh clothing soon.

He was about to set off down the street when the howling of turbines from a city security floater with its search lights scanning the alley came from above. It hovered and started moving towards him as he dived under a pile of sodden packaging. He waited holding his breath, worrying if they had Infra-red cameras.

Rain water dripped off the cardboard onto his face as the floater performed a thorough search of the area. When the floater moved off he could feel his heart pounding. He was about to move when he heard footsteps approaching, two city security men dressed in task force uniforms were searching around the garbage piles.

"They can't have gotten too far. We have the entire area pinned down!" One of them grumbled pulling up the collar of his coat in a vain attempt at stopping water pouring down his neck. A beam of a flash light passed over Roz in his hiding place.

"Come on let's get back to base. It's pissing down and this area isn't our jurisdiction!" the other man said.

"Yeah, OK, you're right. Why the hell should we patrol the streets on foot when they are warm and cosy in their search vans?" The two city guards wandered off back the way they came and Roz waited a few more minutes before racing back to the sanctuary of the hotel.

Roz holed up in his room for eight days, living on delivered junk food and bottled water. To keep himself entertained he rented the reel-player owned by the old lady next door who was a permanent resident. The news reels briefly mentioned a gangland killing a few times but the journalists mostly concentrated on the headlining news regarding recent terrorist bombings. The terrorist groups were bombing the city randomly because the government had banned a bloodthirsty sport called 'The Gauntlet'.

He couldn't understand all the violence over a sport, although as he had never been that competitive himself, he had never really seen the attraction in sports in general. The day after he had carried out the hit, a bomb had exploded in a busy shopping mall killing seventeen people and maiming forty-two. The relief he felt at this atrocity, detracting attention away from his own activities was tempered by the disgust he felt at the terrorist's cowardly behaviour. He wondered why they killed innocents instead of the actual people that had banned the sport.

Marcie, the lonely old lady from next door, often visited him to chat and to watch her favourite reel-player programmes with him. He didn't mind her visits particularly when she brought her cat with her which was a great ball of ginger coloured fur. It felt calming to his touch and he had always liked cats since he was young and had one called Warlock as a pet, it had been skinny and black with only one eye. The other eye had rotted out with disease because his father refused to take it to the veterinarian to clear up the infection.

Rotten old bastard! He thought, meaning his father rather than his pet. On this particular day, Marcie was seated next to him cradling a steaming cup of tea.

"Did you say you were leaving tomorrow?" she asked. Although she tried her best to hide her emotions he could hear the tinge of sadness distinctly.

"Yes, I have a long space flight back to Alim where my home is." He said, not taking his eyes off the screen so that he didn't have to look at her as he lied.

"Well if this is your final night I will make dinner for two so you don't need to order any more that take-away rubbish." She smiled and brushed away a wisp of white hair from her brow.

"That sounds nice Marcie but really you don't want to be bothering yourself making dinner, why not let me cook?"

She tried to argue with him but he insisted that he would cook a nice dinner for them both.

"Okay, dinner at seven then but don't you be cheating and getting one of those filthy take-outs." She cackled and waved a finger in his direction before hobbling to the door.

Roz ventured out into the city to purchase the food, after being cooped up in the small apartment for so long the fresh air felt good on his face. He was smiling as he briskly walked into a large food market full of competing aromas. As he wandered around the various stalls he realised that he would miss Marcie when he left, in the brief time he had known her they had almost become each other's surrogate mother and son. He worried about her health and wellbeing especially living in such a horrible city as Krell. How she had survived to a ripe old age was beyond him. He stopped at a greengrocer and placed a number of exotic vegetables into the shopping basket hanging off his huge arm. The basket was soon bulging with a variety of products including two fresh poussin that had cost him an outrageous number of credits. As he was making an occasion of it he found a small, but well stocked, wine merchants. He was having trouble choosing a good vintage, until his eyes fell on a bottle with a blue triangle and two leaping hunting cats.

"Madeline's family wine!" He chuckled and grabbed the expensive bottle.

As he turned to pay he noticed two men wearing the typical corporate dress of crisp dark suits coming toward him. One placed a heavy gloved hand on his shoulder.

"You will accompany us back to the station house." He commanded.

"I can't right now." Roz replied calmly with a genuine tone, "I'm cooking dinner for a friend. If it's okay with you I will drop by the station after the meal?"

The two men laughed and one of them pulled out a set of handcuffs.

"OK," Roz said resignedly, "if you insist."

He struck the bottle against the face of the man with the cuffs. It shattered in an explosion of wine and blood and the man fell to the ground screaming and reaching for his face. It had all happened so quickly that the other man was still in shock.

"I said I will come by the station when I'm done, why

do you people have to be arse-holes all the damned time?" Roz shouted as alarms started to wail in the store.

"You're a dead man!" The corporate man yelled as he attacked.
The melee was a chaotic blur of hands and feet as the two fighters tried to penetrate through each other's defences. Roz was forced backwards by the ferocity of the attacks and a well-timed kick sent him careering into a pyramid of stacked tinned products. As he scrambled away from the pursuing attacks he knew he was in trouble, whoever his assailant was he had the upper hand, the attacks came in like swift rapiers within a duel. He needed to buy a few seconds.

"Ok, you win! I will come quietly." Roz said trying to get his breath back. He picked himself up from a pile of food stuff and raised his arms above his head in surrender.

"Finally!" The corporate man said with a grin reaching into his jacket pocket to retrieve a set of hand cuffs. A bullet casing danced across the shiny floor and the man blinked twice holding his chest. Wetness spread around his fingers and a dizzy sensation filled his head.
Roz secured his pistol within the folds of his jacket and walked over to the two fallen men and quickly field stripped them of credits and a few weapons before rushing for the exit. Security alarms rang in his ears as he leaped past cowering merchants and tumbled out into the busy streets of Krell.

Marcie waited until midnight for Roz to return, she was dressed in her best blouse and a long sweeping skirt. The sparse make-up she had applied was faded as she had wept a number of times already. She stared with incomprehension at the table that had already been set for two when she had arrived in Roz's room. Just plates, cutlery and wine glasses to welcome her, no smells of cooking, no sounds of greeting, no signs of Roz. She had waited patiently, she had been waiting many years now and was used to it. She had thought Roz was different from the rest of the undesirables living in the hotel; they only seemed to care for themselves but he had appeared to care for her. Obviously she had been mistaken. As the hands on the clock swept across the last lonely seconds of the day she finally hobbled out of his room and returned to her own, closing the door behind her.

Her own room was dead; a mausoleum dedicated to her autumn life, a few pictures here and there; her daughter who had died so young and so many years ago, her husband who had left, unable to cope with his grief. Her favourite chair sat next to the window looking down on the harsh streets below. Here was an impression in the carpet left from her reel player, there her cat was curled up asleep on the radiator. She collapsed into her chair and placed her face in her hands, tears fell from between her fingers as she understood that she was alone once again.

Roz raced through the streets looking desperately for an escape route.

Bastards! Couldn't they just wait another day, why now? Why? He ran round the corner of a street leading on to the Glow and saw a patrol approaching him.

"Terrorist. Open fire!" The guard captain cried out. Roz cursed and ducked down a side street as bullets ricocheted off the corner of the building leaving pedestrians leaping for cover to avoid the gun fire.

"What have we told you Roz? When a city is on full alert due to terrorist attacks, you don't run! If you run the guards assume you are a terrorist and a target." Gidd shouted to him from across the street shaking his fist with anger.

"Not now!" He whispered knowing that Gidd could hear him no matter where he was.

He approached an escalator leading to the underground cylinder tram and leapt down it three steps at a time. It was the early evening rush hour and the platform was full of people waiting to catch the tram home. It was so busy that he estimated he wouldn't be able to fit on the first tram to arrive unless he could make headway to the front quickly enough. He could hear from the squealing of the steel lines that a tram was already approaching and the wall of people in front of him was too vast to get to it. The guards behind him pushed at the crowd, searching the many faces as they passed. They were getting closer to him faster than he could press on forwards himself. Although he had never been a good gambler he had his final wildcard to play. He tapped on the shoulder of a man in front of him.

"Can you smell nerve gas?" His voice was raised just enough so that the people around him could hear. His statement was like an echo in the crowd, people mimicked his exact words and chaos spread through the gathered throng.

The days of watching the news reels had paid off, the public's mood was already panicked and speculation was rife that the terrorists may threaten to attack using nerve agents in crowded areas. Panic rapidly billowed in to hysteria and Roz ducked down and bulldozed his way towards the waiting tram through the people trying to work their way back up on to the safety of the street. The tram was automated and waited patiently, its circuits oblivious to the riot on the platform. He looked back and could see that the guards were being swept away from him. He dived inside the tram accidentally elbowing a passenger in the face. He didn't apologise and made his way down the rows of seats until he found one which had a news reel player. He collapsed wearily into the seat as the tram started down the lines leaving the pursuing guards behind.

The journey took him swiftly through the under-city towards sector five which was close enough to the space port for him to walk the rest of the way. He watched the news reels as they came in and was shocked to notice a live feed of a camera set at an odd angle. Piles of bodies lay around the station platform, some of them still, others were twitching spasmodically. An anchor man appeared in a small window at the bottom of the screen, a bizarre looking fellow with spiky blonde hair.

"This scene of terror is live from the Glow!" He said excitedly.

"At the moment the terrorists have yet to claim responsibility as the innocent people are left dying after the nerve gas attack in the underground station. The cowardly terror group Glaive is suspected to have sparked the attack which has killed so many. Survivors are reporting that a man tried to warn the people in the cylinder station that there was a bomb about to explode and that the pathetic security forces ignored him.

"Why do we pay taxes for such a shoddy security force? Are we safe walking the streets? No! Are we under constant threat from terrorists? In this reporter's humble opinion yes we are! This is Rod Szuzek for Cable 4 News."

Roz turned the news reel off and wondered how long it would take for the authorities to realise that there had not been an attack and that the fatalities had been caused by the stampede he had started. The tram stopped at sector five and he made his way through the station to ground level.

The streets were saturated with people who didn't know if the tramline was safe to use having just heard the news. The people seemed torn between going home and risking death or just waiting around to see what else might happen. He didn't feel like making his way through such a large crowd so he made his way to the road side and entered a waiting street taxi.

"Take me to the space port." He said to the driver who wearing a pale blue smock and sun glasses.

"You picked a fine day for it. The terror group Glaive has just set off a bomb." The driver said as he drove the taxi onto the highway.

"Yeah I know, I've just heard about the gas attack." he said trying to look as convincing as possible.

"Nah, that's old news mate, they have just set off another one in the industrial sector. It's blown all the circuits to one of the nuclear plants. If that mother goes off we won't have to turn the light on to take a piss ever again!" He chuckled. "I hear the fire force is there setting up containment fields and attempting to re-route the safety controls, we should be alright. I hope."

"What?" Roz said in disbelief. It appeared like luck was truly on his side and that all events were a confluence to allow him to escape.

"I don't understand why the terrorists are so cooked up about the ban of a sport." he said as he took off his jacket, the ambient temperature in the taxi was humid and stifling.

"You're not from round here are you son? The Gauntlet games were a good income for the average Joe. I could make up to two hundred credits a night selling game tickets to taxi punters. Not to mention the money I made from gambling on the fighters. Nope those days are gone and now I have to scrape a living ferrying folk up and down the city" He paused. "Not that I condone terrorism friend." He added nervously. The driver was quiet for the rest of the journey to the space port.

The space port was busier than ever due to the terrorist attacks, tourists and merchants seldom stayed in a place where they could be blown up at any moment and were looking to get off planet. Roz reached in to his pockets and pulled out a meagre wad of credits, he had left most of his money back at the apartment and the fresh produce he had bought had taken a large chunk out of what he had taken.

I hope Marcie finds the money I left, at least before the landlord does. He thought glumly.

The realisation of his position finally struck home and he felt like he had hit a stone wall. He did not have enough money to buy a cheap flight and he couldn't ask for money from the Kommando school because it could link them with his mission. Nor could he risk going back on to the streets of Krell, especially, if as he suspected, he was now considered to be a member of Glaive. It appeared that he would have to rely solely on his skills and resourcefulness. One of the port bars opened as he made his way through the amenities sector, it seemed like a good place to ponder over his circumstances.

The bar had been fabricated from cero-steel and dark opaque glass forged onto the alloy walls of the port. Two burly bouncers eyed him for a while before he slipped them twenty credits each to grant him passage into the bar. The interior flashed with a multitude of colourful lights, deliberately tuned so that the customers eyes had to re-focus during their entire stay. Naked women danced and rived against numerous phalluses while scantily clad hostesses offered expensive alcoholic drinks. It was obvious this establishment catered to docked ship labourers who were ready to spend their hard earned wage on sinful pleasures and booze, like a parasite it bled them dry.

It was a long night for Roz as he asked around the bar for cheap transportation or work on board a ship. He had just about had his fill of the drugged up dancing ladies and the watered down drinks when a group of rough spacers entered the bar. Credits seemed to flow from their hands as the girls provided drinks and expensive thrills. The leader of the group clapped his hands as a male stripper danced around the table. The leader watched every motion of the dancer while a female prostitute gave him a hand job under the table. When the dancer had stripped to his bare flesh, the leader pushed the prostitute away with obvious satisfaction on his face and his cronies howled with laughter.

Roz eyed the spacers for a while longer before wandering over to the table where they were sat. He pulled up a chair and ignored the threatening looks he got from the thuggish louts around the leader.

"I thought you might be looking for extra hands." He ventured hoping for the best now that he had thrown himself into a hornets nest. The leader grinned revealing golden teeth and offered his hand to shake.

"I'm Captain Trogan and these losers are my crew." he said gesturing to the rough looking entourage around him. Whoi all laughed in unison.

"I'm Roz." He said and realised he had just given out his real name.

"Stupid fuck!" Brother Brian's words echoed in his mind.

"Well it just so happens I am looking for more hands on deck, what are your qualities?" Trogan asked as he pulled the male dancer nearer.

Roz looked around the bar, to the exit and then to Trogan, "I've done a bit of all sorts but I'm best with weapons and security. I can also pilot a craft."

"Warrior creed, I like it." Trogan's eyes narrowed as he nodded in approval. "We could do with someone on board who can handle themselves in a fire fight, be it ship to ship combat or a ground skirmish."

"What kind of weapons do you have installed?" Roz asked, attempting to keep the captain's attention on him instead of the male dancer who was sitting on Trogan's knee.

"The Raptor has a co-axle laser trident, a forward facing plasma cannon and a bank of insti-missiles." Trogan said while he smoothed his hands over the oiled chest of the dancer.
Roz nodded, he was familiar with those weapon systems and could operate them easily enough.

"Now tell me, are you in some kind of trouble Roz?

You seem a little bit on edge." Trogan looked hard at Roz.

"No trouble at all, I just need some work. I'm not fond of planets and prefer being onboard star ships." He replied returning his stare.

"Well the pay isn't that good but if you work hard we can discuss bonuses and future opportunities." Trogan said tapping his finger against his thin nose.

"That sounds fine to me." Roz said forcing a smile.

"One final question; do you enjoy a little grappling?" Trogan asked as he licked the shoulder of the dancing man.
Roz felt suddenly nervous at the thought of what the question implied.

"I'm red blooded if that answers your question."

"Now that is a shame, a muscular feller like you. What a waste." Trogan groaned shaking his head.   "Okay welcome on board, you can start by buying a round of drinks for the boys. I on the other hand need some private time with this lovely morsel." He winked and shunted the dancing man toward the private rooms.

As Roz approached the Raptor he thought that it looked like an old freight ship that had been pieced together from a handful of other ship types and upgraded more times than a robotic whore. The ship had been painted a green so dark it almost appeared black and rust had formed at the outlets to the thrusters. Trogan gave Roz a quick tour of the hull of the ship, pointing out various parts whilst giving brief stories of how he had acquired them. Roz noticed a ramming spike at the front of the ship and knew pirates often used such apparatus to attach to other vessels before disgorging a pirate crew into a merchant ship.

"What's with the privateer ram spike?" He said pointing to the tubular, fortified spike at the front. Trogan laughed and pulled him away to show him the emergency exit hatch.

"It's merely ornamental, we have never used it, but look at this, it's a type Z emergency hatch; it can pretty much couple up to any craft in an emergency."

Roz tried his best to look interested as the captain continued to drone on. The interior of the ship came as a surprise, it was clean, sparse in design and the cabins were thoughtfully laid out with the safety of the crew in mind. Emergency bubble suits hung in each cabin and a number of them could be accessed in the communal rooms. The primary drive engines appeared to be brand new and had probably been salvaged illegally from another ship. They also appeared to have had several robust upgrades.

"Expecting trouble captain?" Roz asked as he ran his hand down the stealth drive Ion coupling.

"I'm only expecting trouble from you. Only joking! Fucking hell Roz, you can't go out into space if you're not expecting trouble!" Trogan howled with laughter and shook his head.

"I suppose your right. I just haven't seen so much stuff hot wired into a primary drive engine before." He said shrugging.

"Then my friend, you haven't ever set foot on the Raptor before! She's one of the best ships in the quadrant even if I say so myself." Trogan smiled patting the core manifold. Bollocks! Roz thought.

"Well I'll do my best to help keep her ticking over Captain." Roz grinned.

"You do that my boy, you do that. Now if you are ready I'll show you to your quarters. I'm sure you'll find them comfortable." Trogan raised his hand to indicate for Roz to walk ahead of him.

Roz walked before him thinking that not only could he not trust this strange man who led the ship but what kind of death he would do to the captain if he tried it on with him.

CHAPTER 18
The Raptor

On his first night on board the Raptor Roz slept like a baby, the silent drive circuits kept the motion of the craft to a bare minimum. He couldn't help thinking of his travel sick friend Daemon and how this ship would have made his life a lot easier. His cabin was surprisingly spacious if a little rudimentary but it was clean and comfortable.

He woke up early and decided to get rid of the beard that had grown over the days spent on Krell. The water ran cold over his hands as he splashed his face, he took out his combat knife from the folds of his clothing and started to shave. The light in the room was low and he had trouble shaving due to the shadows cast in the mirror. He found that he had to concentrate hard to do a good job and had nearly finished shaving under his chin when he noticed a bump on his neck. It was strange because he hadn't ever noticed it before and he was concerned about diseases he might have caught from the sewer in Krell. What the fuck is that? He thought to himself as he examined the odd bump with his fingertips, it felt like a small square under the skin, close to his jugular.

"Roz we need to talk," Gidd said from the shadows of the reflection. Roz frowned and poked at the lump on his neck.

"This isn't part of me. I can feel it! It's artificial!"

"Leave it alone Roz, it's been put there for a purpose, now let us talk about these degenerates you have joined up with," Gidd said attempting to change the subject.

"It's a fucking corporate chip, isn't it?" He yelled, picking up his blade from the sink.

"Listen I was going to tell you sooner, but they wouldn't allow me to. Just leave it alone and pretend it was never there. Forget about it." The worry was audible in Gidd's voice.

"When did they put it in? Was it while I was in Cryo after the incident on the Rock?" He ranted raising the blade to his throat.

"What are you doing? It is a violation of your contract with Xen if you even attempt to remove the chip." Gidd said his mouth wide with shock.

Roz cut a tiny incision into his neck and slid the tip of the blade into his neck until he felt it make contact with something hard. He prised it upwards and squeezed it out with his fingers revealing a blood coated, thin bluish square. He held it in his fingers trying to examine the tiny structures covering its surface but the light was too dim to make out anything which could answer the many questions streaming through his mind.

"Put it back solider! Or I will…"
Roz dropped the chip down the sink and ran the tap. The blue square swirled around the sink before disappearing down the drain. He looked into the mirror again and noticed Gidd had vanished. A strange sensation danced over his body; it seemed all at once as if a heavy weight was lifting from his mind. He looked at his reflection in the mirror, his blood-stained neck and chest made him look like a lunatic but his eyes were peculiarly clear. For the first time in a long while he felt normal, like the person he remembered being back on his home planet before he had got involved with Xen. He smiled and said, "Welcome back Roz."

The mess hall was at the back of the craft under the cooling ducts and the crew didn't seem to notice the bandages around Roz's neck as he walked into the room. He found a seat away from Captain Trogan, who, to bolster moral among the crew, ate with his ship mates instead of in his cabin. He filled a bowl from the food dispenser near the middle of the table and recognised the brown sludge to be space paste. It was a high calorie food used on long space hauls which could sustain a person for a day as long as they drank plenty of fluids. It didn't taste too bad either and he could feel it expanding in his stomach with each mouthful consumed. The crew chatted about mundane subjects as he half listened to the tales. However one of the subjects caught his attention.

"We are heading into rogue space to the Sia mining colony. It shouldn't take more than a standard space month." Trogan informed his first officer.

"Yeah, it's one of those rogue asteroids, yielding high quantities of Molybdenum, we should get a good price and then we can use one of my old contacts to off-load it." That was Jann, another new comer to the Raptor crew who had joined up the same day as Roz.

"Jann says the colony is always on the lookout for Morphs so with any luck we could do a straight swap for all those drugs I acquired from Krell. Later on tonight Jann's going to tell me about this contact he knows." Trogan said staring at Jann with a frown of distrust.

"That's right captain." He said nervously. Trogan laughed and pretended to inject drugs into his arm. "I dare say the mining yield will decrease after we have made a visit to their little colony."

The others started to laugh as Roz left the table. He made his way back to his cabin to rest his bloated stomach while he pondered over the other newcomer. Jann didn't seem to have any relevant skills to be a spacer and he asked a lot of questions. Roz couldn't help disliking the fellow and suspected Jann was only on board because he was handsome and olive skinned which Trogan obviously admired. The contact story didn't weigh up either and he suspected Jann could be connected to the police authorities which was the last thing he needed onboard.

Roz was soon distracted by his work stripping down a plasma prong, carefully cleaning each part before reassembling the device. A voice from behind him startled him causing him to bang his head.

"Morning Roz." Jann announced loudly before laughing.

"Fucking hell! Didn't your parents warn you about sneaking up on folk?" Roz moaned as he rubbed at his head.

"Sorry Roz! Oh, that looks bad, do you want me to fetch a med-kit?" Jann grimaced at the bulge on his head.

Roz was aware that in spite of his training Jann had been able to sneak up undetected on him and his suspicions grew even deeper.

"No! Now what do you want?" He said feigning anger trying to mask real feelings.
Jann sat down next to him and held out a small flask of brandy. Roz took a few tastes to see if it was laced with toxins before taking a hit.

"It's a bit hard to fit in when you're new so I thought I would get to know you, in the hope I have at least one person I can call a friend on this drifting trash can." Jann took back his flask and took a few hits himself.

"Yeah I know what you mean but in time we will both get to know this crew and then you will have lots of friends." Roz said.

"Are you ex-military?" Jann asked.

Roz rounded on him, anger rising up his spine. "You ask far too many questions for your own good." he hissed. Jann looked horrified, fear danced in his eyes as he backed off a little.

"Look. I was only asking. I couldn't help noticing your military style walk and the way you scan a room for exits before you take another step."
Roz stood and grabbed his tool box and headed away from the prying man, he was glad his rage didn't get the better of him.

"Wait!" Jann cried following him down into the engine room. "I'm sorry, I just wanted to make small talk, most folk are proud of their military background?" Jann shook his head as Roz ignored him and disappeared into one of the service ducts.

Three weeks passed and Jann had kept his distance from Roz, he had befriended the pilot instead and then integrated with the rest of the crew. In a conversation, Roz overheard between Jann and Trogan he had heard Jann say that he had previously worked for the Seinal Corporation as a solider but was discharged after an injury. Roz couldn't find words for the hatred he felt towards Jann even if he was lying about his affiliation with Seinal.

During dinner times in the mess hall Roz developed a habit of studying Jann's every move. He no longer believed Jann was working for the police but was equally convinced that he wasn't an ex-soldier since he certainly didn't act like one. He now harboured the suspicion that Jann could be military intelligence and he slowly convinced himself that it was a fact using the logic that asking a lot of questions would be an inevitable consequence of an intelligence background. He resolved to uncover the history of this irksome stranger and find out if he had lied about his past or was even still active in the intelligence community. Nothing was going to stop him finding out the truth.

The next day Roz followed Jann from the canteen toward the water recycler in the lowest deck. Jann was cheerily humming a tune as he gathered up a number of cleaning tools before shimmying down a rung ladder. When he got to the recycle engine he began to adjust the settings and inspect the various filters removing them one by one to clean them. A foul smell of waste, both vegetable and human, drifted down the gangway to where Roz was hidden. Roz tried his best not to gag recalling the stench of the sewer back on Krell.

Jann slipped into a water resistant gown, tripped the system and pulled the main valve lever which jettisoned the irreclaimable contents of the tank into space. Satisfied that it was empty he re-pressurised it and popped the main hatch before climbing inside. Roz covered his mouth as bile leapt up his throat; he gurgled a little and tried to take his mind off the stench before he made his way to the recycler.

"Morning, Jann." Roz called out as he leaned on the porthole. Jann stopped his cleaning work and looked to see who was speaking.

"Hello Roz, what brings you down here?" He said grinning, leaning on a long swab.

"I came down here to apologise. I feel I've been behaving badly towards you and I was hoping we could become friends."
Jann shook his head and laughed.

"Nah, no hard feelings at all and I'm glad you want to become friends at last. I must admit though that I thought you were a bit of a prick when we first met." He joked and laughed some more while Roz feigned relief.

"Well I'm sorry about that, I guess the last thing you needed was me giving you some shit but there again you must be used to dealing with it down here! I don't know how you can handle the smell; did they teach you to ignore it when you were a solider?" Roz said resting his hands on the lintel of the doorway.

"Not exactly," laughed Jann, "but it toughened me up."

"Yeah, see any action?"

"Nah, I served for a term but I didn't get on the frontline, I was more in the logistics, you know, sorting out stores of gear and food for military columns, that kind of thing. But I still had to go through all of the training." He looked up at Roz who just stood eying him, after an awkward pause he continued with an edge of nervousness in his voice. "I realised it wasn't for me so I left and worked on a delta farm for a few years, that was more to my liking." His eyes glazed as he remembered the better part of his life.

"Oh, you quit did you? I heard you got injured or

something and that's why you left."

"I might have gotten carried away when I was telling the story." He said, the smile leaving his face as he folded his arms defensively allowing the swab to fall to the dirty floor.

"So which outfit did you work for?" Roz pried.

"It was the Seinal Corporation but it really wasn't anything good, just logistics." He said feeling suddenly prone in the metal box, especially now that Roz was almost snarling.

"Don't take this the wrong way, my friend." Roz smiled,   "But I fucking hate the Seinal Corporation and everyone in it from the bosses at the top down to the lowest piece of shit in the pecking order." Roz slammed the hatch shut locking the mechanism in place as Jann banged on the tank and screamed but the noise was muffled by the thick steel plating. Roz ignored his pleas and began to whistle the tune he had heard Jann humming minutes before. He smiled as he pulled the jettison lever propelling Jann into the deep unforgiving cold of space stopping his cries dead...

"Goodbye, Jann!" Roz said waving at the imaginary diminishing figure before he turned around and spent a few minutes rigging the machine to make it appear to be the scene of a terrible accident.

Jann was missing for over twenty four hours before anybody realised he was no longer on board the Raptor. It would have been longer if it wasn't for the pilot wanting an Ion impeller cleaning and raising the alarm.

Captain Trogan gathered the crew together and ordered them to search the ship to see if there had been an accident although privately he hadn't ruled out the prospect of foul play. Eventually one of the crew found blood inside the jettison tank and after investigating Trogan assembled the crew near the water recycle machine.

"I've taken a look at the evidence and it would appear that Jann left the recycle engine on standby before going inside the tank. It looks like the circuits ran the standard routines and purged the tank. Let this be a lesson to the rest of you to follow procedures and not to take shortcuts. I know none of us really got to know Jann but it's customary as part of the Raptor crew to have a wake for our dead companion." Trogan looked sick and he was clearly upset with the loss of the little pet that he had been grooming. "If anybody knows something more about the incident then you may come to me in private with the matter."
Roz admired Trogan's leadership and cunning, the way he was attempting to root out wrong doings if they existed without losing any face among the crew by directly accusing anyone.

"Okay then. The wake will be at standard seven, space time. Now everybody get back to work!" He barked as he peered at his time piece.
Luckily nobody among the crew apart from the captain had any affinity with poor old Jann.

Roz looked out through the viewing port in awe, the cup of coffee held in his hand had gone cold a long time ago and whenever he sipped it he grimaced at the stale taste. Outside, in space, he could see the massive ash blue asteroid drifting slowly and turning end on end. On its chaotic surface he could see tiny lights and artificial structures massed deep in the larger of the craters.

"So we have arrived at Sia." He said to nobody in particular frowning at the installation and imagining the asteroid as a beautiful animal and the colony a parasitic organism upon its grand body. Every so often a shimmer of some kind of shielding system blinked and then faded. The ship banked slightly to follow the path of the asteroid, tracking the colony to keep it steady in an orbit around the centre of gravity. The ships inter-com crackled and hissed for a few seconds.

"Get your shit together we should be docking soon. Well, as soon as these assholes give us the docking code. When we dock I want everybody suited up, armed and ready. Jann assured us that we shouldn't expect trouble but I'd prefer to be ready if any shit goes down." Trogan's voice faded and the inter-com fell silent.

Roz smiled to himself as he thought of Jann's corpse floating around in the middle of fuck knows where and was surprised that the captain even mentioned him, he must have lusted after him even more than he had suspected. He watched a bank of red lights flashing within the installation before heading down to the armoury.

The captain had informed the crew about the drug deal that morning and everyone understood the roles they were to play. Roz had been assigned as the personal body guard to Trogan based on his imposing stature and knowledge of weaponry. Judging by the way the captain had set up his crew for the deal Roz suspected that he was expecting more trouble from the miners at the colony than he had let on to. The Raptor glided through the air-seal shields and into the docking bay of the mining installation. The bay appeared devoid of other crafts and personnel which troubled Roz since the miners could deactivate the air-seal shield exposing the docking bay to the deadly vacuum of space without endangering any of their own men.

"Captain, something about this doesn't feel right." Roz said voicing his concern. The captain nodded in agreement.

"I know what you're thinking Roz but we have done deals like this before. Stick to the plan and we will all be home free."
Roz shook his head and grabbed Trogan's shoulder.

"I can't see a welcoming committee either? They have the tactical advantage." Roz noticed the captain's shoulders rise betraying an obvious sign of doubt.

"Listen to me! These barbarians don't have tactics they are so inbred they can hardly think. We do the deal, we get out and everybody gets their cut. It's what we all want." Trogan hissed, his patience fading fast.

"Trogan, I think you are making a big mistake. I swear we are walking right into a trap!" The seed of doubt had

343

been planted and Trogan started to look increasingly nervous but the lure of the credits if the deal went down jaundiced his judgement. Roz could see the internal struggle playing across the captain's features.

"As captain I order you all to continue as planned." Trogan said. Roz scanned the faces of the crew and saw that most of them thought the prospect of imminent death definitely outweighed the value of their promised cut of profit.

"What if I evened up the odds?" Roz said as Trogan glared into his eyes.

"What have you in mind?" Trogan asked eagerly.

"I say we take off and then ram the dock wall using the Raptors docking spike and take this place by force. We could secure several tonnes of Molybdenum which is worth more than that shit you intended to sell. Then we jump this rock, head for Talon II and sell both the Moly and the drugs to a contact that I know. Hell, I'd even lead the charge myself!"
The captain stared at Roz in disbelief and couldn't even begin to contemplate the insanity of the plan.

"You are totally fucking nuts!" Trogan cried as he shook his head violently trying in vain to rid himself of such a crazy idea.

"The plan is solid and more likely to succeed than the death trap you are sending us to." Roz countered angrily.

"No, it's too risky, there are too many obstacles in the way!" Trogan yelled looking at his crew for support.

"No," answered Roz coldly, "The only thing in the way

is you!"

Roz lashed out towards Trogan, his straight fingers sinking deeply in to his neck impaling his wind pipe and very nearly taking his head from his shoulders. The crew gasped in horror and reached for their side arms and melee weapons as Roz withdrew his fingers with a shower of gore and turned on them; his eyes blazing murderously.

"You know he was leading you to your deaths. My plan is solid! Are you with me?" Roz yelled stepping forward.

The crew members were unable to return his glare and backed away; their hands no longer reaching for their weapons. All of them unanimously felt compelled to assent to his question more out of fear than any true leadership.

Down on Sia, the self-appointed leader of the mining colony, Qwertis, studied the image of the Raptor within the docking bay utilising his live-feed terminal screen. His entourage surrounded him impatiently waiting for his order to deactivate the air-seal shield.

"What are they waiting for?" Qwertis whispered.

"What's that my Lord?" One of his advisers asked nervously.

"What? Oh nothing. Wait!" Qwertis scanned the display. The computer had detected the engines of the Raptor starting up.

"What are they doing? Why isn't the captain adhering to the plan?" Qwertis raged to his minions. All eyes within the room were fixed on the Raptor taking off inside the docking bay. The ship hovered for a second or two in the air before its thrust jets blasted on full sending the craft out of view of the comm eye.

"Holy shit!" Qwertis screamed.

Minutes later alarms wailed inside the colony installation as gunfire and combat raged through the numerous corridors and rooms. Qwertis watched the security monitors cursing like a core trooper as he attempted to coordinate the defence of the installation utilising his minions to the best of his abilities. Throughout the carnage one thing was noticeable; several times he had witnessed a crazed lunatic carving a path of bloody melee through his poorly armed miners.

Qwertis smashed the display screen as the door to the command centre crashed open. He turned to face a muscular man stalking into the room, his suit drenched in blood.

"Wait! I can give you credits, lots of credits!" Qwertis pleaded.

Roz narrowed his eyes focusing them on the quailing man with utter hatred.

"Please spare me. I will give you riches beyond your imagination." Qwertis fell to his knees as Roz approached with a gore stained knife in one hand and a smoking pistol in the other.

"I don't need you. I now have full run of this facility and your riches." Roz announced calmly.

"I'm begging you! Please! Spare my life. I have vaults

brimming with valuables." Qwertis cowered in the foetus position, prone and terrified.

"Show me!" Roz commanded as he edged his knife against the man's jugular.

The rogue asteroid exploded like a collapsing star as the Raptor sped away into the darkness of space its hold brimming with cargo. The only trace of the massacre that had taken place at the mining installation was the plasma stream left by the jets of the craft which quickly dissipated. Roz had overloaded the fusion core of the mining station knowing full well the explosion would cover his tracks. Once again his training had paid dividends since a fusion power plant was no different than a standard nuclear cell; both could quite easily be turned into a bomb. As the explosion buffeted the Raptor Roz assured the crew they were all safe and richer than they could have ever imagined. With the crew behind him bolstered by the promises of further riches, he was now truly the captain of the Raptor and its next destination would be Talon II.

Roz lay back in the captain's quarters he had commandeered, the bed was soft and comfortable but he was a little disturbed by the metal manacles dangling from the chromed bars at the head of the bed. Although he assumed his newly acquired crew would not assault him while he slept he kept the door to his room firmly locked. As a further precaution he had a sidearm tucked under his pillow just in case of a ship board mutiny. A small red light flashed next to the bed followed by the voice of the pilot.

"Captain, we are approaching Talon II. The nav-com has picked up twelve docking ports which one of them do you wish to use?" Roz grabbed his weapon and clicked a switch on the bed side speaker.

"Hang fast one moment, I will come and show you which port." Roz raced through the sections of the ship toward the helm. The pilot had a map of the planet up on one of the many displays. Roz studied it and pointed to a port in the northern hemisphere with a large zone of rain forest surrounding it.

"Take us there." Roz commanded.

"Yes Captain." The pilot nodded.

"Let me know when you about to land." Roz instructed as he set off back towards his quarters. Roz headed past the door to his room and continued on to the life pods at the stern of the Raptor. He leapt through one of the small ducts and closed it shut before firing up the computer which brought up life support systems and the rudimentary navigational controls. This was the only functioning pod as a few days before the approach to Talon II he had disabled the others and ensured that the pilot's computer would not detect when his launched.

The small display depicted the rolling trees below the ship and the port a few miles ahead. Roz nodded to himself and pulled the launch lever firing up the jets of the life pod and sending the craft away from the Raptor at speed. He rummaged in his jacket pocket and pulled out a small black device, using his thumb he moved away the safety cover and pressed the red button beneath. The ion cell of the Raptor began to overload and soon exploded tearing off the rear end of the ship. The front portion smashed straight into the ports safety shields which had been deployed just after the first explosion on board the Raptor had been detected.

Roz guided the life pod in to the thick canopy of the forest and hoped that luck was with him. As the sleek cylinder crashed through the tangle of leaves and branches Roz hit the retro jets to reduce velocity but suddenly realised that he had made a serious error. He had estimated that the trees were of the same approximate height as those surrounding the Kommando school but he was soon undeceived. He was faced with the reality that there was a drop of some two hundred feet to the ground, not the fifty he had expected, he had cut the velocity too soon and the pod was plummeting down. Pulling hard on the stick Roz performed a controlled landing as much as he could manage and braced for impact. The vehicle plunged into the lush vegetation which absorbed some of the momentum but Roz was still struck unconscious.

He awoke with a trickle of blood running down his face from a cut to his forehead and for a moment wondered where he was. His limbs ached and reaching up he felt a painful bump on his forehead, his fingers came away crusted with dried blood. As he came too, he cursed his rashness in not waiting to break the canopy before hitting the jets; it could have easily cost him his life. He realised that as things stood it may have done yet; it had been his intention to hike through the jungle to another one of the docking ports some 30 clicks away but in his condition that could be impossible. He checked for broken bones and to his relief found that he was relatively unarmed other than numerous cuts and bruises.

He set off the explosive bolts holding the hatch on and emerged shaken in to the daylight. The sodden ground of the rain forest squelched under his boots and he surveyed the damage. The crash landing had torn a gouge in to the earth some fifty feet long and a trail of vines and debris hung behind and over the pod. With difficulty Roz moved to the panels that held the emergency equipment but he had to fight constantly against the tangle of vines and leafy plants. By the time he had recovered the survival gear Roz had to stop to catch his breath, his lungs laboured in the extreme humidity of the rain forest. His training had taught him that wherever possible he should use the resources available to him so sweat soaked and fatigued he snapped a nearby vine and sucked at the sap for a few seconds before water trickled into his mouth. The water tasted sweet, it seemed to stimulate and revitalise his ailing body. Feeling more optimistic than he probably had reason to he braced himself for the journey ahead. Using the scar in the ground from the landing to give him a bearing in relation to the docking port they had been heading towards he consulted his compass and began heading in the direction of the second port.

Initially progress was quick and in the course of a couple of hours he estimated that he had covered three kilometres which was good going in such an environment. Slowly however the density of the jungle increased as he started to find areas impassable, he often had to work his way around then estimate the correction required in his bearing. The heat and humidity began to wear him down and even worse his body was starting to feel the effects of the crash landing. His neck and legs were beginning to seize up making his progress slower and slower and more laborious. Eventually he decided that it was folly to continue without resting up, he sat upon a rotten tree branch and covered his face with his massive hands. The oppressive atmosphere and alien noises of wild creatures began to demoralise him, he felt as if he wanted to break down and cry. Traversing the rain forest had been harder work than he had first thought and with many miles still left to cover he realised the forest could quite easily be the death of him. This fugue quickly passed as he remembered that he was trained to survive in such conditions and that his worst enemy was negativity. He could not afford to mope around, he had to keep active. He decided that he would set up camp here, get some sleep and prepare to continue at dawn.

The sun had gone down and darkness shrouded the forest in a vale of shadow and Roz was thankful for was the nightfall drop in temperature. He had found a fallen tree to use as a shelter and insulated it with dead leaves but he had found that sleep was hard to find with the din of animals and insects in the air. Eventually, he dropped off into an uneasy sleep filled with dreams of falling. When he awoke he found that it was still dark, he tapped his timepiece and as the face illuminated he saw that it depicted a time completely inappropriate for the planet. He guessed he had been asleep for some hours but he had failed to align his chronometer with local time and had somehow forgotten that the days lasted 29 hours on Talon II (due to the slow spin of the planet). He realised that he had probably been suffering from a concussion and wondered what other mistakes he had made.

He shouldered his belongings and routed through his kit for the night goggles he had taken from the life pods survival kit. The goggles were poor quality; nothing like the equipment he had used before and they seemed to wash his vision with a heavy green tint which he found annoying.

"Shit!" He yelled into the forest. Anger rose inside him and he kicked off a large clump of bark from a nearby tree and howled into the night like a lunatic. His rage subsided and his heartbeat slowed as the forest descended into an unnatural silence. Roz suddenly felt as if eyes were on him, he scanned the undergrowth for the tell-tale reflection of eyes but did not see anything. A muffled growl rumbled from the trees ahead so he dropped low into a combat stance, drawing his knife and holding the blade towards the night air. His eyes strained searching the forest for any kind of movement, no matter how small.

Something huge crashed against his flank knocking him to the ground and blasting the air from his lungs. He swung wildly with his knife but found nothing other than humid jungle air. As he regained his feet something jumped on his back and he felt furred claws raking against his flesh opening up great lacerations. He scrambled under the weight of the great creature as he slashed and stabbed feeling his knife sinking into yielding flesh. He was pushed once more to the ground and he quickly rolled onto his back using his arms to protect his face and upper body. Looking directly up he could see stars through a gap in the canopy, they looked like green emeralds through the goggles. He could hear the harsh ragged breath of the creature nearby and looked towards the noise straight into the face of a great cat, its body tensing ready to pounce. He prepared for its final assault as its hind legs quivered and it leapt through the air towards him.

CHAPTER 19
Sigra III

Over the course of a year, the civil war on Sigra III had escalated from minor skirmishes in the major cities to a planet-wide war-zone. The Xen Corporations original intention had been too slowly take over control and eventually consolidate the neutral planet but it had all gone terribly wrong when the government split into two opposing factions. One side supported Xen's intentions and the other, made up from patriots, wished it to remain a neutral free-trade world. As with any conflict, it had attracted mercenaries and arms merchants from every part of the local galactic sector to feed like maggots upon the corpse of war. The Seinal Corporation had so far avoided direct involvement in the affair due to the recent merger with their Xen partners but it was common knowledge that they were selling arms to the patriotic rebels.

Over thirty five percent of the planet's infrastructures had been reduced to nuclear ashes from the bombardment from both factions. These strikes had reduced the population by fifty percent as targeting landmasses with little mineral wealth meant that non-strategic cities and urban centres were the favoured strike zones. It was clear to Xen that only a ground war could end the conflict since once the rebels had used all of their ballistic missiles at the outbreak of war they had dug themselves in to bunkers and emplacements. Xen themselves had no further wish to use nuclear weapons or else they would have no inhabitable zones on the planet once they had vanquished the enemy. Sigra III had already been poisoned enough by radioactive isotopes to make conditions for any kind of ground fighting expensive and dangerous. While the ground battles continued Xen were installing numerous atmospheric processing facilities to begin the clean-up for the eventual victory.

Daemon sat in the great hall on board the Goliath, one of the huge mobile battle stations orbiting Sigra III. He wore an all in one black suit and a peaked black cap with gold trimming. On the front of the cap was a silver "X" fixed above the peak, and on his collar were three silver stars showing that he was now a first lieutenant of Xen. Around the long table were military officials, agents, advisors and other high ranking members of the administrative staff. He noticed that Agent Rowson had taken a seat near the head of the table and was looking upon proceedings with a smug look on his face.

Everyone was sat in silence listening to the chair person, a dowdy woman with greyish hair and a hooked nose called Florentine who was Xen's leading Environmental Manager. She had been drafted in recently from Xen Prime to attempt to sort out the entire mess and stop the planet being rendered uninhabitable. Even though she wasn't the highest ranking officer present she easily dominated the room.

"As you can see by these charts most of the battle zones are highly toxic and deadly to breathe without purification units. Areas around some of the rebel held cities that were formally annihilated by nuclear attacks are especially lethal and will require our troops to wear full E.C.A. to attack. The rebels know it is costly for Xen to attempt to penetrate these places due to the toxins, radiation and diseases present in the atmosphere." She said as she pointed to the many displays at the head of the long table.

"Diseases, who the hell released those? I thought we weren't going to utilise bio-weapons on Sigra III." One of the generals of the CORE interrupted. His face was flushed with anger as Florentine glared at him and gestured for silence.

"I have been assured by the board's directors that the official line is that we ourselves have not released any kind of dangerous pathogens. Their presence is being attributed to the rebels starting to utilise bio-weapons due to the lack of anything else for them to use!" She scolded whilst trying to suppress a whimsical smile.

Several other members of staff around the table

started to laugh at this response as they already knew some of those kinds of weapon were being used by Xen on the planet.

"Unofficially, of course, the story is different. It seems that our attacks have not been at all coordinated and that's why Xen have sent me here. We must act as one; this is not a playground for personal advancement." Florentine looked around the table to check that her message was sinking in; Xen would be watching everyone's moves from here on in.

"These pictures were taken this morning. What you are looking at is the devastated city of Golette. The rebels were using the city as a training facility to create more warriors to bolster their depleted ranks." Florentine announced as a picture of a levelled city popped up on the central display screen.   "As of last night Golette was a prime target for ground assault but overnight it has turned in to this waste ground. Who is responsible?"

General Meletong, the commander of the Sigra III civilian legions nervously cleared his throat and stood up.

"The siege of the city of Golette had cost over ten thousand of my civilian soldiers within the last month. A high ranking Xen official, who I shall not name in this meeting, decided to use a six megaton device last night to finish the minor campaign of Golette."

"And why wasn't I notified? Who authorised a nuclear attack?" The environmental officer yelled and banged her fist against the table. "Sigra III has been crippled enough with radiation and toxins. If we carry on with the use of atomics then there will be fuck all left to claim! We can't profit from contaminated resources!" She looked like she was ready to burst into another outburst until agent Rowson coughed and stood up.

"I authorised the attack." He said quietly and stared at Florentine until she sat down. "However, there is no reason for our esteemed colleague to be concerned as the device used was a neutronic bomb. In other words, it was a low grade polluting weapon which has only a short half-life. I might point out that it was fucking expensive too and I would have preferred to use a standard atomic weapon." Rowson grinned and ruffled a few papers in front of him waiting to be challenged but nobody dared to.

"I would also like to point out that statistically speaking we have just removed seven percent of the rebel fledgling forces who would have caused considerable trouble in months to come." With that said he sat back down and smoothed back his salt and pepper hair victoriously. The majority of the staff had started to whisper among themselves until Florentine brought them back to order.

"Presently we have a major situation within the city of Runich. A rebel leader is currently holed up in the bowels of the city. Twenty or so years ago Xen trained this individual to get him elected to the governing body and then plant handpicked Xen sympathisers within the infrastructure of the planetary governmental network. The plan was going well and over the years we slowly got a foothold within Sigra III. However, with the outbreak of the current war he has turned against his allies and become a hero of the rebellion. His reasons for becoming a traitor to Xen are unknown but what we do know is this; he was trained by us and knows how we operate." Florentine paused and took a sip from a glass of water before she continued. "This rebel leader is called Jackabah and we believe he is the leader of the entire rebellion."

The room erupted into nervous chatter with several officials appearing mortified by the revelation that the enemy leader used to be a Xen agent and it seemed prudent to Florentine to adjourn the meeting for one standard hour.

The officials of Xen gathered again in the great hall, the displays at the head of the table depicted a huge sprawling city under which was written Runich. On another screen was an image of a short, bearded man with round spectacles wearing a blue robe. Under the picture of the man, in capital letters, was written Jackabah. Florentine paced up and down for a while under the great screens until everybody was silent.

"Let me introduce Dr. Cole of the science division." She said as a small plump man wearing a white smock waddled to the podium. He adjusted his spectacles and nervously cleared his throat; it was clear that the man wasn't used to public speaking and was more use to the solitude of a laboratory.

"The rebel leader has chosen a very strategic city to hide in. Runich has an extensive network of tunnels, chambers and rooms below the city, all of which have been converted to house a large rebel army and outfitted with various facilities such as machine shops and foundries. To the north a range of mountains and to the south a great river provide natural barriers from a ground attack leaving only two possible attack points. The city also has a large number of Ion power plants within its holdings, any kind of air-strike would cause a rupture to these plants and cause a cataclysmic reaction thus rendering an air attack impossible." Dr Cole paused for a while to allow the information to sink in.

Colonel Kolkorin laughed and shook his head.

"This is ridiculous! I have never heard the word impossible in the same sentence as our air-force. My pilots could drop a bomb on a squat pig from a mile in the sky."

"Silence! Allow the man to finish his briefing." Florentine interrupted. Dr Cole wiped a few beads of sweat from his brow and clicked up a few slides upon the display screens.

"Colonel, let me explain. The reason it is impossible for an air strike to be sanctioned is because of the unique geological make up of Sigra III. It is a planet rich in Ionic ore and its core is contains an unusual abundance of liquid Ionic elements. If one of the Ion plants explodes in Runich it will not only level the city but cause all the other plants to chain react. The science division believe the concentrated effect would surge into the planet itself all the way down to its core. The resulting explosion would literally rip the planet in half.

In turn the gravitational effects would destroy the three moons of Sigra III, all of which are owned by the Xen Corporation."

The displays showed a violent graphic simulation of such an event which brought gasps of shock around the great hall. Florentine joined Dr Cole at the podium and patted his shoulder.

"Clearly we cannot allow this to happen, the losses would be incalculable from the high yielding mining moons alone, not to mention the destruction of the planet we intend to claim." She said calmly as statistical graphs displayed the financial losses to the company.

"It is not just a question of credits Madam Chairman." Agent Rowson called out slamming his fist on the table. "The moon of Honn orbits Sigra III and it is home to one of the largest Xen garrisons in the quadrant. The training facility on Honn would also be lost; as you know gentlemen it produces some of the finest CORE troopers within the corporate universe. The shit we have just witnessed on that colourful animation cannot be allowed to happen!"

Colonel Kolkorin nodded wide-eyed in agreement.

Florentine scowled at the agent and wrapped her knuckles on the podium.

"Thank you Mr Rowson for your additional information but I think everybody present is aware of the consequences of such an event by now."

Rowson bowed and sneered in her direction then looked round the table for more support. The sneer on his face disappeared as he saw Daemon looking directly at him with a gleeful smile clearly hoping to piss him off. Florentine gestured into the shadows of the hall as a tall auburn haired woman stalked out with a precise military stride. It wasn't until the lights of the room illuminated her face that Daemon recognised that it was Sherry???

"What's she doing here?" He wondered. She was dressed in a light armoured E.C.A which was as black as the night. Even from where he was sat he could see the corporal chevron on her left shoulder plate.

"I would like to introduce Corporal Sherry of the four hundred and ninth CORE infantry. We had her shipped up from Sigra III to give you an eye witness report of the present situation around Runich." Florentine said clapping her hands with a proud look on her aging features. Sherry stepped up to the podium.

"Thank you. We captured the township of Tulnep which is four miles east of Runich. Presently we are digging in and constructing a staging post for an attack. The no-man's land in between is sparse and flat so we have a good view of the defences the rebels are assembling on the outskirts of Runich. They seem to be better equipped than we first suspected and we have spotted a number of Seinal designed field artillery weapons which the rebels have somehow laid their filthy hands on." She paused and waited for any questions.

"Using your considerable military knowledge Corporal," Agent Rowson said sarcastically smiling.

"What do you assume our casualties will be if we

attacked with our current strength against the eastern side?"

"It would be a massacre and we would be defeated before the half way mark of no-mans land. We would be cut down on the flat ground with no cover available." She reported keeping direct eye contact with the agent.

Rowson shrugged and began to whisper with Colonel Kolkorin. Florentine raised her hand to call a halt to the numerous conversations starting around the long table.

"That will be all Corporal. This meeting is adjourned until tomorrow, I think you all need to go now and work on possible options to sort out this matter as quickly as possible." She said and switched off the large displays.

Daemon pushed his way toward the podium where Sherry was reading a document given to her by Florentine.

"Corporal Sherry I presume." He said trying to disguise his voice. Sherry looked up from the document and immediately grinned.

"Well look at what the cat dragged in." She said winking and wrapping her arms around him. Now that he was closer to her, he noticed the remnants of a bruise under her left eye.

"Was it a guy or a girl?" He said tracing the slight bruise with his finger. She looked puzzled for a few seconds before laughing.

"It was a guy, we had a small disagreement and he slugged me."

Daemon frowned and pulled an angry face, "I do hope

he is suffering right now."

"Yeah, he's currently in the field hospital nursing a broken arm and a fractured skull." She said cockily before eyeing his rank pins. "I don't fucking believe it! You're a first lieutenant already?" she smiled and shook her head.

He half-heartedly saluted and stiffened his body as if he was standing to attention, while Sherry pretended to strangle him.

"Yes I am and you would have been too if you went to Vex II instead of running off and joining the CORE." He chastised.

"At least my rank has been earned. Your rank is but a ceremonial one." She said smiling proudly and thumbing the chevron on her shoulder plate. He couldn't help agreeing to the logic of her statement and thought better of pressing the subject. "So what are you doing roped up in this shitty campaign?" She asked.

"To be honest with you, I'm not sure at the moment. Nobody has told me yet but I have to attend a meeting in an hour or so. Maybe I will find out then." He said frowning and wondered what his first assignment would entail.

"I have some free time on the Goliath so maybe we can go for a few drinks after your meeting?" She said through a long yawn. It was clear she had missed out on a lot of sleep of late.

"Sounds good but wouldn't you rather come back to my cabin? After all we have some catching up to do." He whispered leaning close to her ear, brushing her neck with his fingers. She hit him so hard that he left the ground and landed in a heap on the floor.

"I don't think so!" She hissed before striding away furiously. His jaw felt like it was on fire and he wondered why he didn't see the punch until it was too late to avoid.

"You deserved that my friend." The demon growled with laughter in his mind.

"Hey thanks for your help, you could of warned me or something." He yelled, knowing he was the only person left in the great hall.

"I hope it knocked some sense into you."

"Whose side are you on anyway?" He said rubbing his aching jaw. The demon remained silent.

Daemon waited in a bleak looking hall at the side of a foreboding rusty door labelled ADMINISTRATION. He had been waiting for over half an hour before the door opened revealing a tall, skinny woman with a short black bob. She wore a charcoal grey suit with a short skirt and black high heels.

"You can come in now lieutenant." She said eyeing him with a blank stare. Her pale white skin and jet black irises made her appear to be like one of those vampires from an old graphic reel. He entered the bland room which had a table and two plastic chairs before sitting down. The woman closed the door and stood in the corner of the room behind him. He was about to speak when the woman shushed him.

"Don't speak just wait!" The door opened again and he turned in his chair and saw agent Rowson storming in with angry features on his thin face.

"Nice to see you again lieutenant, I won't apologise for keeping you waiting because I'm not forced to." Rowson sat heavily in the other seat and brushed a crease in his black suit with his hand.

"I will make this quick. I have chosen you to get your arse down to the base at Tulnep and be my eyes and ears for a while." He raged.

"Don't you have agents doing that already?" Daemon asked.

"That's none of your business, just do as I say and make a report on Colonel Lenz who is currently in command down there. We will proceed after you have made your initial report." Rowson threw a detailed manuscript and a communicator across the table.

"That bitch has it in for me." He growled and suddenly realised he had spoken his thoughts. "Are you still here? Make sure you catch that transport craft. There are more details in that shit I've just tossed at you. Now fuck off!" He pointed to the door.

Roz finally caught up with Sherry in the bar and apologised for his actions. She laughed and told him that she would let him off with a warning this time. The bar was mostly empty which enabled them to talk among themselves instead of shouting over a din of chatter. Apparently Sherry had been drafted to Sigra III a month after the nuclear war. She had started as a private and gained her corporal rank just after Tulnep was taken by force. She rambled on about the many battles before Tulnep which her squad had spearheaded and was clearly excited by the accounts. He was disturbed to hear that many of the surviving rebels had been rounded up and sent for Xen processing. He had been privy to examining film reels involving Xen processing all of which had left him sick to the stomach.

"Why didn't you go for officer training? The stuff we learnt in basic is nothing compared to what I know now." He asked as he gulped down the rest of his drink.

"That would have taken the best part of a year, probably more with travel added into the equation." She stated as she ordered more drinks.

"It was nothing like basic training it was relaxing and fun as well. You would have liked it." Daemon told her not believing the reason she had given.
Sherry shook her head and her auburn locks drifted around her porcelain face.

"Yeah? At what cost? To start hearing the voices? That's what happens as I've been led to believe." Her eyes narrowed as if she was scanning for any emotion upon his face.

"Voices?" He nervously returned.

"Don't give me that crap Daemon, I bumped into Miles a few weeks ago, he said the voices in his head are driving him to the brink of insanity."
Daemon's spine froze and the demon in the shadows of his mind shrugged with open gnarly palms.

"Miles? Where did you meet Miles?" His voice was

fierce with tension. She indicated with a nod over her right shoulder.

"He is down on Sigra III, I don't know where for sure and he wouldn't tell me where he was going even when I asked." She was pained by not knowing.

"So Miles is down there in all this shit as well?"

Sherry shook her head, "Probably not. I think he was travelling to a secret laboratory. He said he wouldn't see any combat. You know Miles, always acting secretive and strange but he didn't seem like himself." She looked around to check that nobody nearby could overhear them. "He said that if Xen were happy to control peoples E.C.A.'s he wouldn't be surprised if they took the next step to controlling their minds."

Daemon couldn't believe Miles heard the voices as well, he had thought that it was just him. Miles had been right about the suits back on the Rock so maybe he was right about this too; perhaps all students of advanced training heard voices. Maybe it was all part of Xen training.

"It's getting late Daemon. I have to catch the first shuttle down at five." She downed the fresh drink in one and saluted him before she left. He ordered another drink and watched her curvaceous body strut out of the bar.

"She is stunning isn't she Daemon?" The demon growled its voice an echo in his mind.

"Stupid question! Of course she is." He whispered to the empty table and looked down in to the remnants of his drink.

The boxy battle pod waited in the docking hanger on the Goliath. It was a heavily armoured shuttle that had been painted black in an attempt to cover up the pock marks from rockets and small arms weapon fire. While its engines idled its weapon systems were auto-tracking the motion of dock workers, the workers ignored the guns or they were oblivious to the weaponry targeting them.   Daemon waited patiently near a group of engineers who were prepping the shuttle for its descent to the planet's surface. Fuel pipes steamed with sub-zero liquid gasses while the conduits pulsated from the pressure of the mobile fuel pumps. He rattled out a number of travel pills into his palm from a white tub and swallowed them with a gulp of tepid water. The water had a chemical, bitter taste due to the on-board recycling techniques. It clawed at his throat like moonshine spirit but aided the passage of the calming little pills to his gullet.

"This is going to be a rough ride." He thought swallowing back a mouth full of bile which had surfaced in the mere thought of the journey down. The gang plate descended as the ion impellers began to swirl and whine.

"I hate these things." He said trying to steady his trembling hands as he made his way up and inside the shuttle.

Fiery plasma trails arched like a rainbow from the Goliath to the upper atmosphere of Sigra III. The battle pod rattled its way through the thin gasses surrounding the planet as fire plumes raced off the nose of the vessel, visibly licking at the viewing ports. Daemon tried to close his eyes and hoped the delicate looking glass was indeed fire proof. He nervously scanned the passenger section and noticed the other eleven people all seemed calm.

Lucky bastards! He thought as he checked his safety harness again. The shuttle settled from its violent turbulence allowing him to calm down and his stomach to settle. He could now see dirty looking clouds from outside the viewing port, to his eyes they looked more like clouds of dust and particles rather than rain. Minutes passed as the shuttle cruised through the sky, and as the little pills started to work his head started to feel numb and his stomach stopped rolling as much. The intercom crackled.

"Hang on everybody, we have just entered rebel…" The pilot didn't finish his statement when something exploded down the flank of the craft. The explosion was strong enough to roll the ship full circle in the air. The passengers held on to whatever they could grab hold of within the split second. Daemon could see many low grade missiles through the viewing port. They were circling like wolves, attempting to find niches in the crafts armour. Another one hit but it hadn't primed itself so it just dented the hull rather than detonating.

Sheer terror began to wrack Daemon's nerves, he was entirely helpless. He didn't know if he was more likely to jettison solids into his underwear or throw up the contents of his stomach as another explosion ripped off a segment off the passenger section. Wind howled inside the hull, the temperature dropped quickly as debris and unfastened passengers became a tornado of chaos. Breathing masks dropped from the overhead bulkheads and he fixed one of them to his face. Even though he could feel the motion of the engines it was almost silent as though his ears had suddenly stopped working due to the crisis. The shuttle limped to the nearest Xen occupied base and landed. It was far from the planned destination. Daemon, the pilot and two others were the only survivors.

Daemon was pulled kicking and screaming from his seat by several dock workers who carried him to a cargo box and sat him down. One of them administrated a strong sedative and started to patch up the cuts and bruises which marred his face.

"You were lucky there mate. You should have seen the other poor fucks we pulled from your shuttle." A kind featured, hulking man said.

Daemon looked over to the mess of the ship and shook his head when he saw the ground crew beginning to patch the shuttle back up.

"Are they insane? That craft won't fly again?" He cried as the hulking man started to chuckle.

"Yeah it will, those shuttlecrafts are expensive and resources are stretched thinly. They will have it patched up and ready to fly by the morning." He grinned and offered a calloused hand to shake. "My name's Tugg, it's not my real name but it's what everybody calls me round here."

371

Daemon's hand seemed tiny compared to the big man's hand.

"Lieutenant Daemon. So where is here? I mean where are we? Am I? I'm supposed to be at Tulnep."

"Tulnep? Never heard of the place, it must be far away. This is Rolands-Port a supply depot for the war effort." Tugg placed an instant adhesive patch on a cut above Daemon's eye.

Daemon pulled out his communicator and clicked a few buttons to contact agent Rowson.

"Daemon, what the fuck do you want? You can't have finished your report already?" Rowson barked.

"There's been a slight technical problem sir. I'm currently at a place called Rolands-Port." There was a pause and then Rowson hung up, obviously in a rage. Daemon put his communicator away and shrugged at Tugg.

"Well Tugg, by the sounds of things I'm miles from where I'm supposed to be."

Tugg slapped him on his back and pointed over to a neon sign stating bar.

"I knock off now, why don't we go and have a few drinks maybe your friend will call back later?"

It somehow sounded like the best idea Daemon had heard for a long time.

Tugg ordered several drinks from the bar and then sat down across from Daemon. The huge man had more tattoos than bare flesh and sported a large bushy beard which gave him the appearance of a gentle giant. The drinks were brought over by a bedraggled bar maid whose clothing was grimy and looked ready to slip off her skeletal frame. She placed two foaming flasks of ale and two spirit shots on the table. Daemon could see that her eyes were bloodshot and her scraggly blond hair hung limply around her face. He couldn't help noticing the needle marks up her arm as she passed him his drinks.

"Hello I'm Casey. I've not seen you round here before handsome, have you just landed?" She slurred and winked drowsily.

"Landed? Yeah, you could say that." He joked. Tugg had his hands covering his face shaking his head.

"I have a spare room if you wish to rent it cheap for tonight?" She said trying to steady herself on the table.

"Err, let me think about your offer." He winked as she shrugged and attempted to strut away sexily, however it looked more like a drunken stagger.

"If I was you I would rent a room at the bunk house, that girl isn't clean." Tugg pretended to inject his arm and followed up his mime by sliding down his chair slowly.

"I am not interested anyway." Daemon answered but Tugg looked as if he seriously doubted his words.

"How long have you been on Sigra III?" Daemon asked as Tugg knocked back the potent shot of red spirit.

"Too long my friend but it's a job and an income. Hell I can't get better than this with a class B in engineering." Tugg Laughed out loud. It was a laugh directed more to himself than a chuckle shared with the

Xen officer sat at his table.

"So what's the latest news planet side?" Daemon said before throwing the shot to the back of his throat. It was hot and sticky and his instinctive reaction was to spit it back out. He swallowed hard, fighting against the fiery fluid which seemed to carve its path down to his stomach.

"Bad on both sides, they gain a bit of ground and loose it within the hour and vice versa. It's a continual struggle on both sides, the only currency they wager are people's lives." Tugg looked glum so Daemon ordered a new round of drinks without forgetting to wink a few times at the loose maid as she collected the empty vessels. Tugg and Daemon drank until the bar closed.

Daemon had taken up Casey's offer of the spare room because he was in no state to find the bunk house. She had to half carry him most of the way back to her room because without support he was bouncing off the corridor walls. Finally they arrived at her room which was in the most rundown part of Rolands-Port. He wandered into the bedsit and noticed that there were no other doors or adjoining rooms. Casey started to undress him and he couldn't be bothered fighting.

"I thought you had a spare room." He said swaying on the spot with his trousers round his ankles.

"It must have slipped my mind. You don't mind sharing my bed do you handsome?" She said as she pulled off her beer stained gown revealing the signs of her filthy addiction upon every ruined vein. He understood the situation and drunkenly attempted to put on a condom for protection. She replaced the half donned sheath with her mouth and when it came loose she tossed it over her shoulder. He could feel her tonsils with every thrust of her head while her tongue spiralled around him frantically. Even though alcohol and stimulants had numbed his body sufficiently he came, a powerful climax which he thought he would never recover from. He lay on the scruffy bed, while she slipped off her knickers and joined him on the bed playing with herself for a while. Daemon watched and sensed his arousal returning, he could see that her fingers were wet. He was too drunk and aroused to resist her as she climbed on top of him and eased him gently into her.

"Fuck it!" he said out loud. But she didn't hear over the cloud of the drugs she had previously injected.

CHAPTER 20
Escape

The communicator bleeped and Daemon tried to work out where he was in the darkened room. He felt someone stirring on the bed and he suddenly remembered what had happened. He fumbled for the communicator and put it to his ear.

"Does it take all fucking day for you to answer your calls?" Agent Rowson yelled. "Get yourself down to the docking port and meet up with Captain Antress. He will supply you with an E.C.A. and make room for you on his armoured column which is passing Rolands-Port. The column is heading for Tulnep, don't miss the transport!" With that said he hung up on Daemon before he could he even reply.

Daemon cursed into the room and scrambled around in the darkness trying to find his belongings. He eventually exited Casey's bedsit and left a tidy number of credits on her bed. The streets were quiet at that time of the morning and Daemon passed nobody other than a drunk who looked to be in a terrible state. Looking at the wasted man he was reminded of the state he had been in last night and he felt guilty for having unprotected sex with such a dire specimen of an addict. He searched in his kit bag as he walked to the dock and popped a couple of metabolism enhancers. You never know what kind of infections people carry nowadays, especially skanks like Casey. He thought to himself.

The route to the docks was convoluted and he got lost a few times in the labyrinth of streets. By the time he had reached the dock he knew he was late and saw that Captain Antress was waiting impatiently next to an armoured transport which was parked near the exit.

"Get this on!" The Captain barked as he kicked an E.C.A. storage housing on the floor in front of him. Daemon was surprised that the suit was brand new. He started to get into it as ordered.

"I've just had to detour an entire armoured column to pick up your dumb-ass!" Antress grumbled as Daemon finished dressing.
Daemon felt the demon crawling up his spine and felt that things might get out of control unless he did something to satisfy its anger.

"We best get this out of the way Captain." Daemon

said evenly turning to face the gnarled veteran. "Just to make things perfectly clear to you and stop any unnecessary conflict in future I feel that I need to point out that the next time you address me like a member of the common soldiery I will cut your fucking balls off and show them to you."

The captain's jaw dropped and his eyes blazed with anger.

"Just who the fuck do you think you are, soldier?" The captain demanded.

Daemon grabbed Antress and pulled him so his face was inches from his own; Daemon's pupils were dilated giving him a fearsome appearance.

"I'm Lieutenant Daemon of Xen and you would benefit by remembering that!" He pushed Captain Antress backwards and watched as he fell over trying to get away from his fearsome eyes.

"Take me to Tulnep." He said finally as he stepped over the captain and boarded the armoured command vehicle.

The convoy of armoured vehicles set off north east towards Tulnep, Daemon had been told that it was going to be a long and dangerous journey. There was little for him to do other than sit back and wait. Captain Antress had sat as far away from Daemon as possible and every now and then he eyed Daemon as though he was a dangerous animal. Daemon couldn't help noticing that he outranked all the officers in the command vehicle, including a civilian intelligence officer, an attractive woman in her mid-thirties. The command vehicle was spacious compared with the troop carriers that made up the majority of the column and he couldn't help wondering what it was like for the regular troops cramped up together with little or no room to stretch.

"Looking forward to a bit of combat hey Lieutenant?" A young sergeant asked between mouthfuls of cold tinned steak. The man didn't look like he had ever seen a battle in his life and would probably wet himself in a real fire fight.

"With any luck the war will be over by the time we reach Tulnep." Daemon said as he stretched his arms. The sergeant nearly dropped his canned food and frowned.

"I fucking well hope not! I haven't even fired my rifle yet, I want to bag at least ten of the rebels before this war ends." The sergeant turned his chair so he didn't have to face the apparently pacifistic stranger and continued to eat.

"Then pray you don't have to fire it. Personally, I think Xen should pull out of this war, the cost of a clean-up will outweigh the profits gained from strip mining the planet." Daemon continued knowing it would probably antagonise the sergeant even more.
Captain Antress had heard the conversation and he looked like he had swallowed a wasp.

"Is that what you think? You haven't been down here in the shit and watched your friends die by bullets from those fucking rebels!" He spat.

"I've just arrived captain and I believe those rebels

are fighting on the ground they were born on. We on the other hand are invaders who vaporised an entire city yesterday morning. It was home to over three million people and I suspect they are lamenting a little more than you are over your lost buddies." Daemon said with no emotion on his face before Antress exploded with rage.

"It's called war dumb-ass! You better find out whose side you're on or you might as well get out now and join your comrades. I could report you for such a traitorous statement Lieutenant!"

"Are you suggesting that I could be a traitor? Not at all Captain, I follow my orders as commanded. However, unlike the CORE I've been taught to think for myself. I'm not conditioned to think of our enemy as being wrong or being intrinsically evil. I am on the side of Xen because I work for them and owe them allegiance. I follow orders, if my orders are to come down here and kill a load of innocent people then I will. However, it's very likely that I wouldn't be so eager like sergeant fuck-wit over there." Daemon nodded to the young sergeant who had suddenly stopped eating. The intercom buzzed interrupting the conversation before Captain Antress could reply.

"Captain, we are entering a possible rebel held township, they may attack the column." Antress gave Daemon a glare as though the conversation wasn't finished.

"Send word to the column, man the co-axles and prepare for an attack." He commanded pointing at the young sergeant to man the gun. The sergeant started for the rung ladder but Daemon pushed him out of the way.

"Where the fuck do you think you're going?" Antress barked.

"I'm going top side to man the gun, anything to get away from this room full of war-mongers." He said before sealing his helmet.

Through the dome that housed the co-axle gun Daemon could see ruined buildings looming on both sides like bare trees in the bleak winter. He switched his headset to the microphones on the exterior of the vehicle so he could listen for any gunshots. A strong wind blowing through the shattered buildings made a haunting, howling sound in his ear speakers which made him shiver slightly in his E.C.A. Xen had certainly done a number on this town, it had obviously been carpet bombed until there were only husks of buildings left standing.

He plugged his suit in to the command module to give him manual control of the gun and immediately the suits instruments detected high levels of toxins and a moderate amount of radiation, probably fall-out, in the polluted atmosphere outside. He winced as he felt a syringe entering his spine and knew the suit was bolstering his body against the radiation just in case his suit was compromised.

Damn it! I'm going to feel that shit later. He thought annoyed that he hadn't overridden the system to prevent the injection before plugging in. It was standard procedure that co-axle gunners were at the mercy of the onboard computers when in a combat situation. The anti-radiation cocktail that had entered his bloodstream would save his life if he was exposed to the elements however the hangover from the drugs was terrible. He remembered the time in the academy when he forced to take anti-rad drugs; he had bounced off the walls for hours during the come down.

The command vehicle rumbled down the main street as he noticed a shopping mall nestled between two ruined buildings. The mall had only suffered minor damage which rang alarm bells in his mind. As he looked on he saw two rebels dressed in mismatched E.C.A.'s exiting the mall carrying heavy weapons. He swivelled the main gun round and switched it to close range before squeezing the triggers. A jet of superheated plasma leapt from the gun engulfing the two assailants before they had even realised that that they were in the line of fire. He watched their bodies dance around in the piercing blue fire and could hear their screams and the sound of their bones cracking due to the immense temperature of the plasma. Their pitiful motions only ceased when the weapons they carried finally exploded putting them out of their misery.

The explosion also demolished the front section of the building bringing it crashing to the ground in a plume of dust and fire. Over the thunder of the collapsing building Daemon started to hear the staccato crackle of gun fire. He briefly switched his visor to infra-red and could see the heat signatures of the rebels swarming from the ruins around the armoured convoy. He called out their positions over the intercom and prepared to open fire.

At that moment the leading vehicle at the front of the convoy moved over a tank mine. The sixty tonne vehicle looked like a child's toy as it flipped through the air hitting and destroying a nearby building. Daemon switched to the rota-gun and sent a hail of armour piercing rounds into a group of charging rebels who had appeared from the mall. The spent casings from the weapon jettisoned more than twenty a second as he kept his aim on what was left of the human beings. Limbs and body segments continued to twitch as the gun carved lines of death through the approaching ranks.

He instinctively ducked away as small-arms fire rattled off the armoured housing encasing the co-axle. He suddenly heard the unmistakable sound of a fast approaching rocket just before it hit the carrier. He managed to grab the gun stanchions before the entire co-axle was ripped from the top of the command vehicle. The motion was sickening as it cascaded through the air, he saw the ground, sky, fire, more sky and then the ground again as it tumbled violently across the rubble-strewn streets.

The battle raged on around him as he checked his suit's readings to see if he was harmed. Although he didn't feel that he had been wounded the suit would tell him if it had administrated any pain killers.

However, it seemed that these new suits were obviously much tougher than the decrepit ones at the academy. Between the armoured housing and the suit, it appeared that he had been left unscathed. He grabbed his firearm and scrambled out of the remains of the burning turret and charged into the chaos of battle. The din of explosions and automatic fire was so loud that he turned off his ambient sensors and rushed into the cover of a nearby building.

"When is it my turn?" The demon asked.

"Soon I think, this place is more your kind of thing but be quiet for a moment I need to think." He gasped as the demon skulked in the shadows of his mind eager to fight and murder. Daemon tried to locate where his comrades were and if he could make it to another vehicle for protection.

"You didn't even give me a turn on that gun. That looked fun."

"Look I told you to be quiet!" Daemon repeated ducking into cover behind a solid interior wall and rechecking his suit harmonics for damage or breaches. Amazingly his suit hadn't even taken a scratch and all systems reported 100%.

"Please! Daemon let me take over. I want to secure a victory for you." The demon blazed with fiery flames leaping from its lava like veins, rushing over the cracks and imperfections of its dark and gnarly flesh.

"No! We will ride out the battle here and when it dies down, we will…" He couldn't believe he was having this conversation with another sentient being living in his mind.

"You're a fucking coward! Don't you want to be the hero?" The demon howled in his mind as it kicked over a pile of skulls, the souls it had gathered from its past murderous actions.

Daemon tried to ignore the demon's tormenting voice calling for him to surrender himself to it over and over again. He felt the rocks in his mind wall crumbling and realised he couldn't win.

"Fine! You take control, but remember it's my body too. If I perish so do you!"

Daemon felt himself drifting out of his body and sighed with relief. Inside the recesses of his mind he found himself wandering down a dark corridor lined with prison cells. He found the darkest chamber and collapsed on a ruffled bed to sleep. Outside, out in the real world he could still hear the sounds of battle so he wrapped a pillow around his ears in an attempt to muffle the sounds. However, he still could hear screams and gunfire and the demon howling with glee.

The lights in his mind prison had dulled to the colour of glowing embers, flickering red and orange lights which cast sinister shadows over the bricked walls and tingeing them blood-red. The roar of the demon was unbearable, he could hear the malice and glee it was feeling. He was tempted to fight for control of his body and to wrest it back from the demon's grip but the intensity of battle had increased and he feared for his life.

"Am I mad? Have I gone totally over the edge and

plunged into insanity?" He wept under the moth eaten blankets and wondered if the demon would ever give his body back. Glimpses of horrendous images flashed before him, even here in the sanctuary of his id a link existed with the demon and it exulted in showing him its achievements. He saw a group of rebels being blown apart from the explosion of a fragmentation grenade, a man's helmet being ripped off exposing his screaming face to the toxins in the air, a young rebel, no more than fourteen years old being torn apart by a shower of shrapnel. The images continued on and on, and now and then he felt his arms jerking from the firing of an assault rifle even though he couldn't see or feel the weapon.

He began to wail and thrash around on the bed suffering from a sense of hopelessness that was indescribable in its intensity. Finally after what seemed like hours the noise of the battle dimmed and the lights in the mind prison illuminated. The demon was returning, the fires from its body licking the cell bars as it made its way down the gangway toward his hiding place.

"It's all yours now my friend, the fun has ended!" It rumbled as it leant its burning skull-like head into the cell. Daemon reluctantly walked back up the corridor rising through levels of his sub-consciousness.

As his vision returned and he became his own master Daemon was confronted with the sight of the street scattered with low burning fires and some of the surrounding buildings still blazing. He staggered around the battlefield with his head throbbing and his ears ringing from the explosions and gun fire. Dizzied he eventually found a medic patching up a badly damaged E.C.A. he looked through the visor and recognised the face of the young sergeant from his vehicle. He held out a trembling hand toward Daemon.

"Thank you again Lieutenant. I'll never forget what you did. You saved my life carrying me out of the burning command vehicle. I thought it was over for me." He gurgled through his chest speaker. His suit had more field patches than actual suit and one of his arms had been completely crushed. The field medic injected a yellowish serum into the E.C.A. coupling and picked up a laser cutter from his kit.

"Sorry son but I'm going to have to take the arm. We will get you a new one when we reach Tulnep." He said grimly as Daemon wandered away. He wasn't in the mood to watch some poor bastard loose an arm.

Ahead of him he saw Captain Antress and headed towards him. The captain smiled broadly at his approach and grabbed his arm.

"Hey, I'm sorry about saying the stuff I said earlier." Antress told him. "If I knew you were that good in battle then I wouldn't have... Look I'm sorry." He said with an air of embarrassment. "No hard feelings I hope. Damn it, I'm going to write up a report and try and get you a commendation of bravery. I've never seen anything like it in all my years in the CORE."

"There's really no need. I would prefer to forget what happened here." Daemon stated as he scanned the number of dead that littered the ground.

Everywhere he went for the next hour he was met by strangers who wanted to regale him with stories of his actions, people wanting to thank him for his part in the battle. Daemon surveyed the handy work of the demon with measured calm, he knew he had to accept responsibility for the carnage he looked upon and the level of savagery displayed. He and the demon were somehow one and although he did not understand it he knew that he had to accept it.

It appeared that at the start of the attack the rebels had had considerable successes. They had taken out the lead and rear vehicles of the column then opened fire with rocket launchers. The convoy had lost six vehicles including the armoured command unit and the tide of battle had been in the rebels favour until Daemon has appeared like some dervish and spearheaded the rally. Leading from the front he had shown no fear and no mercy, his bloodlust had inspired the CORE troopers to victory.

The officers that had survived the ambush had to share spaces inside the already cramped troop carriers, some of which were barely road worthy. The interior of the regular transports were sub-standard, dull grey bulk heads with gaping holes from weapons fire, a few of them were new but others bore many old battle scars.

Make no wonder the casualties from the ambush were so high. He thought as he poked his hand through one of the holes. It was an inconvenience to have to be fully suited in the rickety transports as they made their way down the road but with the vehicles open to the atmosphere they had no option. He turned off the local communicators and tuned into the long ranged frequencies to find out what was happening in other parts of Sigra III. Battles were in progress all over the planet and where things were at an impasse the troops were digging in and preparing for trench warfare. More often than not the transmissions were reports on the aftermath of bombing raids and assessments on the damage caused. Scanning through the bandwidth he stumbled on an S.O.S transmission.

"Calm down corporal! Now start again and try to make more sense this time." Command ordered.

"Dead! All of them fucking dead! Code 303." The corporal claimed with intense panic in his tone.

"Code 303? What is Code 303?" Command asked.

"Intense viral contamination. I am locked down in a store room and I can't get to an E.C.A." The corporal had broken down, he wept into the comms microphone with all hope lost.

"Try to calm down. We are going to get you out of there. Tell me your present coordinates!" Command issued.

"I am at a secret installation in the southern hemisphere. I don't know the coordinates but the base's code signature is The Dairy. Everyone is dying, help us please. You've got to help us!"

The transmission faded and Daemon assumed they had switched to a more secure channel. Captain Antress tapped twice on his helmet. He switched to the local command channel to hear the captain's voice.

"Lieutenant, I have halted the column. We have insurgents holed up in the valley ahead. We are waiting for an air-strike. In the meantime I have issued orders to secure the area."

Daemon nodded once to the captain.

"OK Captain, I'm going to stretch my legs and take a look around."

It was clear that the captain didn't like the idea but agreed anyway knowing full well he couldn't command Daemon to remain seated.

Daemon leapt from the vehicle on to the asphalt and checked his ambient sensors. The air still contained minor toxins from the fallout from the warheads used on the city they had passed through but nothing seriously dangerous. Compared to what he had seen of Sigra III so far this place was a relative paradise. A valley of fading green grass stretched ahead as far as he could see and a few pine trees littered the landscape, most of them intact. He looked on past the armoured column and couldn't see any immediate signs of dangers in the nearby hills. Ground troops were making their way to higher ground around the convoy, the armoured men leapt up the hills like mountain goats thanks to the hydraulics in their E.C.A.'s as they secured the area. He looked again at his ambient sensors and decided to risk popping his helmet, he would be well protected by the anti-rad injection he had received earlier. A rush of cool air washed over his face bringing the musty smell of pine oil and moist grasses.

"So there are places on Sigra III still unspoilt by war." He said to himself.

He clambered up the valley running his armoured fingers through the flora, which brought perfumes of wild flowers to his senses. His suits auto systems complained all the way up the hill, 'SUIT BREACH! SUIT BREACH! REPLACE HELMET!' but he ignored its warnings and found a flat rock to perch on. The rumbling of the engines from the transports down in the valley had faded as he had climbed higher and he was able to concentrate on the beauty and greenery of his surroundings. Looking up he saw murky clouds drifting overhead, swollen with toxic rain. He averted his gaze and attempted to put warfare out of his mind.

He wondered what this place had been like before Xen had come to the aid of the government. He laughed at the thought of it, if this was Xen's idea of helping them it was a good job that they hadn't made enemies of them.

He sat for a while and his thoughts drifted to that summer's day so long ago with Millie. The smell of the glade around him and feel of the wind on his face reminded him of that good time in his life. He tried to remember the details of the dream that he use to have so often but it had been such a long time since he had dreamt it he found that he couldn't recall the details.

Things could have been so different; he could have got a regular job and married Millie. He might have been a father by now, living in peace and enjoying life rather than living amongst all this death.

Why did I join up with Xen? he asked himself yet again. He finished the thought as two dark coloured air cruisers passed in front of the sun thundering over his head towards the hills. Drop canisters shot down from the bellies of the crafts engulfing the hills in the distance in great walls of fire. He looked on in despair as the fires washed away all the greenery within a blink of an eye.

He replaced his helmet and clamped it shut. The artificial vision of the helm dimmed slightly to reduce the glare of the inferno dancing on the charred hills. He witnessed the devastation before him, the butchery of nature itself. He was a witness to the closest thing possible to hell he could imagine, every flower, every tree and every blade of grass was gone. When the fires began to die down he made his way back down the valley towards the convoy.

"Xen have truly lost their minds!" He said.

"And you haven't?" The Demon questioned through a guttural laugh.

"Shut it you!" he snapped but he knew that he had to agree.

He felt that the demon was like the inferno he had just witnessed, destroying all the vestiges of goodness and wholesomeness in him. He knew that he was bordering on psychotic but felt powerless to do anything about it. Xen had made him in to what he was and they were unlikely to help him now.

Down in the southern hemisphere of the planet an

old friend of Daemons was busy trying to escape the chaos of the war torn planet. Dr. Miles had been working in the Xen laboratories since his arrival on Sigra III with ever increasing resentment and anger. His hatred had festered and corrupted him and he had become increasingly unstable. When he had met Sherry they had talked about old times and their hopes for the future and she seemed to sense that he was different somehow. He feared that he had said too much to her about how difficult he found it being a slave to Xen and had muddied the waters by telling her about hearing voices from the implanted chips. They had talked for hours but when she had invited him back to her room to stay the night he had declined fearing that he might reveal his plans to her in the comfort of her bed. He could see in her face that it had upset her and saw her check her anger and shortly after she had left him telling him to take care of himself. Once he would have cared about hurting her feelings like that but he no longer cared.

He had been flown down to a research facility which was colloquially known as The Dairy and had immediately been set to work in the bio-weapons division. He began research into new methods of dispersing viral contaminants and did just enough work to keep his superiors happy. However, this line of work was just a rouse to keep their attention away from his development of a new strain of his Miles virus.

Late at night, when the labs were quiet he wandered in to them carrying his teddy bear Dante. He would pick loose the seam on its back and remove the vials and plates that contained samples of his original Miles virus. He worked ceaselessly at developing a strain for which he could create an antidote. Night after night he finished his work by placing the samples back inside Dante and sewing him back up. Amongst the security guards he quickly gained a reputation as an eccentric and they joked that he was "married to that fucking bear."

Initially he tried mutating the existing strain and had some success in making it more virulent but could not solve the problem of creating an effective vaccine or antidote. Eventually he decided to use some of the test viruses he was working with during the day when he worked on the dispersal technology. All of these viruses, though deadly, could easily be nullified and he hoped that he could genetically engineer similar tendencies in to his new creation through DNA splicing. The problem he had was that the Miles virus kept attacking the foreign bodies he introduced to it even at the molecular level.

Finally, after much experimentation, he was able to isolate stable base pairs in the genetic string and attach triggers that reacted in a similar manner to those seen in the "safe" strands (as he dubbed them). The result was that he was able to activate the triggers through a serum he created which destabilised the base pairs and led to the rapid breakdown of his own virus. An unexpected side effect of this was that during the incubation period the new strain exhibited characteristics similar to those shown in the commonly used Mastavil Strain.

This was the breakthrough Miles had been waiting for and he began running tests on a larger scale and was soon ready to execute his master plan. He took one of the lab rats from its cage and injected it with the virus then gave himself the antidote. He rubbed at the syringe mark in his arm and felt it coursing through his veins. He smiled knowing that it was the only batch he had produced.

Fifteen minutes later Miles was carefully placing the rat's still warm carcass into the air vent and replacing the panel he had removed. He knew there were no vigi-cams or security guards in this area and he had already adjusted the thermostat to blow warm air instead of cold. All he had to do now was to wait for his new biological weapon, which he had dubbed the Miles II virus, to multiply in the rat. Based on his research on the animals in the lab he estimated he had four hours before people began to show symptoms. Once this happened he knew that his plan was pretty much assured of success as it would be unlikely that anyone would realise exactly what was amiss at The Dairy.

Once the symptoms had manifested themselves if anyone was quick enough to make the connection and diagnose that the contaminant was the Mastival Strain they would undoubtedly assume that the appropriate anti-virus drugs would work against it. They would be wrong, the anti-virus would only make things worse and speed up the already rapid death The Dairy would face.

He made his way to the canteen and ordered lunch and a cup of tea. He sat and waited next to his briefcase which contained all of his notes and research material and within Dante three batches of the Miles II virus.

After his meal he checked his watch and mentally went over the tasks he needed to complete to get away from Xen once and for all.

"More tea, Doctor Miles?" The waitress asked him. He hadn't noticed her come to his table and thought it best not to be rude. Not that it mattered, she probably only had a day to live, if that. It was a shame really, she was very pretty.

It is such a waste of life but plans are made to be adhered to. He thought and gestured for a refill. As she poured out the red tea he noticed that her hand showed the tell-tale sign of a slight tremble, he studied her further and noticed her pulse rate had increased at the nape of her neck.

Interesting, it is moving quicker than I suspected. He thought, surprised that it appeared to be more virulent outside of the lab.

"You're on leave now aren't you, Doctor Miles?" She asked, while she mopped her forehead with a napkin.

"Yes Pasie, I am waiting for my ship to dock to go on vacation." He lied.

"A beach holiday maybe, somewhere hot?" She shuddered and seemed to have problems focusing on him.

"Now, now Pasie, you know I am not allowed to tell you." He claimed as the jug of tea slipped from her hand

and shattered against the floor.

"Ohhh!" she moaned uneasily, "I'm sorry Doctor but I think I need to lie down, I feel a little queasy." She never made it across the room. It was if she just decided to lie down there and then in the centre of the canteen. Miles finished his tea and quietly made his way to the secret hanger in the opposite direction from the main dock at The Dairy.

As he walked there he found people lay strewn unconscious over the floors of the rooms and corridors. They were all showing the early symptoms of his horrific new weapon. It was as if all the personnel at The Dairy had suddenly decided to play the child's game of sleeping lions. He had timed everything perfectly, most of the guards were sleeping in the dormitories and only a skeleton shift of guards wearing E.C.A. remained conscious in the installation.

"Now comes the tricky part." He whispered to himself.

He slipped into the administration block and pushed the motionless form of a technician off a chair. The thud of his skull hitting the floor made such a sickening sound that Miles curled his lip in disgust. He sat and uploaded a program he had written and waited for the computer defences to fall. It was then he noticed Tinya sprawled unconscious on the floor, her breath slow and raspy. He had been besotted with Tinya as soon as he arrived at The Dairy but she had taken an instant dislike to him. He pushed back his chair and wandered towards her peering down upon her face.

397

"Tinya you are so beautiful. So angelic and now you are sick and dying. You should have loved me. I would have taken you with me and saved you from a horrific death."

He knelt down at her side and cradled her head in his lap; blood dribbled from her gums and ran darkly down her pale chin. He reached down between her legs and carefully pulled up her skirt. She wore white laced knickers which he slowly pulled to one side. He instinctively peered around the room to see if anybody was watching before he slipped his fingers into her. She was moist and her temperature was dangerously high, he savoured the moment before he removed his fingers and noticed specks of blood on the tips. He couldn't resist the temptation to taste her and delicately put his digits in his mouth. The computer terminal bleeped startling him. He gently lowered her head back to the floor and rushed to the terminal. His fingers tapped through various commands with great efficiency and when he had finished he turned off the light in the administration block and waited by the side of Tinya's unconscious form.

The dock sections fire alarms sounded an alert which automatically pumped carbon dioxide into the hanger bay. All of the on duty guards made their way quickly to the alerted zone safe in their E.C.A.'s. At first through the clouds from the extinguishers they did not notice the people lain all over the place and by the time they did Miles had already accessed the secret hanger and locked it down.

"What the fuck's going on here?" One guard asked nervously.

"How the hell do I know? Are they alive?" Another guard said as he prodded a limp scientist with his firearm.

"Well whatever is wrong, I am keeping this fucking suit on." The first replied.

As more guards arrived they all seemed to shrug together when asked similar questions.

"Where is Sergeant Qulles?" One guard asked. The others tapped the tops of their helms twice which was an off the record military signal for "fuck knows".

"Hey isn't that Corporal Adams?" Someone asked pointing to the door of a supply room just off from the corridor. The corporal was waving his arms around within a store room and was only visible by the circular window in the door.

"I think he's in trouble, quick open the door and let him out!" Another guard issued.

The corporal was frantic; he banged his fist against the glass and tried to wave the guards away. When the door opened he screamed and held his head.

"You idiots! Now you've killed me."

The guards didn't understand and felt a little upset by the corporal's words.

"I was trying to tell you NOT to open the door." The corporal whispered before he broke down crying. The guards patted him on his shoulder in a vain attempt to calm him down and wondered what he was talking about.

The secret hanger bay was at the far end of the installation and had been created for the high ranking officials of The Dairy to escape in case of attack or outbreak. Miles stood in awe scanning one of the docked space craft; it was nearly invisible in the dim light of the hanger, the sleek, matt black hull was built around its main interstellar drive.

"There you are my baby. You don't mind me calling you baby?" He whispered towards the interstellar cruiser.

He had overheard the head of The Dairy speaking of this new craft several weeks ago and it had been simple to hack the computer network to discover the idiot's security password. The ship had been called The Evader, but Miles didn't like that name so simply called it 'My Baby'.

Its function was simple; it was a stealth craft that could evade the most delicate of scanners, a ship that could outrun a standard war cruiser and a ship with a real interstellar drive engine. As far as he knew it was unique and it belonged to the Administrator of The Dairy who was probably lying in his bed bleeding from every orifice, his body riddled with Miles II virus.

Miles had carried Tinya with him from the admin block and dragged her on to the craft before returning to pick up his briefcase and boarding the stealth ship. The interior was made of platinum-molysilicate, a very expensive alloy which aided the evasion of scanners. It was polished to a shine in every room and corridor and produced an almost mirrored effect. He placed Tinya in a cryogenic tube and sealed it off before he started it up and watched as it iced her in seconds.

"Why didn't I make two batches of anti-virus?" he scolded himself, "Mind you, Tinya might have caused a bit of a fuss if I had tried to inject her."

The final feature of The Evader that had attracted Miles to it was that it had its own onboard laboratory should the administrator be escaping from a contamination leak. It was fully stocked and contained enough supplies to provide him with the materials and equipment to make another batch of anti-virus for Tinya. As the craft left The Dairy and headed out into space nothing terrestrial or orbiting Sigra III detected the craft. It vanished into the vastness of the galaxy like a thief into the night.

CHAPTER 21
Reconnaissance

The township of Tulnep had been just about levelled if it wasn't for the rubble and the outline of foundations scattered around nobody would have guessed a thriving township had ever existed there. On the west side of town stood a sprawling prefabricated fortress overlooking the front line to Runich. Daemon noticed it was still being assembled as he strolled through the ruins carrying a pack of gear. He stopped and watched a group of CORE troopers piecing together a wing of air tight billets at the back of the fortress. His suit harmonics began to register toxic compounds in the ambience as it started to rain from the filthy black clouds that swirled in the sky.

One of the troopers gave him a half-hearted salute whilst coupling up his suit's excrement umbilical with a small pump waggon. Daemon laughed at the sight and continued around to the front of the stronghold and scanned the front line. Low rubble walls had been constructed in horseshoe curves spreading out from the fortress for about a quarter of a mile into the flat expanse of no-mans land. Behind some of the walls stood large field artillery weapons and quite a few of them were Fyr-spurs that looked older than he was. It appeared that things had got bad enough for Xen to use these banned weapons in the war. From their condition, it looked as if the CORE still followed the motto of why purchase new when you can use the old surplus.

Behind the emplacements, dark armoured warriors were digging out trench lines and laying rails into the muddied earth. Even though he couldn't see the faces of the troops he knew they must be utterly demoralised, he knew he would be if he was out there with them. He couldn't believe the CORE was being used as regular labourers instead of being the combat machines they were bred for. Given the number of Sigran casualties, he supposed there were no people left to labour on this war-ravaged planet.

He wandered as close to the frontline as he could and stopped when the mud had climbed to the knee joints of his E.C.A. Sherry had been right, the open land in between Tulnep and Runich would be a killing field if Xen risked an all-out attack. He switched his visor to the binocular mode and scanned the enemy fortifications on the opposite front line. The rebels had outfitted the edge of Runich into a machination of murder; field guns, plasma cannons and vehicle mounted machine guns were well protected in emplacements. Daemon shook his head at the sight and sighed as though Xen had already been defeated. He turned to head back and spotted an armoured person heading toward him. The insignia on his shoulder plates were those of a colonel and as he got closer Daemon switched his communications to the local network.

"Lieutenant Daemon is that you? Lieutenant Daemon?" his voice came through the speakers.

"Yes?"

"I thought it was you, Lieutenant, I'm Colonel Lenz. I can't say I'm pleased to see you having heard you've come down here to spy on me but nevertheless I will try to be hospitable." The colonel's gravelly voice echoed around his helmet.

"I wouldn't know anything about spying colonel I'm just here..." Daemon began saying whilst offering a salute.

"Don't salute me, boy! Your current rank is nearly level pegging with me anyway. Military ranks aren't worth a shit anymore." Lenz interrupted.

"I see we are already off to a terrible start, maybe we should have a beer and begin again?" Daemon said in a conciliatory manner.

"Bullshit! Follow me. Let's get you out of this shitty weather before you get stuck fast in that mud you're standing in." Lenz grumbled angrily.

Daemon prized himself out of the thick mud and followed colonel Lenz back to the fortress. They wandered in silence through the smoke rising from the burning shit-pits and trudged through the mud which seemed to be made up of human bones, earth and stagnant water.

Back in the colonel's quarters, Daemon found himself sat opposite the heavily scarred face of a late middle-aged man with piercing dark blue eyes.

"Are you familiar with the ancient game of Chess?" Lenz asked as he smoked a fat cigar.
Daemon had heard of the game and understood some of the rules but had never really played it even through Miles tried to get him playing more times than he cared to remember.

"I understand enough that the situation is a stalemate at Runich. Is that what you were going to suggest?" He said and watched the old man struggling to open a bottle of beer. The colonel nodded grimly and gave him both bottles to open.

"This little campaign is way out of control. I've got administration hammering at the doors asking ridiculous questions every hour of the day. What is the holdup? When will you attack? What do you suppose the costs will be? We can't even send an air strike to fuck the rebels over with all those Ion plants littered all over the city." Lenz looked like he hadn't slept for a long time and stress lines were making his old features even more wrinkled.

"Yeah, I watched a simulation of the chain reaction of

the Ion plants exploding. It was scary stuff. Colonel Kolkorin nearly shit himself when the simulation destroyed the planet." Daemon said stifling a burp from the consumption of the fizzy beer.

"Colonel Kolkorin was never a thinking man, hell only a few years ago he believed the Seinal Corporation was run by an alien intelligence," Lenz said sniggering before his features turned serious. "Listen to me lieutenant, I'm no engineer but I say that theory of the planet exploding is a bunch of horse shit and an intelligent man such as you should be having doubts also," Lenz said quietly.

"I have my doubts but we also have our orders Colonel. If the high council of Xen are banning the use of air-strikes then an alternative plan must be enforced." Daemon stated quoting dogma and then wished he hadn't sounded too much like an agent of Xen.
The colonel pondered for a while and gave him a look as though he was weighing up his trust.

"I will probably regret telling you this." He paused and gave Daemon another glare of mistrust before continuing. "About a week ago I gave an order to begin tunnelling under no-man's land towards Runich. You see I was an apprentice mining engineer before I joined up with the CORE. Anyway, the tunnel is a standard way lane, we haven't excavated too far yet but we have installed a bunker down there as a defence measure."

"Go on?" Daemon said in a commanding tone until he remembered who he was talking too and put his hand up to apologise. The colonel curled his lip slightly.

"It's a question of time, tunnels take time to construct and I don't think Xen is going to give me much time before they order a suicidal ground attack. Those soldiers out there in the mud are human beings, they are my men and they are good soldiers. As far as I am concerned they are not expendable to the whim of some desk jockey back on Xen Prime. I dread the day the order to attack comes to my door."

The despair on the colonel's face was a terrifying sight to behold and Daemon couldn't help but worry about Sherry being caught up in the whole deadly campaign.

"I hope Xen gives you the time you need Colonel, I have a friend down here in this mess." He said as Lenz nodded.

"I know son, when I heard from Rowson, I mean Agent Rowson, that you were heading down here Corporal Sherry advised me that she had seen you up on the Goliath. I hear you went to the same academy. She's a good solider son, a damned good soldier." Lenz picked up his beer and headed towards the door and added, "They are all damn fine soldiers."

"Yes, sir." Daemon replied automatically.

"I just want you to remember that before you do anything – unwise," Lenz said draining his beer and leaving the room.

Daemon looked at the control panels nearby and was tempted to browse some of the latest orders but he decided he had time enough to find out what he was sent down here to do.

Sherry browsed her personal messages on her portable terminal; her eyes could barely focus on the screen due to the long shifts she was pulling on watch and recon. She hated logistical work and groaned at the wasted day she had spent in the mud on the front line recounting the enemy gun emplacements. The messages she had received that day were of the standard sort, one from her father wishing her well and a number from ex-lovers wishing she was in bed with them right now. She was about to turn it off when a new message appeared on the screen.

Hello Sherry,

I was sent to a biological warfare installation, working as part of a team to create a new virus for the company. They were hoping to design a retrovirus which would saturate the surviving populous of Sigra III and create the next generation of indigenous people with suppressed thoughts of rebellion. They wanted me to come up with a way to ensure that everyone on the planet would be infected almost simultaneously. I had been told that the project could go on for twenty years but after one year I would be promoted to Administrator of The Dairy and supervise the work. The Dairy project is highly classified and the Xen Corporation wishes it to remain a secret. If the research had been completed then planet Sigra III would have been a breeding ground of unthinking slaves. Xen would have had a pliable workforce to fill off-world mining positions (which is dangerous life threatening work as you know) and laboratory test subjects. As you may have guessed I've always felt that I have already repaid my debt to Xen and that I have my own plans and ambitions, running The Dairy is not one of them. All this said, it soon became clear that they would never create the agent they were working towards without stealing more of my ideas. Needless to say, I wasn't willing to aid them to create the virus they intended me to manufacture.

I am sorry, but this is goodbye. You will never see me again and the Xen Corporation will consider me to be their enemy. Perhaps you will too should you find out what I have done. Hopefully, Xen will never catch up with me and I hope that if it comes to it you can find it in yourself to forgive me and remember me in a better light than I probably deserve. I feel as if I owe you so much. If you didn't already know you were my first. I ask only one thing of you Sherry. Avoid The Dairy at all costs!

Doctor MILES

Sherry reread the message in disbelief and then checked it to see if it had passed through the standard Xen administration editing and found that it hadn't. She wondered how Miles had managed to bypass the system. One thing was for sure; it sounded as if Miles was in a lot of trouble and with the corporation spread far and wide he would have a terrible task ahead of him trying to evade the clutches of Xen. She closed down her terminal as Colonel Lenz entered the communication room. She stood and saluted, the colonel waved her salute away with a balled fist.

"How many times have I told you? You don't need to salute me when you are off-duty!" The colonel was riled up over something so she fell at ease. "How well, exactly, did you know the Lieutenant when you served with him?" He growled and looked ready to lash out at something with his gnarled fists.

"Pretty well Sir, we met back at the training academy and I was also with him through the great test before I joined up with the CORE. Why?" She asked.

"I'm asking the goddamned questions corporal!" He barked as he rummaged in his pockets for some coffee tokens. He found some and slotted them into a nearby vending machine violently as though the tokens were throwing stars.

"Well you will be glad to hear that your little friend has just shipped down here and he is already getting on my tits!" He handed a cup of coffee to Sherry and then quaffed his cup down.

"When I bumped into him on the Goliath he never said anything about coming all the way down here to Tulnep but there again I don't think I ever mentioned exactly where I was stationed," She said with a thin smile.

The corporal eyed her from the rim of the cup before bursting into a fury.

"That Xen whore dog isn't showing all his cards. I'm not entirely sure why he has been sent down here but I know it isn't to help us!" He raged pointing his finger near her face.

"It's probably something routine after all he has only just graduated." She claimed nervously trying to avoid the prodding motion of his finger.

"Graduated from what exactly? His admin papers say he did officer training but I think he did agency training. Why would Rowson be the one telling me he was on his way otherwise? He has probably come down here to interfere just like that Rowson fucker, he is always too happy to keep popping down for a visit." He crushed the coffee cup spilling the remnants of the dark liquid over his hand. He cursed and tried to regain a measure of calm.

Sherry had never seen the colonel in such a perturbed state.

"Seriously colonel, he went to Vex II for officer training, he is one of us. He was asking why I hadn't joined him there. He would never lower himself to become an agent." She said but started have doubts about her old friend.

"Well I don't trust him, and a friend or not, you shouldn't either. We can't have one of those shit-dicks poking their noses into our military affairs. You got that?"

Sherry nodded in agreement as she picked up her field pack which she had left next to the terminal.

"You will find your so called friend in the command room." the Colonel continued, "Find out his plans and who is pulling the strings above him. I want a full report by zero nine hundred tomorrow!"

Sherry was about to leave when the colonel gripped her

arm.

"If you fail me, corporal, I will have you finishing this campaign dressed in an un-armoured Bubble-suit with the civilian regulars. Have I made myself clear?"
She looked into his dark blue eyes and could see the truth of the threat.

"Yes, sir." She said shaken up and left the communications room thanking the stars above that there were no prying eyes in the room.

Sherry found Daemon in the command room drinking bottled beers and brooding over the local map display of Tulnep. He looked round when she entered and smiled.

"Hey Sherry, I was wondering when I'd see your face. I've had a chat with Colonel Lenz who has been singing your praises. Good on you." She made the distance toward him with her hand raised ready to slap him. He braced himself with only one eye open but made no effort to defend himself.

"You are in deep shit, my friend!" She yelled with her hand poised to attack.

"What's the matter?" He asked as he smiled at her beautiful radiance. She threw her arms in the air and sat down shaking her head.

"You! That's what is wrong. Why didn't you tell me on the Goliath that you were heading here? Tell me honestly; did you train to become an agent or an officer? If I detect you're lying I'm going to slap you so hard that you will probably end up drinking through a straw for the rest of your life!" She said through clenched teeth.

"What? I told you. I went for officer training why would I lie?" He said defensively.

Sherry tried to see behind his green eyes to detect the truth but she knew she was useless when it came to psychology.

"I want to know why you have been sent down here to Sigra III? Why didn't you tell me?" She asked trying to read his sudden smile.

He pulled up a chair to face her and sat down calmly. The demon inside him stirred.

"She is pumping you Daemon, tell her fuck all!"

"Come on Sherry why did you think I was on the Goliath? Of course, I was going to head down to the planet. I didn't know where though. You should have guessed I would end up here. Why did you think you had been asked to brief us all?" Daemon shook his head with wonder; he thought Sherry was smarter than this.

"But why?" she asked with her eyes beseeching him.

"What is this Sherry? Some kind of interrogation? Look, I'm happy to play along, I've got nothing to hide. I've been sent down here to check the defences of this fortified township. There is a lot of money riding on this operation and quite a lot of speculation over the strength of the rebel forces holding Runich." He watched for her response to see if she seemed content with the limited information he had given her. It was nothing that she had not heard already at the briefing and it appeared that she seemed satisfied.

"Sent by whom?" She asked with tight lips and a frown.

The demon stirred in Daemons mind and hammered down the increasingly fragile walls of his psyche. Daemon found himself in a darkened cell naked, with cold chains snaking around his body.

"You're not doing this. I will not let you do this!" Daemon yelled in the darkness of the cell and strived to break free of his bonds.

Regaining some measure of control Daemon laughed and slowly shook his head from side to side to buy some time. It was clear to see that her interrogation skills were rudimentary and he only needed to keep his story plausible to keep her in the dark.

"Lovely little Sherry. You know I can't answer that question; it would be a direct violation of my orders." He said struggling to contain the demon inside him.

She noticed a change in her friend, his pupils had dilated until they covered his iris and his voice sounded strange.

"So why don't you run home to your safe little... SHITHOLE!" The demon bellowed through him.

"What are you?" She screamed as she tried to scramble away from his evil glare.

Daemon tore at the chains and one by one they fell to the filthy cell floor, he had very little time to warn her before the demon took him again.

"GO NOW!" He yelled, shaking her until she ran out of the room and away from his alter ego.

He just had enough time to watch the command room

door slam before the chains dragged him back into his mind prison.

He was hanging limply bound in chains with little enough strength to gain control of his body. The demon approached down the hall of cells, the stench of sulphur in the air around it. It slammed open the cell door and roared.

"Don't resist me Daemon, that little bitch needed to be taught a lesson!" it roared, a heat haze rising from its open maw.

"You're a fool there's a security camera in the command room that has just recorded you. You have given yourself away!" He yelled as he squirmed in the chains, retching from the stench of the angry demon.

"The camera witnessed your acts, not mine!" It grinned, revealing a row of toothpick like teeth. "You leave me no option but to punish you!"

It reached down grabbing a claw full of chains which instantly glowed with the heat from its body. Daemon watched the heat travelling slowly up each link in the chain until it began to sear at his flesh. While he screamed the demon laughed and blew hot fiery air into his face. The agony wasn't localised to one area of his body, instead, it boiled his blood cauterising each and every nerve.

Time had no meaning as he struggled to remain conscious throughout the ordeal and then it suddenly ceased.

Daemon found himself lying on the floor of the command room in sweat soaked clothing. He remained on the floor until he gathered enough breath to move. For the very first time, he felt true terror towards the abomination inside him. He wondered how he could control it when he was around his friends. It seemed to be gaining strength by the day and he was becoming weaker. Would he eventually spend the rest of his life locked away in his own mind? But the question was too terrifying to dwell upon. He finally plucked up the courage to move and headed off to the billets to rest.

Daemon felt like the loneliest man in the universe while he ate his breakfast. Around the table Sherry, Colonel Lenz and a number of other officers were gathered chatting amongst themselves. Sherry hadn't said a word, nor looked at him and he imagined she was still pissed off at him for scaring her witless the night before. The food was unexpectedly good being a mixture of real meat and processed vegetable matter. Apparently, the CORE had special privileges when it came to food and even though the meat was scarce on Sigra III the company freighted in fresh supplies daily to bolster moral, no matter what the cost. Sherry pushed away her empty bowl and was about to leave the table until Colonel Lenz glared at her after glancing at his time piece.

"Stay your ground corporal, and you lieutenant. The rest of you are dismissed." The other officers quickly spooned the last morsels of their breakfast before leaving the table. Lenz relaxed in his chair and lit up a cigar with a cigarette lighter which seemed to produce more heat than a napalm thrower.

"What are your plans for today lieutenant?" He said as smoke settled around him.

"I was hoping to inspect this tunnel you mentioned yesterday. Would that be possible?" Daemon said with a foxy grin as Sherry covered her face with her hands embarrassed by her friend's presuming front. The colonel feigned surprise and nodded.

"I suspected as much but surely you wouldn't enjoy inspecting a muddy tunnel which has collected several tonnes of eradiated rain water?" The colonel said slyly…

"On the contrary, I would be delighted to see the structural design of a way-tunnel to further my studies in engineering. After all, that was the secondary subject that I practised throughout my Xen training." Daemon said with a hint of sarcasm.
"Oooooohh I like it Daemon, the colonel disliked you when you arrived and now he really hates you! Keep that up and I will no longer have to take control of you when you pussy out on me!" The demon whispered in his mind.

The colonel's hand had moved down to the nickel plated side arm, holstered on his belt just below his protruding gut.

"If that's what the Lieutenant wishes then who am I to stand in your way. But let's get one thing out of the way, the next time you bait me I will put a bullet into your disrespectful little head!" Lenz said gripping the ivory handle of his pistol. His eyes were bulging out of their sockets as Sherry banged on the table to distract the pair of them.

"Are you two finished? I don't want to be clearing up brains all morning because a couple of MEN wanted to kill each other. Hell, we are all on the same side. Save it for those rebel bastards out there!" She cried.

Lenz and Daemon eyed each other for a few more seconds before the tension broke and they both laughed at the stupidity of the situation.
"You had me going there, colonel," Daemon said putting his combat knife away. "I thought we might have resorted to something a bit stronger than words."

The colonel looked at the blade and laughed. "Ha! I would have blown your brains out before you had time to use that pig-sticker on me."

"Oh, this knife? Colonel the knife was a feint, I intended on using this!" Daemon chuckled as he revealed a BORE pistol from under the table. The colonel shrugged and nodded proudly at the strategy.

"So maybe you would have blown out my guts but I had my little insurance policy." He said revealing a hand grenade; the safety catch tight in his fist and the pin rattling around his thumb.
Sherry's mouth dropped open. She was mortified that she could have been killed by her commanding officer over a petty argument.

"Well, it looks like we could have both killed each other twice over then." Laughed Daemon, "And taken others with us. You are one tough fucker sir."

"You're no angel yourself, Lieutenant." Grinned Lenz.

"More of a demon than an angel Sir, now with your

permission I'd like to inspect the tunnel."

"Permission granted son. Corporal, be sure to extend our guest every courtesy." Lenz motioned for them both to leave and had his eyes fixed on the pair of them on the way out.

They changed into their combat suits in no great hurry and secured a battle rifle and spare clips.

"What happened last night Daemon?" Sherry asked finally breaking the silence.

He cringed at the recollection but had known that she would ask about it eventually. He watched as she picked up her helm and tested the carbon dioxide expellers.

"All I can say is, forget the old Daemon, I have changed. Or maybe I've been changed. For the worst, it seems but I would never hurt you, Sherry. Please believe me."

She connected her suits umbilical to the liquid gas bayonet and turned to face him with her beautiful features racked in doubt. A hiss followed as the suits tanks filled with super compressed liquid gasses.

"You scared me Daemon. I have never seen you turn like that. Has Xen changed you through advanced training?" She looked up and Daemon saw that moisture had formed in her eyes enhancing the already aquatic blue colour of them. "Because if that is what Xen training does then I am glad I opted for the military."

He put his arms around her and hugged her as tightly as any two people could embrace in heavy combat armour. He found the nape of her neck and kissed her softly. She relaxed a little and brushed his dark hair with her fingers. She rested her cheek against his as he unbuckled her shoulder plate which clattered to the floor. Sherry kissed his lips once and pulled her pistol firing around at the security lens. Now they were alone from prying eyes.

They pulled and tugged at each other's armour, the floor was soon scattered with pieces of heavy E.C.A. With their bodies hot against one another Sherry backed herself to the wall, the alloy cold against her back. He kissed her breasts then her stomach and onwards towards the place where she really wished for his full attention. She gasped and pulled his head into her, raking her nails against his scalp. Waves of warmth slithered through her body and she bit her finger and closed her eyes dizzy with pleasure. A powerful orgasm exploded inside her and she momentarily lost control of her knees as his mouth filled with her cum. She moaned and pulled him up then pushed him away from her and grabbed her knickers.

"What?" He said with his face showing absolute confusion as Sherry put her knickers back on. She smiled and reached for her vest.

"We have a lot of work to do Daemon besides which I've already cum." Sherry nearly laughed out loud at his expression.

He stood in front of her, stark naked and fully aroused as she continued to gather her armour, loving every second of his torment.

"Well, that's just great Sherry. A true little prick tease

aren't you?" He stated not hiding any contempt.

"You have a hand don't you Daemon? Nip over there in the corner, I promise I won't watch." The whole scene seriously amused her. She laughed so hard that the tears that she had tried so hard to hold back minutes earlier cascaded down her cheeks.
Daemon scowled and started to gather his clothes and armour.

"You rotten little bitch. I can't believe you did that to me." He moaned.
Sherry just shrugged her face smug with delight.

"Hurry and get your armour on and then we can go and inspect the tunnel." She stated between bouts of giggles.

The rain fell hard, typical of the torrential storms in this part of the world. The rain water tapping on their armour echoed inside their helms drowning out most communications which was a relief to Daemon since he did not want to talk to Sherry just now. The ground was already saturated and had turned into a swamp of mud and pit pools. Daemon adjusted the settings of his suit to increase the power to the servos in his legs to aid his balance in such bad conditions. The tunnel head had been covered by a prefabricated alloy hut and troops worked inside trying to keeping the storm water from entering the tunnel. The tunnel itself was flooded to the waist and more water dripped continuously from the earthen ceiling. The many pumps in the underground laboured in vain to carry the water elsewhere; it seemed like a continuous losing battle for the little mechanical devices. Daemon noticed that every twenty meters or so the tunnel had been rigged to explode as a failsafe should they lose the tunnel to the rebels.

It had taken over half an hour of wading before they reached the halfway point under no-man's land which had been fortified into a bunker made from Kalumcrete. They entered an airlock and waited for the solvent jets to clean off their armour. Daemon clicked his communicator while the steamy jets ran a programmed cycle.

"So are you going to finish me off then?" He asked grinning in his helmet.
Sherry answered by cranking her rifle and chambering a round. The inner door of the airlock hissed open as Sherry took off her helmet and mouthed the word 'Cock sucker' towards him.

The bunker was basic in design by necessity; the blocky dull grey Kalumcrete walls had set in a matter of minutes so they could only be laid in the most simplistic patterns. The room was dimly illuminated with energy efficient overheads and the stench of musty sweat and recycled air clung to the airways in every breath. The troopers in the bunker had the look of veterans with glazed eyes that had seen too many atrocities deep set in battle worn faces. The troops all seemed to look the same, ugly brutes' every last one of them, regardless if they were male or female. However, they still maintained their discipline and all saluted with great respect as soon as they spotted the command studs upon Daemon's left shoulder plate. A military lieutenant dressed in grey fatigues signalled to them as they entered the command room.

"Good to see you at last Lieutenant Daemon I've have heard of your achievements. My brother Corporal Ganny Bray was on the convoy with you. He claims you fought with exceptional honour and saved the lives of many men, including his own." The lieutenant stated as he shook Daemon's hand vigorously.

"I have to admit it all happened so fast but we all fought bravely that day." Daemon conceded.
Sherry apparently still had a jealous streak in her as she obviously didn't enjoy him being praised and butted in.

"The lieutenant has come to take a look at the tunnel and its progress Lieutenant Bray." Bray flashed Sherry a furious look.

"Corporal, I know why the Xen Lieutenant is here, I just wanted to thank him for saving my brother's life. It's the least I could do!"
Sherry made herself busy at the coffee dispenser, grumbling under her breath and cursing the day she had ever met Daemon. The two lieutenants exited the command room into a private office space to talk further.

Lieutenant Bray rolled out a schematic of the tunnel's construction. Daemon browsed the large negative and estimated it would probably take two whole weeks to complete providing the disintegrator held out. Bray explained the tunnels past the bunker were unstable especially with the current weather conditions.

"It's the goddamned monsoon season on Sigra and we are right in the worst affected area. The nukes Xen used on this planet doesn't seem to have made the weather any better!" Bray was obviously doing his best under the circumstances but was clearly feeling the strain especially with the timeline Colonel Lenz had set him. Bray turned on a large display which depicted a live feed of the tunnel excavation site. A gang of engineers and troopers worked in appalling conditions using an old mine disintegrator. Bray rattled on about conditions, materials and shift rotations as Daemon contacted the demon within.

"Well, what do you think? Have I gathered enough information regarding the tunnel?" He sat facing the demon within a fiery flickering dungeon of a room constructed from his very own psyche, a neutral meeting ground he thought.

"Yes. This is perfect Daemon. We now wait until it's completed." The demon stated tapping a clawed finger on the iron table between them.

"And what then? Considering people are dying every day making that tunnel."

"Your point being?" The demon queried with a frown, its dark oval deathly eyes devoid of understanding.

"Oh yeah, I forgot. Life means very little to you." Daemon shook his head in dismay.

"How can you say that? I have saved many lives during our journey." The demon said matter-of-factly without rancour.

"Yes. But more people die than you save."

"I only save the ones that really count! Remember I could have quite easily killed Sherry last night while you cried like a little baby in your dark retreat." The demon growled in a low rattle as though it would have enjoyed murdering Sherry for its own pleasure.

"So we wait then. Are we done?"

"For now, but I would be on my guard if I were you. I think the Colonel is after your blood and I don't blame him."

Daemon made some rudimentary copies from Lieutenant Bray's files. He thanked him for his information and headed off back to the camp with Sherry. As they entered the airlock Sherry pushed the emergency stop and rounded on him.

"So? Did you get what you came for?" She asked showing signs of discontent.

"Sherry, I'm just doing my duty like everyone else here. I don't know what you think I'm up to but there is nothing to it. Seriously, all I'm looking forward to is having a few beers in the canteen. Will you join me?" He said, ready to don his helm.

She sneered at him and clamped her helmet shut without deigning to reply.

Daemon shook his head sadly and secured his own helm. As he stood waiting for the airlock to run its cycle he heard the click of her local communications.

"Let's have some beers and maybe later. Well, I might finish off what we started."

Daemon couldn't help but hope so.

CHAPTER 22

Spaceman

The preliminary planetary scan showed no life forms on the small blue moon other than those in the small Delta-farm commune. The moon had no official name and though it may have had a number designation or at least some kind of signature it hadn't been recorded on the Evader's flight database. The tiny sphere of rock orbited a huge gas giant, a planet with an immense gravitational pull but with no other notable features apart from its spectacular purplish blue colour. This tiny backwater of space hadn't been bothered by any major corporation for decades as there wasn't any profit to be made from this ragtag collection of sterile moons and planets. The colonists on this moon were most probably the sixth generation and had probably never seen travellers or merchants within their lifetimes.

The colony appeared to be made up by four anti-matter shield domes. Two of the domes contained crops, one livestock and the last dome held the living quarters. The domes protected the colonists from debris from space and the lunar surface dust storms, caused by the gas giant's gravity well. They also had a contingent of industrial particle emitters which quickly rendered meteorites and space crafts that ventured too near into harmless dust. The emitters could only be utilised on a planet or the moon without any other life forms as anything outside of the emission zone would be vaporised.

This Delta-farm differed from the giant corporate installations on numerous planets which grew exotic plants and livestock to be sold profitably on the great interstellar market. This colony was purely self-sufficient and only grew enough to sustain the humans living there. There was practically no waste and everything was recycled, including body matter to be used in the crop fields.

Miles browsed the life signs and counted sixty-four heat signatures within the domes and no reading of any type which could be construed as being any serious weaponry other than the great particle emitter installations. He considered the amount of inbreeding the colonists would have been subjected to and surmised that the gene-pool would be spread rather thinly. However, after being isolated for so long in the absence of diseases they would be perfect subjects for his experimentation.

The Evader's stealth shields would allow him to slip past the particle emitter undetected so Miles tapped in the landing coordinates and switched to auto-pilot. He couldn't believe his luck in coming across such an opportunity, a settlement of unarmed colonists to harvest. He rushed down to the cryo-chamber and peered through the curved glass at Tinya, still icy cold and riddled with the life-threatening Miles II virus. She was safe for now but he cursed himself and hugged the cyro-tube.

In his haste to escape The Dairy, he had not examined his antivirus for the full range of side effects. Because of the secretive nature of its development, there was no way he could have done fully. It was only when he had performed a routine medical check upon himself he had found that he had become sterile.

He kissed the cold glass and pulled up his white smock and started masturbating to the visage of Tinya within the tube. When he ejaculated against the side of the glass he broke down and wept knowing he couldn't ever spawn any children himself with his seedless fluid. Miles had spent a month in the onboard laboratory during his journey through space in the attempt to reverse his affliction but nothing he had tried seemed to work.

The Evader landed undetected about a mile away from the delta farm commune and the innocent colonists were in total ignorance of the evil that had come to their doorstep. Miles browsed the armoury noting that it had several varieties of E.C.A. which the

Administrator had collected over his long life. It appeared that he had been somewhat of a collector as there were some vintage suits including an old P5 Hazard model. These were from the golden era of corporate expansion and were built to last and very durable in extreme conditions. The only alteration made to the P5 was the bayonet fitting to adapt to modern day couplings for the boots, gloves and helmet. It must have been the Administrators favourite as it had been used only a month ago according to the suits battle-log read out upon its archaic L.C.D.

Miles couldn't resist using the P5 so he clambered in through its old frontal hinge system and warmed up the suit. The hinge hissed shut and unlike modern suits, it took a while for the operating system to flicker into action bringing up old-fashioned fonts on the helm display. An educated sounding computerised male voice told him the suit was ready to use. Miles was used to hearing the monotone female voice which had replaced the old voice over a hundred years ago. He walked the suit to a full mirror and peered at himself for a while.

It was a dull grey colour with flashes of green trimming and a hell of a lot chunkier than modern suits. It felt a little top heavy but he presumed he would eventually get used to its balance. Miles liked the brassy fixtures; the gauntlets and centurion style helmet but frowned at the gaudy gold cooling fins sprouting from the back of the suit. You had good taste Mr Administrator, it's a shame you were a callous prick.

Miles put the Evader on maximum security and left

the stealth shield on. He clambered down the ships belly ladder and leapt onto the moon's dusty surface. Several dust devils swirled on the surface kicking up a convenient dust storm that would quickly cover the evidence of his passing. He walked the featureless land until he could see the shimmering domes ahead. From then on he crawled slowly through the deep dust deposits obscured from sight.

Imogene sat under a small group of Os-Os fruit trees sheltered from the heat of the Sol-lights high in the shield dome. She liked to play here because the air smelled and tasted better, plus the shade of the trees made this a magical place. Her parents forbade her playing here because of the proximity of the shield walls. There was nothing stopping a person walking through the shields into the vacuum of space and they feared she might trip up or accidentally or run through the shields. The last time her parents caught her playing here they had punished her severely, her fruit ration was cut for a whole week and she was made to stay in the habitat for over a month.

Outside Miles watched the shimmering image of the little blonde girl, a girl of eight years maybe ten. She was talking to something in her hands which he couldn't make out due to the shifting shield wall. Whatever she was saying he couldn't hear from out here so he moved closer still and flicked a talk-bug through the shields.

"… and one day we will go to the stars and live in the heavens and we wouldn't be made to plant crops or peel Gannypods anymore and then I will marry a starman and drift from star to star. I will be the queen of the stars and you can be my space advisor." She whispered to her spaceman dolly which she cradled like a newborn baby in her arms.

Miles nearly wept in his helm; he was sterile and could never sire a daughter.

If I can't create an heir then I shall adopt one! He thought erratically. A distant cry shook him from his thoughts.

The girl dropped the spaceman dolly in panic at the sound of the voice calling for her.

"Imogene? Imogene?" A female voice echoed in acoustic of the dome.

The girl ran off towards the centre of the dome and when she had covered most of the ground towards the centre of the crop dome a woman appeared at the Ion arc entrance. She waved to her daughter.

"I hope you have been playing in the crop fields and not near the orchard?" The woman shouted in a parental tone.

Imogene ran to her mother's arms and hugged her midriff for a while. They talked for a while but the talk-bug couldn't pick up what they said even when he boosted the amplitude. Miles waited until they walked through the ion arc into the main habitat. He crawled forwards and tested the shield with his gauntleted fingers before passing the barrier. The dust that had collected on his suit was captured in the field and he watched for a second as the motes wandered upwards.

Miles thought that it was beautiful and shook his head at how many people neglected to appreciate the beauty that science could create.

He looked around and saw the discarded spaceman doll face down on the ground. He picked up the drab white toy and looked at it.

"Hello Spaceman, been left behind have you?" he asked.

He placed it at the base of the tree, seated with its back against the trunk, then searched around the soil for the talk-bug and found it amongst a few leaves that had been shed. Picking it up he looked around for a better place to secure the device and spotted an old rusted wheel cart; its wheels were half-embedded in the rich soil as if it had been abandoned. He plucked a ripe reddish fruit from one of the trees then knelt down next to the cart and carved a smiling face into the fruit's flesh with the suits las-cutter. Pleased with his artistry he placed the talk-bug as its nose then positioned the fruit under the shadows of the cart. Finally, he fixed a small Vigi-cam on the handles looking towards the tree where the spaceman was propped up and the distant ion-arc. Satisfied he carefully crawled back through the shield dome.

Back on the Evader Miles stripped down an old bubble suit to fit a young girl. He worked through the night making sure the new seals worked and fitted a medical compressor to the back of the new suit. It looked rather heavy so he tested its weight remembering she wouldn't be strong enough to carry a full kit. Dissatisfied, he redesigned and scavenged smaller parts from more modern armour to reduce its bulk. Where parts could not be scavenged he machined a number of parts which he cut from some of the lesser bulkheads of the Evader. Finally, the lightweight suit hung limply on the work manikin, it was ugly and drab.

He looked at it and stroked his chin. "It needs to be coloured!" he said out loud with a trace of excitement, "Pink maybe? No! I know!"

Miles took down the new bubble suit and spray painted the entire thing an off-white, near as possible the same colour as her little spaceman doll. Before he left the ship he brewed himself up a quick stimulant, laboratory quality and not a hint of caffeine.

Miles made his way to the same spot he had been the previous day and waited and waited like some patient lizard waiting to catch an insect. Just as he was about to give up hope he saw Imogene rush through the ion arc into the crop dome. She skipped to one of the vegetable patches and pulled up a root vegetable before sneaking off towards the orchard. It looked as if she was searching for something and Miles smiled to himself. Finally, she came to the little grove and spotting her dolly before sitting down beside it.

"There you are!" she said and brushed the dirt from the fist-sized tuber in her hand. Once she seemed satisfied she bit into the vegetable spitting out the skin. Miles could hear her humming a song to herself between mouthfuls and now and then she pretended to feed her dolly.

"Last night I dreamed you came and found me and hugged me so tight that I became you!" She giggled and the holding the little space man made him dance with glee.

Miles could see her clearly now, the vigi-cam live feed was perfect with her sat central in the cameras focus.

"Imogene, over here, under the cart." He called through his intercom to the talk-bug. Miles had re-wired his voice transmitter to synthesise the educated male voice of the P5 suit he wore.

Imogene looked around wondering where the strange accented voice came from. It was a tone she had never heard. Miles grimaced. The accent of the commune was totally different from the Uni-language spoke in the corporate galaxies.

"Who is that?" Imogene asked with a smile of wonder on her face.

Miles switched the synthesised voice off and tried to mimic the accent spoken by the commune.

"Under the cart, I am here, can't you see me?" He asked.

Imogene crawled towards the shadows of the cart dragging the little space man for comfort. Her brown eyes searched the shadows.

"Hello, Imogene." The smiling fruit stated.

Imogene wasn't smiling anymore; her face had taken on a curious yet cautious frown. She looked over towards the Ion arc to see if her brother was around playing a trick on her but Tadd was nowhere to be seen.

"Do you want to see the stars?" The fruit asked her.

She giggled nervously and looked around her again.

"You sound funny, who are you?" She asked in a tone betraying that she instinctively sensed danger.

"I am a spaceman. I will never harm you." The fruit smiled.

"Your mouth doesn't move when you talk and your nose looks silly." She stated.

Miles tried to think fast, he didn't want to take her by force, it wouldn't be right.

"If you wish to come along with me I will show you the stars." The smiling fruit was pitching to one side. Miles cursed to himself as the vibrations of the little nose speaker overbalanced the fruit.

Imogene perched herself next to the cart then grabbed the fruit and shook it to see if something rattled inside.

"Imogene stop that! I am delicate you might break me." He pleaded trying to keep the impatience from his voice.

She pulled the talk-bug from the fruit and discarded the organic matter over her shoulder. She studied the small device in her fingers mopping off the juice with the cuff of her shirt.

Miles was unexpectedly pleased that she had seen through his childish ploy. So you're intelligent. Good! You will make a fine daughter. He thought.

"Where are you really? This isn't you." She stated with a great big grin.

"You got me. I am actually outside the dome. Look to the left of you." She shot a look to her left and saw a shimmering figure stood outside the shield wall. A bulky alien made from metal. She smiled and waved.

"Hello, Mr Spaceman." She said as she waved some more. The stranger waved back and lifted up a small space suit.

"This is your's Imogene. But it's only yours if you wish to come with me." The alien said.
She looked in awe at the shimmering suit.

"Shall we see what you look like in your new space suit?" The alien asked.

"Wait! I haven't decided if I want to come yet." She said slyly.

"No Imogene you haven't yet. Do you want more time to decide?" The alien crumpled up the suit and put it back in a sack.

Imogene nearly screamed at the alien taking her chance away to see the stars. She stood and got as close to the shield wall as she could before the static began to raise the hairs on her head.

"I want to come. Please, I want to come! I don't like this place!" She pleaded.
Miles handed her the bubble suit through the shield wall but remained where he was instructing her in how to properly put it on.
She had nearly finished getting inside the suit when a thought came to her.

"Can spaceman come with me?" She asked holding up the dolly.

"Of course, he has his own suit and can survive outside the dome, I don't see why not." The alien said reassuringly.

When she had finished putting on the bubble suit the alien held out its hand through the shield which she reached out for and grabbed.

"Now it feels a little funny going through the shields but don't worry. I am here."
Imogene started to walk through as an itchy sensation washed over her.

"I don't like!" She said.
The alien crouched and gripped her hand stronger.

"You are nearly there, just another step and you're through." Miles couldn't hide the impatience in his tone. He was so close to gaining a daughter.
She was through the barrier and the itching feeling stopped immediately. Imogene walked through the dust, deep to her knees, hand in hand with the alien. She had dreamt of walking in the forbidden zone numerous times from daydreams to night time visions. The dust devils swirled around them as they walked the mile to the Evader.

She felt like she was walking on air, the alien was making her dreams come true. After an hour of walking, Miles sensed the Evader was close. He tapped his arm terminal and cancelled the stealth mode of his craft. A large and mighty ship crackled into view, arcs of dissipating lightning illuminated the sleek black hull of the Evader. Imogene hugged the alien and danced in the dust, excitement couldn't even describe how she felt.

"This ship is yours Imogene, Queen of the Stars!" The alien crouched down in front of her and pretended to kiss her hand in a noble manner like a fairytale prince.

Inside the ship Miles kept his P5 on, he didn't want to reveal the fact he was human under his bulky garments. He led her on a small tour of the Evader and explained she need not wear her bubble suit inside the ship. At first, she was reluctant to remove her spacesuit but he promised to show her the pilot controls and once she was ready he briefly showed her the local star map on the navi-display. Then he took her to one of the private quarters on the upper deck.

"This is your bedroom, Imogene. Here is your bed." Miles said pointing to a cryotube. "It is a magic bed that makes all of your dreams come true. Do you want to see if it comfy?"

Imogene climbed into her cyrotube and lay there while the alien explained they were due to go into interstellar drive and could go anywhere she wanted. The alien sat next to her tube and read a story to her before he gently closed the cryo and iced her for transit. With this done Miles visited the armoury then returned to the piloting chamber and tapped in a new flight path. His finger hovered over the enter button for a while as he considered what he was about to do.
His brain went over and over the plan of action. No! Not yet. Rest first. He had neglected his original plan the moment he had seen the girl. He should complete what he had come here to do. He clumped his way back to the armoury, removed the P5, popped a tranquillizer and fell asleep on one of the medical beds.

Miles slept more than twelve hours and felt

extremely groggy when he awoke. After making himself breakfast from the ship's canteen he took a little of the stimulant he had made. He looked around at his surroundings; he was sat at a lonely table with three other empty tables around him. He drank freshly steeped tea and absentmindedly stroked the three lumps on his neck. One of the lumps was the original Xen chip they had placed in him years ago, the one which brought the voices, the other two lumps were chips of his own design. They merged with the original chip and scrambled the voices so he could now choose whether to hear their council or not. More importantly, they prevented Xen decrypting his true location in the galaxies. With breakfast out of the way, he busied himself in the ship's laboratory and cooked up a batch of low-grade nerve gas.

The Evader lifted from the moon's surface, its jets billowing fine dust all around the craft. It hovered for a while until just enough dust could be picked up by gravitational winds to create a thick obscuring screen. The anti-static of the stealth shields kept the dust away from the hull so that its shape wouldn't be revealed by settling particles. Slowly the craft skimmed the surface of the moon heading in circles around the colony until the dust storm covered about six square miles of the moon. The colonists were blind to the world outside the shield walls and since storms like these occurred every once in a while would have no cause for alarm.

The auto-pilot kept the craft low enough to avoid the particle emitters and turned the craft 180 degrees landing it half inside and a half outside the crop dome. Its invisible gang plate descended onto the soft earth. Miles waited for a moment scanning the interior with image enhancers to ensure that nobody was working the field. He held a dart rifle loaded with tranquillizers and a cylinder of the homemade nerve gas was attached to the utility belt. The P5 allowed him to leap over thirty feet from the Evader into the cover of the orchard where he waited.

Miles didn't have to wait very long before the P5 detected motion from the Ion arc that entered the habitat dome. Three men wandered into the crop dome dressed in overalls burdened only with long tools they used for cultivation. They chatted gruffly to one another while they walked then one of them laughed a little, the sound echoed around the dome.

Miles unfolded the rifle's bipod and targeted one of the farmers. It was hard at first using the old P5 targeting system and he performed three dummy runs before he even attempted to fire his first dart.

"Ow!" Roul cried dropping his tools and rubbing his shoulder. Something tiny and metallic fell to the floor.

"What's the matter Roul?" Donnie asked.

Wegg seemed to find the situation amusing until Roul dropped to his knees.

"Roul?" Wegg said with a worried frown as Roul fell face down in the dirt.

"Shit!" Donnie screamed holding his leg tightly.

Wegg crouched down to take a look at Donnie's leg and pulled out a tiny prong of metal.

"Fucking hell Wegg, watch what you're doing!" Donnie complained.

Wegg held up the piece of metal to the light to take a better look.

"What is it? Gods, I feel funny." Donnie said before he crumpled to the ground his eyes rolling back until they only showed the whites.

Wegg peered around the dome nervously patting at his friend trying to wake him up. The final dart struck the last farmer right in the back of his neck and the toxins worked quicker there it seemed. By the time it had taken Miles to run to the farmers they were all out cold.

Miles examined them and crushed the larynxes of the two smaller farmers and tied up the other one with Billy-tape. He was a well-built man, six foot tall by Miles estimation, broad on the shoulders and rugged in appearance. The tag on his overall read Wegg.

"Ok Wegg, you're going to have to do," Miles whispered to himself. Miles knew he would be out cold for a few hours so made his way to the Ion arc.

The habitat dome contained a huge ugly drab grey alloy building. From the Ion-arc he could make out a few emergency airlocks attached to the side of the living quarters. He watched two females carrying water skins wander through another ion-arc which connected to another crop dome to the north. He ran to the first airlock and pushed the control switch. The airlock creaked open revealing the lock space, he entered and waited for the machine to run its cycle.

He noticed that the inside of the habitat had been carpeted with weavings and the walls were adorned with animal pelts and other rustic hangings. His P5 ambient senses picked up echoed voices from a room just off the main corridor so he readied his weapons and peered into the room. Four old ladies sat crossed legged on stuffed cushions, they chatted idly as they busied themselves weaving.

They won't put up any fight but they may warn others, he thought. Miles stormed into the room and the old women looked at him with a mixture of fear and awe.

"Scream and I will kill you all. Move and I will kill you all!" The metal man stated.

They seemed to understand and nodded in unison. Miles moved with his rifle trained on them and looked into another room which seemed to be the habitat canteen and kitchen. It was large enough to seat about thirteen families. A slim woman sizzled vegetables on a heated plate and hadn't noticed the bulky armoured man at the doorway. He raised the rifle and aimed at the back of her neck, he squeezed the trigger which dropped her in a matter of seconds.

"Stay here." He commanded to the four women then headed into the kitchen getting the Billy-tape out again and carefully restraining the unconscious woman.

Miles went from room to room, killing or restraining his victims dependent on his needs, it wasn't long before he had six unconscious females aged between twenty and forty. He dragged each female to the airlock, under the watchful and fearful eyes of the older women who shivered each time he passed them. He spent another half an hour carrying and dragging his prizes back to the Evader, including the male Wegg.

Miles thought about killing the remainder of the colony but something nagged at his soul.

"Maybe I will leave them be," he decided, "I have already stagnated the gene pool by taking six females and a prime male. Not to mention killing another eight. Yes! I will leave them to survive with what they have. Maybe they will piece themselves back together in a few generations? Doubtful, but at least I offer them the chance of life."

Miles iced all of his specimens and plotted a new course to a far distant planet. The Evader cruised away from the colony until it was far enough away from the emitters for him to engage the main thrust jets and establish a safe orbit around the moon. Once in orbit, he jettisoned a transmitter buoy purposely so that Xen could eventually pick up his last location and coordinate.

He closed his eyes and accessed the Xen chip inside him.

"Dr Miles where are you, please report your position and surrender yourself?" The voice asked immediately.

Miles grinned to himself.

"Far from your clutches, however, I have left something for you to discover. Nothing much I admit but it will show you whom you are dealing with." Miles said mockingly.

"The virus you released at The Dairy killed over a hundred people, Dr Miles. Why would you do that?" The voice asked; this time its tone seemed angered.

"I've spent most of my teenage life and beyond creating viruses for Xen and you stole every single idea I created with that fucking chip you surgically implanted in me!" Miles spat. He was so angered that he hit the pilots console with his palm. The voice went silent for a while and Miles held his head shaking away his rage.

"Come home, Miles. Xen needs you!" The voice whispered.

"Oh, I will come home but not in body. I'll be back in spirit! When the corporate engine grinds to a halt and you find that my virus is destroying you, then, then you will know I have returned!" Miles opened his eyes breaking all communication with the Xen chip.

Miles hit the auto-pilot button and The Evader took control warming up its drive engines. The ships interstellar drives howled and shook the craft causing static discharges to leap from the hull's exterior. As The Evader jumped and swayed finding a safe course to take to its destination Miles quickly made his way to his private quarters and leapt into a cryo tube before the sickness took hold of him. Miles was iced as The Evader leapt into true drive leaving only an orbiting transmitter buoy and a stagnant Delta-farm upon the dusty moon.

CHAPTER 23

Recuperation

Roz rolled away from the swiping claws of the jungle cat then threw his full weight into the side of the beast. Pain shot through his body as he knocked it off its feet and landed on top of it on his wounded side. He wriggled his body trying to pin it down and free up some space so he could strike a killing blow. Grabbing a handful of fur he levered his leg and rolled on top of the creature and buried his blade deep within its flesh. A stench of stomach gas filled his nostrils and the great creature thrashed under him then fell still. He lay on top of the creature for a minute feeling nauseous then took a look at his opponent. It was a magnificent animal with vibrant orange fur and long curved teeth. Its paws were about nine inches wide with two double edged talons coated with a pungent clear fluid. Roz rubbed his fingertips on the talon then sniffed the oily residue, it smelt acrid and odd. He felt another wave of nausea passing through him and his stomach cramped up. His vision began to blur and he slumped down against the soft fur of the cat before passing out.

An old woman wept as she rocked in her favourite chair near a blood-stained window. Behind her Madeline ran around frantically, her head hanging from a thread. At the foot of the old woman, Karli swept up broken glass and blood from the floor of the filthy apartment. Gidd stood next to Karli drinking viscous red fluid from a glass tumbler and laughing insanely between gulps.

A blue electronic chip swirled down a sink as Gidd smiled and winked within the reflection of a mirror.

Explosions tore people apart, people with hollow faces in total disbelief and horror. Daemon vomited blood into a huge receptacle, a great bowl that overflowed as he continued to disgorge red fluids.

Daemon? Daemon wiped his mouth of gore and looked up. He grinned revealing pointed bloodied teeth with eyes of pure black as Karli mopped the overspill from the receptacle her face full of despair.

Karli? She stopped her work and took off her clothing slowly. When she was naked she turned around. The flesh on her back was marred with the scars of a whip. Daemon caressed and probed the welts with an evil grin on his face. Twisted horns sprouted from the top of his head as Karli moaned with pleasure from Daemons touch.

LEAVE HER ALONE! Roz cried, as darkness took him again...

Roz awoke in a small room adorned with dried animal skins and bones over the walls. The room smelt of putrefied fat and bile. He tried to lift his head but his body refused, he tried once more in spite of the pain and sickness it caused him. He managed to elbow his way up to a sitting position on a bed seemingly made of furs and leaves. A tumbler of discoloured water stood on a low side table and looking at the crusted rim he dimly remembered drinking from the vessel but an hour ago just after he had thrown up. He looked down at the bed and noticed a receptacle half filled with watery vomit stinking in the humid heat of the room.

He had vague recollections of someone caring for him over many days but it all seemed like a bad nightmare. He had drifted from dreams into what he presumed was real events, or was all this a fabrication of his mind? Was he still in that terrible forest? Had he really killed a great wild animal?
He shook his head in confusion and tried to concentrate. He clearly remembered the crash landing in the great rain forest but little else. He looked down at his body and saw that lacerations, cuts and infections covered his body and that a yellowish paste had been smeared over the wounds which oozed stinking discharges. He closed his eyes and soon fell into a dreamless sleep.

Out in the forest, a woman walked carefully holding a brace of groundhoppers which she had cleaned and gutted about a mile away from her home. She knew the scent of blood would attract large predators towards her but she seemed to have an understanding with them. She felt that they looked upon her as a fellow predator and gave her a wide birth unless the instincts of hunger took them. Only under those circumstances would she be tested and end up having to fight in bloody melee. She tried to remember how long she had been in the forest as a wild woman; too long she presumed, long enough so that she couldn't even remember how she had got to this wild place. Something prowled to her flank, it had been following her for a while now, slowly and very cautiously. Probably a Zol-cat she thought moon's but she wasn't sure. She dropped one of the ground hoppers and hoped the beast would be satisfied with her offering. She hadn't got more than fifteen feet away before a large feral creature leapt out and took the ground hopper disappearing into the forest within a blink of an eye. She sighed in great relief.

"You're getting rusty Chinn that was no Zol-cat!" she thought. The rainforest had changed over the last year or so; it seemed new beasts roamed around and some of them she hadn't had the chance to name yet. She had heard rumours from the merchants at the trading posts she visited once in a while that laboratory installations had been set up deep in the forest, laboratories that upset the balance of nature by experimenting with genetics. She doubted the rumours and thought the strange and new beasts had always roamed the rain forest but had migrated north due to the urban spread of cities. She reached an embankment and clambered over the small obstacle to set eyes upon her home. The hut she had built with very own hands stood at the foot of a rocky verge, a trickling stream meandered but ten feet from her home. She smiled and relaxed now that she neared her sanctuary.

When she walked through the entrance she saw that the man had moved and propped himself up. His body perspired like a crushed sponge leaving the blankets sodden with moisture. She knelt at the side of the bed and smoothed a wet cloth over his chest and cheeks. "Handsome devil aren't you? Even in the throws of toxic sleep." She smiled and blushed at thinking of such things. For heavens sakes Chinn, you're old enough to be his mother.

She brought down a handcrafted mortar and pestle from a low shelf and worked some herbs, toadstools and fruit juices into a paste. The wounds were healing by her estimation and his body was fighting the infections and poisons that defiled him. He would soon be better she thought.

Unexpectedly his hand shot out and gripped her throat but with a grip as weak as a kitten.

"Who are you?" He croaked.

She pushed his hand away gently and a smile crept up her cheeks forming a perfect crescent.

"Hush little man. You are safe. Be thankful for my

help!" she said.

Roz peered at her through a fevered haze. He could see that she was much older than he was; her face was marked with scars, her eyes wrinkled slightly at the sides like avian feet. Even so, Roz suspected she would have been pretty in her younger days but the toil of survival had carved its blemish upon her.

"How long? I must go..." He whispered, interrupting his sentence with a fit of coughs. He tried to elbow himself up further but she pushed him back down upon the bed.

"Not long at all. A few days, maybe more, time really has no meaning out here." She said softly shrugging her shoulders.

Roz tried to say more but was too weak. He passed out and Chinn changed his dressings and prepared a meal by a low burning stove.

Two more days of tormented fever passed before Roz could get out of bed. It was early morning and the sun was streaming through the open door. Having got to his feet he noticed the woman had prepared his breakfast and left it on a low table next to the bed. His stomach growled as he spooned down the warm meaty broth and as he ate he could hear singing, or at least what sounded like singing, coming from outside the hut. He finished the last spoonful and painfully walked the distance to the door of the hut. He guessed it would be at least a week before he was well enough to resume travelling to his destination. Even that depended on being able to get enough rations from the hut to sustain him on the journey.

The singing hadn't stopped and seemed to come from within the forest. He leant against the frame of the door and felt the cool breeze of the morning forest bringing the scent of damp earth and ferns. The singing was louder now and coming from somewhere close. He laboured with every step following the singing until he came to an overhang of rubbery plants. He parted the great leafy stalks to reveal a pool of water twenty or so feet down in a natural bowl. A naked woman sat in the shallows of the algae-covered pool bowling water over her long salt and pepper hair. Her dark olive skin glistened like dew in the morning light. She turned and looked up towards him and he bashfully averted his eyes from the scene.

Chinn watched him looking away and wondered why he did it before assuming that it must be some kind of custom of his culture.

"Are you feeling better?" She asked as she crushed the water from her hair.

"Yes. Much better but I am still weak." He admitted.

She stood up and brushed off the algae that had gathered on her waist.

"Good. You are strong." She paused and added, "What is your name?" whilst wrapping a blanket of fur around her nakedness.

He paused for a while in deep thought. The fever had taken its toll on him and remembering things seemed hard. For some reason he felt that he should not tell her, it was as if he was expected some internal warning telling him to lie but none came.

"Roz. Yeah, Roz. I had almost forgotten!" He chuckled in remembrance of his own name.

"Don't worry… Roz. I often forget my name. The forest does strange things to a person. My name is Chinn by the way." She wandered up the embankment towards him.

He no longer covered his eyes now that she was clothed and Chinn understood that his strange reaction had been something to do with her nakedness. However, she still didn't understand why he had done so.

Roz offered his hand to her as she approached the last part of the climb but she refused and looked at him strangely. Roz didn't realise he had insulted her warrior-hood by offering his aid. She looked at the strange man and wondered if the females of his race were helpless.

"Come on let's get you back inside before you fall over!" She said reversing the roles and helping him back to her abode.

They talked all morning about his ordeals in the forest after the crash landing. She laughed when he told her about the great hunting cat attack.

"A Zol-cat? Is that all?" She laughed again pointing to the furry blanket she wore. "What do you think this has been made from?" She really had the giggles and Roz couldn't help but join in, he found it impossible to be offended by her behaviour, it was clear to Roz that she was a great warrior and demanded respect.

"Well I killed it at least?" he laughed.

"Only the one?" she asked and pointed to several

452

more furry blankets around the hut and laughed more. "Zol-cats are the least of your worries out here. There are greater predators that roam the forest, some standing a few feet higher than you." She threw the blanket to the ground and grabbed a few garments to wear.

He turned away while she changed. He guessed she was fifty or fewer standard years old, a good eighty years left in her probably. Maybe more if she had a good genetic bloodline but who could tell with the hard life she had endured out in the wilds.

"You can look now." She announced with a strange smile on her face. She wore a macabre collection of grotty animal pelts sewn together with great skill.

"I am hungry, are you? She asked.

His stomach rumbled at the mere mention of food and he nodded. She busied herself in a draped-off area which smelt of wood smoke and dried meat. After a short time, she produced several cuts of smoked meat and prepared them with a sprinkle of herbs and a delicate smear of honey. They ate and talked more, mostly about Roz, but now and then a small tale about Chinn.

A week had passed in the sanctuary of the hut. Every now and then Chinn went hunting, gathering fresh meat and foraging for fruit and nuts. She taught Roz how to smoke the meat in order to sustain its shelf life and showed him some basic survival skills such as broiling salt from the fat of several animal species. His assistance in doing these menial tasks gave her more time to hunt but Roz formed the impression that she taught him these skills so he could remain there with her. Early on the eighth day he announced to her that he had to leave, she didn't weep but she was clearly upset.

"Your life until now sounded horrible. At least when you kill something out here its survival and not some kind of contractual kill! Stay! I want you to stay!" She pleaded.

He had broken every rule in the Kommando covenant, he had told her about the Kommando School and the assassinations in the name of Xen. He took hold of her shoulders and locked eyes with her.

"Listen I would like to stay but I need to get back right now. I am already late and I need to finish what I started."

Chinn shook her head in dismay.

"You can't leave. You wouldn't survive two days in the wild." She stated matter-of-factly.

Roz knew she was right and that he couldn't survive out there, not even with the meagre skills he had learnt from Chinn.

"That is why I need you to come with me." He said without expression.

Her face contorted in confusion, she sat down staring wildly at her kit bag.

"You ask too much from me Roz! You are talking about miles of unexplored rainforest. Dangerous places even I avoid."

Roz knelt in front of her and held her legs.

"Chinn I don't want you to come with me. I need you to come with me."

She didn't know how to take his words and she stood puzzled wondering if he required her assistance to get away from her or if he meant something else. Roz saw the play of emotions on her face and sought to ease her concern.

"Chinn I meant it as a compliment. I want you with me but I don't want to put you in any danger."

She remained stunned into silence for a while before she hesitantly tried to put her feelings into words.

"Roz, you can imagine the years of solitude I have harboured. It has been a lonely life out here in the wilds. I have never been needed before, it's a new, perhaps, I should say, an old emotion I had forgotten about."

"Will you come with me?" He asked.

She looked down upon him into his bright icy blue eyes and felt other old, forgotten sensations through her body.

"The journey will be dangerous, maybe even life threatening, but I will come anyway, now that I am needed again. Especially, if it you who needs me." She smiled ruffling his hair.

Early the next morning Chinn organised the rations, water skins and equipment needed for the journey. She checked through Roz's remaining possessions and tossed away his electronic compass explaining instruments of its kind didn't always work in the forest due to the amount of iron ore in the indigenous rock. Roz sat outside the hut sharpening the knives she had given him and then moved onto cleaning the hunting rifles with natural lubricants. Chinn stepped out of the hut carrying several packs of equipment. She was dressed in heavy pelts with a rifle slung over her shoulder and knives close to hand.

"Take off your clothing Roz and wear these." She threw him a bundle of pelts and leather twine. He stared at the bundle for a while a little embarrassed about stripping in front of her.

"When you're out here it is best to smell like the forest. The clothes you wear at the moment smell of man." She noticed his reluctance to strip and added. "I will cover my eyes if you wish. It is your custom yes?"

He smiled and nodded nervously wondering why he was so reticent to show this woman his nakedness. Chinn peered through the gaps of her fingers watching closely as he undressed. She felt a warm and fluttery sensation in the pit of her gut from his muscular body marked with scars from numerous battles and; oh yes, a big fellow indeed.

When he had dressed and all the fun had gone from peeking at him she walked around inspecting him, she retied a few knots and tugged loose some of the pelts that were far too tight. Chinn then packed him up, distributing the weight of weapons and packs equally. Satisfied she playfully bumped into his shoulder testing his agility and balance. He didn't budge and she seemed satisfied that his strength had returned.

"Ready to go?" She asked as she smeared a mossy clump around his neck and forehead. The moss smelt like a mixture bitter lemons and a mild detergent. He sniffed at it suspiciously.

"Bug repellent." She explained and did the same to herself.

It was nearly midday and Roz needed to rest yet again. He had rested twice already, not used to the relentless heat and humidity or the intense activity. Chinn granted a rest stop but she was clearly getting impatient with stopping and starting all the time. He collapsed on a low rock, sweat dribbling off his cheeks as he panted what seemed to feel like his last breath.

"You will have to slow down a little Chinn. I can't keep up the pace." He spluttered through intense pain in his chest.

She made some kind of sign with her hand which he assumed signified something to do with 'washing her hands of him'.

"We have to move quickly Roz, if we stay still too long, predators will pick up our trail and attack us." She paced back and forth eager to get moving again.

"I don't think I had recovered as much as I thought." He said offering an excuse, "Anyway I'm used to short bursts of speed, not endurance running. I am an assassin for fucks sakes! I stalk my victim slowly and when the time is right I am swift." He trailed off as his words obviously had no meaning to a woman of the wilds.

"Ok, I will slow down a little but we need to move now. This is Zol-cat territory and I am in no mood to fight right now." In her exasperated state, she hadn't noticed a large beast had stalked up behind her in the undergrowth.

Roz saw a shape rising behind her shoulders and adrenaline filled his veins burning away all the pain he was suffering like a cleansing fire. He leapt towards Chinn and pushed her away from the line of attack of the strange bipedal beast. It reared up in front of him, towering over him and putting on an intimidating display. Roz faced it reaching for two large curved knives used for clearing away through the jungle. The beast roared at him and took a step forward.

Chinn had picked herself up and had levelled her rifle at the creature carefully taking aim and shooting it in the head stopping it dead. Roz jumped at the report from the rifle and stood looking down at the beast. He suddenly felt drained and the pain returned. The creature, whatever it was, was far bigger than the Zol-cat he had killed weeks before; it had scales like a reptile and sprouts of fur at its joints. What remained of its head had the appearance of an overgrown canine. He felt Chinn's hand on his shoulder, soothing out his tense muscles, her head resting against his arm.

"Thank you." She whispered. Roz shrugged, it had all happened so fast he didn't have time to think about his actions.

"You were right; it's my fault that it attacked. We must keep on moving." His tone was distant.

"It's a Zangar. We have these creatures on my home world, that much I do remember. What it's doing here is anybody's guess." She crouched near the animal and carefully removed its musk gland from behind its ears.

"Rub its musk on your wrists. Zangar are solitary creatures and generally avoid one another until mating season. The scent should avoid other attacks by Zangar."

Roz did as he was told without question.

Chinn had slowed down her pace but Roz still needed rest periods between sessions of running but these were taken by walking slowly rather than stopping. Roz was glad that Chinn had relented since the incident and was happier to let him recover when needed, otherwise, he suspected, she would have run him into the ground. It was late in the day, barely two hours before darkness fell in the rainforest. They had come to a small clearing with a ridge of rock blocking the northern passage. Chinn had asked him to wait while she scouted the area and Roz had watched her like a hawk as she checked the surrounding forest for danger. She stopped near the rocky face and seemed to disappear into the stone itself.

"Chinn?" He hissed in panic. There was no reply. He scanned the clearing again. He was about to scream out her name when she reappeared from the rock and waved towards him.

"It's all clear. Come on quickly." She called.

Roz ran the distance and she grabbed his arm and pulled him through the rock face. A strange sensation fizzed on his skin as he passed through the false rock into the darkness beyond. She held his hand and guided him in the pitch black as he counted every footstep he took.

"Chinn, what is this?" He whispered in the dark. He hated surprises; in fact, he hated anything unknown.

"Be quiet!" She whispered.

Fear gripped him as her hand slipped from his. He blindly swept his arms in front of him trying to re-establish contact. For what seemed like an eternity he was alone until, eventually, he heard a mechanical clinking sound which echoed in the tunnel and daylight began to filter through the gap of a door that Chinn had opened. Through the open door, he could see a depression leading down to a wide circle of trees in a natural basin. High rocky crags loomed on each side isolating this section of the forest. In the centre of the overgrown area was a prefabricated alloy building with a few armoured vehicles next to it, twisted up in the vines and plant life.

"How the fuck did you find this place?" He asked in awe.

Chinn scowled at the language he used, the same scowl she always used when he said the word fuck.

"By accident I suppose. I felled an A-lope with my rifle and the beast disappeared into rock. I searched and found my hand could enter the rock, curiosity took over and I walked through." She said laughing at his expression.

"The section of rock is a holograph, strange really

they are seldom used nowadays. They were too costly to power." Roz explained. He paused at the implication that this meant the installation still had power and it could therefore still have an air-lifter.

"The building is empty but most of the rooms are locked. I think it has been abandoned for a good number of years, don't you?" Chinn asked while gesturing Roz to follow her.
They walked cautiously towards the building and Roz stopped in front of an old X.A17 armoured vehicle used to transport troops. The boxy vehicle had been decommissioned over twenty years ago due to a fault which would have been too costly to recall and repair. Roz had forgotten which company built the faulty machines but had seen them in operation on training film reels.

"Roz! Come inside." Chinn shouted from the door of the installation. He walked to the door and cleared away a moss covered plaque that read: SUPPLY DEPOT B7. It was dark inside so Roz pulled out his flashlight and looked for a coil box.

"It's safe Roz, I've used this place to hole up several times before. The large predators keep clear of this place. It's a man place you see?" Chinn smiled in the dim light not understanding what he was looking for. He was fiddling inside a metal box attached to the wall cursing a few times while he worked.

"And then there was light!" He said flicking the mains power switch in the coil box. The lights flickered for a while and then illuminated the main room. Chinn had readied her rifle in panic.

"It's ok Chinn. It's just light that is all." He hugged her to try and calm her down. When her body relaxed he removed her rifle from her.

"I need some time here Chinn, why don't you settle down for a while? Try and rest." Her eyes were wide with the fear of the unknown.

Roz closed the main door and settled himself down at a console terminal. The installation had been in standby for twelve years, all the data logs had been wiped apart from the last few entries in the system.

COLONEL KEBLA: (Dated twelve years and two months ago)

20:12: When the rescue team arrived the science team had preferential treatment as always. They were airlifted first. My troops were held at gunpoint until they evacuated the science team. Not that any of us could put up a fight. My troops were stripped naked, tagged and then airlifted. I chose to stay, they granted me my dignity due to my rank.

21:42: They really pulled a number on us here. I am pretty sure now that all of this was planned. It started three days ago when my troops began to feel ill. At first, we assumed it was jungle fever until they began to drop like flies. Corpses were gathered and burnt in the pit. Most of the science team didn't understand what was happening at first. It wasn't until half my troops had died they began to panic. The science team worked around the clock for a cure or something that could slow the process down. Everything they tried failed.

22:04: Feeling pretty bad now. I am glad I never married but I feel so alone now. I know Xen will not return to this place so I have encrypted a file hidden in the data logs. Somebody clever could upload the information if they wish. In all my years of service, I am convinced Xen has kept me downtrodden, it had taken me over sixty years of service to achieve the rank of colonel. It all seems for nothing now. Why didn't I follow in my father's footsteps? I could have owned my own plantation by now with many more years to live.

22:34: I am doomed. I can feel the virus working in my organs and bones. I have hours to live, a day at the most. Whoever finds this message I ask only one thing. DO NOT OPEN MY ROOM. It will be marked with a red cross. I believe even in death I will pose a threat to anything living. Which brings me to one conclusion, Xen wants the virus to be released on this world. Why? I have no idea.

23:25: I suspect this will be my last entry. I am to be another death in the name of Xen. I hope they rot in Hell!

********* NO OTHER ENTRIES *********

Roz scowled at the screen for a while. He searched the database but found nothing else. Maybe Xen knew the colonel would try and leave some indication of what had happened here. He was about to give up hope until he typed in the word 'red cross' and a file appeared on the display. He was still unable to open the protected file so Roz scanned through the colonel's last logs again and paused on the word 'Hell'. He knew that all systems like these had secret firewall protections which worked in the background operating systems. He attached the file to the firewall program which had been dubbed 'Clean Sweep' and the file opened.

SUPPLY DEPOT B7: Planet Talon II
Depot Commander: Colonel Kelba
Drill and Field: Sergeant Topma

Science Administrator: Dr Kelmon
Science team (Hons)
Dr Frak, Dr Yessur, Dr Ulran, Dr Inz & Dr Mullindow

Science team (secondary)
Student Hesloch, Student Finch, Student Colmah, Student Miles & Student Xu.
Recon & Squad Leader: Corporal Tanc
Private's:
Downs, Benz, Choe, Logan, Vimnark, Tess, Olan, Grendow, Sejid, Xann, Gltz, Faver, Taggen, Jurin, Myr-legg, Tobin, Sanli, Jani-Mari, Ol'Kahn, Jubbie, Corritz, Shobeck, Hannz, Lupie, Krotte, Florin, Pengal, Rassie, Dorach & Blitzburr.
Maintenance :-
Quirtiz, Pula, Inviss & Welmach.

Roz stared at the list of personnel and wondered why the Colonel had encrypted this file. Maybe he wanted to tell their families about the criminal activity that happened at supply depot B7? He couldn't make head nor tale of the list and decided to print it out. Chinn had already bedded down in a rough bedroll and was fast asleep now that she knew this place to be safe. Roz bedded down next to her and reread the list he had printed.

"Come on Kelba, what do you want me to do with this list? There must be something in this list you want me to see." He shook his head and cuddled up next to Chinn, she moaned a few times in her sleep before he drifted off to sleep beside her.

CHAPTER 24

Return

Roz knew he was dreaming of a day that had passed by when he was back at the Xen academy in one of Mistress Suix's boring lectures. She was droning on about corporate sabotage and the directives in place to keep the Xen Corporation safe. Roz's attention waned and he looked at Daemon, who was sat to his left, nursing his head and complaining of being hung over yet again. It looked like he had been up half the night shagging that Cian again; mind you, he mused, she was pretty damned hot so who would blame him?

In the seat next to Daemon sat a slight man with receding hair and jet black eyes. He didn't wear a normal jumpsuit like the rest of the students, instead, he wore civvies clothing. Roz was unnerved by the fact that you couldn't make out where he was looking. He leant over to Daemon and whispered to him.

"Who is that strange fucker sat next to you?" Roz asked.

"That's Miles, or should I say, Doctor Miles. He's been chipped already. Not to mention he's already completed the great test." Daemon told him.
Roz leant forward to get a better look at the odd man. He remembered feeling hatred towards this man called Miles, it was probably caused by jealousy due to the fact he was sat next to his best friend.

"I don't trust him. He looks like a corporate arse-hole!" He stated.
Daemon laughed and elbowed Roz playfully.

"Nobody trusts him, Roz. Would you trust a man that's been chipped already? Besides which, his field of intellectual pursuits includes bio-engineering. He's one of Xen's favourites by all accounts so you better not get any ideas of having him "slip" in the showers." Daemon stated.
Roz settled back in his seat and pretended to listen to Mistress Suix wondering what that freak had done to be so favoured by Xen.

Roz woke with a start and sat up in his bedroll his eyes unseeing in the total blackness of the room. The auto systems had turned down the main lights and he could hear that Chinn was still fast asleep. He reached out, fumbling for his flashlight and clicked it on. He searched for the print out he had taken and re-read the list of personnel, his eyes stopped and focused on the name 'Student Miles'.

"I wonder; are you the same Miles? It's a stab in the dark but we will see!" his mind was suddenly active.

He threw his bedroll aside and rushed to the computer terminal pressing the space bar and waiting as the screen came to life bathing the room in a soft blue light. His fingers were hovering above the keypad eager to type in the word 'Miles' when Chinn groaned and clambered out of her bedroll. She stood naked in the middle of the comms room stretching out her limbs.

"Roz? Are you ok?" She asked shivering in the cold of the installation, rubbing the sleep from her eyes. He looked back to the screen and away from her feminine form as a warmth grew in the pit of his stomach and his heart beat faster.

"Erm, yes, I'm fine. I just had a nightmare. I think." He said uncertainly while he tried to suppress his baser instincts.
Chinn padded over to his chair and wrapped her arms around him.

"You need rest. You have studied that thing all night. Come and rest." She smelt of the forest mixed with her own feminine scent. Her hug was tight around him and her long dark hair tickled his chest.

"Type the word! Type the word!" something inside him called out, he paused, balanced on the brink, unsure whether to follow the urges of his body rather than his brain. He sighed deeply knowing that now he had started thinking about if it was indeed Miles he couldn't be at peace until he found out one way or another.

"Give me ten minutes and I'll come to be with you. I need to find out one more detail."
She kissed his shoulder twice.

"Ten more minutes!" She said archly in a mock commanding tone as she made her way back to bed. He admired her athletically toned body in the dim light and was tempted to join her immediately.

"Type the word! Type the word!" The inner voice screamed and Roz succumbed and typed 'Miles'.
He smiled and felt the tension drain from his shoulders when no records were returned but it appeared his relief had been premature. The computer asked if he wished to search the external drives and Roz frowned as he hadn't been aware this system had any other storage devices other than the ones in the room. He pressed "Y" and the computer searched again and displayed that it was somehow connected to an old P.D.U. which was somewhere else in the installation. The display depicted a data sheet on Student Miles, including a picture of him. The striking difference in his appearance was that the picture had been taken before he had had those strange feral eyes implanted. He almost looked human.

"So you are the same Miles! Obviously, the good colonel was onto you before things went to shit."
The colonel had written several comments below his

data sheet; one dated three months before the virus infection at Supply Depot B7 and the other obviously written before he locked himself in the red crossed room. Roz read them with a sense of dread.

09:03: Xen has shipped in five students to aid the science team here. All of them seem to check out with the information Xen have provided me apart from Student Miles. For some reason, his qualifications have been edited by Xen under directive 32D and he seems to have a two-year gap in his history profile. This time there isn't even the usual directive editing, just a gap with no explanation. I will have to maintain a vigilant eye on him while he remains here.

23:44 : I should have killed him the day he arrived. Something just didn't ring true about him and the silence from Xen should have warned me. I am ninety-nine percent sure he engineered some kind of viral agent for them then released it. Whatever the virus was it immobilised and killed quickly. This has all the hallmarks of a 'great test' and I suspect Miles has more than passed his test here! The key code for the red crossed door is KEL65 but you won't find my corpse there simply because I am not infected. I probably will be soon though but before I go I'm determined that I will find that bastard Miles and make him wish his mother had kept her legs crossed!

Roz gawped at the display for a while with his jaw agape. He looked up towards the door to the main installation then down at Chinn who had fallen back to sleep; a soft purring sound emanated from her.

"Right then Colonel Kelba what have you left for me behind that locked door?"

He silently padded across to Chinn to make sure she was fast asleep then, satisfied, he headed to the main door of the installation. He winced as finally, the auto-systems detected his presence and the lights started to flicker on. He scuttled through the door quickly and began to search the corridors and rooms for a door marked with a red cross. The installation was bigger than he had first suspected but eventually, after a thorough search, he found a heavy steel door marked with a small red cross. He typed the code into the keypad and the door hissed open. The room beyond was a small hanger containing a jet black air-lifter and next to it was an empty air-lifter pad. The aircraft was vaguely cone-shaped with a rotary blade system above its main body. The eight Scimitar forged blades formed into a shape similar to the spokes of an umbrella.

Roz couldn't believe his luck; this aircraft could more than make the distance back to the Kommando School. He hooked up the power cable and set the aircraft on charge hoping after all these years it was still operational. He made his way back to Chinn and slid by her side listening to her groan a few times before settling back into her harmonic purr. After an hour of excited wakefulness the installations auto systems turned down the lights but still he couldn't sleep. He remembered flying in an air-lifter as a child with his father, both of them were passengers and although he had never piloted one he reasoned that it probably

471

couldn't be too hard. Roz hadn't realised Chinn was awake until she spoke to him.

"What did you find?" Chinn asked from the darkness. Roz nearly jumped from his bed clothes.

"I have found something, something that will get us both out of this stinking forest." He grimaced realising this 'stinking forest' was Chinn's home but luckily she hadn't taken any offence by his last comment.

"Are you going to tell me?" She asked as she snuggled next to him. Even in the darkness, he could sense she was smiling. She felt warm against him and he tried to think of explosives and sharp assassin weapons in the vain attempt of not becoming aroused.

"In the morning I will tell you." He said rolling onto his stomach to hide his arousal. Her leg smoothed over him, her breasts pressed against his back and her lips were moist against his neck. Chinn hugged him tight and settled herself for sleep.

"I liked it better when I was needed." She whispered in the dark.

"I do need you Chinn, nothing has changed." She seemed satisfied and drifted off into deep sleep.

Chinn awoke the next morning to find an empty space where Roz had slept. At first, she felt a sense of panic until she smelt food being prepared. She dressed and followed its scent and found the canteen mess hall. Roz was busying himself cooking breakfast, he had numerous pans over a hot plate, stirring and frying up preserved meat and beans. He noticed Chinn as she entered the canteen.

"I have raided the stasis pods and found lots of abandoned food. It's all tinned goods but I suspect it will taste OK."

Chinn made herself comfortable on a round table for two which Roz had already set. Shortly after Roz came over to her holding two pans.

"I think I might have overcooked the beans but this meat stuff looks alright." He pointed a spoon at four fat slabs of brown reconstituted griddled meat.

They settled down to breakfast and started on the relative feast of food before them compared to the usual meagre rations they were both used to. Chinn was soon feeling full and she watched Roz scooping up food with his spoon, he was all smiles and seemed different from the previous day when she had introduced him to the hidden installation. It seemed to her that he had reconnected with his own world and had all the confidence that brought.

"We leave today but not by foot," Roz said with a grin.

Chinn sipped a mouthful of the filtered spring water that tasted bland to her, not having the unique taste of the forest she used too, involuntary she screwed up her face in distaste.

"You will get used to processed food and water in time," Roz said noticing her dislike to the water.

"If we aren't walking out of here how are we travelling?" She asked looking for answers in Roz's face.

"Come on, I'll show you." He grabbed her hand and nodded over towards a door.

Chinn felt tense as he led her through the mazy installation and Roz gripped her hand reassuringly. He understood that she wasn't used to manmade constructions like this having been so long in the wild and that she intrinsically distrusted them. When they arrived at the hanger he pointed towards the air-lifter hoping she would recognise such a craft but instead she looked puzzled.

"It's all very pretty Roz but all I see is a black metal cone with four legs and some kind of weapon on the top. Is it a weapon of some kind?" She asked seriously. Roz shook his head for a moment and then starting to nod in answer to her question.

"It's a transport really but, yes, it is a weapon too I suppose. But we need it more for transport." Roz said and then added, "Well I just hope we don't need it as a weapon."

Chinn wandered over to the machine and smoothed her hand over the cold body of the air-lifter noticing that it did have armaments. Roz threw her a bundle of clothes.

"They are old army fatigues. You won't need your forest pelts anymore."

She looked at the bundle with distrust then shrugged and started to change, first into the underwear and then the rest of the dark green clothing. The clothes somehow felt unnatural on her skin and didn't follow the form of her body as the pelts did but she attempted to hide the fact that she didn't really like them. Roz started to load the air-lifter with equipment and rations that he had salvaged from the stasis pods as Chinn busied herself tying up her hair in a top knot using leather lace.

"I found some pistols as well and a couple of BORE carbines. Not that we will need them but its best to be armed if the need arises." He handed her the weapons and quickly showed her how to operate and reload the firearms.

Roz opened the main hanger and watched the great concertina of metal alloy folding away revealing the sky. Chinn pointed up into the sky with a smile.

"Halneques! Aren't they beautiful?"
Roz looked to where she was indicating and saw three birds of prey hovering on the thermals. The birds must have had a wingspan of twelve feet or so coloured with bright and dull green feathers; their talons glinting in the morning sun.

"Halneques hey? We will become one with them using this machine." Roz said with glee.
Chinn held his hand tight and kissed his cheek.

"I have always wanted to fly. You are a dream come true Roz."
Roz blushed and patted her back.

Roz warmed up the rotors and brought the air-lifter online. The onboard computer asked for a flight code, he tapped in 'KEL65' hoping it would work.

"Welcome Colonel Kelba." The feminine computerised voice stated. Roz brought up a map of the planetary sector, then connected to the satellite uplinks and waited a while as it initialised and started updating with twelve years of progress from the last time it had been used. He scanned the map for a while until he found landmarks near the Kommando school and placed a locating tag over it.

"Wow!" he laughed, "It even has autopilot! This couldn't be easier if they came over to pick us up." He engaged the flight path and clicked the autopilot. "Damn good job! I wouldn't be able to fly this fucker very well!" Chinn tutted at his language and he grinned and blushed slightly.

"Auto-pilot engaged." The computer stated.

Chinn sat wide-eyed next to Roz and placed her hand in his, he squeezed it to help calm her while the air-lifter made its final checks.

"We will be home soon and you are more than welcome in my home," Roz said.

The sound of the blades overhead rose to a crescendo and the ship lurched in to the air. Chinn grimaced as the craft took off feeling her stomach turn over as it lifted above the installation. She squeezed hard on his hand as she started to feel ill and Roz leant forwards to open a small side window and stroked Chinn's back as she was sick through the open window. It seemed that Chinn shared Daemon's dislike of travelling and Roz was relieved that he had recognised the signs of travel sickness. He leant towards Chinn giving her a bottle of water which she took and cleaned out her mouth. Her hand was hot and sweaty as the forest rushed under them; a sea of greens and browns specked with the colourful plumage of forest dwelling avians.

The air-lifter had covered over one hundred miles in a

little less than forty minutes when the proximity alarm bleeped. As the craft automatically slowed its pace in response Roz scanned the displays for a possible enemy or anti-aircraft devices. He thought he spotted what looked like three possible emplacements but was uncertain due to the outdated display. He erred on the side of precaution and decided to land the craft manually. The air-lifter responded oddly to his controls and it lurched from side to side a few times before he eventually landed it with minimum damage. When the blades stopped their motion Chinn and Roz leapt from its metal body.

They stood at the edge of the forest, the main road headed into a local township that Roz recognised. He knew that they could easily walk the distance to the Kommando School from here. Before they left he salvaged the flight recorder and set the craft to explode, covering the links back to the B7 supply depot. Chinn was unusually quiet as they walked towards the town.

"Don't worry Chinn. You will be welcome in the school."

Chinn looked appalled and upset.

"Who said I am joining it? I agreed to guide you back to the school that is all!" She shook her head and wandered ahead of Roz. He caught her up quickly grabbing her shoulders to slow her pace.

"Chinn wait. I haven't planned any of this but it feels right. I need you by my side. I have never been surer of anything in my life. Please, come and see before you make your decision?" Roz pleaded but Chinn pushed him away with sudden violence.

"I am not a murderer Roz! I survive from the land, part of the natural cycle of things of this world. I can't become an assassin and see and do the things you have done." Tears formed in her eyes and she refused to look him in the eye.

He struggled to comprehend her words. She had the perfect skills to become an assassin, better than he could ever be. It didn't make sense to him why she was behaving like this.

"Besides, I have been living too long in the wilds to ever fit in with your way of life. Can you see me shopping in the local shop for clothing and food? No!" Her arms were folded across her chest and the tears were long gone.

"I imagine it will be hard but in time you will fit in. Chinn, you had a life before the forest and I want you to be part of my life."

His words fell on deaf ears. Chinn sat down on an old oil drum at the side of the road and began to count up the rations and equipment that she carried. He felt a panic as he realised she was going to leave him and return to her forest home.

"Chinn! Stay with me two more days and if you wish to leave after that I will organise a transport back to your home." He took her hands and looked at her. "Please, just two days."

Chinn looked to the forest and remained silent for a while and Roz sat down in silence with her while she made her mind up. Chinn was so far from home, she estimated it would take about at least a week of dangerous travel to get back to her forest home through an unfamiliar jungle.

"I will stay two days then I will return with your aid of transport."

Roz agreed and they shouldered their packs and walked the few miles into town.

The Kommando School stood upon a great forested hill with most of the installation buried below the ceremonial buildings and the great temple. Chinn was surprised how beautiful the gardens were around the temple building with a number of water features and exotic plants giving a sweet scent to the air she breathed. Some of the plants she recognised but others she had never seen before. Roz acted strangely in the proximity of the school, he seemed to show her around the buildings and gardens as if they were on their very first date.

A tall man dressed in a black robe wandered from a utility building and spotted Roz and the strange women stood in the meditation garden.

"Well look at this." The man smiled and bowed, Roz bowed back to the robed man.

"Master Vaul, I have returned. This is my friend Chinn, she will be staying with us for two days." Roz stated.

The man frowned as he peered upon the woman whom Roz had brought to his sanctuary.

"Indeed. Presumably, she will be staying in your

quarters. I honour your decision but I trust that I will have to remind you of the rules within this enclave."
Roz bowed again to signal his agreement.

"So you have returned at last. Welcome back Roz, you will not need debriefing we have already received word that the deed has been done. When you are more settled come and see me. I hope your, friend, finds everything to her pleasure."
Roz thanked the robed man who, after they had both bowed, wandered away towards the temple.

"Who was that?" Chinn asked watching him walking away serenely.

"Master Vaul is one the heads of the school. I only ever met him at my initiation but I think he knows pretty much everyone here."

"He seems nice enough. I thought he might have objected to me staying with you." Chinn stroked Roz's hand.

"Being part of the Brotherhood has its privileges." He laughed and grabbed Chinn's hand excitedly and took her to the canteen section in one of the utility buildings. Roz knew that Chinn wouldn't be welcome in the secret installation below the façade of buildings but she would be made to feel at home in the communal areas. They ate in a large room filled with benches and at first Chinn seemed nervous in the company of so many strangers but after an hour or so she began to settle down. Roz told her of his friends from the Xen Academy and how he had struggled to fit in with the intellectual side of training but had finally become accustomed to it.

"So Daemon went to officer's school?" She said between mouthfuls of steamed vegetables.

"Yes, he went there after the academy. I kept in touch with him via messages while he was there and I was at the Kommando School." Roz smiled remembering his old friend and the old days.

"And you didn't want to join him at the military school?" Chinn asked with a frown.
Roz paused, his hand holding noodles on chopsticks stopping in mid-air; he lowered his head down and stared at his plate of food trying to find the right words to explain things to her.

"The heads of the academy thought I was better working alone and transferred me here. I suppose they didn't think I was the right material for leading others. Maybe they were right, anyway, I was glad of the decision. I was never a commander." He said matter-of-factly. "And if I hadn't been transferred here I would have never met you." He smiled meeting her eyes.
Chinn concentrated on her food blushing with the attention and his kind words.

That night they slept together in true comfort, they wrapped themselves around one another keeping each other safe and warm. Chinn had finally made her mind up. A life without Roz was a life she couldn't live, no matter what she had to sacrifice to keep with him. She remembered all the nights alone in the hut in the deep forest and now that she had a taste of love again she refused to return to the meaningless and lonesome life she used to lead. Roz had little trouble persuading the heads of command at the Kommando School to retain her. His master witnessed true potential in her and some of her skills surpassed the master's skill levels, especially in the field of survival techniques.

Chinn had proved herself a capable killer due to her experiences in the jungle and all they needed to work on was her psyche and her archaic morals regarding the assassination. It was common for assassins to work in pairs or triplets in the field, about forty percent of the assassins operated in groups at the Kommando School. Working in couples had been dubbed the buddy-system, it was more likely a pair would stay alive due to the bond they had and the fact two was always better than one to get the deed done. Given time she would be a worthy and valuable addition to the Kommandos.

They spent one more night together before Chinn was due to be conditioned. She was nervous about the procedure but Roz tried to allay her fears telling her that it had made him who he was. However, when she left in the morning he couldn't but help shed a tear and hope that she would come back the same person.

Master Vaul sat in his dimly illuminated chambers watching a religious film reel on his desk display. He always felt a sense of ease and comfort watching the familiar scenes of the martyr's flagellation and prepared himself for the release of seeing the trepanning of the saviour.
A message flashed at the bottom of the screen disturbing his meditation. He reached towards the

console and clicked the message, which paused the film reel and displayed who was attempting to contact him. He sat up straight at the unexpected name from his past. He quickly walked to his door and secured it against any unexpected visitors then returned to his desk. He clicked the link on the message which brought up a live feed of the Xen intelligence ship orbiting above Talon II. The visage of a terrible man appeared on the display.

"Vaul? Is that you?" The man's twisted face moved closer to the camera apparently to get a better view, "Oh I see, I take it that you're Master Vaul now?" He mocked with a crooked grin.

"I think you already know that Hellus," Vaul nodded, "it's been a long time since we last crossed paths but I'm sure you and your intelligence friends know everything about me."

"Not everything Vaul, some things are best kept known just between the two of us."

Vaul remained silent and gestured to him to continue.

"It seems we have a problem on Sigra III and much to my disgust we need your help." The man looked sickened that he had to stoop to asking for Vaul's aid. Vaul remained calm even though he detested Agent Hellus.

"Shall we use the usual drop? We obviously can't speak on this channel." he asked.

"Yes, we will use the usual drop." Agent Hellus agreed with a curt nod of his head. "Have you anybody in mind for a..." Hellus paused to find the right word, "special mission?"

Vaul produced a feral grin, "Yes. It just so happens I have somebody in mind for the kind of contract you'll have in mind."

CHAPTER 25

Meltdown

One of the privileges of Daemon's rank was that he was entitled to a private room away from the main billets. This had proved to be a blessing considering what Sherry and he had been doing most of the night. He yawned and noticed the heavy scent of sex still pervaded the small room. He could see Sherry washing herself through a haze of steam in the compact shower cubical and he listened to the song she was humming. He recognised the tune but could not remember the name of it or where he had heard it before. Reaching into a side drawer he pulled out the tub of metabolism pills he kept and washed one of them down with leftover stale beer from last night. It seemed to be a bit of a habit for him to be taking these pills recently and he was concerned that although Sherry might be the sexiest woman to walk this planet her highly charged sexual appetite meant she could be carrying all manner of infections. The fact that he could have infected her with something from Casey did not even occur to him.

The shower turned off as Sherry walked from the cubical grabbing a towel to dry herself. He knew she would be bitchy in the morning so walked past her without saying a word and entered the shower. She muttered something which he didn't quite catch before the noise of the water drowned out the rest of her grumbles. The water was scorching hot and then icy cold, he tried to turn it off and realised he had to exit the cubicle before it did that. Having fought his way from the shower he stood naked and cold in the small room looking for a towel. The only towel in the room was around Sherry's shoulders and she was pretending not to notice that he needed it before he froze to death. Daemon reached for the towel but she moved away from his hand.

"Sherry, give me the towel!" He asked in a tone of voice reserved for giving orders. Sherry was obviously amused by his plight and answered his order by giving him a rude gesture with her fingers.

"Give me the fucking towel." He shouted as they pulled and tugged over the cloth like playschool kids over possession of a rag doll.

"Get you own!" Sherry screamed as she hugged it tight to her chest. Daemon grabbed hold of her and dragged her to the door before pushing her out into the corridor.

"Fine, keep the fucking towel. I will keep your clothes." He said with a grin and slammed the door. Sherry banged on the door for a while as he changed into his fatigues. The banging stopped and he suspected she must have got bored and risked running through the complex naked to the billets where her belongings were.

Boy, am I in trouble. I don't think I will get a warm welcome at breakfast. Mind you, I bet I have scored points with the troopers for providing them with morning entertainment. He thought as he dressed. He looked at his time piece and realised how late it was.

"Shit! I'm late. Come to think of it so is Sherry. She is going to kill me!" He whispered to the empty room before grabbing a small field kit from his solitary locker.

Sherry had been placed on a warning for being late to drill and as punishment had been given latrine detail that day with no breakfast. Consequently, Daemon ate his breakfast alone in the canteen and having learnt of her fate couldn't help but feel sorry for her out in the mud cleaning up excrement. If she had as bad a hangover as he did she probably would have thrown up in her helmet at least once by now.

Colonel Lenz wandered into the canteen and sat down facing Daemon before lighting up his customary cigar. The colonel blew the spent smoke over Daemon's face and breakfast in an obvious attempt to annoy him.

"Right, listen very carefully you Xen parasite! I hope it

was worth keeping Corporal Sherry up all night to miss my beloved drill formation." The colonel said making Daemon wince and put his hands up to apologise.

"I am very sorry commander we were…"
The colonel angrily cut him off.

"I know what you were doing! I don't need a goddamned rundown on last night's performance. My corporal is outside in the pissing rain clearing out shit tanks when she should be on patrol supervising the elite." The colonel said while pointing the fiery end of his cigar at him.

"Look, we have somehow got off on the wrong note. That much is clear. I have been sent here to oversee the operations of your fortified position and my report will be a good one." Daemon announced.

"What fucking report?" The colonel said stubbing out his cigar and sneering at Daemon with a hint of nervousness. Daemon leant forward and stubbed out the last trace of smoke from the cigar.

"I just follow orders Colonel, like every other officer of Xen. The administration needs a report so I will write one. Personally, I think you're doing a damned good job here, under the circumstances." He allowed his words to settle before adding. "Maybe when they understand your situation here the Administration will delay the order to attack. That's what you want isn't it?"
The colonel didn't look pleased with it at all, in fact the mere mention of a report had seriously rattled him. A petty officer in clean green fatigues rushed into the canteen and saluted to the officers present.

"Colonel Lenz, Sat-Com has just picked up a heat signature from Runich. We think it could be a weapon system." The colonel scrambled from his seat and gestured for Daemon to follow.

"Come on let's go and earn our pay!" The colonel stated grimly.

The operations room was a hive of activity with officers and technicians monitoring terminals and gathering information. The room had already started to take on an air of panic as numerous displays were uploaded. The colonel elbowed himself to the front of the largest display which depicted a feed of Runich. A bright fiery heat bloom emanated from somewhere in the city. One of the admin workers enhanced the image which seemed to be a rocket of some kind launching from the edge of the buildings.

"When is this feed from?" the colonel demanded.

"About five minutes ago, sir." The technician replied.

"About five minutes? More or less? Dammit, I need to know when." Lenz yelled.

"Errr, four minutes and fifteen seconds, sir." The hapless man replied.

"Where is it now?" Lenz asked nervously.

"Tracking it now. It's reached the apex of the parabola!" An admin worker shouted in panic.
The colonel's face washed out to pure white.

"Tell me that isn't a nuke. Convince me that it isn't a nuclear weapon." The colonel said using a tone suggesting impending doom for them all.

Daemon's immediate thoughts were on Sherry out

there on the open ground. The trail of the rocket arced away from the city in the general direction of the base. The colonel grabbed the comms and tapped in the local frequency.

"All personnel seek immediate cover. Repeat, seek immediate cover! We are tracking a missile launched from Runich. If you can make it below ground I suggest you do so now!" Sweat dribbled from his brow as he stared at the rockets climbing image.

The missile, having reached its programmed apex had started its arc down to the ground. The anti-aircraft guns at the base volleyed an assault against the enemy missile as it made its way closer to the fortified position. Daemon thought of the brave men and women manning the guns attempting to bring down the weapon. He also pondered over the fabricated alloy base they sheltered within. The walls may as well be made of paper to a nuclear weapon.

"It's spinning out of control. It's too heavy at the front!" Sergeant Colex stated but he knew it wouldn't make that much difference if the warhead chain reacted.

"Where will it hit?" Colonel Lenz demanded,

"It's going to miss the base but not by much. Someone check my calculations." a voice called out. All was silent for what seemed a lifetime until someone else called out, "Yeh, about two clicks to the east, impact in about thirty seconds."

Everyone watched the live feed as the missile spun wildly before it hit the ground about a mile east of the base. A stony silence issued as all the officers stood watching the image of the crashed rocket. All of them waited with dread for the device to explode.

A few seconds passed.

"Is it a dud?" Sergeant Colex asked with a smile on his face but he was the only one who smiled in the room.

"I'm hoping it's just a shot across our bows. It may be a warning." The colonel said but he was obviously unsure of his own words.

Another few seconds passed and a few sighs of relief rang out before Daemon pointed at another display. "It seems you have some very brave or very stupid troopers driving toward it. Call them back colonel. I doubt any of them have the training to disarm an atomic device if that's what it is."

The colonel grabbed the comms.

"Turn that vehicle around and head the opposite way now! Don't stop driving!" But the colonel's words came too late. A small sphere of bluish light began to grow from the crash site, the vehicle already showed signs of intense heat upon its armour. They watched in horror as the sphere expanded slowly growing in size and the men burst into flames.

"It's not a nuke Colonel," Daemon stated. "I think they have armed the missile with an Ion reactor core. There is going to be a lot of heat for a while but it won't explode." He knew of such improvised weaponry from his training exercises and he suspected this attack was the last resort assault.

The vehicle that had driven out towards the crashed

missile was a bubbling molten wreck. The sphere of blue light was over a thousand feet in diameter before it halted its expansion but the heat it emanated was still fierce. All nearby electrics shorted and most of the defence guns and structures were ruined outside the eastern perimeter of the main compound. Small fires erupted around the operations room and every display crackled with static before shorting out.

"We are blind. Orders colonel?" Sergeant Colex blurted.
Everybody in the operations room noticed how the temperature was climbing and some of the metal walls began to hot-spot.

"Right everybody to the armoury now! It's the most protected part of the base and we can get heavy E.C.A.'s there." The colonel ordered.

Bright fiery heat started to penetrate through the walls as everyone evacuated the operations room. Most of the overhead lights had blown in the corridors making it hard to navigate towards the armoury. The entire base seemed to be a hubbub of panicked voices shouting and screaming in dimly illuminated corridors.

"Silence! It's this way." Daemon heard the colonel's order from somewhere in the darkness to his left.

The walls of the installation had begun to glow with numerous heat blemishes. Daemon slipped on the hot floor and realised the soles of his boots were melting. Most of the personnel of the building had all had the same idea which made the armoury cramped with people all elbowing for room to put their suits on.

Daemon was one of the last into the armoury and had to manually lock the main door hoping it wouldn't fuse shut in the growing heat.

He grabbed the first available E.C.A. and found fortuitously that it was a heavily armoured suit and not one of the standard combat units. He sealed his suit and heard the hiss of air and was able to breathe again without coughing from the gas of the superheated metal walls. Headlamps illuminated in the armoury and he could hear numerous clicks of local communications being turned on. Daemon focused on his own suits integrity and noticed the air tank was only half full.

"Why aren't these suits refilled after use?" Daemon grumbled into the local comms to no-one in particular. He felt a tap on his shoulder and realised it must have been the colonel.

"Daemon? So you made it? Good. How long do you think that thing will burn?" The colonel asked trying to keep a measure of calm.

"Not long but I suspect we would be all bubbling pools of flesh if we hadn't got here." Daemon guessed. "Open the interior airlock door. The air-lock is the most fortified place in the building and it will give us all some more room."
The survivors all complained about the idea worried about what would happen in the event of an outer door breach.

"You heard the Lieutenant open the interior door of the airlock!" The colonel issued.
Daemon heard the clicking of communication circuits to

private channels and saw the colonel motioning to retune his set.

"You better be right Daemon!" The colonel stated with a threatening tone when he established communication.

Daemon laughed, "Colonel if we all get cooked to death in here then you have my permission to kill me."

Sherry waded through the steaming pools of rainwater that had collected in the underground tunnel. She had heard the colonel's order to seek shelter and managed to dive into the tunnel before the missile struck. It was now clear that whatever the weapon had been it had somehow raised the ambient temperature even down here. After about twenty minutes of running, falling and wading through the tunnel, she had managed to get to the underground bunker. Lieutenant Bray welcomed her into it once the airlock had finished its cycle.

"What the fucking hell's going on up there?" Bray asked his face contorted with tension and stress. Sherry took off her helm and saluted the lieutenant.

"Some kind of weapon has been dropped on the base. It could be nuclear judging by the heat it is giving off." Sherry guessed.
Bray sat down on the closest available seat, his hands clamped firmly over his face.

"Nuked? Where the fuck have the rebels got a Nuke from?" Bray had finally broken down, he had hit rock bottom and tears had formed in his eyes.

"I didn't say it was a Nuke, I just think it might be." Sherry crouched at his side and hugged the lieutenant.

"Gods in the heavens we could be stuck down here. Not many people in command know of the tunnel's existence." Bray burst into free flowing tears. Some of the troopers had come into the reception room and witnessed their commander in his moment of weakness. Sherry knew she had to react or else she risked losing the men to panic.

"Pull yourself together Lieutenant! We still have command and a good contingent of troops down here. The fight isn't over yet." Sherry yelled hoping he would show some signs of taking command of his gathering troops. Bray was desolate and had already taken off his command badge and thrown it across the floor.

Sherry understood she was now in command of the secret bunker by default. One of the troopers picked up the badge and gave it to Corporal Sherry to take the lead.

"Take Bray to the billets and tuck him into bed. Make sure he is kept guarded at all times, just in case he feels like taking the easy way out. Do not let him take his own life, he will be processed as a coward and punished accordingly, do not let him take the easy way out." She instructed.

Two troopers picked up their former commander and carried him off toward the billets without question. Sherry held the command badge in her gauntlet. Acting-Lieutenant Sherry, yep, that has a damned good ring to it! She thought.

She noticed a lot of other troops had sought
sanctuary down in the bunker. They must have gone to
ground before she had reached the tunnel head. She
had their attention and knew she had to get them
acting like soldiers again. She looked out at them and
pinned the badge to her shoulder plate.
"If any of you behave like Lieutenant Bray then I shall
personally see to it that your families are sent vid-tapes
of you being spaced for your cowardice. You are
soldiers of the CORE. You are the best. And I expect you
to act like it." She looked round letting them all know
that she meant business and started her new command
with a quick head count.

Over one hundred and fifty troops had gathered in
the bunker but it had been constructed to hold four
times that number. She tried to establish contact with
the command section but was not surprised to find that
the communication lines had burnt out between the
base and the underground bunker. She hoped someone
above ground had survived the rebel attack.

Back in the armoury, the interior door had to be
manually overridden. Daemon ensured that everyone
was fully suited up before the smallest of gaps was
opened so they could see if the airlock had been
breached. On inspection, it turned out that the outer
door was severely melted and a few holes gaped in its
thick metal body. However, in the time it had taken
them to override the interior door the heat had died

down. A glow of bluish light could be seen coming from the east but the door was already cooling down.

"I think it's burnt itself out or started burning its way into the ground. A single core shouldn't get too far before it collapses into itself but it will burn for a while yet. It should be safe enough to move outside now." Daemon told Lenz starting to open the interior door more so he could climb through.

"Wait! The rebels might have another missile ready to go." The colonel said while he held Daemon back.

"Well, I'm not staying here and waiting for another volley of fire. I doubt the airlock could stand up to any more damage. I don't think we have any option other than to evacuate from here." He nudged the colonel's hand away and clambered through into the air-lock. Everyone else seemed to agree as nobody wanted to stay within the metal tomb.

"Right everybody arm themselves with as much as we can carry. And the next time we build a base like this let's build some fucking bunkers first!" The colonel called out to the troopers.

Everyone laughed nervously but privately agreed with his logic. Daemon inspected the outer door, it had fused to the frame and the melted holes were not big enough to escape through.

"Bring a cutter first. We are going to have to laser-cut our way out and it might take a while."

Daemon supervised the cutting as the colonel organised munitions.

"I'm very surprised you didn't need my help back

there Daemon but you did well to keep our shell together. If it means anything I offer my thanks". The demon echoed from the deepest region of his brain. Daemon turned off his comms.

"Do you think they will use another one?" He asked.

"I doubt it. Hell…"

Daemon cut the demon off.

"Don't use that word. I'm not happy with that word, especially now the base has been subjected to hell fire!"

"I mean to say: I don't think they will attack with such a device again. I suspect they couldn't or their ruse of destroying all of the Ion plants simultaneously will fall to its knees. If they don't have enough Ion plants left to reach critical mass it will only bring an air-strike from Xen." The demon claimed.

"Ok, what do we do now?" Daemon asked.

"First get us out of this shit hole and then we order reinforcements and while we wait for them to arrive we go to that underground bunker." The demon said with a sinister giggle.

"Then what?" Daemon said with an angry tone.

"Then I will tell you what you have chosen to forget. How about that?" The demon bargained.

The communications light pulsed in Daemon and he was forced to abandon his dialogue. He turned his comms back on.

"Right let's go and see the extent of the damage. You lead the way, hey Daemon?" The colonel said in jest. Daemon was surprised to see that the troops had finished cutting through the door and realised that he must have been in discussion with the demon for far longer than the few minutes he thought had passed. The dilation of time experienced in those episodes started to worry him.

"No. You're right I will go first," Daemon said distractedly while he chambered a round in his battle rifle.

He stepped through the hole that had been cut, carefully avoiding the still glowing edges and looked east towards the bomb sight. A small bluish glow still radiated from the missile crater but it was fading by the second. It seemed unbelievable that this was the only remnant of the devastating rebel missile; the attack had been an unequivocal success. The base had been totally devastated; it looked as if the camp had been made from cheap plastic as buildings stood warped and melted. In places, it was still glowing and smouldering and the only recognisable surviving structures were the power plant, the armoury, the reception and the air-lock. The colonel climbed out behind Daemon and stood surveying the scene for what seemed an age before saying anything.

"If we are the only survivors I'm guessing over two thousand troops have died in this assault. We are sitting ducks if the rebels attack." The colonel clicked his long range circuits.

"This is Colonel Lenz. We have been attacked and our base of operations has been totally destroyed. What are your orders?" He waited for a few seconds for the transmission to bounce.

499

"Colonel Lenz? It's a relief to hear from you, glad you survived. We watched the whole thing from the Goliath. Your orders are to hold the position. Reinforcements are already inbound, they'll be there shortly." Command crackled.

"Roger that, we'll stay put. Over." He clicked to Daemon's private channel and continued. "Well Daemon we've taken a bit of a kicking and I'm hoping they haven't got another core to fire at us. Get the men together; we can be expecting drop ships any moment." The colonel said peering around the devastation.

Even as he spoke, a high pitched whining sound came from the skies as five William Hadley drop pods and what appeared to be a command sphere started their decent. Daemon assumed Xen was no longer taking any chances, he knew the William Hadley's could withstand a direct nuclear attack, due to the apt shields they had installed.

The colonel came over to Daemon's side and elbowed his chest plate.

"Well son, I'm betting my command is going to be relieved. They won't take kindly to this happening on my watch. It looks like you may as well write whatever you wish in the report because my career is over." The colonel sighed and added. "Yep, I will be commanding a desolate supply moon at the arse end of space within the month."

Daemon knew that he spoke the truth, Xen was quick to promote after a victory but swift to demote after failures.

"I don't have the words to console you colonel and I guess you'd know they were hollow anyway but I won't be pinning the blame on you in my report. I hope they will be reasonable when I tell them of your cool-headed command under such circumstances." Daemon proffered.

"Thanks, Daemon," the colonel said but he doubted Xen could ever be reasonable, "but this has to be the biggest massacre to date in this campaign. I will be lucky if I don't see the wrong end of a firing squad." The colonel looked at the approaching craft with resignation.

The drop pods howled as their heavy thrusters slowed their descent before landing in a line formation. The command sphere landed in the middle of the drop pods still glowing at its base from the entry through the upper atmosphere. The survivors rushed towards the structures seeking sanctuary in case the rebels fired another weapon at the camp or started a land assault. Daemon followed the colonel towards the command sphere.

Sherry led a small reconnaissance squad through the humid tunnel having decided to evaluate if the radiation levels above ground would allow the troops in the bunker to leave its confines. All the squad members were feeling the side-effects from the anti-radiation drugs Sherry had insisted they took before performing such a dangerous recon mission. One trooper had to be carried back to the underground bunker barely thirty meters down the tunnel when his body had gone straight into toxic shock with the high dose of Metabol.

After this aborted attempt, they soon proceeded again and found much to their puzzlement that the radiation readings were as low as they had been before the attack. The evidence indicated a nuclear weapon had not been used so Sherry was now curious to see what, if anything, of the base survived and signalled that they were to continue onwards. A few grumbles started to come over the comms regarding her order, some dissenters complained how ill they felt and that they shouldn't have taken the Metabol until they had encountered any radiation.

Sherry was feeling just as bad as the rest of them and wasn't inclined to tolerate their shit; she gave them a harsh dressing down using choice language before leading the way. Soon daylight filtered into the tunnel from the entrance ahead and she made a hand signal to stop her squad before she made the final distance to open-air.

"OK, we head out and make a quick sweep and return. Nobody is to spend more than two minutes above ground. If one of us falls, leave them and return to the bunker. That includes me! There's something I don't like about all this. Check for viral and biological materials in case the bastards have started using them. If they have then we'll need to quarantine ourselves." Sherry stated to her squad and began creeping forward.

As she neared the exit her comms unexpectedly came

back online and she heard local communications heading back and forth. Confused she made the final few steps to ground level and looked out. The first thing she witnessed was the row of drop pods and a command sphere obscuring the view of Runich. She looked in the direction of the base and saw it was completely ruined but noticed elite Xen troopers sweeping the area with a contingent of armoured support vehicles. It was then she realised an elite trooper had a rifle nozzle against her helm.

"How many survivors are below?" The elite trooper stated in a fierce tone. Sherry dropped her weapon and put her arms in the air reluctantly.

"About one hundred and fifty, I have assumed command of the underground bunker." She replied. The trooper signalled to other nearby troops to stand down.

"All the officers are in the sphere. Go there now and we will see to the troops below." The trooper said.

"So it's safe?" Sherry asked.

The trooper understood her meaning and held out his hand as he let out a low laugh.

"It wasn't an atomic device." He stated as Sherry took his hand. "Intelligence claims it was an ion core from one of the power plants." He helped her up from the trench.

Sherry felt even sicker now that she knew the Metabol had been a waste of time, the come down off it was severe, worse than it felt now. Sherry moved off towards the gigantic sphere, she knew her rank would be dropped right back to corporal as soon as she entered the drop sphere but she kept hold of the lieutenant's badge in the meantime. She dreaded having to rejoin the ranks and having to face the men she had ordered to take the drugs. They would undoubtedly berate her for it at every opportunity something they would never dare do to a lieutenant. As she wandered towards the sphere two razor craft flew over the destruction towards Runich. She waited just long enough to witness a few explosions from within the city before entering the new command post.

Colonel Lenz could feel the tense atmosphere inside the command sphere. He felt like a convicted man on the long walk to the execution chamber enduring the final seconds before the hangman pulled the trapdoor lever and ended his misery. Daemon had tried to reassure him but the colonel had already convinced himself that the grilling he would receive would be worse than the death penalty. They waited in a grey metal reception room while command reviewed the situation and analysed the disaster that had taken place.

"Colonel, you can still save yourself. Choose a fall guy and I will back your words up. Maybe that dumb fuck sergeant?" Daemon stated but the colonel shot him such a look he decided to drop the idea.

"Lieutenant I'm offended at your suggestion. We in the CORE don't just fuck each other over. We accept responsibility for our actions and their consequences.

Sergeant Colex has saved my life twice, he may well be a dumb son-of-a-bitch but he is loyal. My career is already ruined and I don't want to bring my finest officer down with me by acting like a coward." The colonel growled and added,   "Maybe you can be my fall guy. Hell, I don't even know you." Daemon didn't know if the colonel said it in jest or if he was actually considering dropping the blame on him. In any case, it really didn't matter who was to blame, the day had been a total disaster and the high command would decide who their own scapegoat would be.

A petty officer opened the door to the meeting room, saluted them and gestured for them both to follow. The room was hazy with smoke and the stench of confined men. It was small in comparison with the reception and sported a long metallic table with a bluish glass top. Daemon looked around the table and immediately noticed two Xen intelligence agents amongst the rest of the seated people of various military ranks.

Colonel Lenz elbowed his side and gestured to the man sitting at the head of the table. Daemon had to squint to see the man's face through the smoky atmosphere before he recognised Colonel Kolkorin from the meeting on the Goliath. Daemon suspected that he had unwittingly just found himself at the centre of a court-martial and quickly saluted his hosts in an attempt not to antagonise them.

From the corner of his eye, he noticed a sudden movement from Colonel Lenz then saw that he had pulled out his sidearm. Everything seemed to happen far too quickly, Colonel Kolkorin's head disappeared in a mist of blood leaving a limp body in his chair; a cigar still smoking in what was left of his mouth. Daemon heard two more shots to his side and turned to face the colonel and saw that he was saluting the rest of the gathered entourage and placing his firearm in his mouth. Daemon cried out in horror and was momentarily blinded by the muzzle flair from the pistol.

He stood blinking in shock covered with the colonel's blood as Lenz's body slumped to the floor in slow motion. To Daemon's horror, he thought he heard a mumbling sound coming from his ruined mouth and face. Daemon couldn't believe his senses and stumbled towards Lenz and distinctly heard a sound, he realised that Lenz wasn't dead; he had somehow fucked up his own suicide.

"Finish... me... off!" Colonel Lenz somehow whispered; his tongue hanging from the gaping hole in the side of his face. Daemon was unable to fulfil his request since the officers were now on their feet pointing pistols at himself and the prone figure on the floor. Daemon threw up his hands in case they thought he was part of the colonel's murderous plan.

The hour that immediately followed had been the most intense in Daemon's life as he faced an interrogation from one of the intelligence officers at the meeting, an Agent Anderson. It reminded him of the Pseudo-met training back at the academy when he had to master his fear or risk losing his life. He had used some of the basic breathing techniques learnt then during the interrogation that took place. It helped to calm him down and answer their questions clearly knowing that unless he convinced them otherwise he would be accused of being Lenz's co-conspirator and would face spacing or worse. After they had satisfied themselves that he was not directly involved they asked him what he thought had driven Lenz to such actions.

Daemon told them of the signs of stress he had seen in the colonel since he had first met him and how after the attack he appeared to be a broken man. They were interested to hear that Lenz had mentioned Kolkorin in disparaging terms and believed that he may have held him responsible for the death of his men.

When the meeting was formerly ended Daemon asked if Colonel Lenz was dead.

"Hell no! He's been taken to the medical facility and placed on life support until we can determine how much damage he has caused to himself. We'll use all of the medical science at our disposal to make sure that bastard doesn't die on us. We'll do whatever it takes to make sure that we can make him stand trial for what he has done." Anderson told him vehemently.

"What? But surely he'll be executed once they find him guilty. Why not let him die?" Daemon asked surprised at the news.

"Let him take a cowards way out? Never. He must be made an example of."

"But the cost of keeping him alive must be

507

astronomical. It seems like madness." Daemon stated shaking his head.

"The cost to a corporation like Xen is negligible in purely economic terms, however, should it be known that an officer of the CORE was able to get away with such an act of treachery its reputation would be irreparably damaged. Xen must, and will, be seen to be strong."

Daemon thought it best not to get embroiled in an argument of politics considering what he had just been party to and simply agreed with Agent Anderson before excusing himself.

He wandered down to the canteen to fortify his nerves with a few strong drinks and noticed, to his delight, that Sherry was there. He could hardly believe that she had survived and hugged her firmly before he sat down at her table. He worked his way through a third of a bottle of whisky as they told each other about what had happened in the last few hours.

"So," she concluded, "they debriefed me, stripped me of the rank of acting lieutenant and bumped me up to being a sergeant instead. I've got to say that I'm a bit pissed off they didn't make me lieutenant but I guess I should be happy enough to receive any kind of promotion."

Daemon fingered her sergeant's pin and smiled.

"Well, I doubt the amount of ass you'll kick will change whether you are a sergeant or lieutenant." He laughed as she slapped his hand away and pretended to clean away his fingerprints from the shining metal.

"I guess that depends on who becomes my new superior. I can't believe Colonel Lenz did it." Sherry had taken the news badly and Daemon could see that she loved the colonel in a fatherly way and obviously looked up to him as a role model. "And you had no idea what he was going to do?" she asked her eyes starting to water.

"None at all. He just double tapped Colonel Kolkorin then shot himself before I even had time to react." Daemon repeated for maybe the fourth or fifth time.

"I just. I mean. Why? Why would he have done such a thing?" Sherry said as she pushed her meal around with her fork no longer in the mood to eat.

"Responsibility can do strange things to human beings. Even though the bomb episode had nothing to do with the colonel he seemed to take it personally. Maybe he did want to avenge them. Maybe we'll never know." He shrugged hoping Sherry would understand the strains he had been under and saw that tears now ran freely down her face.

"I know one thing for certain. I would never turn my gun on myself even if I had murdered a high-ranking military officer." She said angrily.
Daemon shrugged again and spooned a good mouthful of the beef stew into his mouth. Sherry pushed her meal to her side and picked up an ice cold beer to cool her brow.

"You said you sought sanctuary inside the tunnel. Are they still cutting under no-mans land?" He asked hoping to get her attention away from Lenz.

Sherry nodded and gulped down some beer.

"Yeah, the lieutenant had strict orders to finish the digging. The tunnel is still being excavated. Why do you ask?" She replied with a curious frown.

"I think we should go and find out if they are still digging." He said. Sherry shook her head.

"I can't go! I have been placed under orders. I'm to report in soon. I'm going to be leading squad four." Sherry stated with a grin of true satisfaction.

"Yeah! Well, what if I could get you and squad four to accompany me on a special mission?" He asked watching every emotion on her beautiful face.

"Oh yeah, let me know how that goes hotshot." Sherry laughed. "But I really do need to go." She hugged Daemon and kissed him on the cheek before wandering off towards the onboard billets.

Daemon decided to stay for a while and drink a few more beers. He grabbed two from an ice rack and returned to his seat to ponder over who was the highest ranking officer on board the command sphere now that the good Colonel Kolkorin was pushing up daisies and Colonel Lenz was immobilised.

"While you are thinking it over I think it's a damned good idea to check on the tunnel. We need that tunnel Daemon!" The demon stated.

In Daemon's mind, they were sat in a room almost identical to the bar he was sat in. The only difference was that the demon sat opposite him and the off-duty officers and troops had been replaced by dead rebels with all manner of gruesome wounds. The dead rebels peered over to Daemon's table with expressions of hatred towards the pair of them. One of the dead wandered from the bar dragging her entrails behind her. Daemon tried to ignore the souls in the bar around him knowing full well this vision wasn't real.

"I'm leaving tomorrow. Fuck this war!" He said. The demon erupted in white hot flames in true anger and shook its head.

"I don't think so Daemon! Look around you." The demon gestured around the room with its bloodied claw. "You can't just leave all this behind and forget about it. I'm the only one who can keep you from seeing such things all of the time. The tunnel is the key Daemon and by the gods, you will follow your orders even if I have to take control of you again! Don't you want all of the dead to leave you alone? You know I can do it for you." The demon grinned and balled its clawed fist causing all of the dead souls to evaporate within a screaming fire. The bar was now scorched and lifeless and they sat alone.

"That's a nice trick," Daemon said sardonically, "maybe I should learn that one."
The demon snarled curling up its beast like jowls which revealed numerous rows of toothpick teeth.

"I presume Xen intelligence knows of the tunnel by now?" Daemon asked. The demon shook its head and grinned.

"Of course they do. That bitch Sherry told them all about it. It would have been easier to follow the original plan and have you sneak you into Runich somehow. The tunnel's existence merely cut a corner in the path to our glory but we don't need it. I dare say they have performed a planetary scan of this zone after the explosion which would reveal the tunnel anyway. Not that it matters. After all, it was the tall intelligence agent who interrogated you who gave us the orders. I'm surprised you didn't recognise him." The demon claimed.

"What Anderson? I've never seen him before. You seem to forget that I'm left totally in the dark when you are in control. All of these plans are yours alone. You're going to have to fill in the blanks.   Say I sneak into Runich what then?" Daemon could not reconcile himself to the fact he had somehow blanked out the mission parameters. Worse still he was struggling to separate reality from the fabrications of his mind; had he really received orders or had his alter ego created the plan. The demon cleared its throat and attempted to answer his question.

"We meet up with this so called hero of the rebels and find out what he plans to do with this world. If he fails to reveal his secrets then we simply kill him and plant a new rebel leader in his stead. A new leader who can bring down the rebellion from within! Or we capture him and drag his carcas back to Xen for interrogation." The demon looked as if it didn't actually know how it would play out.

"OK. We'll do it." Daemon said flatly.
Slowly the bar returned to normal, Daemon drank the last mouthful of beer and headed off to the private

room he had been issued on the command sphere for a much needed shower.

CHAPTER 26
Breaking Storm

Jackabah sat alone in the observation room deep below Runich. He hated being below ground because he felt trapped but he hated wearing a survival suit above ground even more. He had watched with distress as his home planet was laid to waste by the corporation scum until it became impossible to live on the surface without protection from the radiation and poisons. He had watched with joy at the destruction of the Xen military base but it was a short lived exultation when the drop pods and the sphere descended.

He knew damned well the William Hadley drop pods could withstand another assault; not that he had another weapon to throw their way. His entourage of loyalists had explained they no longer had propulsion units to launch another ion core. It had cost the rebels six brave lives pulling the ion core out of the reactor power plant and placing it in the missile. They had died hideously before they could even witness the fruits of their labour.

It won't be long now until Xen counter attacks, he thought to himself. I doubt that bullshit scare story of ion plants destroying the world will hold out much longer.

Jackabah had been trained by the best tutors Xen intelligence could offer but all the skills in the universe couldn't change the fact the rebellion was practically unarmed. They had survived for this long partly because of his training; he had disseminated the kind of disinformation that would set alarm bells ringing at Xen and have their finest minds coming up with simulations and statistics.

The console before him buzzed and new information flickered up on the screen. Reports were coming in that Xen had just dropped a few carefully placed electromagnetic pulse bombs which had scrambled two of the ion power plants rendering the cores dormant and destroying one of the forward communications posts. The city of Runich had thirteen ion plants left, not enough to support the scientific meltdown theory anymore. Jackabah was tempted to proceed with the meltdown of the remaining power plants anyway and to destroy Runich in a huge fiery explosion to prevent Xen gaining anything from the city.

He gritted his teeth and tried to think calmly about the situation. He knew that the destruction of the city would only come at a massive loss of life for the poor rebels; it wasn't worth the loss of life, no city was. Merely hours ago he had managed to strike a victory against Xen but it was only one small battle in the war.

Now his command hung by a thread, the chain of command had numerous weak links and Xen were probably getting ready to instigate a ground assault to clear Runich street by street. Engrossed in his self-destructive thoughts he hadn't noticed Melinda enter the room, she however, had noticed that her great leader was demoralised.

"We have made preparations for you to leave Runich Jackabah, there is a cylinder train waiting for your escape." She whispered close to his ear.

"I cannot leave yet but I want as many as you can muster to board the train and leave this place." He said in a commanding tone attempting to regain some of his former command despite shaking his head in despair.

Melinda gasped in horror at his words.

"But if you don't leave the rebellion is finished! You must escape to carry forth the power of the people. Runich is lost, you know that, but you can counterattack in another town or city and keep those bastards on their toes. You can't allow it to end here!" Her voice carried the tone of a true loyalist but it was wasted on his ears. She couldn't understand why he would give up now after all her kinsman had laid down their lives with honour to follow his orders. It was his reluctance to allow Xen complete control of their home planet that had led to taking a stand at Runich.

Jackabah needed some time to himself to gather his thoughts; somehow he had to develop a plan to get his people out of the mess he had primarily created. Although if he died keeping the Xen dogs from his city, then he would have Martyrdom to fall back on and the rebellion would continue in his name.

"Melinda! Please leave. Let me gather my thoughts!" He barked. She blinked a few times at his anger and rushed out of the room. When the room fell silent he tapped up the map of Runich.

The map displayed the two fronts that would need to be defended, to the east lay the drop pods and seven miles to the west a smaller Xen assault force was assembled. The area to the north was ringed by the Gewl Mountains in which he had stationed some gun emplacements. To the south the great swift running river of Othei afforded the city some protection. With the meagre weapons available holding the east and west fronts Runich would fail quickly, that much Jackabah understood. He further studied the map for a while hoping he could somehow create a plan of action.

"The river!" He shouted out aloud starting to perform calculations on screen before he tapped the communications.

"Get me another ion core, I have a plan. We may as well use power plant six, that's the last plant above ground. Also, begin construction on a submersible, use an old amphibious vehicle and convert it." He ordered.

The loyalists didn't understand at first but followed his orders to the letter. He gave a silent prayer for the brave souls who would be ripping out another ion core. With that done he grabbed his cap and rushed off towards the workshop.

517

The workshop always amazed Jackabah; it used to be an underground reservoir until the outbreak of the war when it was converted to be used as a foundry, machine shop and fabrication assembly. He walked along the work cells counting the civilian vehicles being converted into armoured transports and mobile field guns. He shaded his eyes from the plasma cutting and welding which worked around the clock to produce these rudimentary weapons of war. He also noticed the fatigued but brave faces of his engineers. The master of the shop approached him, he appeared very angry and upset and Jackabah braced himself for the venting of his fatigue.

"I've just had word you intend to rip out another ion core. Are you fucking crazy? If that bastard sparks in here it will fry us all!" The master spat the words with vehemence.

Jackabah held the man's arm and attempted to calm him down.

"Tony, you are master of the shop and you know I will always listen to your words of wisdom but we are on the precipice now. We must put aside caution and take risks we previously would not have accepted." As always Jackabah's voice carried absolute conviction but Tony seemed to be about to disagree with him.

"Please Tony," Jackabah pleaded pre-empting him, "just listen to what I have to say. I have a new plan, if, after you have heard it, you think it is hopeless then I'll take your word for it and order the evacuation. But I think we can destroy the Xen forces here and win a

518

major victory which will send the Xen dogs running with their tails between their legs."

Tony leant his head against the shoulder of the rebel leader his body quaking with tension and stress.

"You ask too much from your people Jackabah! Moral has swan dived with the arrival of Xen reinforcements and now you ask us to risk everything again and pull out another fucking reactor core." He whispered still clinging to Jackabah's shoulder.

"Tony, you're my friend and you know that I wouldn't put our people in danger unless I was sure we can spark a chain reaction of rebel attacks planet wide. As soon as the other rebels hear of our victory and how we achieved it they will follow suit and we will hear the howls of victory from our kinsmen." Jackabah tightened his grip around Tony bear hugging his words home.

"Very well," Tony said. "Tell me of your plan." The engineers had started to notice the strange spectacle and paused in their work, it wasn't often they saw their great leaders showing any sign of weakness. They watched on as the two men whispered to each other over the next few minutes and watched as Jackabah made expansive motions with his hands and how Tony stood up tall and proud in response.

"I hope you're right," Tony said in earnest when Jackabah had finished. "I cannot stand any more of this war. Every day I hear of my kinsman dying in all quadrants of this planet all in the name of rebellion. I will do what you say no matter what the cost to me." Jackabah knew that Tony was as good as his word as he had lost his brother Greg when they removed the first ion core.

"Take today and tomorrow off Tony, you need to rest. How long have you gone without sleep?" Jackabah asked. When he didn't receive an answer he presumed it had been too long, especially considering the fact he hadn't had time to truly mourn the loss of his brother. The master of the shop staggered away in tears and some of the workers dropped tools and aided him back to his quarters. Jackabah commanded the rest of the workers to return to work and continued towards the foundry area.

The stench of molten metal was thick in the air as the rag-torn labourers scurried around pouring glowing liquid alloys into small moulds scattered around the shop floor. Men, women and some of the older children worked in appalling conditions keeping the foundry alive and the production of base castings steady to support the machined parts used in all manner of vehicle and weapon conversions. Jackabah felt sick to the stomach as he wandered through the foundry area.

"My people deserve more than this! Xen will pay for the atrocity of this war!" The rebel leader vowed as he continued right through to the other side of the workshop and headed off to the underground docks.

The docks were a disarray of stacked packing crates as the workers laboured around the clock to unload the cargo of food, medical supplies and weapons that were brought in by a secret cylinder train. All of these goods had been bought at a great price from the ghastly gunrunners and seedy merchants who thrived upon a sickly planet torn by war. The workers here all had the signs of drug addiction, stimulants to keep them going and narcotics to send them into brief moments of stolen hazy sleep in the little time off work they had.

The plight of his colleagues made Jackabah's flesh crawl once more. His people had been reduced to shells, voluntarily risking themselves to the seduction of the peddler's chemical highs just to keep working for him. Perhaps it was no wonder that they submitted themselves to such risks given what happened on a daily basis on Sigra III. Maybe even drugged labour was preferable to facing the harsh realities of what was happening on the surface.

It appeared that the new shipment of armoured suits, ammunition and weapons had finally arrived. Some of the packing crates sported the emblems of the minor corporations that had fed on this hideous war. The riches that were left on this planet were lining the coffers of true parasitic merchant scum. It was like feeding time at the zoo, the bloated corpse of Sigra III feeding the jackals.

Jackabah considered what would happen if he leaked to Xen the fact other corporations were aiding the rebels. Perhaps it would start an interstellar corporate war and ease the pressure on them. More likely it would lead to the shipment of supplies being cut.

"Don't bite the hand that feeds you!" He whispered to himself. What was important was that these new supplies should give the rebels a better chance of

521

holding off the CORE troopers for long enough for his plan to be executed.

Daemon left the sanctuary of the sphere and walked down to the tunnel head. The morning light filtered over the mountains to the north casting great shadows over the new base and the ruins of the previous installation. He passed a few patrols on his way but ignored them like they did him. He noted that the earth of the tunnel entrance had baked to a solid mass under the fierce heat of the rebel attack as he headed for the underground bunker. Most of the rainwater had evaporated inside the tunnel allowing him to make good headway. It wasn't long before he was safe inside the confines of the underground bunker.

The demon had been correct about planetary scans from the orbiting Goliath, Xen intelligence had noticed the deep underground tunnel under no-man's land and placed a new lieutenant in charge of their excavation to be aided by Daemon himself. He met with the new lieutenant in charge of the operation and discovered he was a real corporate arsehole; it was obvious he had never even witnessed the field of warfare.

"We are steadfast Daemon. The tunnel should be completed soon." The arsehole lieutenant stated with a lop-sided grin. It was almost as if he was supervising a factory rather than a secret military operation. Daemon scowled and levelled his eyes at the new lieutenant.

"How long do you think it will take to complete?" He asked.

Daemon had seen the planetary scan read-outs and knew the renewed excavation didn't have far to go before reaching some kind of void or cave system under the no-man's land.

The lieutenant paused calculating the cutting process verses the time estimation.

"I suspect we will reach the voided areas this time next week. While we are on the subject of the voided areas what do you presume they are?" He asked with more curiosity than needed.

Daemon narrowed his eyes with growing anger.

"Lieutenant, just dig the fucking tunnel! The voided areas are none of your business!"

The lieutenant backed away from Daemon disturbed by the fleeting glimpse he thought he had seen of Daemons pupils fully dilating, obscuring the colour of his iris until the whites of his eyes nearly turned black with inner darkness.

"Yes. Of course, I will, erm, get back to it then." The lieutenant physically quaked in his boots and broke eye contact with the terrifying man.

Daemon wandered over to the console terminals and punched in a series of codes bringing up a display of troopers working the excavation head.

"You have five days to complete the tunnel!" Daemon stated before leaving the room. On his way out of the bunker, he stopped to talk to Corporal Kell who saluted and asked what he needed.

"The new lieutenant is a tit! If he doesn't finish that tunnel in five days' time, you have my orders to put him to death. Is that clear corporal?" The hard-faced woman nodded and saluted.

"I understand your orders first Lieutenant Daemon of Xen!" She punctuated her words by chambering a round in her firearm and wiggling her trigger finger. Daemon smiled and headed off back to the central command sphere.

The operations room in the sphere was abuzz with activity as console technicians and commanding officers paraded around the room gathering and organising incoming information. The Xen assault group to the west of Runich was crossing the seven miles of no-man's land and the rebels were putting up quite a fight. General Joss had already sweated through his army issue shirt as he watched the battle through the aid of circling air-recon crafts. Daemon picked up two coffees and gave one to General Joss. The General took the beverage without looking at his fellow officer.

"The rebels are tearing us apart?" General Joss stated almost dumb-founded. He watched with shocked disbelief at the numerous displays of Xen armoured vehicles under an onslaught of heavy resistance. "We have to take them on both fronts! Prepare our eastern force and make it quick!"

Petty officers began to relay orders for the eastern army to prepare for a full attack. Daemon watched the lower display screens which depicted troops on full alert in the William Hadley drop pods assembling in the staging chambers. He was about to leave the operations room when a Xen intelligence agent grabbed hold of his arm.

Daemon turned and faced the tall stern looking man, his eyes hidden by dark reflective glasses.

"Leaving so soon Daemon?" Agent Rowson asked with no expression on his stony face. Daemon leant closer to the agent.

"I was about to gather up Sergeant Sherry and squad four to make sure they don't get caught up in this mayhem. Off the record sir, I don't believe General Joss knows what he is up against and how to plan a surface battle." He whispered.

Agent Rowson nodded once and placed a toothpick in his mouth to chew.   "Is that so? And your plans for squad four?" The agent asked.

A bright explosion on one of the displays distracted the pair for a few moments. An armoured Xen vehicle had just bought it by a well-aimed rocket.

"I plan to take squad four to the underground bunker which will be my staging area." Daemon explained as the agent re-focused his gaze upon him.

"Ah, the tunnel! But the tunnel isn't complete. It could take days, maybe weeks to finish." It seemed the agent had done his homework, he had obviously seen the tunnel on a planetary scan.

"I suspect it will be completed in five days. That's another reason I'm going below ground, I'm going to make sure it's finished." Daemon tapped his sidearm to make it clear to the agent he was going to use extreme force to relay his orders.

"Before you scurry off Lieutenant, you might wish to know I have followed every move of your career so far.

I'm impressed at the moment; however, I will be very upset if you let me down." The agent mimicked Daemon and tapped his sidearm as a threat.

Daemon had to hold back the demon clawing its way through his brain, in the attempt to stop his alter ego tearing off the agent's head. Agent Rowson noticed the change in the lieutenant and took an involuntary step backwards.

"I think you better get out of here before the good general has you lead his eastern army into Runich!" The agent said with a slightly nervous tone. "But one last thing Lieutenant, we want that bastard alive!"

Daemon staggered away from the operations room, he had managed to trap the demon in a dark chamber within his psyche; out of harm's way for a while.

The entire command sphere was on full alert with officers and troops packing the corridors in a display of poor planning. He headed towards the billets and hoped Sherry hadn't already been assigned to the current attack. The city of Runich would be a citadel of guerrilla warfare by now. Every building would be a fortress and every available man, woman and child would fight like cornered rats.

In Daemon's opinion, the Xen military had stupidly played right into the rebel's strengths. If Xen occupied sections of the city and tried to push on further it meant they couldn't risk using air assaults in fear of hitting their own troops.

I bet Jackabah is rubbing his hands together in joy right now. How stupid can Xen be? Unless, I'm missing the bigger picture of course. Daemon shook his thoughts from his head and entered the command billets.

They were like any other sleeping chambers apart from numerous live feed displays and communications terminals. He spotted Sherry studying the current ground battle and could see that she was probably wondering why her squad hadn't made the big push towards Runich.

"Hello, Sherry." He said. Sherry turned around to meet Daemons gaze.

"Lieutenant?" She frowned and seemed a little confused by his presence.

"You are now under my command. Gather up squad four and meet me at the underground bunker." He said ready to leave until Sherry became angry.

"What are you talking about? I was to wait for orders to attack Runich. I don't want anything to do with you or that fucking tunnel!" She barked.

"Listen! I won't bother reminding you of my rank or reminding you of the consequence of disobeying a high ranking Xen commander. Just do what I say and I promise I will provide some real combat for you." He smiled loving every second as her anger switched to a display of emotional breakdown.

"Daemon! I want to fight on the streets of Runich. I don't want to spend weeks in a dark tunnel." Sherry screamed and clenched her fists until her knuckles were white with rage.

He leant forwards and grabbed hold of Sherry's tunic

and pulled her towards him.

"Gather your squad and get down that fucking tunnel, Sergeant!" He barked as his pupils dilated and became almost lifeless.

Sherry shook her emotions away and saluted. The demonic creature facing her saluted back before it headed off to the sphere's armoury.

The armoury was the biggest he had ever seen, a veritable warren of armoured suits, firearms and equipment stacked upon shelves and hooks. Daemon felt like a ten-year-old in a giant toy shop with festival cash to spend. Two auxiliaries aided him whilst he selected items to pack upon three floating lifters. Some of the equipment was experimental or newly developed versions of equipment he was familiar with. He felt that now was not the time to distract his squad with new toys to play with so only selected equipment they would have been trained to use. He was about to leave the armoury when his eyes drifted upon some mean looking advanced carbines. They were sleek, very light weight, bull-pop in design and fitted with sniper scopes and silencers. His resolve deteriorated at the sight of such beautiful weapons so he grabbed two carbines and as many clips as he could personally carry knowing that Sherry would undoubtedly want one of those sexy bastards.

"Take these lifters to the underground bunker." He ordered to one of the auxiliaries. He filled a carry case with Geo-charges to aid the excavation of the tunnel while the auxiliary guided the lifters out of the armoury via a handheld remote. The last thing on his shopping list was a prototype armoured suit he had trained with on the Goliath. It was one of the new command light weight E.C.A. combat suits with shielding units to protect the head instead of the standard armoured helm. Daemon laboured under the weight of his personal items and equipment on his way to the underground and wished he had commandeered another of the lifters.

Sweat dripped from Jackabah's brow onto one of the many keyboards scattered before him. His eyes darted from one display to another the horror of siege warfare evident on every screen. Calls of distress and reports of minor victories drowned out his thoughts as the numerous voices of his rebel army crackled and hissed over the local communications. The fighting units had fled to the inner city when Xen had entered the city on both fronts. The snipers and rocket positions had halted the advancing Xen forces, east and west. However, the rebel's rudimentary weapons were having a tough time penetrating the armoured Xen divisions but had at least forced them to rethink the attack. The western front seemed to be holding its own but the eastern defence forces were on a steady withdrawal. Jackabah quickly punched a private code into the comms and hooked up a live feed to Commander Koff on the eastern front.

"Koff?" Jackabah asked unable to recognise the commander due to the amount of mud and debris which had marred the visor of her combat suit.

"Yes sir," Koff replied raising her carbine to her shoulders and firing off a quick burst.

"How goes the battle? Are you still holding to the east?" Jackabah queried hoping for good news.

"We have had to withdraw to Commerce Square but the Seinal Corporation bank buildings are providing good cover. We could do with some reinforcements and some more armoured vehicles to push them back." Koff stated.

The live feed was a little fuzzy and Jackabah realised the Xen forces were already setting up communication scramblers.

"I can spare three vehicles and a gun emplacement, will that help?" Jackabah said and wished he had more to send.

Commander Koff's helmet nodded.

"We will use them wisely oh-honoured leader." The commander stated in a loyal tone.

Jackabah wanted to weep for this glorious warrior woman. Her predecessor had perished under intense plasma fire while manning a field gun just an hour ago. The rebel leader pulled some of his central defence force to aid Commander Koff in defending the eastern attack.

Melinda had entered the room while he relayed orders to his central defence force and she seemed very excited.

"Our engineers have managed to pull out the ion core at power plant six. It hasn't sparked and the recent shipment of protective suits has saved their lives." She said beaming with joy.

Jackabah silently thanked the heavens hearing this news.

"Prepare the core in the hot-cell like we did last time but follow the procedures to the letter. We can't have that thing sparkling in the underground." He said with a worried frown. He hugged Melinda and kissed her once on her cheek.

"Start evacuating the children to Tell-brook via the underground cylinder train," Jackabah instructed her. "Give the greedy merchants whatever they want if they can guarantee them safe passage but don't tell them of our plan. They will pay for their greed!"

Melinda took out a pill box and swallowed a few stimulants then offered the box to Jackabah. He noticed how tired she looked and took a pill himself. She watched him become absorbed with the battle consoles for a while before she hurried off to begin the evacuation. Jackabah picked up the communicator and tapped in a direct line to the engineering department. An engineer answered the call.

"Is the master engineer around?" He asked.

"He is in the foundry organising the casting of some vital parts for the submersible. Do you want me to go get him?" The engineer said with a heavy sigh.

"No, that won't be necessary. Could you find out how far we are with the submersible?" Jackabah said.

"I dare say another day or so, maybe more. Especially if the parts don't cast right, we threw the patterns together this morning, we aren't even sure the special alloy will run." The engineer explained and then shouted at his apprentice. Jackabah didn't catch what he said but it sounded like the apprentice had just screwed up something.

"I am going to have to go; Max has just welded the wrong part on an attack vehicle. It's happening more often now. Everyone is just too tired." The engineer complained before the line went dead.
Jackabah tapped the communicator and then realised the engineer had just hung up on him.

"The cheeky bastard! These engineers have no manners." He said out loud then started laughing at the absurdity of the situation.

Everyone was working themselves to exhaustion to aid the cause and it was inevitable that mistakes would creep in. He slumped into his seat and hoped that he wasn't making critical errors himself. He felt the stimulant working through his tired veins but the drug struggled to revive Jackabah's fatigued body. He balled his left fist and cupped his right hand around it before closing his eyes and offering a quiet prayer.

I need more time Lord! Just give me a reprieve and allow my people a final strike against these infidels.

A short time later it appeared as if his prayer had been answered, a storm front had broken over the Gewl Mountains and the monsoons were rushing towards Runich. The weather display depicted a mighty storm head coming from the north which would slow the enemy forces down and reduce combat visibility.

"Thank you oh Lord!" he whispered.

The rains hit Runich hard. The detritus of war was subject to a fearsome and destructive lightning storm. Rainwater turned the scorched earth to mud and flooded the basements of destroyed buildings. Sheet lightning descended all over the city and the deafening peals of thunder sounded like the horns of Jericho. The weakened structures crumbled at the cacophony of sound and fell into the foundations below. The rebels and Xen forces dug into whatever cover they could find to avoid being hit by falling masonry.

It seemed the city had been put under temporary ceasefire as conditions became too severe to wage war. Both sides took advantage of the reprieve to service weapons and battle armour. The Xen freight vehicles trundled over the no-man's land to the east and west with only the threat of getting stuck in the mud rather than rebel gunfire. Now that Xen had dug into the city outskirts the freighters formed a vital supply line that provided ammunition, field guns, vital medicines, food and water.

The rebels had been busy earlier in the day destroying strategic buildings and attempting to block the main thoroughfares with the rubble which now covered main roads and routes into the city. In the area near Commerce Square where the street by street combat has been most intense a strange scene now played out. Rebels and Xen troops shared a meal under a bubble tent when only half an hour before the storm they had been fighting one another. It was as if the rains had washed away their animosity as enemies regaled each other with tales of the hardships they had endured.

In all wars, it is a rare thing to witness opposing factions welcome their enemy into camp to share provisions. But war does strange things to people. It brings out the very worst of man but sometimes the very best of which humanity could offer.

Before the rebels left the bubble tent they thanked and shook hands with the Xen troopers exchanging trinkets such as insignia and chocolate. Both sides knew only too well they will be killing one another as soon as the storm lifted but for now they were safe together in the eye of it.

The geo-charges had made good headway in the excavation process gaining Daemon precious hours. He supervised the half-naked troopers who laboured upon the tunnel head using the new plasma cutters that he had commandeered from the sphere's armoury. The newly installed air-scrubbers worked around the clock to clean the air of carbon dioxide and dust in the newest section of the tunnel. The carbon dioxide didn't really bother the advanced cloned troops but the dust had been a problem until now. The cloned troops had been grown with a special organ which could process shitty air by removing unwanted toxins and extracting additional oxygen. However, the dust had got everywhere, blinding them, choking them, clinging to them and clogging the machinery.

Sherry leant on a dented sledge hammer and watched the labour force. Her face was a picture of absolute dissatisfaction. Daemon had tried his best to cheer her up during the last two days in the bunker but her intense mood swings had started to grate on his nerves.

"Not long now Sherry, maybe a day or so." He said half-heartedly. He had to admit to himself that he was tired of all the digging.

"You said that yesterday!" She groaned and launched the sledge hammer against the adjacent wall. The hammer smashed a lump of baked earth from the wall which cascaded to the ground.

Daemon shook his head in disgust at Sherry's tantrum and clicked the ambient temperature unit. It showed that it was just over forty degrees Celsius making the tunnel like an oven due to the heat from the plasma cutters and the poor ventilation. He couldn't help notice Sherry had sweated through her vest which had all but revealed her breasts. Under normal circumstances, he would have probably been aroused by the sight but he was so tired he just wandered off to the bunker for a shower. On his way, he passed several troopers planting explosives on the tunnel walls. The explosives were a contingency to allow them to blow up the tunnel should the rebels discover and try to utilise it.

The shower was cold as all surplus power had been diverted to the war effort. Daemon cursed as the freezing water splashed against his body but had no cause for complaint as it was he who had deemed hot water an unnecessary luxury. He returned to his bunk to dry off and saw that Sherry had followed him back and was presently sat on his bed cutting cross-hairs in the bullets to use in her side arm.

"Why are you doing that?" he asked as he towelled himself down.

"I've heard a rumour that the majority of the rebels are wearing bubble suits and not any kind of real armour. No need to look for penetration." She said without raising her eyes.

He shook his head thinking what a sick bitch she had become. Cross-haired bullets caused more tissue damaged as they expanded when they hit the target but they wouldn't even get through armour. She was looking to make a right old mess of somebody.

What troubled him more was that he knew damned well the rumours were propaganda spread by the Xen intelligence to increase the moral of the troops. The problem was everybody in the Xen attack force had been so caught up in the rumours that they actually started to believe their own lies. Her bullets would be useless if she came upon a fully suited rebel.

"You might want to alternate them. You know, just in case." He advised knowing it was useless to tell her that the rumour was bullshit.

"This is just for up close and personal." She laughed. "You know, just to make things interesting." She threw the loaded pistol onto his bed and unclothed herself before jumping into the shower.

Even a cold shower had seemingly made him feel more human than before as the sight of her beautiful naked feminine form had resonated with him. He jumped into bed and rolled onto his stomach to hide his arousal and let his mind drift away trying not to think of her wet and glistening in the shower.

When Sherry had finished the shower she saw Daemon was fast asleep face down on his narrow bed. She felt like waking him but decided to listen to the communications before settling down to sleep. The transmitter extension ran the length of the tunnel to the surface but with the recent rains, the signal was barely audible.

She listened to the siege of Runich and wished she was fighting alongside her fellow troops. Not that they were having a good time of crushing the rebels from what she heard, especially in Commerce Square where the battle was thick with blood on both sides. She tried to imagine the sprawling ruined buildings, sniper fire from random windows of the burnt out husks, armoured vehicles laying down covering fire while medics attempted to rescue injured troops through the fog and smoke of heavy plasma guns.

"I could have been an overnight hero if it wasn't for Daemon holding me back here!" She said and then cursed as Daemon stirred in his sleep. She had forgotten how loud one tended to talk with noisy ear comms on.

She removed the earpieces and checked on him; he was still sleeping but his mouth worked in silent conversation. Sherry leant closer to hear the low mumble, assuming he was dreaming. She was surprised to hear that he seemed to use two entirely different voice tones and that they seemed to be having some kind of conversation. She couldn't clearly make out what they were saying but it unnerved her the more she listened. Sherry nearly screamed out when his eyes suddenly flicked open and stared at her, they were jet black surrounded by a tiny circlet of white.

"Haven't you got anything better to do sergeant?" the Demon said in a feral growl.

Sherry leapt towards her bed and grabbed hold of her sidearm from the bedside cabinet. The demon's eyes followed her as she nervously grabbed her clothes and edged around the bed towards the door.

"Leaving so soon Sherry?" He asked in a passive tone but it still wasn't Daemons voice that she heard.

"Yes. I thought I would check on the tunnel." She lied trying to keep an element of calm in her voice.

"The tunnel? Yes, that's a good idea. Once that's completed we can get this mission finished and leave this shit-hole planet!" He said in an understanding voice.

Sherry had got to the foot of the door, but she was curious about this other Daemon; the creature that surfaced and became him.

"Where is Daemon?" She asked raising the pistol.

The creature didn't give her time to fire a single round, it closed the distance to Sherry, disarmed her and pinned her painfully against the door in a fraction of a second. Sherry couldn't believe the lightning speed which it moved and she swore she hadn't blinked. She wrestled against its iron grip as it stared into her eyes almost studying her.

"Threatening a Xen officer is a court marshal offence sergeant, you know that?" It hissed releasing its grip. "Go and check on the tunnel! And the next time you do something as stupid as raising arms against me I will disembowel you and show you your own innards."

Sherry watched this bestial creature who inhabited Daemon's body pick up her pistol and empty the magazine before giving the weapon back to her. She took the empty pistol and fled through the door gathering speed in her run towards the sleeping billets. She would spend the rest of the night with the regular troops, far enough away from the psycho that slept in the officer's residence.

When Daemon arose the next morning he had no recollection of the events of the night before and wondered where Sherry had got to. A message glowed on his terminal and upon opening the message he found that Colonel Lenz had perished during the night. Apparently, the tough old bastard had regained a measure of consciousness and turned off the life support machine. The medical crash team couldn't revive him and Daemon wondered if he had died with a smile on his face. In some ways, Daemon was glad he had finished himself off as he suspected that Lenz would have been sent to the plants if he had survived.

While the rebels were assembling their new weapon and Daemon continued the excavation of the tunnel

Runich was being sliced like a cake. Rebel-held zones slowed the advancing Xen troops at such a cost of life that the high command was threatening to pull the plug on the entire siege. General Joss had twice asked to pull out his troops and carpet-bomb the city until it was razed to the ground then nerve gas the rebel underground. Xen intelligence declined both his requests and continued to supply General Joss with troops and weapons.

Although Xen intelligence was displeased with the slow progress of the taking of the city they knew that they would eventually win. For each man who survived the battle, they would gain a battle hardened veteran who could be harvested from this siege and added to the Elite Xen fighting cores. The invaluable experience these war veterans gained would be utilised in theatres of war upon other worlds.

The Xen Corporation was actually making a steady profit from the outdated arms and drug sales they supplied to the rebels which they would never be able to sell otherwise. The rebels were simply handing over all their gold reserves not realising they were lining their enemies company coffers. The kickbacks alone could pay for Xen to supply the procession of troops that were being butchered by their own weaponry upon Sigra III.

What the rebels and the common soldiery failed to understand was that Xen didn't want to end the war. They wanted it to continue until Sigra III had been pillaged of all of its strategic resources and reserves.

The cost to manufacture a standard battle rifle in a mechanised plant cost twenty-two Xen credits. Selling just one obsolete battle rifle to the rebellious scum on Sigra III gained Xen a net profit of over three hundred credits. War in the eyes of a major corporation was simply transferring one lucrative economy into another type of profit.

The Xen Corporation had moral flexibility; they were as happy to sell grain as guns. It didn't make an iota of difference as long as the money poured into the various deposit accounts. Everything was a commodity to be bought and sold and that included its employees. If they were not bright enough to realise this concept then they were a disposable commodity. It took a special individual to transcend into the upper echelons of the corporation; it only took an ordinary one to die for it.

CHAPTER 27

Assignment

Master Vaul watched the passing traffic of ground cruisers on the main street of Morden from the window of a taxi. His journey from the Kommando School had taken all morning by jet-craft to the city of Morden. It was the third largest city on Talon II in terms of population but Vaul had always felt an affinity to it and thought it was the greatest city on the planet. In terms of art and culture it was unequalled, besides, it also had the best restaurants in the quadrant including his favourite The Ta'rgg which boasted fresh jungle crab daily. The only thing that spoiled his mood was the fact he would be meeting with Agent Hellus, Vaul found him distasteful in the extreme; a despicable man whom he had been forced to work with against his will many times. Even now when he bore the acclaimed title of Master of the Kommando School it appeared that he was still subject to the man's influence.

Hellus was the archetypical intelligence agent who stayed well away from the limelight but seemed to have a hand in most things. The only occasions you ever got to see him usually meant something serious had driven him out from behind his desk. He had an army of spies and agents working for him and was renowned as being a master string puller and manipulator.

One of the things that unnerved Vaul about dealing with agents was the fact you were never sure who actually ranked the highest in the intelligence community. He had contemplated this many times before wondering if rank system actually existed in the agency or if every agent held an equal rank, a collective of intelligence networks working as a single unit. Whatever the situation was in the Xen intelligence hierarchy he instinctively felt that Agent Hellus was some kind of unofficial top dog and needed to be treated with caution.

The main streets of Morden were awash with bright flickering lights that played across the bustling crowds of rich, well-dressed people. But all this façade of splendour was a veneer upon a dangerous underworld, walking but two minutes from any main street revealed a seedy and dangerous city of crime and corruption. This juxtaposition of culture and crime was the main reason Vaul loved this city, the rich stayed to their parts of the city and the villainous folk stuck to theirs. It was a perfect balance of society, the paths of the two groups very rarely crossed. He remembered recruiting several individuals from the darkness of Morden City a few years ago all of whom he had moulded into perfect operatives.

The drop point for their meeting was an exclusive restaurant minutes away from the grand square, it stood on the cusp of the two worlds and was consequently shunned by the city residents but provided a sanctuary for Xen operatives. The ground cruiser parked outside the plain looking building which to the eyes of any casual passer-by appeared to be an old auction depositary rather than an opulent eatery for powerful corporate members. Vaul looked at his time piece and realised he was early. He preferred to be late. Keep the bastard waiting and let him stew a little he thought. The driver of the ground cruiser waited patiently while Vaul browsed a local newsreel.

When Vaul was satisfied that he had kept the agent waiting long enough he slipped the driver a bunch of bank notes and casually wandered towards the doorway. A chain cannon hidden above him tracked him at the entrance as the doorman asked for the relevant codes of entry. The door opened smoothly and noiselessly and the alleyway filled with bright light and the echo of voices from within. The doorman took Vaul's coat and ushered him into the reception which was filled with varied Xen officials from off-duty officers to planetary ambassadors. As the maitre-d' scanned the list for his name Vaul noticed Agent Hellus sat alone at their usual table. Even from here he could see Hellus was in a terrible mood and as he approached the table Hellus was already ranting.

"I'm not an idiot Vaul! You have deliberately kept me waiting. I know damned well you landed over three hours ago."

Vaul sat down and began to fiddle with the cutlery on his side of the table ignoring the agent's anger.

"Calm yourself Hellus. I merely got caught in traffic coming out of the port. It's a very busy time of year." Vaul said with a mixture of contempt and calm in his tone.

Hellus silenced the newsreel he had been watching and sipped the last dregs of wine from his glass.

"Well I'm a busy man! I will get straight to the point and then you can get the fuck out of my sight." Hellus stated angrily.

Vaul blanched at his coarse language and gestured for him to wait a moment as he ordered a drink and first course. This only added to the agent's rage and had Hellus trembling in his shoes. A nearby waiter took his order and refilled the agent's glass in an attempt to calm the angry man down.

"You may be the master of THAT school of assassins but you can't abuse your position and keep vital executives standing with their dicks in the wind." Hellus moaned between guzzles of wine.

"I've already explained myself Hellus, you really should try and calm down. The wine is rather excellent don't you think?" Vaul asked savouring the agent's discomfort as much as the vintage he was tasting.

Hellus' reply died on his lips as the waiter approached with the first course of Halneque wings in a mulled sauce. Vaul breathed in the aroma before he tucked into the sweet meat.

"We have a problem on Sigra III the planet that we are currently bleeding dry," Hellus said with a mouthful of chewed meat.

Vaul was disgusted by his barbarism and merely nodded as Hellus continued.

"It just so happens that a rebel leader who calls himself Jackabah is holed up in some rat infested city and is threatening to blow all the ion plants simultaneously. He claims that it would create a chain reaction right down to the core of the planet and it seems some of our scientists believe that it could actually happen. The threat, be it a bluff or otherwise could, in theory, cause a planet-wide earthquake which could tear the planet in sunder."

Vaul nearly choked on his meal and started to laugh at the agent's words.

"Look. I am no scientist but even I can tell the threat is just not credible." Vaul said pressing his serviette to the corner of his mouth.

Hellus shook his head gravely and produced a small printed schematic which Vaul took from him and scrutinised.

"At worst it would be a tiny planet-wide earthquake; nothing more than a tremor. Please don't tell me you have dragged me all the way to Morden to show me this?" Vaul said with underlining disgust.

"You're not seeing the whole picture Vaul. If this scumbag rebel chain reacts the ion plants it would not only destroy all the processed ionic ore but it could be construed as being a major victory to every rebel on the planet. Your so-called tremor would be physical evidence that Xen could lose the war and provide a rallying call to other would-be heroes on other planets.

I don't think I need to add that ionic ore is getting harder to come by since the merger of Xen and the Seinal Corporations. Every sub-corporation has embargoed their own stocks and refuse to sell to any major corporation." Vaul tried to interrupt but Hellus continued his diatribe. "There is enough processed ionic ore on Sigra III to see us into the next century. Not to mention the raw ore we could reap. We can't have every rebel leader on Sigra III destroying the stuff we intend to collect! Xen intelligence is having a hard enough time to convince the military faction that this exploding planet scenario could be viable. Now do you see the picture?"

Vaul nodded in agreement, he had heard rumours of the depleting ionic stocks within the Xen foundation.

"O.K, Hellus, I see where you are coming from but where exactly do my assassins fit into this scenario? It sounds like you have left it too late to infiltrate the rebels. They would never accept the arrival of strangers at this juncture." Vaul asked with careful curiosity. Hellus smiled and raised his glass in a mock toast.

"You know our methods too well Vaul. Our preliminary plan is currently in operation on Sigra III, we have a Xen lieutenant in the process of tracing and retrieving this so-called rebel leader before he tries to blow everything to kingdom come. What I need is a contingency plan, a tasty bit of wet-work for your hired killers just in case the lieutenant fails in his mission." Hellus said while winking.

"A duel operation, running side by side? And what happens if my assassin meets with your lieutenant?" Vaul asked.
Hellus grinned and raised an eyebrow.

"I don't think I need to answer that question do I Vaul?" Hellus said in a measured tone. "Events would be allowed to run their course naturally."

Vaul nodded in understanding as the agent passed him the relevant documents. Hellus ordered his coat and left Master Vaul to the second course of his meal.

Chinn had been training all morning until the heat of the midday sun became unbearable and her stomach growled for the want for food. She found Roz in the canteen section of the Kommando School; he had been studying ancient poetry most of the morning within the meditation temple. Chinn spooned the fish stew hungrily into her mouth as Roz recited a few passages he had memorised that morning. She feigned interest for a while before attempting to change the subject. After emerging from the conditioning she had been placed straight into training and after three weeks she felt tired from the rigorous nature of it. Although her mind had been opened up to accept the necessity of killing the enemies of Xen some vestiges of her beliefs still existed. Her solitude in the jungle had made her psyche strong even now she was having second thoughts of staying in the school with Roz. Although she missed the smell of the forest and the daily routine of survival she didn't miss the food. The food in the school was delicious due to the master chefs who prepared the daily meals.

"I have some down time coming up. I thought we could spend the day exploring the woodland around the school. I haven't had time to see the pine trees." Chinn said. She had been used to the trees in the rain forest that dwarfed those around the school and she wanted to understand their nature.

"I don't see why not. To be honest with you I haven't really explored the woodland around the school yet. It will be a damned sight less dangerous than the rain forest and we might even get to see a night caller." He said. He noticed how tired she looked and a day in the woods would do her the world of good. Chinn started on her second course of mushroom pate and rustic broken bread.

"I hear Master Vaul has just returned from the city." She stated with a frown. Roz nodded and closed his notebook.

"Yes, I saw him arrive in a ground cruiser. He looked to be in a bad mood he didn't even bother to bow in greeting." Roz said while he stirred a cup of herbal tea.

549

They hadn't noticed Master Vaul approach them in the canteen and he overheard the last comments and cleared his throat to announce his presence.

"Yes, I apologise, it was rude of me not to offer a greeting but my mind has been on other things of late," Vaul said as he placed a small brown wrapped paper box on the table in front of them. Chinn's heart dropped seeing the box on the table as she knew it contained mission information.

"I want you both to study the information in the box and collect what you need from the armoury. As you already know, if asked I did not give you the box and the contents are for your eyes only. A starshifter will be waiting for you in the grounds at dawn so make sure you are both ready to board it." Vaul stated before leaving them to finish their meals. When Vaul had left the canteen Chinn shook her head in dismay.

"I'm not ready for a mission Roz. I failed the last two psycho-evaluation tests." She whispered across the table.
Roz didn't know what to say; he had assumed the school would allow them more time to hone Chinn's skills before sending them on a mission.

"I will see Master Vaul and explain we aren't ready." He was about to leave the table when Chinn grabbed his arm and stopped him from going anywhere.

"No. Master Vaul must have his reasons for sending us. Maybe the mission is an induction mission for me and he wants you with me as an advisor?" She said.
Roz wasn't sure. He thought it unlikely that they would

send them both out on what would be little more than a training exercise. They opened the box in their sleeping chambers and found nothing could have prepared them for the contents of the box.

That night Roz and Chinn made love like it was their last night alive. As he drifted off to sleep Roz had a premonition that he would wake up to an empty bed before dawn and find a letter on his pillow explaining Chinn's reasons for returning to the forest. But when morning came he found that he had been wrong to doubt her. His alarm buzzed and the nightmare of Chinn leaving him washed away in a tide of joy. Her dark brown oval eyes and smile was his first image of the morning. They had carefully studied the contents of the box and the numerous papers and schematics were still scattered over the bed linen. They gathered what they needed from the armoury and packed the equipment into carry sized packages. While they showered they heard the howl of descent jets coming from the grounds of the school.

Roz had never seen a Starshifter before but had heard rumours of these swift crafts from his Xen training. Starshifters were the fastest shuttle crafts to date. They sported no weaponry at all but could basically outrun most military vessels in space. He also knew that he would not have to suffer the indignities of travel sickness as they were equipped with onboard cryo-tanks. The bulky craft whined in standby in the courtyard, it appeared to be a compact ship, probably entirely built around an interstellar drive engine. The interior was cramped but they were quickly shown to the cryo-tubes by the flight attendant. The flight attendant was the most bizarre incarnation of humanity that Roz had ever seen. It appeared to be part man and part machine with transparent tubes pumping pale coloured liquids around a withered body. A mechanised exoskeleton provided its motor functions and Chinn had to cover her nose from the stench of stagnant atrophied flesh which tainted the air around the man-machine. They couldn't wait to be iced just to get away from the nauseating stink. As they clambered into the cryo-tubes, the ship's hull began to shake on take-off. The flight attendant leant over Chinn's tube and spoke in a metallic voice.

"Sleep now. Wake later!" It stated mechanically before shutting the lid of the cryo-tube.
She felt something prick her spine and moments later she felt the narcotics working through her system bringing a drug induced smile to her face. Her vision faded to darkness and she felt the ambient temperature dropping.

"Sleep at last!" She sluggishly mumbled before her body shut down.

The starshifter leapt through space at phenomenal speeds, it would only take a fifth of the time taken by a standard star cruiser to reach Sigra III. During its travel, it was able to pass through some of the most dangerous areas of space with impunity as opportunist privateers would have no chance of catching the shifter off guard. By the time the privateers even noticed the shifter on the long range scanners it was already rocketing into the distance. Any rudimentary missiles fired at it eventually burnt out in the futile attempt of hitting the fleeing craft. Starshifters were a commodity of the richest corporations in the universe, the amount of fuel burned in a single trip would be more than the average daily profit margin of any minor corporation. Xen being one of the major corporations of the known universe had many such crafts at their disposal. It was, after all, the safest option for interstellar travel.

Roz regurgitated what appeared to be concentrated bile into a receptacle held by the stinking flight attendant. The man-machine patted him on his shoulders while making reassuring mechanised sounds. Roz shivered frantically in the open cryo-tube trying not to throw up again. He had been thawed out too quickly which had brought on painful side effects.

"You wake now. We approach Sigra III and drop you off in the Goliath." The sinister cybernetic man stated.

Roz nodded as he slowly climbed out of the tube and staggered over to Chinn's cryo-tube to find that it was empty.

"Where is Chinn?" He asked angrily.

The attendant didn't understand anger or any other emotion, there was very little humanity left in the shrivelled husk.

"Friend thawed first. Little power to thaw out both tubes at the same time. Most power used on drive engines." It answered robotically.

Roz made his way through the cramped corridor to

the helm of the ship and found Chinn drinking sugary tea. She appeared to be well and not suffering from any side effects. She smiled at Roz and patted the only seat available for him to sit down. He chose to remain standing for a while to see the approach to the Goliath. It was a massive craft shaped like an open lotus flower set in high orbit over Sigra III. The planet itself was a dun colour and even from the high reaches of space, he could make out great storms raging over the planet.

A door hissed open at the front of the Star shifter and Roz stared as a chair slid out holding what he assumed was the pilot. It looked like it had grown out of the pilot's chair and although it appeared similar to the flight attendant it was recognisable as a withered old woman with scraggly white hair. She was attached to the chair by numerous tubes and an artificial lung at the side of the chair pumped air into her chest rendering her voice relatively normal compared to the attendant.

"I am sorry we had to thaw you out quicker than normal Roz but one easily loses track of time in space." She said with a wispy ancient voice.

Roz was glad that he could not see her face clearly in the half-light as he thought that if it was as ravaged as the rest of her it would be enough to put someone off their dinner. A hiss and a gurgle filled the uneasy quiet as the lung provided her with more breath.

"I like your friend Roz, she is very clever and pretty too. If I was one hundred years younger and not attached to this chair, I would have fallen for a woman like her." The pilot said with a cackle.

Chinn laughed but Roz recognised it was a nervous laugh.

"You best be gathering your belongings we dock in sixteen minutes and I can't wait around. I have to go to Dandibah to pick up some corporate officials." The pilot said with a groan.

The docking process was a quick affair, their credentials fast-tracked Roz and Chinn straight through the security clearance zone. A petty officer met them at security and led them with haste to a small briefing room. The officer appeared to be fresh out of school, his young man's moustache looked more like a comb of hairs and his face was marred with acne. He began to read off a series of scripted questions, with mostly routine yes / no answers but a few overcurious non-regulation questions had been spliced into the questionnaire.

Roz assumed the young officer wished to impress his commanders by asking the more prying questions and made it clear that he didn't need to answer them. The young man persisted in an officious manner and overstepped the mark when he unwisely asked who the intended target was to be. Roz informed him that the terms of the contract meant that he would have to consider killing the petty officer for his curiosity. By the time they headed off to the docking ring the young man had broken down in tears and begged for his life. Chinn was clearly upset by the threat Roz had made towards him but understood they couldn't reveal the details of the mission. He had noticed her silent mood.

"Come on Chinn, liven up. I wouldn't have really killed him I just wanted to give him a new life skill. The skill of minding one's own business when talking to individuals with a class three security clearance. There are many in our line of work who wouldn't have thought twice about popping the young officer there and then for asking mission-related questions." Roz said.
Chinn shook her head and stopped in the corridor. He cringed, waiting for her to explode in anger.

"I can't be you! That young fellow will probably struggle to sleep for weeks after your threats. He will be looking over his shoulder for the rest of his life thinking you are going to come back and murder him." She was flustered and upset.

He tried to calm her down but it spurred her to continue her outburst.

"I am going to follow this contract to the end. I will pull the fucking trigger if need be but this will be the first and last time! I just can't find it in me to be so frivolous in threatening or actual taking of human life."

Roz hoped her words were a spur of the moment reaction, to be forgotten as time went by but it seemed clear she wasn't happy being an assassin. He hugged her and she struggled at first before slowly relaxing in his arms.

"If you leave the school after this mission then I will leave too. Maybe we could use my savings and buy a farm on Talon II, near a forest if you wish?" He said knowing that he had accumulated a substantial amount of credits already. She nodded in his arms and hugged closer to him.

The docking ring on the other side of the Goliath was used for direct transit to Sigra III. The bay was filled with battered drop craft and merchant ships, not one of them manufactured for interstellar travel. Roz and Chinn passed a stack of packing crates which were being re-stamped with minor corporate symbols. The crates held weapons that had yet to be re-branded and still sported the big X of the Xen Corporation. A port manager showed them to a stealth craft at the far side of the docking ring which was dwarfed by the bulky military transports but appeared to be newly manufactured. It was vaguely disc-shaped and its sleek black surface was covered with strange shiny prongs.

"It might look like its straight off the production line but it's like that because it's never been damaged." The port manager said gesturing towards the sleek ship and started to explain the science behind these types of invisible crafts. He mentioned that it had only arrived for field service at the Goliath about a month ago but had already had over fifty drops. As he garbled on about new technology a female pilot approached holding a small carry case.

"Greetings! I'm Stephanie. I will be your pilot for today. I had a transmission about an hour ago. It seems you need dropping off in the mountain range north of Runich." The pilot said in an easy manner as if she was just exchanging banter.

Chinn nodded and gestured toward the stealth craft, "Have you piloted it often?" she asked.

"Oh yeah, we're well acquainted." She laughed, "I will get you down in a jiffy, don't you worry your pretty heads. We aren't expecting trouble today." She grinned seductively before ascending the gang plate.

Chinn growled at Roz's open-mouthed expression as his eyes followed the curvaceous pilot up the gang plate.

"I didn't know you liked blondes, Roz!" Chinn said as she dug the heel of her elbow in his ribs.
Roz tried to appear as if he wasn't interested in the young woman but his red flustered face gave away his obvious attraction to the young pilot.

"No. I prefer brunettes!" He said with an embarrassed, childlike expression.

"You better be honest with me! You wouldn't want me to snap her pretty head off would you?"   Chinn said in a tone of seething jealousy.

Roz shook his head then narrowed his brow.

"Wait a minute! What were you saying before about frivolous taking of human life?" He said with an open grin knowing he had her in a corner.
Chinn frowned and pushed him in the direction of the gang plate.

"This is different Roz! Remember I have spent years in the company of wild animals. You don't want me getting all primordial on this floozy over mating rights?" Chinn said but spoilt her threat with a giggle.

Roz shook his head and laughed out loud.

"Don't worry. You still have full mating rights. Maybe it's just rutting season." He ventured and slapped

Chinn's bottom.

Chinn waited until they both got to the top of the gang plate and then barged into his side. Roz staggered away from the impact and nearly fell the full ten feet to the ground of the docking ring. She helped him to his feet and grinned.

"There won't be any rutting going on, my stag! There is only one alpha Doe in this relationship." She said before kissing his cheek.

Roz looked over his shoulder at the height he would have fallen if he hadn't stopped himself and wondered if Chinn would have really hurt him. Chinn's loving eyes answered his last thought.

The interior of the stealth craft was strange to behold. It had strange mirrored walls made from some kind of alloy Roz wasn't familiar with. Stephanie prepared the ship for take-off while the passengers strapped themselves into the seats. The pilot returned to the passenger section and made sure everything was in order.

"Right, the flight won't be too long. When the red lights come on you will notice the craft slow, the gang plate will descend and I want you both quickly off my craft. When we land, the ship will become visible to defence weapons and probably the odd sniper, that's if there are any around on the mountain side so get out quick." She stated with a wink before returning to the helm of the ship, closing the door behind her.

Both assassins donned their helms and warmed up their life support, the suits had lightweight armour so not to encumber them. They hoped that wouldn't need heavy armour where they were going but they would probably require their wits about them. Roz felt the rumble of the ship as it penetrated the upper atmosphere of Sigra III and even without looking through the viewing ports he knew there was a violent storm below. The display in front of Roz depicted weather patterns of blizzards and heavy snow at the drop zone. He recalibrated his suit, changing its colour from black to white. Chinn noticed and did the same.

"Tingly!" Chinn, she said through the communicator, laughing. When the suit re-calibrated it vibrated all over due to the change in its polarity. Roz assumed she liked the sensation as her suit changed back to black and then to white again.

"Stop mucking around!" He said and then joined in with her laughter. The pilot had been correct, it didn't take long before the hull interior changed to the red lights.

"Twenty seconds!" The pilot announced over the ship's comms. A howling wind entered the hull as the gang plate descended. Yellowish snow spiralled into the craft as the assassins leapt out of their seats and dropped to the snow bound rock. The ship waited until they had got to a safe distance before activating its leap jets which rocketed the craft into the air vertically. No sooner had it reached thirty or so feet the craft disappeared within its stealth shields.

Visibility was low on the mountainous basin so they had to rely on the suits sonic display for a while until they reached suitable cover to ride out the storm. Chinn found a jutting overhang of rock which provided a good place to camp for the night about half a mile away from the drop zone. Roz inflated a bump-tent and scrambled inside out of the hideous swirling blizzard. Chinn remained outside for a moment as she scanned for life signs using an instrument which detected heart beats.

When she was satisfied the area was safe, she crawled inside the tent to join Roz.

CHAPTER 28

Infiltration

Sherry sat on a low outcrop of stone that was still warm from a previous plasma cut. She watched Daemon working the tunnel head, his muscles labouring with the weight of the cutter. There had been an accident that morning involving a super-heated plasma cell explosion which had literally melted the core trooper using the tool. Daemon had taken over after the accident in an attempt to increase the ever declining moral of the troops.

Sherry inhaled the Koll-weed she was smoking and felt the narcotic feathering out her stress levels. She had exchanged an old fashioned side arm for the packet of Koll-weed which was like gold dust on Sigra III at the moment. A core trooper leant on Sherry's shoulder; the female soldier was totally fatigued from her exertion over the morning and was still upset by the loss of her friend. Sherry thought her behaviour was a little strange since it was rare for a trooper to show any emotion at all. She assumed it was the combination of fatigue and sorrow provoking such an unusual reaction in a trooper spawned for war. Daemon powered down the cutter and passed it to a nearby man. Sweat dribbled off his face and chest as he plodded over to sit with Sherry. He noted that she cringed in his presence which was happening quite regularly since they had been underground. She had been acting strangely for a while but he couldn't fathom out the reason.

"Bastard granite!" He mumbled as he towelled himself off with a grimy rag.

Sherry shrugged and ignored him; she knew the rock had changed from soft sandstone to granite making it increasingly difficult to cut. Daemon patted the female core trooper on her shoulder in the attempt to reassure her but it didn't seem to help. She carried on staring at the place where her friend had died not six hours ago. Sherry placed her arm around her and rocked her for a while but that didn't help either.

"I think we better get her on a shuttle ship home," Sherry said.

Daemon noticed Sherry's use of the word her; troopers were rarely referred to as anything other than "troopers". These clones didn't even have names; they just had numbers and model types. He wondered where home would be for a trooper that had been born into the CORE. The only home they knew was the frontline or guardhouses stationed on some backwater in a remote part of the universe.

"I think it might be better is she remains here, let her rest in the billets for a few days. That'll give her a chance to get her back on her feet. A 'malfunctioning' trooper will probably be put down if you know what I mean?" He said knowing Sherry understood his words.

"Or sent to the plants!" Sherry mumbled. She stood up and helped the woman to her feet.

"Come on, let's get you to bed for some rest," Sherry said as she half carried the limp trooper away to the bunker.

Daemon watched as they left the tunnel and saluted the sickly trooper. His arms felt like dead weights and his body was crashing under the stimulants he had taken over the last few days.

"I notice I'm doing all the work as usual!" He said to the demon. It didn't answer and had been silent over the last few days due to the amount of time the tunnel was taking to excavate.

"Maybe I'm finally rid of you!" He tested but it still didn't answer. He smiled and hoped it was gone forever. It had been silent for a while now and he felt a little different in himself. Calmer but somehow empty? A great crashing sound from the tunnel head washed away all his thoughts of the demon.

Not another accident! He thought as he raced to the tunnel head and heard a cheer from the workers.

"Contact sir!" One of the troopers stated gleefully with a salute. Daemon saw a dark void behind the great hole in the tunnels face. He felt all the troubles of the world lifting from his shoulders as he snatched up his rifle.

"Get a squad down here and guard this entrance, once we've got it shored up I'm going to risk a look at what is on the other side." One of the workers rushed off towards the bunker while the other six braced the rock face with pneumatic jacks then readied their rifles. Daemon ducked under the lip of protruding granite and the light mounted on his gun revealed a humongous chamber ahead, the beam was speckled with dust motes from the cutting. The chamber smelled stale and cool air replaced the heat from the half molten rock around the entrance. His boots hissed as he clambered through the superheated hole bringing with it the stench of burnt plastic. The chamber beyond appeared to be some kind of disused reservoir that had long since run dry. He dropped to the floor of the colossal chamber and made a quick sweep of it.

Sluice gates and rusted pipes poked into the chamber at various places and a great recess in the centre was about twenty metres deep with a walkway around the lip. He looked back to the pinpoints of light from the trooper's guns at the tunnel entrance just to reassure himself of an exit point in case he ran into a patrol of any kind. He slowly started to walk forwards, taking care to keep his footsteps silent. Most of the massive pipes he encountered went upwards into the rock. He cursed silently to himself and thought of all the equipment he would need to bring down here to move a squad through the pipes. If he had studied the planetary scan map correctly he was presently in a derelict section of the under-city. Daemon's light scanned over an old maintenance hatch which had been invisible on the preliminary scan and wondered where it led to. He investigated further and realised that this old hatch could be opened easily using only meagre tools. Buoyed with this finding he raced along the chamber back to the cooling entrance that still glowed like the embers of a low burning campfire within the folds of darkness. Sherry was waiting by the tunnel's entrance and even in the low light, he could make out the excitement on her face. The last time he saw such glee on her beautiful face was just over a week ago when she was on top of him in the folds of sexual pleasure.

"Action at last Lieutenant!" She stated as she cranked a live round into her assault rifle. Daemon shook his head and clambered back through the smooth rocky entrance.

"Seal this entrance temporarily we need to re-examine the planetary scan data before we make our move into enemy territory." He ordered and saw Sherry's face drop glumly. She began ordering her squad to seal the tunnel head and to wait for further orders although it was done with lacklustre enthusiasm.

Daemon grabbed hold of her shoulder and smiled.

"I think we have a potential unguarded access point into the underground system. It will be easier than I first thought. So, please, stop with the theatrics. I need you and your squad combat ready, give them all a few hours to rest up. We will be going in soon. You can hold me to that as a promise." Daemon listened as she relayed his orders.

He smiled broadly and gestured for her to follow him back to the bunker.

"Daemon we don't have time for that!" She stated flatly.

Daemon looked aghast at her; he couldn't believe she would even think he was gearing up for a fuck at this crucial juncture in time.

"Sherry! I just want you to study the maps so you can prepare your team. Sometimes I wish you would think like a professional soldier and not be so obsessed with the contents of your knickers!" He said with jest.

Sherry laughed along with him but he could tell he had overstepped the line so he quickly dropped the joke. As he turned his back on her Sherry quit her laughter and narrowed her eyes towards him. They both walked in silence through the tunnel towards the bunker passing armed guards every ten feet.

"We're going into securing the rebel leader. Everyone else is expendable." He informed her.

Sherry merely shrugged as though she knew what the mission would be already.

"We must somehow capture this rebel leader and get him back to Xen for interrogation and then I suppose they will either kill him or buy him off to end this insurrection. It might be the case that Xen just kills him and replaces him with a more trusted agent but in any case, it is our job to secure him." He said without understanding the true politics behind the mission.

In the bunker, Daemon brought up the planetary scans on a large display screen. Sherry opened a bottle of fizzy fruit and downed it in a matter of seconds as she watched him tracing a series of faint lines along the scans.

"I knew it!" he said triumphantly tapping the display. "I found a maintenance hatch that the scans hadn't picked up. According to this, there isn't any sign of a tunnel behind it but it has to go somewhere. Look! I think it's been obscured by this main duct running above it. I think that the hatch could literally open up straight into the abandoned sections of rooms and pipes in the underground system. We could map them out and make our way through them."

"There could be miles of maintenance tunnels to get through are you sure you want to spend time mapping them?" Sherry said and then continued before he could put a word in edgeways.

"If you are right why don't we use it to gain access then cut through to this pipe section that leads all the way to that elevator?" She said as she traced her finger along a pipe section heading north-west. Her finger stopped at a dark black tiny square which looked a likely candidate for an elevator of some kind.

He looked carefully at the route she had shown. It was a direct route whilst the maintenance tunnels could well be a labyrinth of tunnels. Even if they led to the habitat section mapping the tunnels could take days.

"Getting into that pipe could cause problems, such as escape route back if it turns out to be a dead end." He claimed.

Sherry smiled and shook her head, "If it's a dead end then I think it's safe to assume that we won't be running into anybody and could get back safely. But if it isn't who says we need to come back the same route? I say we go right to that dark square and hope it's an elevator to the upper habitat. With any luck, we might even walk right into the rebel leader's office of command!"

He was unsure but it was a better plan than mapping out a maze of tunnels. Time was a precious resource and they couldn't afford to waste it.

"Ok Sherry, you've won me over. I don't think we'll be lucky enough to stumble straight on to them but once we are in we may get away without being confronted. They won't suspect that Xen troops could make it into this network without storming the main entry points. From what I've heard even they have started wearing Xen E.C.A.'s so we might be able to walk straight past them once we are in. We will have to raid the armoury again for harness equipment to gain access to the main pipe but on the whole, I think your plan is sound." He said with still an element of doubt.

Sherry nodded and headed off toward the command sphere. He watched her leave and then refocused on the tiny black square upon the planet scan.

"Let's hope you're an elevator!" He hissed.

"It appears to be abandoned," Chinn whispered into the comms as Roz entered an old weather station. It was dark inside and they relied on their suits vision intensifiers to navigate the maze of empty corridors and rooms. At one stage in the war, the rebels must have field stripped this complex for any available components. All that was left were nuts, bolts and washers that lay scattered in the rooms and corridors. It had taken them all morning to traverse down the mountain side, the blizzard storm had raged all the previous night but had cleared by morning. Luckily they had run across the weather station and checked it out hoping the old building had some means of transport down to the city of Runich. It would be a long climb down the mountain if the building hadn't Roz contemplated.

"There's a manhole cover," Chinn stated and pointed to the rusted metallic circle set in the floor. Roz nodded and prised the heavy cover from its bonds while she readied her firearm upon the darkness below. A rudimentary rung ladder ran down a deep circular shaft may be descending over forty meters.

"That ladder could be booby trapped, let me go down first" He suggested.
Chinn nodded once and prayed that it wasn't as Roz secured his firearm and scrambled down the ladder. She watched as he disappeared past her range of vision. She listened to his breathing via the comms hoping the rebels didn't have a base down there.

"It seems to be an old store room, with an elevator... Wait... Yeah, it's been electronically sabotaged but I might be able to re-route it. Come on down." He said.

Chinn quickly joined him in the room below and she saw Roz at work with a box full of circuitry. Electronics wasn't Chinn's forte, she knew how to kill and how to survive in a rain forest but a box containing numerous wires seemed beyond her skill capabilities. She continued to watch him add a small power supply to the fused wires and within seconds the elevator lights illuminated.

"I think that will do it but we haven't got long on the battery." He stated as he tested the elevators mechanism before entering.

The doors closed as they entered the spacious metal box and it began to descend. It was unknown territory below and it was possible the rebels could have guards posted at the exit. They both dropped down into a crouch and readied themselves for trouble, assault rifles trained on the double elevator doors. The doors opened revealing a room beyond.

A rebel wearing a poorly armoured bubble suit didn't have time to arm himself before the two assassins dropped him. The assault rifles made a series of dull popping sounds which made the poor man jig around on the spot before landing in a heap on the grubby floor. Roz and Chinn filed out of the elevator cautiously keeping their weapons trained on the only door out of the room.

"Look at that piece of junk he was wearing, the suits

571

servo must have muffled the noise of the elevator. Lucky break!" Roz called into the comms. "Drag him into the lift while I check out what is through that door."

He looked at her as she paused over the dead man, whose helmet was scattered over the floor along with fragments of bloodied cranium. He could almost feel Chinn's distaste of having to murder an unarmed man so he tried to pull her away from staring at the corpse but she shrugged him off. She played the image over and over in her mind but couldn't comprehend the meaning of such destruction. He walked over and dragged him into the elevator himself as she moved away trying to bring her breathing back to normal.

"Chinn, I'm going to scout ahead, I want you to remain here." He said but her helmet shook from side to side.

"I will follow you as long as you hold your word. This is the last mission you'll do and then we both retire." She stated with an almost imperceptible anger that actually frightened him.

"This is the very last time, I promise." He said holding her arm for reassurance. Chinn had started to realise how many more murders would have to be carried out before she and her partner could see the forest again.

Roz moved towards the door and opened it up a fraction to see what lay beyond. Through the small gap, he could see daylight coming from the end of a long room. A large gun emplacement was being pushed along rails towards the open mountain by two people in poor quality bubble suits. He was about to make a move until he saw another man seemingly supervising the labourers who appeared from the front of the large rail gun. To the side of the room was a tram sat upon a steep gradient which disappeared down into the very depths of the mountain below the long chamber. The tram was open and loaded with heavy looking shells and Roz saw two other men come out burdened with a shell apiece.

Chinn ducked below him and peered out when he gestured for her to take a look. He held up three fingers and counted them down; when all his fingers made a fist she nodded. The two assassins used a basic fantail attack leaving a scattering of spent casings behind them. Chinn on the left of the attack had to pick her shots carefully against the two men carrying the hi-explosive shells. Within seconds of the attack commencing all five rebels lay on the ground with multiple kill shot wounds. Chinn trained her weapon on the open tram just in case other rebels were inside. Roz was making his way around the right-hand side of the rail gun to provide cover from another angle when a heavy blasting sound echoed in the chamber and he was knocked clean off his feet.

He landed a few meters back and saw another rebel with a shotgun coming from the front of the big gun. He scrambled for his firearm and noticed his shoulder plate had been sheared off with the impact of the heavy bore. The rebel cranked the ridiculously big shotgun and aimed for a headshot against his floored assailant. Roz managed to mouth a curse with a complete recognition that his time in the universe as a sentient being was finally up.

But the shot never came. Instead, the rebel stood still for a few brief seconds and the weapon dropped to the floor from his hands. The rebel's body fell on top of the weapon revealing Chinn stood behind him with a bloodied knife dripping thin pinkish fluid. Roz remained stunned and wondered if Chinn was, in fact, an angel coming to collect his soul.

"Roz?" She screamed and rushed towards him.

Her mind raced over the possibility that her soul mate could be lost forever. She pawed at her lover, tears cascading down her cheeks within the claustrophobic helm she wore. He could here Chinn's voice distantly, like the muffled sound of people talking behind a thick screen of plaz but he couldn't move his body to respond to her calls. He was stunned but realised that his assailant may have used poisoned pellets.

He tried to call out to her, "Poison, He's poisoned me." but his throat was constricted and a harsh rasp came out instead.

Chinn noticed his suit has been compromised with small tears in the shoulder section of the suit. She tapped the arm brace of his suit which opened revealing a data stream of information that she read through her blurry and tearful eyes. She saw that he had set his suit to manual override of the life support and quickly turned it back on.

"You're alive." she cried as she patched up the holes in his shoulder section.

His suit detected the presence of the poison and adjusted the harmonics to release an anti-toxin of metabol. Roz felt the drug swimming through his veins like a jolt of electricity the pain of which was almost unbearable. His body began to spasm so his suit administrated a small dose of Quat to combat the pain. Everything became brighter for a few seconds and he somehow found himself in a standing position on his own two feet. Through laboured breath he stood for what seemed to be a few minutes to him when in fact it was seconds.

"I need to sit down again!" Roz snapped through the comms. He tried to remove his helmet but Chinn stopped him and guided him to a pallet of boxes. He felt his heart banging against his sternum and it didn't subside even when he was in a sitting position.

"I hate Quat... I didn't know... Our suits... contained the... filthy stuff..." He said between great breaths of air.

Chinn didn't understand as she had never been under the influence of Quat but she tried her best to calm him down not knowing that it would be like trying to calm a Zol-cat in the full throws of the mating season.

"Why was your suit in manual?" Her helmet shook from side to side in disgust.

"I don't trust the damned things that why. When you have been wearing an E.C.A. suit for as long as I have you tend to keep them in manual and adjust them when YOU please." He sighed and waited for her reply knowing she was going to lose her temper.

Chinn rabbit punched his chest unsatisfied with his

statement.

"You could have died from toxic shock! If your suit was in automatic it would have countered the poison immediately. It's damned lucky I was here." With that much said she wandered away leaving him to his own thoughts.

She's right, he thought slowly recovering himself, maybe I will keep it in automatic for a while. Especially now I know the rebels are using toxic munitions.

The minuscule amount of Quat wore off quickly and he could feel his heartbeat returning to normal. He started to walk in the direction Chinn had walked off and soon found her near the exit surveying the mountain side and the ruined city below. Another rail gun sounded from somewhere up above them and a second or two later a building in the city below blew up in a plume of smoke. It seemed the rebels had a number of strongholds in the mountain and were bombarding the Xen forces below.

Another blizzard was blowing in from the east blanketing the mountain in a white mist which would make a mountain descent impossible. Roz returned to the tram line and entered the driver's compartment. It had a simple control system consisting of just up and down.

Chinn field stripped a few bits and pieces from the dead and together they began to disguise their own suits to make them appear a little more like the poorly armed rebels.

"It looks like we can take the tram line down into the

mountain. I suspect it will take us down into the rebel underground. My only hope is these disguises are good enough to allow us to walk amongst them." Roz said with a great amount of doubt in his voice.

Chinn shrugged and set the tram in motion. The tram line was old and severely water damaged. It made a terrible racket as it screeched and rattled down the line. Roz frowned at the numerous shells that occupied the cargo space.

"Perhaps we should have unloaded the tram before setting off." He gestured towards them.

"On the other hand, it could make for a good distraction." She said while making an explosive gesture with her hands.

Roz nodded and set a plasma charge in the centre of the shells. It wasn't long before the tram pulled into its station. Four rebels waited on the platform close to a stack of supplies and munitions.   One of them was leaning against a support strut half asleep and the others did not seem to show much interest in the return of the tram.

Roz and Chinn exited the tram and pointed back towards the compartment and began to wander to the only exit. While they walked away nervously they could hear the rebels complaining about the lack of unloading that had been done.

"Hey! Why is it still full? Don't they want anymore?" One of them called over.

A mighty explosion answered his question. Roz and Chinn had managed to run the final steps to the exit and dive away from the great fireball that smothered the tram station. Half stunned and covered with dust and small pieces of rubble they managed to crawl into the shadows of what appeared to be a bunk house. Its occupants were now clambering out of their beds in response to their rude awakening. A woman wearing a sleep mask rushed to Roz's side and began to perform first aid as the others ran to the tram station.

"Are you alright? What the hell just happened?" She asked then suddenly noticed the sleek black combat suit under the dusty disguise.

"What the? Who the fu.."
She didn't finish her words as the servos in Roz's gloved hand crushed her windpipe. As the rebels were distracted fighting the fire in the station the pair of assassins moved away unnoticed heading through a reinforced door then jamming it shut behind them.

"That's no damned good!" Daemon roared. It had taken most of the morning to assemble the lifting booms to access the main pipe beyond the maintenance hatch. There had been a lot of confusion assembling the lifting apparatus mainly due to the so-called elite troops having no engineering experience. The troopers all had their heads down in shame and Sherry tried her best jury rig the equipment in a bleak hope to salvage the current problem.

"I told you! You can't make two entirely different jigs to bond with each other, not without machining and welding." Daemon stated as he grabbed hold of Sherry's shoulder plate.

"Go back to the command sphere and get a new jig and this time get all of it, don't just grab this and that." He took off his helmet and sat down on a small packing crate.

"You're the expert why don't you go and get the stuff!" Sherry said in anger knowing it would take over an hour to get to the sphere and back again.

"Fine! Fuck it! I'll go and get the proper lifting equipment. You just make sure that these arseholes don't do any more assembling. The last thing we need is for them to burn out their tiny brains trying to fit a square plug in a fucking round hole." He stormed off towards the tunnel leaving the demoralised squad to ponder upon their inadequacies.

The air lock ran its cycle as Daemon powered up his E.C.A. He trudged down the tunnel wondering how he got into this mess.

"You are just tired, Daemon." The Demon whispered.

"You've been quiet, I thought you had abandoned me. Not that I like your company or anything." He quickly pointed out.

"It's just a minor hiccup. It won't be long now until we grab that son of a bitch and drag him back to Xen for a damned good torture session". The Demon seemed to be in a good mood, Daemon could feel its excited tone due to his hand trembling.

"It would help if I didn't have troops and a sergeant with shit for brains."

"Now, now Daemon, you're losing your temper again

and you know it's easier to control you when you are angry. Stick to the plan, it is solid. Sherry might not be the brightest star in the universe but she is a killer and that's what counts in a situation like this. And if you're splitting hairs, it was SHE who came up with the better plan. Live with it and keep control of the situation". This was very unlike the Demon. Daemon wondered why it had taken a shine to Sherry all of a sudden.

Daemon clambered out from the tunnel to the surface; the pollutants of war had almost drowned out the great sphere and the Hadley's in a haze of purplish mist. Armoured vehicles were being airlifted to the base by great hovering vessels. Nearby troops waited patiently to enter the new vehicles and he made his way past them to the command sphere. He rushed through administration and headed towards the armoury and almost bumped into Agent Rowson coming out of the logistics chamber. The tall man grimaced seeing Daemon and he gnawed at a splintered toothpick.

"I hear you have broken through into the underground rebel facility. I do hope you're not going to be long in recovering our man. The ground war is: how can I word it correctly," Agent Rowson was saying before Daemon added his own words.

"A massacre." He said.

Agent Rowson nodded in agreement.

"Not the exact word I was looking for but it is fitting all the same. It seems General Joss is digging his own grave with his lack of expertise in ground warfare. Already the company costs are making board room meetings very tiresome. It seems Xen is over budget in this tiny sector alone." Rowson smiled sadistically as he gnawed on the last splinter of his toothpick.

"I suppose Xen is thinking about pulling out the ground troops and bombing Runich to oblivion." Daemon proposed.

The agent nodded glumly and began to rummage through his pockets for something else to chew on.

"You're on the right track but not quite. The new boardroom gossip is to bring in gas moles and nerve gas the entire underground rebel facility." Agent Rowson stated almost half-heartedly.

"Nerve gas? That wouldn't work. The rebels have bubble suits to stop that kind of thing."
The agent heard his words and shook his head.

"Well, it seems Xen has been playing around with certain mixtures and the nerve agent they plan to use can quickly eat through protective clothing. They call it Mulch agent. Because that's what it does. It reduces human beings to its base biological matter." Agent Rowson had the complete demeanour of being totally disappointed.

"I bet they spent all night coming up with a name for that gas." Daemon stated shaking his head.

"Yes, I can imagine they did." Agent Rowson stated as he shunted past him and headed down the corridor.

"Wait, why haven't they released the gas moles yet?" The agent stopped but didn't turn around to face him.

"Cost my friend. It's far too costly at the present moment. However, I don't think you have very long until they add up the cost of losses and bring down Mulch upon Runich." The agent continued down the corridor leaving Daemon with serious doubts over his present mission.

I need some more advanced suits. He thought.

Back in the reservoir Daemon began to coordinate the assembly of the correct equipment at the main pipe entrance. He had outfitted squad four with better suits which he had stolen only an hour ago from the officer's private armoury. With the jig in place they began to lift the squad members up into the main pipe along with munitions and some exotic equipment commandeered from the private armoury. He knew time was of the essence as it probably wouldn't take long for the Xen officials to decide to use extreme force and gas the underground rebel installation. The last thing he wanted was to be turned into his own base biological components due to an outbreak of Mulch gas. Eight troops, one sergeant and First Lieutenant Daemon clambered into the main pipe and headed straight for the black square on the map hoping for some kind of reprieve.

"Why the new suits Daemon?" Sherry asked as she laboured through the pipe just behind him.

"The new armour has been granted by Xen to get the mission done!" He barked but Sherry didn't seem satisfied.

"But why have we been given them now?" Her tone had all the questioning hallmarks as though she hadn't been told something important. He was running out of ideas to put her off the scent.

"We will be up against the elite of the rebel forces. Xen can't throw us up against such odds without offering us better armour." He was glad that he was a good at lying since Sherry bought it and remained focused and stopped questioning him. He heard the forward team checking back over the communication lines as they crossed each side duct and wondered if he would have been better working alone. This so called elite squad bumbled down the main pipe making more noise than a drunken engineer with an oversized tool belt. It seemed what passed for elite soldiery within the Xen ranks at the moment was nothing more than school boys who had just learnt how to fire in the correct direction. He hoped that they would show their skills in a real fire fight.

The main duct was seemed to be longer than it appeared on the planetary scan and being bent over in the confined space soon began to make every muscle scream as they relentlessly travelled meter by meter. It had been over an hour before the forward team acknowledged a room beyond the pipe. They secured it and waited for the rest of the squad to catch up. Daemon shimmied down out of the pipe into a spacious room which seemed to house a disused power generator.

Several other pipes led away from it and a metal door barred the way to what was hopefully the elevator. The power generator had been gutted for components and had a great square had been burnt out of the main boiler tank. One of the troops threw a breaker switch illuminating the generator room fully.

In the light the squad appeared to be armoured matt black bugs in the new E.C.A. suits. Daemon had seen the new suits field tested against a bunker bomb before he came to Sigra III. The new armour could withstand a direct hit with only minor damage and only required rudimentary repair work afterwards. It was very robust, genius in design, but far too expensive to outfit a battalion, not to mention a legion. One of the troopers pointed up at a rusty plaque upon the door spelt out the words "maintenance elevator".

"Well done Sherry, it looks like your hunch has paid off. I just hope the elevator is still wired to the rebel power supply." Daemon said patting the armoured O2 tank on her back.

"We have power." One of the squad members stated as she fiddled around in the servo box near the elevator door.

Sherry pressed the call button and waited while her squad readied themselves for trouble exiting the elevator door. Daemon fell into rank with the rest of the squad allowing his sergeant to hold command for a while. The doors struggled at first against rusted gears but opened up revealing an empty and spacious lift beyond.

Squad four ascended in the elevator to sub-level 2B. They scrambled out into what appeared to be an old service depot scattered with stacks of rotting crates and rickety shelving units lining the massive chamber.

Daemon noticed the shell like remains of an old fork lift truck sat rusting against one of the dusty walls. Its wiring and pieces of its engine had been left spewed out on to the water logged floor. Water constantly dripped from the porous ceiling suggesting a pipe full of rain from the storms was leaking through above the sub-level the squad had found. A door opened at the other side of the chamber and squad four scattered into the shadows. Two teenage males wearing rag torn boiler suits entered the chamber with flash lights.

"I swear there's a box of cutting disks in here somewhere. I found them last month when I was scavenging for vehicle parts." One of the teenagers said his voice trembling with fatigue.

"There had better be. I hate these old sections they give me the creeps. Last month I found some scanks holed up in sub-level D. They tried to attack me but they were dusted to the eye balls. I got out of there as quickly as I could." The taller of the two replied.

"Yeah that happened to me a few months ago. Filthy skanks. There were a load of them holed up under the old refinery. They asked me if I had any reds but I ran off before they could surround me." The smaller of the two said while laughing nervously.

"Don't they know there's a war on?" The tall one barked as he searched the darkness of the laden shelves with his flash light.

"Beats me, maybe they are too high to even realise. We cleared them out of the refinery mind you. I think Commissar Nell put them to work in the foundry making bits of shit for the field guns." The nervous one claimed before an assault rifle was shoved rudely into his face. From the dark shadows squad four had circled the two young men. Fear crawled over their innocent faces as numerous bug-like machinations began shouting threatening commands at them. The two teenagers were roughly dragged and handcuffed to a support stanchion. It didn't take long to interrogate them as the aggressive pressure they were subjected to and the blatant threats of total and forcible removal of their manhood soon broke them.

"We should kill them. If we leave them alive they could give away our mission." Sherry hissed into the comms.
Daemon shook his head, by all rights they should kill them but the two young men weren't going to be an immediate threat, especially if they are tethered down within a disused warehouse.

"No, I think we can leave them be. Nobody will find them for a while and by the time they are found or reported missing our mission should be complete." He ordered much to the disappointment of his sergeant. She seemed far too eager to depress her trigger finger for his liking and in good time she would get her chance soon enough.

It soon became clear that the two young men had spoken the truth under interrogation; they had not only told squad four where to go to find the Rebel leader but how to get there avoiding as many guards as possible. Daemon was glad he had allowed them to live; bumping into them had been the luckiest break over the past month. It would have been a different story if the teenagers had been older and more reluctant to give away such information to the enemy.

He had detected a slight hatred towards Jackabah within the voices of the two young men. Maybe like everyone else in this hellhole they just wished for the war to end and aiding the enemy might accelerate such an outcome.

Fires burned all over the city of Runich as razor crafts finished a devastating sweep of bombing raids. The rebels had been crippled and only pockets of resistance still held out in the night as waves of Xen troops secured great chunks of the city. The only buildings that seemed relatively intact were the Ion plants which sat unscathed surrounded by skeletal buildings and piles of endless rubble. Xen squads were capturing more abandoned anti-aircraft gun positions by the hour. It looked as if the rebels had finally given up, or their numbers could no longer establish the city.

A Xen field commander looked up toward the great mountain as an aircraft screamed over the mountain side and destroyed the last of the troublesome rail guns. Some surviving groups of rebels surrendered their positions after the bombing raids. Depleted of ammo and resources they walked the last few feet into the hands of their enemy. Shackled and war torn they were gathered up quickly and secured into armoured vehicles to be processed. The last remaining rebels that could fight witnessed the Xen troops pulling back. Orders had been circulated among the Xen troops to allow the rebels one final chance to surrender.

Agent Rowson leered at the military officers rejoicing and drinking aerated wine. The command sphere had been abuzz within the past hour and the good General Joss was lapping up the congratulations. Rowson looked towards the huge display screen depicting a meeting room on the Goliath full of Xen hierarchy clapping in unison.

This all seems very good general but we need Jackabah alive and in chains before we start opting for hot soapy showers with one another. Agent Rowson thought having seen this scene many times before. He had a nagging feeling that this little war wasn't over yet.

He hated every second that passed and hoped Daemon hadn't already fucked the mission up. He hoped to see the general's face when one of his intelligence officers brought the rebel leader in alive and ready for interrogation. It would be even sweeter if Jackabah had one final plan which would send General Joss to the firing squad or the plants.

Agent Rowson stood and stretched his limbs before elbowing his way through the gathered people and out of the command room. He wandered down the corridors towards the shuttle station and boarded the next shuttle to the Goliath and away from Sigra III. As the shuttle left orbit and the Goliath appeared on the scope he held out a small communication device and almost willed it to ring.

It remained silent.

CHAPTER 29

Endgame

Jackabah watched as the last cylinder train left the station, and heard the lines whining and echoing as the train was enveloped by the darkness of the tunnel. Derris, one his aides, stood at his side attempting to focus upon a clipboard of records. His vision had deteriorated within the last month due to working in the poorly illuminated underground.

"That's the last of them my friend," Derris said as he continued to check through the notes and records. Jackabah stretched his aching muscles and let out a great sigh of relief.

"I'm hoping that's all of them. If we have missed any they aren't going to be leaving Runich." Jackabah stated while looking at the empty briefcase which had been filled with golden ingots only five minutes previously. Derris noticed his leaders frown directed at the empty carry cases.

"Was that the last of the gold?" Derris asked but he suspected that he already knew the answer.

Jackabah shook his head and then begrudgingly nodded; there no longer seemed to be a reason to lie about it, especially to old friends. For most of the last twenty years working as a Xen operative he had spent his time lying to people and manipulating them, it was second nature to him now.

Derris managed a grin on his wrinkly old face and noticed Jackabah looking back into the dark cylinder train tunnel.

"The children are safe now my friend, stop worrying," Derris said calmly as he patted Jackabah's tense shoulder.

Safe for now, but tomorrow? Maybe not tomorrow, thought Jackabah.

The refugee trains had been coming and going for the last four days transporting the children, the sick and the wounded away from Runich. The cost of which had all but depleted the little wealth the rebels had left.

"Well there is one good thing to come from spending the last of our funds: we won't be seeing those filthy merchants again now they know the money has dried up," Derris said with glee.

Jackabah nodded and laughed for a few seconds before his frown returned.

"Why didn't you go?" Jackabah asked his old friend.

"I'm too old for travelling and besides I wish to die here in Runich, my birth place and where I have enjoyed my retirement although it has only been a brief retirement." Derris said and chuckled to himself. He had only been retired for a month or so before the war broke out on Sigra III. He was quickly drafted in by the rebels due to his logistical and management skills which they had on throughout the conflict.

"So what now Jackabah?" Derris asked as they walked up the eerily quiet platform.

"Now I go to seal our fate!" Jackabah whispered to himself leaving the deserted station.

The walkways of the underground were silent as Jackabah made his way to the dry dock. Only a small number of guards remained below ground now that the majority of the people had been evacuated. A few pockets of resistance left above ground kept the Xen troops away from the underground entrances, they were fighting like cornered rats but only had a limited amount of ammunition left. Jackabah's thoughts went out to the brave souls above; the last of the rebellious warriors sacrificing themselves to keep those Xen bastards on their toes. He would see to it that they had vengeance!

Jackabah arrived at the dry dock and saluted the sleepy guard. The guard merely nodded, too lethargic to even return his leader's salute. Welding flashes and grinding disks created sparks that flickered in the great chamber. The stench of hydraulic fluid, diesel and welding vapours saturated the air making the rebel leader cough. The engineers and scientists scurried around the submersible vehicle trying desperately to finish constructing the vengeance weapon. Tony, the master of engineering noticed Jackabah entering the dry dock and waved him over.

"Well it's nearly done Jackabah; I just hope your calculations are correct." Tony smiled.

Jackabah grinned and bear hugged the older man.

"I had the science team working on a simulator. The science is right my friend and the good news is that the simulator produced better results than I had first imagined." Jackabah claimed.

Tony looked to the science team who were gathered in a small group punching endless numbers into a portable terminal. Tony shook his head angrily.

"When did we change Jackabah? I remember the time when we didn't put all of our trust in computers or brain box scientists who don't factor in the cost of human life to build the technology they are obsessed by." Tony barked.

Tony was clearly upset and tired after such a marathon effort on the submersible so Jackabah didn't answer him. The master of engineering pointed to a group of young men that appeared to be sunburnt, who was sat on a bench glaring at the abomination of metal being constructed in the dry dock.

"The fucker nearly sparked when we assembled the ion core into the submersible. We were damned lucky it didn't chain react but the work crew got a suntan!" Tony angrily mentioned.

Jackabah nodded but the engineer hadn't finished.

"Those men won't last the week. The amount of radiation their bodies have soaked up would be enough to power Runich in its hay day!"

Jackabah remained silent as Tony stormed off towards

the exit as he gathered the science team around him.

"How is it going?" he asked.

"Good morning Jackabah. We have new information for you. From the new data, we have taken from the core we have performed some recalculations of the simulation." Dr Goll claimed with a wiry smile.

Jackabah tried to silence the science team who were eager to give him the results where they stood. He gestured for them to follow him to a quieter corner where they could speak and not be overheard by the engineering staff.

"What information? I was under the impression that the device would explode over ten times its own strength when it reacted with the water in the river Othei." Jackabah whispered as he nervously looked towards the busy engineers.

"It's more like twenty times, however, we didn't figure on the sheer amount of water present in the river of Othei. The river of Othei is over two thousand kilometres long, not only that it is very deep and you know it is wide. We are talking about millions of tonnes of water which will literally turn to plasma when our weapon chain reacts."

The grin had dropped from Dr Goll's face and had been replaced with a questioning and almost puzzled frown. He described the expected results using scientific words, figures and even gave a small lecture on matter theory. Jackabah tried his best to understand the technicalities but the pieces of perplexing information just rattled around in his mind, not seemingly going anywhere, nor make any sense.

"Enough!" Jackabah shook his head and attempted to make sense of what he just been told. The science team stopped their banter and waited in silence while their great leader struggled with the problem.

"So, basically, the river will turn to super-heated liquid and literally destroy all of Runich?"

"It will destroy Runich and an area of hundreds of square kilometres of the river land, maybe even more." Dr Goll corrected him and waited for his words to sink in before continuing. "Nothing will be left but a huge crater where Runich once stood and a deep and wide canyon following the river line."

Jackabah closed his eyes and buried his head in his hands.

"When I first came up with this idea you told me the bomb would only wipe out the surface. And now you're telling me the underground and possibly even the mountains will be utterly destroyed? Not to mention a great section of the river Othei and its surrounding lands?" Jackabah whispered through the gaps in his fingers.

"Yes!" Dr Goll said with finality.

"Who knows of these newest findings apart from me and your team of scientists?" Jackabah asked.

Dr Goll took an involuntary step backwards and shook his head in disbelief.

"What? You still plan to use this terrible weapon? What of us and your loyalists. By sending this weapon into the water you will be killing all of us not to mention other townships on the river which haven't yet been subjected to the Xen tyranny!" Dr Goll said while raising his voice.

Jackabah was shocked by the doctor's outburst; he had become used to total loyalty and sacrifice. If others reacted in the same way the entire rebellion would grind to a halt as they tried to get away from the blast zone. Even worse they could even revolt and try to destroy the bomb. He contemplated the various possibilities in a moment and decided upon a course of action.

"No, but I need to stop any unwarranted panic spreading through rumours. Who knows about it already and is the device active? Do we need to deactivate it?"

"Yes, we had to activate it to get the final readings but it should only take a short while to deactivate it again. No-one else was present when we brought it online so the knowledge is only confined to ourselves." Dr Goll informed him looking relieved.

"What about Tony? Are you sure he doesn't know?" Jackabah asked ascertaining the final bit of information he required.

"Absolutely not." Dr Goll affirmed.
This was all that Jackabah needed to know he pointed at the six scientists and shouted out   "Saboteurs!" He leapt out of the way as the sleepy guard stirred at the exit and levelled his assault rifle at the science team and depressed the trigger.

The firearm sprayed an arc of bullets which quickly

mowed down each and every scientist. The engineers nearby dropped their tools upon hearing the gunfire and witnessed the white smocked people being gunned down like bowling pins on a strike. Blood spatters covered Jackabah from head to toe. The guard quickly ran to the rebel leader and made another sweep with his firearm finishing off the hideously wounded science team. Jackabah wiped the blood from his face using his sleeve cuff and patted the guard on his back for his quick response.

"Those bastards said they were going to sabotage the weapon and defect to Xen. They also tried to persuade me to come with them!" Jackabah said before he cleared his throat and spat in the direction of the dead. The guard also spat at the dead science team before changing the magazine in his assault weapon. Jackabah eyed the engineering staff and ordered them back to work.

"Burn those traitors." He instructed the guard.

Jackabah headed to his office of command which had doubled as his living quarters during these troubling times of war.

So I will die here, he thought grimly now that he decided upon his fate and that of all the remaining rebels. "It will be a fitting end to our struggles nonetheless and a glorious one. I will strike fear into the hearts of our enemy. I will rain down death upon the Xen Corporation. Others will take up my cause, not only on this once beautiful planet but other planets will take up the sword and fight against corporate tyranny! The

rape of resources will be put to an end once and for all."
In his bravado he hadn't noticed the numerous armed
guards saluting him as he entered his private quarters.

"Good morning Jackabah. I have been monitoring the
defences at the underground entrances. I have four
teams of demolition experts on standby ready to seal
every entrance into the underground." Melinda
informed him. She saluted and then patted the seat in
front of the consoles for her great leader to take
command once again.

Jackabah pinched the bridge of his nose between his
thumb and forefinger and wondered why she hadn't
boarded the last cylinder train out of Runich.

Some leader I am. I didn't even persuade Melinda to
leave this place. Well, now she has sealed her own fate.
Now she will die here with me! he mused.

"You have done well Melinda, thank you." he simply
said to her.
The numerous display screens depicted the last of his
forces holding back the swarms of Xen troops that
marched against them. Jackabah opened a line of
communication to the dry dock. One of the engineers
answered.

"How long until you can get the weapon in the
water?" he asked. The engineer looked over his
shoulder and then looked back towards the com-eye.

"Not long now, we are prepping the submersible as
we speak." The engineer replied. His face was marred
with grime and his left eye was bloodshot, probably due
to an arc-weld accident.

"As soon as it is ready to swim, no matter what happens, get that bomb in the water," Jackabah commanded. The engineer nodded and closed communications.

Melinda detected the tension in Jackabah's voice and attempted to sooth him by massaging his shoulders. He relaxed a little but his eyes still darted from one display to another, watching and listening to the final resistance via the com-eyes placed at each battle scene. He noticed sector five had been compromised, Xen troopers were scavenging around in the rubble obviously looking for an entrance into the rebel underground.

Let them find it, we are all dead sooner than later. He thought bitterly.

A voice communication buzzed on one of the live lines. Jackabah leant forward in his chair to answer it.

"Great leader, we have had to fall back into the underground, sector five is overrun. Also..." The rebel officer paused for a while. "Also, the demolitions failed to explode. It won't take them long to find an entrance. We will defend stair 5B for as long as we can." The officer said through laboured breath.

"Do what you can Sergeant. May God give you and your squad strength in battle". Jackabah said and ended the transmission. He felt overwhelmed with utter bleakness even though his greatest victory was at hand, even though it would be a pyrrhic one.
Melinda gripped his hand tightly and he could feel cold sweat on her palm.

"We are doomed! It won't take the Xen dogs long before THEY come crashing down the tunnels towards us." Melinda cried with panic in her voice.

Jackabah wrapped his arm around her and hugged her tight to him. He hoped the engineers had finished the bomb and had set it out into the river Othei. He hoped that he would at least have the satisfaction of being vaporised rather than shot.

Melinda raised her head to face Jackabah, all the blood had drained from her face and her eyes were wide. Jackabah tried to speak but she put her hand over his mouth.

"Shhhh, listen!" She whispered.
Jackabah concentrated on the ambient sounds of the room. Over the humming of the terminals and the battle transmissions, he heard thudding sounds coming from behind the great metal door of his command chamber.

"Gunfire!" Melinda hissed. She ran to her field box and quickly assembled an assault rifle.
Jackabah leapt out of his chair and realised he was unarmed; he had always hated being armed so had never carried weapons. It appeared that he would now live to regret it.

"There is no way Xen have got here already! Sector five is a long way from here." Melinda screamed.

Jackabah punched up the live feed to the com-eye in the corridor outside his room. The live feed depicted a small group of armoured Xen troops marching down the corridor towards the entrance. Bullets from his bodyguard's weapons simply ricocheted off the bug-like armour creating great flashes of light. Each Xen Warrior continuously fired their weapons towards his guards as they marched step by step towards his sanctuary. Blood spattered over the com-eye cutting off his view. A hideous silence descended as Melinda readied her rifle towards the chamber door.

"They must have found another way down here. Damn it, I thought I had every entrance covered." Jackabah said in a sheer panic.

Fuck this! I don't want to be killed by Xen dogs! He thought and whispered a silent prayer for the engineers to hurry and end this all.

"Run Jackabah! Get out if you can. I am going to take as many of the Xen dogs with me as I can before I see the bright light!" Melinda barked as she chambered a round in her assault rifle.

My brave Melinda Jackabah thought sadly watching the brave woman taking a stand for the cause.

The great metallic doors were ripped off the manifolds that held them in place by a blast of heat and fire. The shockwave from the explosives used on the door had knocked Jackabah to the floor. Melinda raised herself up from the console that she had collided with and opened up with her firearm. Two warriors in black carapace stepped through the smoke and fire as bullets from Melinda's weapon bounced off their advanced armour. Melinda screamed as a hail of bullets ripped her torso from her legs. She coughed and spluttered choking on her own blood as Sherry aimed and fired a single round into Melinda's head. Jackabah shook his head with hatred.

"You evil bastards! You evil Xen bastards!" He cried as he dropped to his knees and wept for Melinda.
Squad four secured the corridor as Daemon walked the last few paces towards Jackabah. Daemon took off his helmet and leered down at the broken man who wept before him.

"You wouldn't even believe the shit I've had to endure to capture you Jackabah. I'm Lieutenant Daemon and you are now the property of Xen!" Daemon stated as he secured the limp rebel leader in hand chains.
Sherry had moved to Daemon's side and prodded Jackabah with the hot end of her firearm.

"If our lieutenant hadn't been here I would have torn you in half like I did that bitch over there!" Sherry said with amusement in her voice as she pointed to Melinda's corpse in two separate pieces scattered over the floor.

Jackabah curled himself up into a trembling ball and muttered curses though his tears. Daemon didn't seem amused at all by his sergeant's words.

"Sherry! Back off. Sometimes I think you enjoy killing too much." He barked.
Sherry obeyed and moved towards a bank of consoles grinning inside her helmet. Daemon rummaged through his armoured field belt and found his Xen-Com. He punched in a series of codes and set the device to live feed.

Agent Rowson was sat at one of the cafes on the Goliath and had ordered another drink from the waitress who was collecting empty glasses from a nearby table. The waitress took his order and returned promptly with his drink before she attempted to engage him in small talk.

"It's quiet today. There must be a meeting on or something?" The tall brunette waitress said.

Agent Rowson folded his newspaper so he could see her name badge.

"Good afternoon Corel. I was wondering if you could help me?" Rowson asked with a false smile on his face and a pleasant tone in his voice.

The waitress seemed pleased that a high-ranking official had even bothered to talk to her, or even noticed her.

"Yes, I will help you, what do you want?" The beaming waitress stated.

"You can help me by... fucking off!" Agent Rowson spat.

The waitress blinked a few times as his words settled into her skull and she realised the agent was just another bastard like all the of the Xen officials she had met in her lifetime. The waitress leant near enough to smell Agent Rowson's aftershave.

"Enjoy your coffee." She said while smiling and winking.

The waitress wandered away while Agent Rowson tilted his coffee cup to peer upon its dark liquid surface for any impurities she may have left for him.

The dirty bitch. He thought.

There wasn't anything floating on its surface but he would be damned if he would drink it now. He shoved the coffee cup across the table and continued to read his newspaper. While he read an article about purchasing real estate on Itriss II, the breast pocket of his corporate suit vibrated. He dropped the newspaper to the floor and quickly rummaged in his jacket for his Xen-Com. He peered at the display which read 'Incoming call. Sigra III. Project: Nightstand.' His fingers eagerly punched in his clearance code.

"We have him. We need a route out of here." A small visual display depicted Lieutenant Daemon within a dimly illuminated chamber. Agent Rowson wanted to jump out of his chair and do a little victory dance; instead, he remained stony faced and unemotional.

"I have a lifter on standby nearby Runich. In the meantime I will contact one of my operatives and find safe route of escape for you., Stay fast Daemon! Well done. I will contact you in…" Agent Rowson glanced at his time piece and then continued, "ten minutes. Be damned sure you are at the pick-up point once I have arranged it!" The agent stated before ended the call rudely.

He pressed the hot-line button on his Xen-com and waited several seconds before Agent Marcus answered his call.

"Marcus. I need an evacuation zone in Runich. I have an operative in the underground that has captured Jackabah alive." Agent Rowson told him.

Agent Marcus was manning a terminal in the command sphere outside Runich on Sigra III.

"Hang on a second." The agent's fingers danced on the keyboard of his terminal and quickly located several points of evacuation within the ruined city of Runich.

"The best point of exit is at the old library in the inner city. Xen forces have just captured this area and secured it." Marcus stated while he browsed a stream of information about the area in question.

"They have planted a beacon there and I'm sending you the beacon code now." Marcus tapped the send button on his terminal and the beacon code appeared almost instantly on Agent Rowson's Xen-com display screen.

"I've got it! Send the Sul'Hudeen to the beacon coordinates and at all costs wait for Lieutenant Daemon and his prisoner." Agent Rowson commanded before he clicked the end button. He settled back in his chair and idly punched in a direct line to Daemon.

"It's all arranged, the beacon code is 90A-56A-902." Agent Rowson waited a few seconds for Daemon to align the beacon.

"Roger that. It shouldn't take long for me to get there providing we don't run into any trouble." Daemon answered while he prepared his squad to move using hand signals alone.

"Don't fail me now Lieutenant, you are too damned close to failing now." The excited agent warned. "I can't wait until your squad is safely on board the Sul'Hudeen."

"Liar. You just want the package" Daemon stated with a grin.

Agent Rowson forced a feral smile, his teeth grinding from side to side.

"Ok then, pleasantries aside I hope you have an accident with an airlock on the Goliath. As long as Jackabah has strength enough for interrogation, the rest of you can rot."

Before Daemon could counter Rowson depressed the end call button and relaxed in his chair.

Daemon managed to put his Xen-com away before gunfire erupted in the corridor. Squad four were all firing down the corridor at two rebels covered by shield units. Sherry and Daemon crouched in front of Jackabah to use their own armour to protect the prisoner before levelling their own rifles at the incoming targets. The two glowing red enemies danced down the corridor wielding a variety of melee weapons as bullets ricocheted off them as though they were heavily armoured tanks.

Plasma knives found niches in the armour of squad four and the two rebels cut a deadly path through them. The pair had left each troop bloodied and incapacitated as they continued into Jackabah's command room where Sherry and Daemon nervously watched the massacre unfold.

"Where the fuck did the rebels get shield units?" Sherry cried into the comms while she unloaded her entire clip against one of the rebel targets.

Daemon was too flabbergasted to answer her and

didn't even bother to fire his weapon knowing it was utterly futile. Suddenly one of the rebels suddenly halted, not more than six meters from Daemon and threw up its arm to stop the attack.

"Daemon?" The shielded rebel stated in confusion. Daemon recognised the voice even though it was muffled from the interference of the violent motion of the red shield.

"Is this some kind of trick?" Daemon hissed as he shook his head in disbelief. He couldn't believe his ears but he swore that the voice belonged to Roz. Sherry used the sudden pause to load her firearm.

"Does this rebel bastard know you?" She barked into the comms. The rebel stood motionless in the doorway.

"It seems you have just made my mission very difficult. I really don't want to kill you Daemon, just the little shit who cowers behind you!" Roz stated but his tone seemed more friendly than threatening although he remained in a stance to spring back into battle. Daemon now understood it had to be Roz.

"Roz, you know I can't allow you to kill Jackabah now that we've captured him alive. You also know I will probably die trying to protect him so where do we go from here?" Daemon said calmly. Sherry finally remembered Roz from the training facility and the fact that he killed a squad of Seinal core troopers bare handed.

"So this is Roz: the Quat man!" She stated through the comms. Daemon answered her question by nodding and was glad his old friend hadn't heard her malicious comment through their private channel.

"Listen Daemon this is our last time out. The last mission we need to perform and then we retire. Just let me kill that son of a bitch and we can go our separate ways." Roz pleaded but his friend shook his head in denial.

"Roz, Xen plan to use a horrific nerve agent down here and the clock is ticking. We have a ship waiting on standby to take us to the Goliath. Come with us or you will die here along with your colleague." Daemon stated trying to peer around Roz's bulk to get a better view of his companion who lurked in the shadows.
Roz moved aside slightly and gestured towards Chinn.

"I knew you had kept something back from us Daemon you traitor! When did you plan on telling us about a nerve agent?" Sherry growled into the comms. Daemon shrugged and hoped she wouldn't allow her rage to influence the present situation.

"Sorry Daemon, I forgot to introduce my friend." Roz was saying gesturing towards the second figure. "This is my lover and the reason why I have chosen to retire." He stated as Chinn waved with one hand, her other pointing a pistol at Daemon's un-helmeted head.

"Roz! We need to get to the ship before they release the agent." Daemon reiterated. "There will be plenty of time for more formal introductions. Our priority is to get out of here alive at the moment. When we are on board we can discuss the matter of your final contract. Now let's get the fuck out of here!" He calmly stated with closed eyes.

"Ok. We will talk on the ship but I can't promise you I will allow that rebel to live." Roz warned.

"Alright, your threat is duly noted." Daemon said laughing and picked himself up from a squatted position. "Sherry, secure the prisoner! Put him into the emergency bubble suit. Roz and... whatever the fuck your name is follow me!" Daemon barked pointing at Chinn as he made his way to the main corridor where his entire squad had been attacked. The plasma knives had cut through their armour as if it hadn't been there and those who hadn't died of their wounds immediately had bled out.

"Look at the fucking state of my squad. You don't realise how much paperwork that's going to cost me... you... you pair of psychos." He shouted.
Roz could only gesture an apology with his hands.

The beacon they followed wasn't far on the map display but it was still difficult to navigate through the maze of tunnels. Daemon couldn't believe he had convinced two stone cold killers to back down but knew the standoff would be short lived as soon as they boarded the Sul'Hudeen. He had to come up with some options before they got there or else more blood would be shed.

CHAPTER 30

Termination

The dry dock was quickly filling with water from the sluice gates and the engineers watched the submersible bobbing up and down as the water reached a sufficient level to birth the weapon. Each and every engineer knew they would die when the bomb detonated although they hadn't been told so. They understood enough about blast waves to realise what the implications of an ion bomb exploding underwater would be. The violence of it was enough to paint a very clear picture in each and every mind. They had built this device and they understood its capabilities and they had lost many of their best friends in the process of engineering such a terrible weapon.

Hard liquor saved for such an occasion was being shared out equally among them all. They raised toasts to former kin and friends, then finally to the fucking rebellion and their once beautiful thriving city. It was a celebration similar to a wake and many tears needed to be shed. However, not one mention of Jackabah had passed their lips.

The submersible disappeared in a wash of underwater caterpillar engines and made its way out into the vast river Othei never to be seen again on dry land. Its navigation computer provided a path to its destination and the terrible countdown which would reduce Runich to a mere myth had begun. This scorched earth gesture would become a bedtime story to be told and passed down through many generations of the surviving families that had been lucky enough to board the refugee trains. It would be a legend for the rebellion but a tragedy for the people who had once lived and breathed freedom within Runich.

The rally point Jackabah was being led to was filled with Xen troopers who had an insatiable capacity for taking pictures of themselves with many of the wounded, captured and dead rebels. They had been doing so for the last couple of hours after securing the stronghold but still the morbid practice fascinated them. Daemon and his new found team emerged into a seedy throng of military personnel. It appeared the troops had been warned not to intervene and gave the small group a wide birth. Daemon immediately spotted the great Sul'Hudeen, a starlifter craft which had been painted metallic blue down its sleek hull. Its engines idled on standby waiting desperately for the lieutenant and his prisoner. Boarding the vessel was an efficient and quick procedure, as soon as Lieutenant Daemon passed his credentials and gestured to his entourage the ships personnel rushed them all inside and secured them into the passenger bay.

Roz noticed his old friend consuming a number of travel pills before take-off and he smiled realising Daemon hadn't yet overcome his affliction and assumed he never would. The thrust jets howled and shook the entire craft as it leapt upwards from the battlefield. Sherry had secured a seat next to Roz and had already begun to chat to him while Chinn scowled and looked ready to throttle her. Daemon tried to ignore the scene but couldn't help overhearing Sherry's textbook methods of securing a bed for the night with a fresh male.

It looks like it is open season on new cock and Sherry looks very hungry today. Daemon thought to himself as he noticed Chinn was near breaking point; he decided that he had better intervene.

"I have a Xen agent ready to pick our prisoner up as soon as we reach the Goliath. I will try and arrange a cover story with him so you can still claim the kill and be on your way. I suspect the rebel leader will mysteriously disappear into Xen oblivion anyway." Daemon said hoping his words would satisfy the assassins until Jackabah was safely in the hands of Agent Rowson.

"If your agent can convince me that our target is "dead", even if it's merely on paper, then we will both be satisfied. But, well, you know what will happen if the agent doesn't play along." Roz drifted off allowing his friend to fill in the blanks.

Daemon nodded and stared into his friend's hawk-like eyes; the eyes of a true predator and killer. He was glad when the ship suddenly banked hard so he had no choice but to break contact from those terrible blue eyes. The ship rumbled and rattled for a while and then fell silent as it broke the atmosphere into space. The pilot of the Sul'Hudeen lazily announced over the internal communications that they would shortly arrive at the Goliath.

"Roz, when we clear this shit up, can we go for a drink or something? I need to catch up with you and maybe pick your brain on a few matters." Daemon said as he fiddled with the safety harness of his seat.

"If it all goes well then I don't see why not." Roz shrugged and eyed the prisoner for a while who had been forced to wear a black sack over his head during transit.

Agent Rowson waited impatiently at the docking ring on the Goliath along with a twenty strong squad of CORE troopers. The massive blue docking shields that protected the inhabitants of the space station displaced for a few seconds while the Sul'Hudeen emerged into the dock. Agent Rowson smiled with glee even though it was against his nature.

"About fucking time too!" He whispered under his breath. The troopers fanned out into a horseshoe formation as the Sul'Hudeen landed. When he was satisfied his guards had taken their places he drew a large automatic pistol and crossed his arms behind his back to conceal the firearm. The ramp of the ship hissed with escaping pressurised gas before descending to the metallic level. Daemon walked down the ramp noisily still wearing his combat armour, his helmet tucked neatly under his arm. Agent Rowson scowled and noticed Daemon was unarmed and alone.

"Where is the prisoner, Lieutenant?" Rowson demanded.

Daemon held up both of his hands and dropped his helmet to the floor before he continued his walk towards the agent.

"The prisoner is secured but we have a slight problem." Daemon stated.

Agent Rowson stamped his foot like a spoilt child.

"Hand over Jackabah now or I will have you sent to the plants." Rowson barked.

Daemon shook his head from side to side.

"It would appear Xen has sent assassins to kill the rebel leader as well as sending me to recover Jackabah alive. There seems to be a conflict in protocol here and I'm not sure which one to follow. Do I allow these Xen assassins to finish their mission or do I have to kill the assassins to complete mine?" Daemon said as he raised a quizzical eyebrow.

Agent Rowson violently shook his head.

"Let's get this correct. I'm assuming the assassins need the death of Jackabah and you somehow met up with them somewhere in Runich?" Rowson spat and held up his hand to continue his speech,

"Tell those back stabbing murderers that Mr. Jackabah is to be taken into Xen custody and their mission is now over. It has been superseded by your own!" Rowson said attempting a manner of calm and authority but Daemon responded with a flat shake of his head.

"I have a better suggestion. You arrange it so that official records show Jackabah was killed by them and they will release him into your custody, minus his index finger and the gold ring the rebel wears on it." Daemon stated and waited patiently for the agent to see the light of his proposition.

Agent Rowson looked to be on the verge of tears, the great walls of his planning were starting to crumble and fall.

"Fine, the once great leader of the rebellion is dead. Now hand him over!" Rowson sighed. He couldn't believe that it had come to this.

Daemon arched his neck towards his suits communicator.

"We are good to go, bring out the prisoner." He commanded.

After a brief moment, Roz and Chinn brought out the prisoner and marched him out into the waiting throng of troops. Sherry stayed behind on the ship preferring to remain out of sight so that the agent didn't remember her face.

"Take off that bag. I need to see this so called great leaders eyes." Rowson said trying to conceal his distrust of being given the wrong man.

Daemon snatched off the black cloth bag revealing Jackabah to everyone present.

"Satisfied?" He asked still clutching the cloth bag.

The agent smiled as he peered into the tear-filled eyes of Jackabah. He walked behind him and looked down at his restrained hands staring at the gold ring he wore.

"This is what you need?" he asked Roz gesturing to it. Roz nodded in reply. "Well you better take it then." Roz took out his knife and cut Jackabah's finger off as he screamed in agony. Rowson stooped over the former leader looking into his face and basking in his pain.

"The rebellion is not over! Just wait and see my grand finale!" Jackabah hissed to the agent before spitting at him.

Agent Rowson wiped the residual splatter from his face and turned to his audience of guards.

"It has a voice? Isn't that sweet? Well, we have a grand finale for you and I'm glad to say you needn't wait very long to see it." Agent Rowson retorted with a great amount of glee in his tone.

"Are we done?" Daemon asked but the agent seemed very busy all of a sudden and simply waved them away. Daemon winked at Roz and gestured for him and Chinn to follow before communicating to Sherry to meet up at the nearest bar.

The silent computerised countdown had reached the last ten seconds onboard the submersible vehicle. The weapon drifted slightly on the undercurrent of the river Othei using its stability impellers to keep it anchored at its pre-programmed destination. The central processing core of its computer components ran its program unaware of its own destruction and the eminent cataclysm it would unleash upon the land. In the last hundredth of a second before the countdown reached zero the computer realised its own demise was imminent. Something science had searched for throughout the history of computers occurred for the brief period before its processing core burnt out; a computer became sentient.

"SHIT!" The fledgeling being thought before it reached a temperature exceeding one million degrees Centigrade.

The city of Runich was silent apart from the howl of razor crafts circling above the city. It was the few pilots of these vehicles that witnessed the strange anomaly coming from the great river. The river seemed to shine with blinding luminance. The pilots attempted to shield their eyes as the river turned from a bright electric blue to a river of white light. A river of plasma clawed its way up and down the rivers current quickly reaching other settlements untouched by Xen's war. Each inhabitant was oblivious to the galloping of the horseman of the apocalypse in the guise of a blinding, burning death.

The city of Runich was plunged into a violent

earthquake as the superheated plasma ate and cut through the banks of the river and into the foundations of the once great metropolis. The drunken engineers who danced in the dry dock were probably the first to be vaporised. A suitable death granted to the constructors of such an evil weapon.

Landslides from the great mountains cascaded upon the northern outskirts of Runich meeting the shockwave of the explosion and sending a plume of rubble and dust straight in to the atmosphere. The chain reaction from the great ionic bombardment collapsed into itself, sucking the air and the very land into its epicentre. It was like god had risen up from the centre of Sigra III and embraced the surrounding land to its holy bosom. The four William Hadley drop pods and the great command sphere rolled on the tilt of the land towards what seemed to be the birth of a fledgling star. Everything that fell into the hellish sphere of fire was instantly crushed within its molten core. Millions of tonnes of material were absorbed around its burning circumference with each passing second. The life of the angry ball of light was brief on Sigra III but it died satisfied.

It didn't take much time before Xen sent a recognisance craft down to where Runich had once stood. The pilot of the craft reported a great and deep rift in the land and a large perfect black sphere which still smouldered within the crater. The once mighty river ran at a trickle and could no longer truly be called a river but the crater would eventually become a lake known as Lake Runich. The craft's scanners estimated the weight of the black sphere to be more than sixty billion tonnes although it only had a circumference of eight hundred meters. At over three hundred times the density of Uranium of was probably the densest material ever created by mankind to that date.

Agent Rowson had his back to the bloodied form of Jackabah who was tied down to an interrogation chair. He hadn't been able to gain any relevant information from any of the questions he had directed to his prisoner. Even the nail he had driven through Jackabah's scrotum hadn't initiated much of a response. Rowson himself was in the midst of dreaming up his next persuasive tactic when an auxiliary ran into the torture chamber.

"Agent Rowson, I've been ordered to..." The auxiliary broke off his sentence and nearly brought up his lunch when he noticed Agent Rowson's prisoner and what the poor bastard had been subjected too. Rowson rounded on the auxiliary angry at being disturbed at such a pivotal moment.

"Well spit it out!" He shouted at the man. The auxiliary suddenly found his voice and tried his best to ignore the pools of blood and urine under the interrogation chair.

"Runich is no more, it's been attacked." The nervous auxiliary whimpered.

"What do you mean it's no more?" Rowson said incredulously.

"It's gone. There is nothing left. It's been utterly destroyed." The auxiliary looked like he wanted to get away as soon as possible.

Rowson shot a look at Jackabah his eyes shooting daggers.

"What have you done?" Rowson demanded.

Jackabah peered through his hazy vision and looked to the nail through his genitals and the pool of his own blood before making eye contact with his evil tormentor.

"Sigra III is free!" He shouted startling the auxiliary. Jackabah grinned as blood dribbled down from the corners of his mouth.

"This is only the beginning. My people will hear of the victory against Xen at Runich and others will follow my example. Every rebellion on Sigra III will cut your Xen forces in half..."

Jackabah continued to rant as Agent Rowson drew his machine pistol. He aimed low and depressed the trigger and moved his arm upwards cutting Jackabah in half. The auxiliary witnessing the scene doubled himself up and finally threw his lunch to the floor in a series of violent stomach convulsions.

Rowson noticed the vomiting auxiliary and emptied the last of his ammo into him. He looked to his empty machine pistol, dropped it to the floor and made his way to the docking ring to board the next starship away from the Goliath and the shit hole known as Sigra III.

He couldn't imagine what the Xen Corporation would do to him given the loss of Runich. He decided that he would be damned if he was going to end up in a vat of antibiotics trailing tubes of liquid feed entering his naked body while he grew organs for Xen. He had a contact on Vargo I where he could hide from Xen for the rest of his natural life.

As soon as he boarded a starship he made his way to his passenger room and cut out a hard lump from under his skin. He dropped a small black device down the sink and then washed blood from his hands and patched up his left shoulder. He stared at his own reflection for a while and somehow felt better. All he saw in the reflection was a dangerous and calculating man.

"That's it. No going back now. Fuck it!" He assured the image in the mirror.

Sherry waited silently at the bar, she had waited on the Sul'Hudeen until the docking ring had fallen silent before heading there and was wondering if Daemon and the rest of them had already been and gone. It wasn't until Chinn sat down if front of her that she realised something was amiss.

"Sherry, I just want to say, before you get any funny ideas, I just want to say Roz is mine, he isn't available or on the market so to speak!" Chinn waited patiently until Sherry realised what she was referring to.

Sherry had heard this so many times during her life and her career. She understood what Chinn was insinuating and noticed how old Chinn looked compared to herself, Daemon and Roz.

"Well, you can sleep easy tonight because I'm not

interested. Besides, you're probably old enough to be his mother." Sherry said with a mocking tone.

"Play nice Sherry, you don't want to lose your pretty face so early in your career. I wager that you have banked your career upon that very asset alone." Chinn whispered across the table and balled her gnarled fist. Sherry smiled as she watched the aggression building in Chinn.

"But of course, your right. Let's be friends, for the time being, we don't want to upset the harmony of our group. Where are the boys by the way?" Sherry asked. The sudden change in conversation allowed Chinn to relax a little.

"Roz and your friend have ventured off somewhere else to find a private place to talk. They said they wouldn't be long and would meet up with us here later. Your friend Daemon seems to be a very troubled man; I sensed depression in his voice." Chinn said as she ordered a round of drinks from a pretty young waitress.

"Daemon can run hot and cold like the air conditioning but he wasn't always like that. When he was younger in the training academy he was a friendlier person. War can do strange things to people, especially if they hold any rank of responsibility." Sherry smiled to herself as she remembered the younger and happier man.

"It sounds like you loved him once. Maybe you still do?" Chinn said and as she said the word love she felt the warmth from her stomach to her heart.
Sherry nearly choked on her drink and had to mop

alcohol from her lips.

"No, I have only loved one man in my life and it wasn't Daemon. With me and Daemon it was just sexual chemistry; we just wanted each other. We fed off each other's lust and literally fucked it out of ourselves whenever it got the better of us." Sherry claimed and stifled a burst of hysteria.

Chinn shivered in disgust.

"I know." Sherry laughed seeing Chinn's reaction. "You can call me whatever you wish; whore, slut, whatever. It makes no difference to me. I am what I am. As far as I'm concerned the universe is filled with sexual endeavours and I just don't feel I can settle down with one life partner." Sherry said with a wink.

Chinn couldn't understand such a statement and wished she had never heard such a beautiful woman saying such things.

"Maybe you will find somebody who will change your mind?" Chinn said but she saw how Sherry shook her head in flat refusal to even contemplate such a concept.

"Welcome to the modern universe Chinn. Fuck me; have you lived your life in the woods or something?" Sherry said then noticed a handsome off-duty officer wander into the bar.

"No offence Chinn but I have urgent business over there."

Chinn looked in the direction in which Sherry pointed and spotted a tall, blonde haired officer at the bar. Chinn watched as Sherry strutted over to the officer like a feline in heat. The officer had already noticed Sherry and was already smiling.

It was quiet up on the sixth deck. Through the solid plaz window the northern hemisphere of Sigra III was visible. The atmosphere around the planet was a murky orange colour as a storm swirled silently just over the mainland. Daemon and Roz stood facing the window in silence as they watched the numerous transport ships heading down to the planet. It looked as if the Xen military were using every available craft to transport troops and weapons down to the rebellious planet as quickly as they could muster. A nuclear weapon bloomed somewhere on the mainland visible from the orbiting space station.

"It looks like Xen are cutting their losses," Daemon muttered. He had heard of the rebel weapon used at Runich from an officer they met on the way up to the sixth deck. He had also received new orders from Xen to board the next star flight to Xen Prime.

"It looks that way. I'm glad you are being pulled away from this carnage." Roz said before another bright light radiated from the planet.

"Are you struggling with voices other than your own thoughts?" Daemon asked quickly and was ready to dismiss such a silly question if Roz started laughing. Roz shot him a glance and then returned his focus to Sigra III.

"I did for a while." Roz drifted in silence for a few seconds and tried to remember his own struggle with apparitions and voices inside his mind.

"I found something under my skin and cut it from my flesh. It was a chip of some kind and when I flushed it down the sink I heard nothing more." Roz said in monotone as though he wished to forget his life before finding the Xen chip.

"A chip like Miles had?" Daemon eagerly prompted.

"Maybe, I don't really know. I wasn't that technically skilled if you remember? Anyway, I didn't study the fucking thing after I cut it out of me." Roz said angrily and tried to calm himself down by focusing on the stormhead spinning in the toxic atmosphere of the war-torn planet.

"If you plan to stay in the Xen Corporation, which I know I don't, then I would forget about chips and just carry out your life and orders as a Xen officer," Roz warned.

Daemon didn't know what to say in response to this he wondered if he could stay in the folds of the Xen Corporation or if this was a waking call to flee.

"Roz, I see, hear and think terrible things. It's like something is living within me and it drives me..." Daemon drifted off.

How can I explain to my friend that I have a demon living inside me, a demon that forces me to take actions that I wouldn't normally? He thought to himself struggling to comprehend what he had become.

Roz looked to his friend and noticed he was struggling for words to explain something he didn't fully understand.

"Daemon chipped or not, we are capable of terrible

625

things. Even after I removed the chip I still performed hideous tasks but at least I had a choice. I don't think it makes much difference. Humans without Xen training are capable of murderous deeds so what make us different? It's the fact we are trained to be more efficient in methods of murder." Roz said as he put his hand on the cold plaz, the cool of the synthetic glass soothed the heat of his flowing blood.

Daemon pondered on his words, surprised that Roz would come out with something almost philosophical. He had clearly changed since they had last seen each other.

Maybe he is right? Maybe it's all purely human nature. Who rightly knows? He wondered.

"Come on my friend, let's have that drink," Daemon said.

The bar was empty save for Chinn who was sat drinking alone. The table she sat at was strewn with empty vessels and she was about to drink a fresh beverage when Roz and Daemon sat down. Roz smiled and held Chinn's hand for a while having missed being without her for only a few hours. Daemon frowned and looked around the empty bar.

"Where is Sherry?" He asked.

Chinn's eyes were bloodshot and she tried to manage a sentence through her intoxication.

"She… went about an hour ago… with…" She tried to focus on the spot where Sherry and the officer had sat before mustering a drunken shrug. "She must have gone... with him..." She slurred.

Roz raised an eyebrow towards his old friend.

"That figures!" Daemon said moodily and looked to his timepiece. "So what are you going to do in retirement?" He asked.

Roz smiled and gripped Chinn's hand stronger with excitement.

"We are going to buy a small farm near a forest or maybe an old Delta Farm. Somewhere stable, and away from politics and Xen." Roz said with a glazed expression of wonder and dreams.

Daemon grinned but had his doubts.

"Will Xen allow you to do that I wonder? I couldn't imagine the punishment of breaching the Xen contract." He said solemnly.

Roz shot him a dangerous glare and his face contorted with rage.

"To hell with Xen, I've survived on the run with ease. I have been a killer, a pirate and have survived in a great jungle full of wild beasts. Yeah, I think we will be alright. Besides which I don't plan on advertising our absence to Xen at all. First, we were caught in the machinations of corporate employ, then we vanish, it would be like we never existed." Roz claimed with anger in his voice.

"Roz I don't doubt your intentions," Daemon advised "but plan your actions before you just take off. You will need money, and a lot of it to purchase new identities and money to purchase a bit of land. What I'm trying to say is; do you need money to help you?" Daemon said using his best voice of reason.

Roz seemed deep in thought almost digesting each word his friend said.

"We need no charity." He finally stated.

Chinn was oblivious to the conversation even though she sat at the same table. She wasn't used to drinking and found it increasingly difficult to focus on her own thoughts not to mention the enveloping chat between old friends.

"Look Roz, I'm in with Xen for life my friend and I can't possibly spend the money I earn. Please let me give you something towards your new horizons." Daemon pleaded knowing his friend would soon be in deep shit.

"Maybe your right, we probably need all the help we can get." Roz conceded.

"I won't be long; I will just access my account and print out a trade docket for you. You will be able to cash it at the docking ring here on the Goliath." Daemon said before he made his way to a banking terminal on the precinct.

Roz watched him leave and paranoia crawled up his spine. He knew Daemon could easily muster a lot of guards and arrest him and Chinn on grounds of premeditated A.W.O.L. But he waited and rode out the nagging feeling of being betrayed by his old friend.

Daemon returned in less than three minutes, he sat down and pushed a trade docket across the table. Roz's eyes widened as he read the figures on the docket.

"This is far too much Daemon. I can't allow you to give me this amount." Roz said with a tear in his eye but

628

Daemon stood suddenly and saluted to his old friend.

"Take it and make a better life for the both of you. I'm sorry but I must leave now. My starship has docked and I'm supposed to be already waiting to board. Farewell, my friend." Daemon said before he rushed out of the bar.

Roz wiped a tear from his eye and peered once again to the six-figure trade docket then realised that he would never see his best friend ever again.

Epilogue

Miles dropped the fire axe to the floor and wiped off the blood spatters from his face plate. Quat and adrenalin burned in every vein in his body as he stepped over the numerous unarmed corpses of men, women and children. He noticed he hadn't quite finished off some of his victims but left them to twitch in the last throws of death. He couldn't believe how easy it had been to slaughter a ship full of colonists bound for the furthest reaches of space. It was an odious task but he knew he had to do this deed as he needed more Ion cells to fuel the Evader and more resources for his venture into the unknown.

The colonist's craft had been painted with rainbow colours and named The Wooden-Stock and was destined for a small delta-farm community on the outskirts of known corporate space. The colonist ship was obviously an ex-military transport that had been stripped down to become a freighter and passenger ship. The military signature down its vast hull had been mostly obscured with fancy pictures and luminescent paint which Myles found most distasteful.

"Fucking colonists! Yeah, you won't be dancing around bonfires and fucking your friends now! Will you?" He ranted but all he heard in reply was the groans of the terminally injured fighting for their last breath.

The Wooden Stock had a variety of resources on board including hydroponics, planting seeds and machinery of an agricultural nature. It wasn't long before he located the ships Ion cell's and discovered numerous cryo tanks with several occupants still inside. He realised the voyage out here, to the arse end of space, must have taken this rudimentary craft many years to reach the edge of corporate space. Using the Evader's star-drive it had only taken Miles nine months to arrive at the very edge of the abyss of known space. His ship still had plenty of fuel but he had a nagging feeling he would need more to find the perfect habitable planet to finally settle on. Running across such a drifting craft was an opportunity which he refused to miss. Besides he felt he needed more genetic material to add to his stock of human resources.

It had taken the best part of two days to reap the required stock from the colonist's craft before the Evader's umbilical uncoupled from the Wooden Stock. Myles allowed his ship to drift in space while he made sure he had pillaged enough from the colonists before he set a course into oblivion. The Evader's navi-com had drawn a blank on the space beyond this point.

"It seems I'm far from the hand that once fed me," Miles said to the frost covered glass of Tinya's cryo-tube. The icing process had finally obscured her once beautiful form. He would have to be patient until he witnessed her in the flesh once more and even then he knew it would be a long time until she finally grew to love him.

He knew the danger of thawing her out due to the infection she carried; the Miles II virus would spread quickly to his other prisoners and wipe out his stock. He made a mental note to prepare anti-virus serums better than the last batch he made which had rendered him infertile. The cryo-tube next to Tinya's housed his little princess Imogene, his adopted daughter. He could just make out the tiny human being through the frosted glass, her blonde hair had mostly obscured her face and her flesh had taken on a bluish tone.

"Little Imogene." Miles drifted in thought. He knew she already trusted him so settling upon a planet shouldn't cause much of a problem. She will make a fine daughter.

Before he had placed her in cryo he had taken various blood samples and studied her D.N.A. She was of good stock and strong for her frame size, blonde haired which was now a rarity in the universe due to mixed race breeding. She was genetically unadulterated but a little inbred. He understood that she needed to be vaccinated once thawed, protected against the common ailments that the septic life that now passed for humanity in the corporate universe were now immune to.

Imogene's ancestors and relatives had been alone in space a long time, his first calculations had been wrong and he now realised her genetic line had lived at the delta farm for over seven generations, maybe eight. The men he gathered from the delta farm would also need such vaccination. He had a lot of work to prepare before even attempting a mass thaw.

Later that day he decided to leave the vicinity of space occupied by the Wooden Stock. He had all he needed now and was ready to move through the invisible corporate barrier into deep uncharted space. His pulse rate increased as he made his final preparations. Where he was going was directly into the unknown. He thought about how many crafts had ventured further than he was but knew they wouldn't have been a corporate craft or he would already have details of their ventures on the Evaders database.

Miles tapped in a new course on the navi-com and hovered his hand over the execute button. His hand trembled and his thoughts became a bombardment of excitement, fear and worry. He closed his eyes, took a deep breath and gently touched the dreaded button.

The Evader's engines powered up slowly, he could almost feel the sparks of ions smashing against catalysts deep in the reactor core. The ship leaped sideways upon a discharge of plasma vapour which nearly threw Miles from the pilot seat. The countdown had started as he made his way gingerly to his cryo-tube; he had to navigate through a maze of equipment, canisters and old fashioned cryo-tanks which now cluttered every corridor and room on the Evader. The ship powered itself forwards in one jolt which took him off his feet and he bumped his head against a drum of tuber seeds. He rubbed his head and felt warm fluid under his hand, the impact had nearly knocked him unconscious but with the conclusion of the countdown imminent he quickly found his feet and raced his way to sanctuary.

It took twenty seconds to power his cryo-tube up to an operational level before he could clamber inside. The computerised feminine voice had already reached the ten second mark as he closed the hatch of his cryo-tube. He quickly strapped himself into the safety harness and felt a needle enter his spine. Miles giggled to himself as the drugs clawed at his consciousness and he felt his thoughts slipping away from his brain. He didn't feel the intense cold wash over his body or the Evader's star drive reaching its pinnacle.

Lucinda unhooked a latch and carefully opened the secret smuggling hatch on board the Wooden Stock. She listened for a while before venturing out on to the engine deck and noticed the ship had been set on standby. Only the overhead lights and the life support were operational in such a mode. The young woman made her way through the ship, passing mutilated corpses as she went. She reeled in horror at the fact the victims were barely recognisable, their faces smashed, torsos separated from their limbs and heads. Panic twitched in every nerve fibre as she attempted to deduce what had happened to her friends, relatives and her parents.

Lucinda had never before seen such atrocities and hadn't been educated in the ways of the universe. Her teachings had been of love, peace and harmony and such bloody murder had yet to be imprinted on her mind. Her head pounded with fear and her heart beat against her chest in rapid throws of dread and terror whenever she turned a bend in a corridor or opened a closed door. She hoped and wished she would not suffer such a miserable ending as everyone else on board the colonist craft. It wasn't long until she found the mutilated corpse of her father, his dead hands still clasped tight around the amulet of life he wore. His once stark white shirt had been corrupted by his own life blood which had formed a jellied pool of crimson at the seat of his pants.

"Father." She cried as she knelt at his side. She attempted to revive him but his body was solid with rigor-mortis under her gentle touch. An abundance of tears washed down her cheeks as she tried to understand the meaning of death. In her short lifetime she had only ever heard about death and it was generally old age or sicknesses beyond cure which had taken people from her life. She had been saved from such torments of the mind in her past and believed that each soul had travelled to a better place. None of the teachings now made any sense; it was like an awakening of mortality and she realised death could easily be reaped under such brutal circumstances.

It had taken several traumatic hours before Lucinda became accustomed to the events that had taken place on board the Wooden Stock. She made her way to the cryo chamber and realised most of the tanks were missing. She wept when she noticed the empty void where her mother's cryo-tank had once been. All that was left was a few trailing power cables and gas pipes which still dripped oxidising liquid that vaporised before hitting the floor.

"Mother?" Lucinda whispered as she realised she was the only survivor on board. Her mother had been in a deep sleep during the event that had struck the colonist craft. The rota system allowed every member of the Wooden Stock moments of down time in their journey towards Utopia, sometimes months at a time.

"Where have you gone? Why have you been taken?" Lucinda's words merely echoed around the empty unhearing chamber. Her questions could never be answered by the cold, dark superstructure.

A week drifted by while Lucinda studied the operating manuals she had found. Her parents were primarily skilled in agriculture and relied on other people to engineer, navigate and care for the ship, so technical knowledge had never been passed down to her. Luckily she had been taught how to read so she could at least absorb the technical information from the manuals found in the navigation chamber. The information may well have been written in another language because she didn't understand very much of the literature provided. However, a small and brief technical sub-script allowed Lucinda to send out a distress signal. The transmission she sent was rudimentary, in fact it was nothing more than an out of date radio message, programmed to repeat every minute that passed.

"S.O.S... DRIFTING COLONIST CRAFT...SIGNATURE... WOODEN STOCK 437902650XB... NEED URGENT HELP... ONE SURVIVOR... S.O.S..."

Printed in Great Britain
by Amazon